The Divine Path
By
Allen J Johnston

Melinda

I would love to know
what your favorite scene
is. Feel free to let me
know on Facebook.

Allen Johnston

Acknowledgment

I truly could not have done this series without the amount of work my amazing wife, Amber, puts into this. She creates the covers for my books and navigates all the programs that are needed to help this make it to print. She spends hours at a time as if this was her own work. To say she is amazing is shamefully not enough to really describe her. I would also like to thank the man who raised me. My father, Gary, taught me the value of honesty and hard work. It is because of his lessons that I am what I am today. I could not be prouder of that man. I would also like to thank David Baumgardner for just being amazing. Whenever life offers me a curve ball, he always has a way to still hit it out of the park.

CH1

Kade slept lightly, unaware as the silhouette of a man struggled to take shape in the corner. The man shook with the effort as he strained to become more than a faint image. His eyes found what they searched for lying in the bed.

"Kade...save...Doren. Kade...,"the fading form said before disappearing.

Kade's eyes came open as he searched the room for...what he could not say. He listened, but the only sound was that of his dragon breathing deeply just outside his window. He shook his head and dismissed his unfounded unease and smiled to himself as a peacefulness filled him.

Kade enjoyed the happiness that he felt flowing through his body. He sat up slowly, trying to recall why he was in such a good mood. Something about his dreams came to mind but there were no details to help solve the mystery. He gave up trying to recall his dreams and happily bounded out of bed.

Moving to the window, Kade barely saw Rayden's ears rising and falling on the other side of the glass. He watched, and for some reason he could not explain, found it funny and laughed. The world looked alive and felt amazing. He pushed open the window and leaned out, looking down on the dragon. The smile on his face turned into a devious one as he turned and scanned his room. Soon, his eyes found what he was seeking.

Kade crossed the room and pulled a feather from the pillow and then returned back to the window as quietly as possible. He reached out and slowly ran the feather along Rayden's ear. At first, the dragon didn't move. Kade stifled a laugh and tried again. The ears started to twitch. Kade let out a small laugh as he continued his game. Rayden gave a huff as his ear twitched a little more dramatically. Kade laughed loudly, finding this the most humorous thing he had seen in years. The dragon's head shot up and then quickly looked left and right. Kade's laugh was long and genuine. After considerable effort of getting himself under control, he turned back to the dragon and stopped as he connected with it.

Rayden was radiating happiness like the sun radiates light. He moved closer to the dragon and looked deep into its eyes, analyzing the feelings that flowed through the link. Rayden just sat there, staring back. Kade could swear the dragon had a new look in its eyes.

"What has you so happy?" Kade questioned. Rayden just looked at him, not quite understanding what was being asked. After a moment, Kade realized he was going to get no answer and let it drop. "Anyway, how would you like some food?" he asked, moving onto a subject he was sure the dragon would understand. Rayden was fully awake now as he jumped to his feet and looked at Kade hungrily.

Kade noticed his clothes lying across the chair in the corner. He tried to remember taking them off but drew a blank. Shrugging his shoulders, he quickly dressed and hurried out front to his waiting dragon. Many minutes later Kade had produced Rayden's morning meal, which consisted of ten or so pieces of hot, juicy meat. He lost count, his mind threatening to wander constantly as birds sang from the trees.

You are becoming too spoiled, Kade thought with a grin. He was more than ok with it, though. Feeding the dragon was easy, as its palate was not one that was difficult to satisfy. He knew that no matter what he did, he could feed the dragon meat three times a day for years, and it would still be craving the next juicy morsel he would conjure.

The sound of female voices drifted to Kade as he stood staring up at the clouds. He smiled as he thought about seeing his mother again and even more so of seeing Darcienna. He grinned from ear to ear without even knowing why.

Kade walked back into the home and listened for the women to ascertain where in the house they were. It did not take long to figure out that the voices were coming from the kitchen. He wondered if they were making breakfast and felt his stomach growl at the thought of something other than his own cooking. He started toward the kitchen, and the closer he got, the more he could tell that the women were excited about something other than food.

Kade slowly worked his way down the hall, paying close attention for sounds of danger in their voices. As he entered the room, he came upon his mother and Darcienna standing side by side with their backs to him. Upon entering the kitchen, it was clear there was no threat of any kind. He relaxed as his mind took a devious turn. He stood there grinning for a moment, considering what he wanted to do to his two victims. He decided on something simple as he stepped up and clapped them both on their shoulders. Almost in unison, they gave a squeak and jumped, giving him the reaction he was hoping to see. Darcienna glared at him for his childish prank, and her look said all of that and more. Judeen took a deep breath and let it out as if to say, "This was nothing new." Kade started to laugh and then stopped as his eyes fell on the silky, black creature that was curled protectively around his books.

"I can't believe it," Darcienna said, recovering from being startled. "He showed up just after sunrise. He seemed injured with

3

the way he walked half sideways and then laid down on the ground. He still won't let me near him."

Kade reached down and slowly ran his hand over the silky, black fur, checking for injuries. Chance did not react at all, but instead, seemed to soak up the affection. Kade was about to stand up when his hand brushed something that the creature was curled protectively around. He instantly recognized the feel of his sack of books and realized the Transparency Calling was still in place, keeping the books hidden. Kade felt for the calling and let it dissipate. The books faded into view. Judeen gasped but Kade ignored her.

He felt his good humor slowly evaporate. The very books that he had entrusted Darcienna to keep watch over were sitting there on the floor. He felt frustration grow as he glanced at her. Obviously she did not understand how important these were. His gut was in a knot at the thought of coming so close to losing his precious pages of knowledge yet again. He turned on Darcienna and was about to vent his frustration when he thought about how she had probably dropped them while saving his life. He chastised himself for not checking for them sooner and decided to keep his words to himself.

Besides, he thought, *how many times have I forgotten them?*

Darcienna was watching him intently, waiting. It was obvious that she was concerned with how he was going to react. He made a mental note to make sure she understood how critically important the tomes of knowledge were and gave her a genuine smile. She smiled back weakly and visibly relaxed as she let out her breath.

After all, to her, they were just a few books, Kade thought. *Clearly not worth much compared to the lives she was saving.*

"He keeps my books safe for me," Kade explained, answering the curiosity he could see in his mother's eyes. "It's a long story," he said, seeing that the look was still there.

"Everything with you is a long story," Darcienna said. Kade could only shrug.

Turning his attention back to Chance, Kade looked over the

animal and then the books. He noticed that there were several jagged tears in the bag. He reached for the sack, and as usual, the animal gladly gave way to him. Darcienna gave a grunt but said no more. Kade opened the bag carefully, lifting the pile of books out by the strap and placing them on the table.

"Those can't stay there," Judeen said in that tone that indicated there was to be no arguing. Kade took a deep breath and let it out as though in relief. He placed the books back in the sack and put them in the corner, out of the way. Judeen nodded her approval.

Kade was looking at his furry little friend as he prepared to give it its reward for keeping his books safe. He had barely noticed that the women were both standing completely still, staring into the far corner of the room. Kade followed their gaze but saw nothing. Or...was there a faint shimmer? He did his best to dismiss any concern, but as much as he tried, he was unable to ignore the intense sense of urgency and dread that he felt descend on him.

All three looked from one to the other but none said a word for fear of confirming something they did not want to admit. The knot in his stomach began to grow by the moment. His eyes lost focus as he concentrated on the feeling. Yes, it was the same thing that woke him up but he was not awake enough to realize it at the time. Now, he was certain it was...something not to ignore. In an instant Kade, went from being filled with happiness and freedom to one of dread. He locked eyes with Darcienna and then turned to look at the book.

"Son," Judeen said, her voice thick with concern from the look she saw in his eyes, "what are you thinking?" Kade took another deep breath and held it for several long seconds and then let it out when he had come to the only conclusion he knew had to.

"Mother, I fear my..."

"Our," Darcienna said firmly as she took a step toward him, making it clear she was not going to be left out.

"Our journey is not yet done. When I performed the calling the previous night, I connected with other Master Chosen. I think it best if I seek one out just to make sure all is well," Kade said, finding

5

it hard to keep eye contact with her. He did not want to see the worry and concern that was building by the moment. "I am sure it is nothing but…," Kade said and then looked away before she could see the doubt in his eyes.

Kade reached for the sack and gently laid it back on the table. He gently rolled the edged of the sack down until the books were exposed. The one he wanted was on the top. It was the smallest, but right now, the most important.

"What is that?" Judeen asked.

"It is the next step in my plans," Kade said as he stood, studying the books that held immense amounts of knowledge and power.

"Our plans," Darcienna corrected him once more.

"Our plans," Kade said with mock frustration, his mood lightening just a little, knowing that she was still going to be at his side. He turned and locked eyes with her and gave her the ever slightest grin. She returned the look.

Turning his attention back to the books, Kade continued to look them over, as if trying to muster the courage to touch them. He could feel his palms start to sweat at the thought of loosening the binding. He did his best to remain calm and relaxed so as not to worry his mother or Darcienna.

"What is in them?" Judeen asked as she reached for the closest book with the demon image on the front.

"No!" Kade yelled as his hand shot out and gripped his mother's wrist so tightly she was sure to bruise.

"Kade!" Darcienna scolded.

"Mother," Kade said, ignoring Darcienna. He breathed a deep sigh of relief but would not take his hand off her wrist until she had moved back from the deadly traps. "You must never ever, ever touch any of these books without my permission. They were your father's," Kade said as he looked at her. That was all he needed to say for her to understand the lethality of them. This was one of the rare times he could recall ever seeing his mother lose her composure, even if it was just slightly. It took a while for the color to return to her face, but eventually it did. Kade took a moment more to get the sick feeling out of his stomach before continuing.

"This book," Kade said, gently removing the small, black book from the pile, "tells me the locations of some of the other Chosen. Master Zayle had told me that if anything ever happened to him, I should find them." Kade turned to his mother as a thought occurred to him. "Did Grandfather," Kade started to say and then paused. This was the first time that he had actually referred to Zayle as his grandfather instead of his teacher. He felt sadness trying to work at him, but he quickly dismissed it. "Did Grandfather ever tell you anything of the other Chosen?" Kade asked firmly, meaning business.

"Never. He said he would not ever put me in danger by giving me knowledge that could harm me. You know how he was with what was best to know and what was best to leave unknown."

Kade understood this more than he wanted. His mind drifted back to his talk with his father the previous day. *Should he know what his father was trying to tell him?* he asked himself. He shook his head, dismissing the notion completely.

"Why do you have to find them?" Darcienna asked.

"I need to make sure that they are able to stop Morg or we will never be safe. I am certain everything is okay now that they know who is behind all the deaths but I will not be able to relax until I am certain. And...," Kade said and then paused for several long moments while his mind worked. Zayle's warning about other Chosen was firmly planted in his mind. He hoped this was the correct decision as he weighed his options. He looked Darcienna in the eye and continued. "I cannot explain why but I feel like this is the correct thing to do," Kade said finally. "Zayle had told me of a story where several of the strongest Chosen had once imprisoned Morg in the mountain of Drell. I suspect that is why Morg wants to kill anyone that has the ability to channel any type of power," Kade said as he watched Darcienna for her reaction. "Or maybe it is pure revenge on

7

any Chosen alive. I can't really say for sure."

"Then why kill Jorell?" Darcienna asked innocently. Kade stopped and stared at her for several long moments as he pondered this.

"That is a good question," Kade said as his eyes lost focus while he chewed on this latest mystery. "I don't know," he said as he locked eyes with her.

It was obvious that this kind of talk worried Judeen as she slowly worked her hands as if to wash them. Kade recalled this from his childhood. His mother would wring her hands ever so slowly and increase how fast she washed based on how agitated she was. Right now, she moved slowly, but he was sure that it was going to pick up as their talk continued.

"When do you think you will be leaving?" Judeen asked, her voice a practiced calm.

Kade did not answer for a long moment as he thought about the peacefulness he would be leaving. He turned to look longingly out the window. Taking a deep breath to say the words he was going to hate hearing come from his own mouth, he continued.

"Today," he said, accepting a fate he knew he could not escape.

Kade did not need to see his mother to know she was wringing her hands tightly and fidgeting with her dress, straightening it, even though there was not a wrinkle anywhere. He dreaded turning and looking her in the eye. He did not want to see the worry and sadness he knew was going to be there.

"Can't you stay for at least another day?" Judeen tried to ask as casually as possible, but any son recognized when a mother was pleading. Kade's shoulders sagged. He was tempted, but he knew the longer he stayed, the harder it would be to leave. Besides, the dread he felt building in him was almost palpable. Better to go before he found a way to rationalize to himself that it was ok to stay.

"No. That would give Morg another day to succeed in what he is planning. If the Master Chosen are unable to stop him, I am sure he will come after me. When he does find me, and he will, you and father will suffer for it," Kade said as he gently reached out for his mother's hands and looked into her eyes. "And you know I can't have that. I need to leave so you and father will be out of danger. You know it's true," Kade said as Judeen looked away. With Zayle as her father, he was certain he did not need to explain any further.

"But you are a mere apprentice. How can you be needed by a Master Chosen?"

"Apprentice or not, I must do this, Mother. It is the path the Divine has laid out for me."

No matter what ugly truth Garig was trying to tell him back at the clearing, he knew his parents loved him deeply. He could feel it as easily as he could feel the warmth of the sun on his skin. For that reason alone, he had to leave to keep them safe.

"But, would it not be better if you stayed here while you studied? You are still only an apprentice. What makes you think you even have a chance to stand up to Morg?" Judeen asked with as steady a voice as she could muster. Kade watched as her eyes glazed over and he knew instantly that she was recalling the power that Morg could wield.

"Zayle."

"My father?" Judeen asked as she focused on her son again.

"Zayle believes I can stop him. I am not certain I was only meant to save you. I can't shake the feeling that there is more. I must try. I must at least try for Zayle. Part of me thinks he gave his life for me," Kade said as he turned to face Darcienna. "You don't have to come." He knew her answer but he had to at least try one last time.

"When do we leave?" Darcienna asked with one hand planted firmly on her hips while the other held her child. The look in her eye said she was very ready for this battle. Kade smiled despite himself.

Feeling affection for her that he could not explain, Kade just nodded while doing his best to hide his eagerness to have her at his side. He paused momentarily as he considered her motives for wanting to continue with him. He knew she wanted revenge for

Jorell, but he just could not shake the feeling that there was more to it. Was it possible that he was the reason? He could only hope.

"We leave after I learn some of this one's secrets," Kade said as he held up the small, black book.

"You don't even know what is in there? How do you know it will help?" Darcienna asked as she reached for the book and then hesitated, recalling Kade's dire warnings.

"No!" Kade exclaimed, jerking the book away from her. "You must never touch any of these books without my say," he said, repeating what he had said previously. "You do not want to see what happens if you do," he added in a very firm voice. He was on the verge of anger. "With this, you could unleash something so terrible it could easily kill us all." Better she be scared of all books instead of opening the wrong one. "See this book," he said, pointing to the one with the creature in the circle. "This one would unleash that demon on the front. One touch of its poison, and you would die the most horrible, agonizing death possible," he finished in a dire voice.

Darcienna shuddered at the thought. She swallowed hard as she took a small step back, not taking her eyes off the demon. After a moment, she tore her eyes off the book to look at the Apprentice Chosen.

"Kade," Judeen said critically. "Why are they in this house if they are that dangerous?"

"They are only dangerous if they are opened, Mother. I am the only one who can handle them," Kade said as he looked back at Darcienna. She had to understand this if she was going to travel with him. He was even willing to force her to stay if she argued. She must have seen the conviction in his eyes and nodded once in acceptance of the law he had just laid down. She swallowed again, and Kade was satisfied.

"What are in the other books?" Judeen asked, seeing Darcienna's discomfort and changing the subject.

"Well, they range from powerful callings to information about Morg. This one tells of monsters under his control. Here, take a look," Kade said as he handed the book to her. Judeen appeared as if she were ready to flee.

"Are you sure it's ok? I don't want to set off any traps," Judeen said, eyes wide. This was the third time Kade had ever seen his mother lose her composure.

"This one is safe. Zayle never placed any callings on this book. I guess it never mattered if anyone ever looked at it. All the rest of the books have protection callings placed on them. And this one," Kade said, holding up the black book, "is only attuned to me. I don't think anyone else can open it," he said, turning the book over in his hands. He thought back on the message Zayle had left for him. It occurred to him that he had yet to open it and became nervous to do so.

Judeen took the book about Morg and started to thumb through it. Even knowing it was safe, Kade still found he was tense until the book was open. She stopped on page sixteen and stared at the picture. Kade saw the look on her face and was about to ask, "What" when she turned the book toward him. She gave a tilt of her head as her way of asking, "What is this?" Kade studied the writing for a bit and then translated.

"I think it is something that can change shape. They have average to high intelligence and can assume any form," Kade was saying when he noticed the way his mother was off in thought. "What's wrong?" he asked.

"I may have encountered one of these," Judeen said in disgust.

"Why do you say that?" Kade asked.

"Let's just say that we noticed a stranger in town, who was asking lots of questions about you. Your father followed him, but when he thought he had him cornered in an alley, all he found was a mangy dog. It was shortly after that that Morg took us prisoner. He knew who we were immediately."

"Well, you are safe now, Mother. We are going to keep it that way," Kade said. She sighed.

"Can it turn into a dragon?" Darcienna asked.

11

"I don't think so. I suspect they are limited by the amount of ability they possess," Kade said as he studied the picture. "According to what it says here, some have more ability than others, so I guess it is possible, but I just don't know. It also says that some may have difficulty holding a certain shape over longer periods of time," he added as he took the book from her and thumbed through it. He stopped as he studied another image and then turned it for his mother to see.

"I had to kill two of these," Kade said as he watched her eyes widen. Darcienna slid around to look at the page. She put her hand to her mouth and quickly found his eyes.

"How did you survive?" Darcienna asked.

"Well, to be more correct, it was the dragon and me. We killed it together. That is how I survived," he said as his mind called up the image of the grimalkin.

Judeen slowly shook her head as she studied the picture. Kade considered showing her the invisible giant but thought better of it. She did not need more to worry about. He handed his mother the book and turned his attention back to the black book in his hands.

Kade sat down at the table and very gently pushed the other tomes of knowledge away, preparing to open the small, black one for the first time. He felt nervous as a warm flush went up and down his body. Even though the message from Zayle said this was safe and keyed to his touch, until he actually opened it for the first time, he was not going to be able to relax. He placed his hand on the cover, preparing to open it. Just as he started to grip the edge, he heard a chirping, whining sound that startled him. It took a moment for his head to clear, and when it did, he realized the sound was coming from behind him. Turning, he saw Chance sitting up and instantly recognized that look.

"Between you and the dragon I am going to be worn out making food. But, thanks to you, I have these," Kade said as he indicated the books. Darcienna instantly stiffened. Kade winced, seeing her reaction, knowing she was going to take this badly. He sighed to himself and turned to Darcienna. "I did not mean...," he got out before she held up a hand.

"I was supposed to keep your books safe and I forget them. I set them down when I called on my shield. I should have remembered them," Darcienna said, making no excuses for her mistake. Kade could not help but to respect her for it.

"I won't have you beating yourself up over it. You saved my life along with my parents', and that was much more important. And besides, we have the books."

"Thanks to Chance," Darcienna said, chagrinned.

"I won't hear any more of this. Just promise me that you will help look after them, and we can be done with this," Kade said firmly.

"I can do that," Darcienna said, brightening a little. She loved a man who was willing to take charge. It made her feel safe and secure. She smiled at his back. Out of the corner of her eye, she noticed Judeen watching her closely. She reddened slightly without looking at the wise woman.

Turning back to the silky, black creature, Kade performed the Food Calling. He tossed the piece of meat to Chance, who easily caught it in the air. Chance began eagerly chewing with pleasure. Kade turned away from the animal, grateful for the distraction, but it was time to do what he knew he must.

"Maybe you two should stand back a little. I really don't know what is going to happen," Kade said.

Judeen complied immediately while maintaining an air of confidence. Darcienna looked at Kade for several long seconds and then breathed out, resigning herself to the fact that no matter what she said, he was going to open the book. She wanted to tell him no or find a reason to put this off, but the look in his eyes said it had to be done. She had to trust him sooner or later and this was as good a time as any. So far, he had kept them safe. But, it was not what he said that had her so worried, it was the look in his eye and the way he handled the books that had her ready to demand he stop immediately.

Taking a deep breath, Kade placed his palm on the cover of the book. Again, he was surprised that it felt like smooth leather, even though he would swear it appeared to be rough looking bark. He held his breath as he slowly untied the strap that was holding the book closed. There was a power at work here, and the closer Kade got to opening it, the stronger its presence was felt. He took another deep breath, curled his fingers under the cover and slowly pulled the book open. There was a resistance, as if something were holding the book closed, but it was not enough to keep Kade from opening it. He felt a great building of power as a vibration started to pulse through the book. Every muscle in his body was as hard as a rock while he waited for whatever was going to happen, to happen. And then…he was at the mercy of Divine Power as it flowed.

"Kade?" Darcienna asked, her voice thick with concern. It might have been the fact that he was holding his breath that had her so worried, or maybe that he was clenching his jaw as his eyes started to instinctually close. But, regardless, she was scared for him and wished she could throw that black book in the nearest volcano.

Kade never heard her, his concentration on the small tome of knowledge peaked. He laid the cover on the table, but before he could pull his hand away, the calling activated fully. He tensed hard and held his breath as a blue spark shot forth from the book to crackle across his hands. The energy was almost too bright to look at as it leapt from finger to finger until it had covered his entire hand. His fingers twitched involuntarily as the muscles spasmed rapidly. Darcienna's hand shot to her mouth as she stifled a scream. The time it took for the calling to verify his identity seemed to take forever, and Kade's chest ached from the breath he was holding as he waited for the calling to finish. The light disappeared, leaving Kade with hands that were numb and a racing heart like he had run for days. He let out a shaky breath and appeared as though he were going to collapse from exhaustion.

"Kade?" Judeen asked with worry.

"Kade, are you okay?" Darcienna asked as she grabbed his arm with both hands, ready to unleash her healing power. She eyed that small, black book like it was a viperous snake that she wanted gone.

"Yea, I think so," Kade said as he flexed his fingers. "That was powerful. Zayle was not taking any chances with that one. I dread to think what would have happened to the person who tried to open that with that calling active," Kade said with a glance at his mother and Darcienna.

He took another nerve-settling breath and let it out as he turned the first page. As soon as his hand touched the paper, he felt another calling activate. This one was gentle, but as he was not expecting it, it frayed his nerves. He tried to keep steady but his hand shook slightly. He clenched his fist tightly to hide it from the women, but something told him he was too late. A tingling sensation ran across his scalp. Kade's eyes glazed over as the information about the Chosen, Valdry, was implanted in his mind. "I know where one of the Master Chosen is," Kade said in a trance-like state.

"Kade," both women called together.

"There was a calling placed on the page. As soon as I touched it, it activated and sent the information directly into my head. I should be able to lead us to Valdry," Kade said, feeling as though he had just awoken. He was returning to normal quickly but it was still hard to think. He stood, trying to get his mind to clear.

Judeen seemed to fidget ever so slightly as though she wanted to say something but was unsure if she should. Kade smiled a disarming smile as he ducked down to make eye contact with her. Her eyes were toward the ground as she attempted to keep Kade from seeing the look on her face. He gently lifted her head by her chin.

"What?" Kade asked as gently as possible.

"I saw you. I saw how you reacted. Kade, that stuff is deadly. What did my father get you into?" Judeen asked as her eyes started to moisten.

"Mother, it is the way of things now. It's just…Mother, it is best if I did not explain. You must trust me," Kade said, doing his best to reassure her.

15

"I never realized how dangerous the Divine Power was until I watched you just now. You could die," Judeen said and then paused. "You could die at any time, couldn't you?"

Kade sighed. There was no way of getting around this. His mother would know if he tried to downplay it. She had seen. It would take a blind person not to see how tense he had been. He cursed himself for being such a fool for letting her watch.

"Yes," Kade said in resignation. "That is the price I must pay for using the Divine. At any time, if I do anything wrong, it could end horribly, but I am careful, Mother, I am."

Judeen looked away as a slight tremor pulled at the corner of her lips. Her hand went to her mouth as she tried desperately to keep from weeping. She failed but only barely. Kade cursed himself ten times over for being so thoughtless and allowing her to watch.

"Mother," Kade said, but she held up a hand to forestall him.

"Kade, I think it best if we were on our way," Darcienna said. He opened his mouth, ready to agree with her when his eyes lost their focus as a voice screamed frantically in his head.

Help! I am under attack! Morg is..., and then the voice faded. Kade gasped as he squeezed his eyes shut hard. His hand shot out to catch the edge of the table to help steady himself. The pressure in his mind was immense for just a moment and then it was gone. He breathed a deep sigh of relief and focused on not letting his knees collapse.

"Kade, what is it?" Darcienna asked. Her eyes were wide with horror.

"I think Morg is attacking another of the Chosen," Kade said as he closed his eyes and focused hard with his mind. "I think I heard one of them calling out for help. He was cut off," Kade said, his head turned, as if this might help him hone in on the message.

"What if that was the Chosen you were going to see?" Darcienna asked.

Kade did not answer. He was afraid to answer, fearing the worst. He needed Valdry to be okay. Right now, that Master Chosen

16

was his best and only plan.

He exhaled in exasperation and turned to look at Darcienna. She looked back and her heart went out to him. He appeared worn down and stress was taking a toll on him. She wanted to wrap him in her shield and keep him safe forever. She wanted to protect him from the world and let him find peace, but with a heavy heart, she knew this was not possible, yet. It hurt to know that he was not going to be able to find a release from this torment anytime soon, if ever. She could see that this was the way of things for him, and he was not even aware he was suffering. He was used to his nerves being on edge. He was used to tensing, expecting danger at any moment, especially while using the Divine Power. What hurt the most was seeing him struggle not to lose who he was. She felt sadness momentarily grip her, and she fought to hide it.

"Darcienna," Kade said, agitation in his voice. "Woman, where are you? Darcienna," Kade said again as he snapped his fingers in front of her eyes.

"I…I was just thinking that we should really get under way," Darcienna said, knowing that to say she felt pity for him would be a disastrous thing to say. In the short time she had known him, pity was the one thing he was not going to accept. "Pity is for the weak," Kade would say.

"That is what I have been trying to do," Kade said, shaking his head as he exhaled in exasperation again. He took another deep breath and let it out to help recover from the mental assault.

Kade gathered up the books and stacked them in a pile, preparing to cinch the strap tightly. Darcienna put her hand on his arm but did not take her eyes off the small, black book. Kade saw what she was looking at and tilted his head as if to ask, "What?"

"Kade, I don't like that one. You have what you need from it. Can we leave it here?" Darcienna pleaded, glancing from Kade to Judeen. "I would prefer if we did not keep it if we don't need to." Kade looked up at his mother who was staring at the book. She appeared to be on the verge of protesting greatly when she saw the

17

look in Darcienna's eyes.

After taking a deep breath, Judeen said, "Keep it in your room."

Kade quickly raced to his room and pulled a board loose from behind his bed, laying the book in the wall. After slamming the board back in place, he ran out of the room and stopped at the table. He carefully cinched the books tightly and then gently lowered them into the sack. He took Marcole from Darcienna and handed him to his mother. He grabbed Darcienna by the hand and turned to go. She pulled him to a stop before taking even one step. When Kade gave her a questioning look, she tilted her head toward Judeen. Darcienna took Marcole back, waiting for Kade to say goodbye. Feeling like a fool, Kade pulled his mother into a deep hug and held her for several long moments until she relaxed and melted into that hug.

"Be careful, Son," Judeen whispered into his chest.

"I will, Mother. I will." *Rayden, be ready to go! We leave now!*

They handed the boy back to Judeen and raced out the door to the waiting dragon. Kade cupped his hands for Darcienna to mount. She wanted to hug him and relieve the torment she saw in those eyes, but she knew he would not accept it. They had no choice. They needed to go.

"Tell father I had to leave," Kade said as he cast a quick glance at his mother. She disappeared into the house to hide her grief. "Get on," he said impatiently as he held his cupped hand together, waiting for her to mount.

"Kade," Garig said as he stepped around the corner of the house. His gaze was on the ground as if he were avoiding looking his son in the eye. His words were heavy with emotion.

Kade paused, seeing a look in his father's eyes. He slowly dropped his hands and after several long seconds, took a step toward Garig, waiting. He feared what his father was going to say, even though he had no idea what it might be. But, one thing he knew more than anything was that his father was on the verge of continuing the

18

conversation they had started the previous day in the clearing. He wanted to tell his father not to say it, whatever it was. Something in him screamed, "Leave before he speaks." He knew, without a doubt, that he should mount the dragon as fast as possible and ride like the wind away from words that were on the verge of changing his life. Even though every thread of every fiber of his being screamed at him not to listen, he was rooted to the spot. His head was pounding as his heart beat like a drum. Boom, Boom, Boom Kade felt in his chest.

Garig was struggling, and for a moment, Kade felt sorry for him. He saw his father's agony and felt compassion for him. He was about to tell his father not to say another word to relieve him of his suffering when Garig let out the breath he was holding, and his shoulders slumped in resignation. Kade wanted to scream "NO" but could not get himself to speak. He knew that his life was about to change forever, and he just could not keep from listening.

"He said...," Garig started to say and everything went into slow motion. His father walked slowly along the porch as he spoke, his eyes glazed as he agonized over a distant memory.

Kade could hear the birds in the distance as everything became surreal. He could feel the cool air on his face as his father was turning toward the open door. Garig stopped as he agonized over the knowledge he was about to impart. Kade knew to the very bottom of his soul that this moment was going to be one that defined who he was and it scared him.

"He stood there holding you for so long," Garig said with a grim look on his face, not able to look at his son with what he was about to say. "I stayed still, not making a sound," he continued as he moved to stand in the doorway, his back to his son. "For the rest of my life, I will never forget those five words I heard him whisper. The lesser of two evils," Garig said and then walked into the cabin without even a glance back.

Kade felt like he had been hit in the gut. His stomach twisted in a knot, and he thought he was going to be sick. His mind whirled out of control, and he wished he had never heard what his father was trying to say. He hated himself for listening. He knew he should have left, but now, it was too late. He was always going to remember that this is what his grandfather thought of him. His heart ached desperately. He felt like he wanted to get on the dragon and ride for days. He wanted to flee this land and never look back. He clenched his fists in anger, feeling a swirl of emotions wracking his mind, heart and soul.

Why is fate so cruel to me? Does this mean I am as bad as Morg? Kade asked himself. *Why? Why would Zayle say that about me? How could he think that? What does he see that he did not tell me?* Kade agonized as he continued to stare at the ground.

"Kade," Darcienna said softly as she lightly touched him on the arm. He flinched hard as he looked at her. He opened his mouth but could not find any words. He stood there gaping like a fish out of water as his mind searched for something to say, some way to keep her from running from him.

How can she stay with me now? How? he thought.

"I am sure there is more to this," she said as she slid around to look him in the eye. So much compassion and trust was almost too much for him to comprehend.

Kade shook his head, trying to convince himself he would think on it later, but he knew better. It would be on his mind always. Darcienna waited for him patiently, unsure what to do to help with his agony. She slowly moved her hand on his arm as if to sooth him, and it seemed to help just a little.

"Let's go," he said as he tried to be strong.

Would mother and father ever really be comfortable with me? he asked himself. *Well, mother might be, but father was another thing. Did he consider me a bad person? He had to know me better than that. But, why would he not look me in the eye? Was he afraid to see that what he was saying was the truth?* As much as Kade tried to focus on mounting the dragon, his mind kept seeing the goodbye he received from his father. After what his father had said, he was not quite sure if he was welcome long term. Short term was something he knew was okay. He tried to clear his mind and focus on the current task of Valdry.

CH2

Darcienna was very grateful for the seat in front of the wing instead of behind where she had been for the last several rides. Now, she was not going to feel as if she were about to slide down the dragon's tail with every step that Rayden took. She settled in for the journey, waiting for Kade to give the dragon the signal to go. She waited patiently for him to get situated while his mind struggled with the latest dilemma.

Kade fought the urge to look back at the cabin and gave Rayden the signal to go. The dragon turned and started with a slow lope. Kade urged it to a greater speed, afraid that every second he lost was a second he desperately needed. Against his better judgment, he stole a glance back to see if anyone was watching. There was no one in the doorway, but one of the curtains swayed slightly as it fell into place.

Kade watched as the land moved beneath them in a blur. Time slipped by as his mind tortured him over and over with the consequences of his decisions; some good and some painfully disastrous. He closed his eyes, and the image of his father standing with his back to him as he spoke was as clear as if he were standing right there in front of him. If that was not the image haunting him it would be the image of Zayle lying in a pool of blood. Or maybe he would see the many injuries his parents suffered because of him. He clenched his jaw hard one time and then focused on the land again as it flowed past.

"Kade," Darcienna said soothingly in almost a whisper, feeling tension come and go too frequently for her liking. Her voice, in that soothing tone, helped him find release from his torment. He melted and leaned back slightly, his mind fatigued from being overworked. Darcienna found that she was also able to relax, now that Kade was not trapped in his own thoughts.

Hours passed swiftly as the dragon continued on at its easy pace. The land was soon cloaked in darkness. Although Kade was considerably more at ease, his mind continued to drift back to his mother and father. He wished he could be there for them, but he knew   he   would   only   put   them   in   peril.

"Do you know the Chosen we are going to see?" Darcienna asked, breaking the long silence. It startled Kade, but he was grateful for it.

"No. I learned about him for the first time when I opened the black book."

"How do you know he will help?"

"Because Zayle seemed to think he would, or his information would not be in the book. At least, that is how I see it," Kade said with just a touch of doubt in his voice.

As the dragon continued on in its rolling lope, both riders returned to their own thoughts once more. Darcienna mulled over what Kade had said about the Chosen they were going to meet. Something about this made her uneasy, but she could not quite put her finger on it. Maybe it was the unknown, but it seemed that nothing except danger surrounded the Chosen. And, of course, more danger meant Kade was going to try to keep her safe by trying to send her away. It was a pattern she was recognizing, but she would deal with that when the time came.

Darcienna opened her mouth to ask a question but hesitated, unsure if she wanted to know the answer. She watched the way the muscles in his back flexed as the dragon moved while she considered her query. In the end, she decided that it was best to know now before things had progressed too far along.

"Kade, what did you do when you were in Corbin?" Darcienna asked casually.

"I was only there one time. My master was not interested in letting me have much fun," Kade said as he thought about how hard he used to push Zayle to let him go, even if it was just once a year. For reasons unknown to Kade at the time, Zayle was keeping him secluded to keep him safe. "I ran into someone I became friends with while I was there," Kade said as he smiled. He recalled the man who was quick of wit and had a knack for dragging him into situations that he knew better than to be involved with.

"What did you and your friend do?" Darcienna asked. Kade sensed a slight bit of tension and turned to look into her face. He only saw her looking back at him sweetly. Shrugging his shoulders, he casually answered the question while facing forward once again, clearly enjoying the memory.

"Well, first, we went to Dagios where they make the best food ever. Then, we went to this tavern where they put on the most exotic shows I have ever seen. It's actually quite amazing," Kade said as he shot a glance over his shoulder. His mood was brightening considerably.

"I know," Darcienna said under her breath.

"What?" Kade asked as he let his eyes take in the distant horizon.

"I was thinking there had to be more," Darcienna said. She

24

held her hand out in front of herself as if to check for dirt under her nails.

"Well, shortly after we got to the tavern, Turk, that was his name, started to feed me drinks the likes of which I have never had. And wow did they have a kick," Kade said as he chuckled. "I could hardly stand after two," he said and then tilted his head to the side, looking up as if trying to find a memory. "I remember meeting someone, but I can't quite recall the situation," Kade said as he narrowed his eyes, trying to pull the memory to the surface.

"A man?" Darcienna asked as she looked off into the woods.

"A woman," Kade said simply.

"Do you even remember her name?" Darcienna asked with an ever so slightly sarcastic tone in her voice. Kade was too much in his own head to have caught the tone.

"I told you, I was too drunk to remember. I couldn't recall her name let alone her face but I know it was a good time," Kade said, completely unaware of the change in her mood.

"That explains it," Darcienna said, a tightness in her voice.

"What was that?" Kade asked absentmindedly.

"Nothing," Darcienna said as she took in a breath and let it out slowly.

"Why so many questions?" Kade asked as he turned to look back at her again.

"No reason. I was wondering what you do for fun. Just trying to pass the time is all," Darcienna said easily, all signs of her displeasure gone. Although he did not pursue that line of question any further, he did ask another of his own that caught her off guard.

"What did you do the last time you were in Corbin?" Kade asked as he shifted, trying to find a more comfortable position that would ease the riding sores he was developing.

"I went there with my teacher. She had some things she had to do, so I thought I would go along," Darcienna responded, careful to omit details she would rather keep to herself. Unfortunately, Kade continued to blunder blindly along the path she was trying to avoid.

25

"So, what did you do for fun when you were there?" Kade asked with a smile.

Darcienna heard the tone in his voice and shook her head, rolling her eyes. She looked at the back of his head and considered smacking him for even suggesting something along those lines. Just when she was seriously considering actually putting her hand upside his head, she stopped and thought about her night. She did meet someone, but it was not like he was implying. It was not like he was making it sound.

Sure I did not know him, but it was different, she thought. *He was special. It was not as if I had been with more than one guy. That mattered. It did.*

"I normally go shopping or watch some shows," Darcienna said tight lipped.

"Is that all?" Kade asked teasingly. "You and some of your friends did not go out for some fun?" he pressed playfully, missing the dangerous tone.

"No," Darcienna said firmly. She tried to hide her anger but the implications were grating on her. "I don't have any friends in Corbin."

"You did not shop the whole time. What else did you do?" Kade asked, oblivious to the storm that was brewing directly behind him.

"I already told you that I met a man when I was there the last time. What else do you want me to tell you?" Darcienna asked tersely. She immediately regretted her frustration. He really had not done anything wrong besides be oblivious, as all men are.

Kade sobered instantly as he remembered the other man she had talked about. Why did it bother him all of a sudden? He was teasing her and implying that she might have fun meeting people, but now that she had, indeed, done what he was implying, he found himself becoming agitated. The ache that slowly built in his heart made him regret his line of questioning. He was trying to decide how to crush this jealous feeling that was building in him when he paused, sensing he was missing something. There was a piece of a puzzle that just would not fall into place. It was right there. Something about her. Something she was just saying. Maybe the way she was saying it?

"Kade, what's wrong?" Darcienna asked, sensing his mood change.

"Nothing," Kade said as he tried to grasp what was right in front of him, and then it all evaporated like it was never there.

Darcienna considered pressing but decided it would be best if they left it alone. They rode in silence for a while, each in their own thoughts. Kade was deep in his own mind, trying to grasp what he was missing. It felt important, but why? Darcienna started to wonder if she had said something that might have angered him. She was considering asking him, but after a few moments of consideration, she decided to drop it. If he wanted to talk with her about what he was thinking, he would. Little did she know he was still trying to grasp what was eluding him. Finally, he shrugged his shoulders and gave up as his stomach grumbled. Darcienna started to fidget at that moment, shifting several times, trying to find a comfortable position to sit without success. After a few moments of this, Kade turned to look at her.

"You okay?" Kade asked as he saw a pained look on her face.

"Kade, I know we need to get to Valdry as soon as possible, but my legs are cramping horribly and my backside is killing me," Darcienna said as she shifted again while grimacing. Kade narrowed his eyes in thought as he replayed the call for help in his mind. He was about to plead for her to suffer just a little longer when she continued. "Kade, we need rest. And, we have no way of knowing who it was that was calling to you." This last brought Kade up short.

"It never occurred to me that it would be anyone other than Valdry," Kade said as he looked into her eyes.

"It could even be a trap. You just don't know. I think we should rest for the night and start fresh tomorrow. Besides, I am starving."

"You make an excellent point. Okay, I think this is a good place to rest," Kade said as he brought the dragon to a stop. "We have about eight more hours of dark, so we shouldn't be bothered."

Kade jumped to the ground and turned gracefully, clearly getting used to this. He offered his hand to her. She looked at him, trying to see through the front he was putting up, but he was too good. She shook her head, accepting that she was not going to solve this mystery and reached out to accept his hand as she started to slide down toward him. She missed his hand and fell into his arms. Kade was unprepared as the weight of her pressed him backwards. The long ride had taken more of a toll on him that he realized as he scrambled to regain his balance, but his boot struck a root from a nearby tree and they started to fall. He wrapped his arms around her to protect her from the impact.

As soon as the pain from the jarring landing subsided, Kade opened his eyes to see Darcienna's face just inches from his. He became very aware of her body pressed against his and started to feel sensations grow to a dangerous level that would soon shut down the logical part of his brain. He felt her breath against his face and inhaled, enjoying her intoxicating scent. He felt himself start to melt as his eyes wandered over her lips, feeling the urge to taste their sweetness. His hands started to move down her back as if they had a mind of their own. He was on the verge of losing all sense of right or wrong and just letting go. Darcienna slowly slid up as she moved closer to his lips, sliding her hips along his. His breathing was far from steady, and just when he was on the verge of letting go completely, the thought of her with the other guy caused jealousy to flare in him.

Is this thing with me temporary until she can go back to this other guy? He asked himself.

"I can't do this," Kade said as he lifted her off and rolled out from under her.

"What did I do wrong?" Darcienna asked, completely at a loss. "Kade…," she started to say, but he waved her to silence.

28

What he wanted to say was that he wanted her more than he wanted life itself. He wanted to pull her into his arms, look deep in her eyes and then lose himself in her kiss. He wanted this so much that his heart ached. But, if she found the one she was looking for, the pain he would feel would crush him beyond recovery, and he knew this more certainly than anything. He knew what it was to feel the loss of someone that meant everything to him. He was not going to watch her go into the arms of another. He could not think of a more hurtful thing to do to himself than to believe that he could have her only to lose her at a later time. She was more than just a piece of flesh. She was Darcienna.

She sat on the ground, confused, studying Kade, trying to read his thoughts as the expression on his face changed rapidly. She was sure she could see love in his eyes when he looked at her. But in the next instant, it would change to such sadness that she could feel tears threaten to well up in her own eyes. Then, it felt as if a wall a mile thick was growing between them. The wall grew and grew as she watched. Her heart felt as if someone had reached in and was squeezing little by little.

Do you not want me? she agonized as she looked at him. *Why would you not let me in? What is it that you are not telling me? What would it take to get you to open up to me and be mine?* she asked as she stared at the ground. She could see as clearly as day that he wanted her. He wanted her in many ways and she wanted him also, so why fight it?

Darcienna stood and dusted off her clothes. She turned away to hide her face and took several steps without looking back. Well, she intended not to look back, but after a dozen steps or so, she glanced over her shoulder. She saw him watching her, and for just a moment, she saw him looking through a crack in that wall and then it was gone. She stopped and stared down at nothing, trying to convince herself she was not hurt. While she watched, a single teardrop hit the ground and sent a small puff of dust into the air. She wiped her face and swallowed hard. He had his reasons. When he was ready, he would bring down that wall, but for now, he had his reasons. She just had to be patient and be there for him. The more her mind followed this line of thinking, the better she felt. She stole a glance at him and saw him standing as still as a statue.

Kade watched her walk away and confusion clouded his mind. His gut said he had made a mistake. *But, how could protecting my heart be a mistake?* he asked himself. *Am I wrong?* he pondered as his eyes slowed crept along the ground until he was looking at her.

For a moment, he could have sworn she was looking at him, but when he focused on her, she was standing still, staring at the ground. He wanted to go to her and confess how he felt. Yes, this felt right. Either she was going to forget this other guy and be his or he would have no choice but to send her away at the earliest possible moment before there was no turning back for his heart. One way or another, he would have it figured out before he got too hurt. He decided that this was, indeed, the right decision. He turned, and before he could take one step, Rayden roared. Kade felt his heart leap so far into his throat that he almost choked.

"Blood and ash and all that is Holy with the Divine, Rayden!" Kade swore loudly as he clutched his chest. "Do you ever stop eating?" he asked angrily, recognizing the hunger that came through the link. He regretted his words instantly. He dropped his head to his chest, feeling the disappointment through the connection. Rayden sank to the ground and dropped his head heavily onto his front legs as his ears wilted. "Do I have to mess up everything?" Kade asked, cursing himself for not thinking before he spoke. It was a habit he just had to break. His dragon had just spent the day carrying them without complaint, and now that it wanted to eat, he rebuked it.

Darcienna narrowed her eyes as she contemplated what he had just said. *Was he referring to me, also? Did he think he made a mistake by pushing me away?*

"Rayden," Kade said as he dropped to his knees and gently stroked the dragon's head. "You know I love you," Kade said, and then his eyes focused past the dragon to lock with Darcienna's. "You mean more to me than I ever expected," he said as he refocused on the dragon. "I am not perfect and I am going to make mistakes, but if you can accept that, then I will always be in your life," Kade said as he looked past the dragon again, but there was no one there. He wrapped his arms around the dragon's neck and hugged. "Please forgive my rudeness. If you can find it in your heart to accept my apology, I am sure I can feed that deep pit you call a stomach," Kade said as he stood and stepped back. He almost started laughing as he ran his hands through his hair. It was probably the one and only time he would be okay with the dragon drenching his hair with slobber.

"Would you like something to eat?" Kade asked as he turned to look for Darcienna.

"Food would be great," Darcienna said as she moved out from behind the dragon. "You going to make us some?" she asked, as she thought about the beautiful words she had just heard. She could not help but to smile as she recalled the way he had looked past the dragon and locked eyes with her for just a moment as he spoke. Even though he meant it for the dragon, she could not help pretending he meant it for her, also.

"Yes," Kade said, grateful that he and Darcienna were talking, again.

Kade made a piece of meat and went to hand it to Darcienna, who waved it away for the dragon. She always put others first, and it made him love her even more. She had an amazing heart, and if he was worthy, it would belong to him.

If only I am worthy, he thought as his father's words rang in his ears. He shook it off and focused on attempting to satisfy Rayden's hunger. After feeding nature's best devourer of food, he turned his attention to Darcienna.

"I can't believe that such a simple calling would turn out to be so useful," Kade said as he handed the next piece of steaming meat to her. She took it graciously and sat on a fallen log, waiting for him to join her. "I wish Zayle would have taught me this one, sooner," he said as he sat next to her.

"Maybe he didn't because he knew that you would become as big as a cabin if he did," Darcienna said, more her old self. Kade felt such an immense relief wash over him that he did not care that he had dropped his food on the ground. The tension was gone as if it had never been.

"Here," Kade said as he tossed the dirty piece of meat to the dragon. Rayden was clearly not picky as he snapped up the food with a slight bit of sand flavoring and swallowed it without chewing.

Kade made another chunk of meat and return to sit next to Darcienna. He smiled, happy that she was looking at him again with those heart-stopping eyes. He took several large bites and noticed the disapproving look from her at his eating manners. After two more intentionally large mouthfuls, he took two smaller bites. Darcienna gave just the slightest hint of a smile as she seemed to focus on her own meat, but something told Kade that the smile was meant for him. He sighed and proceeded to eat the rest of his food, not in small bites, but not the large chunks he had previously taken, either.

"How long until we reach this other Chosen?" Darcienna asked.

"About half a day's ride," Kade said past the food in his mouth. Darcienna gave him another disapproving look. He took a deep steadying breath, then swallowed the meat in one big gulp and repeated, "About half a day's ride."

For reasons he was not able to fathom, she still had a reproving look. He just shook his head, clearly lost as to what he had done wrong now and looked around to see if any streams ran past. He wished he had the foresight to bring some water, but once again, he found himself thirsty without anything to drink.

"What are you looking for?" Darcienna asked.

"Water," Kade said.

"Why don't you just conjure some?"

"Because it is a food calling, not a drink calling," Kade said with a hint of irritation.

"How would the Divine know the difference? If you wanted

to create grapes, could you?" Darcienna asked simply.

"I suppose," Kade said, pondering her line of thinking.

"Then, if you can make grapes, which are used to make wine, then you should be able to make wine, right?"

"Maybe," Kade said. He narrowed his eyes as he studied the idea. "It is worth a try," he added, curiously. He stood and closed his eyes, eager to test out her idea. He performed the calling while picturing a nice bottle of sweet wine. Within seconds, he felt the liquid materialize in his hands and proceed to splash on the ground, getting his legs wet. Kade jumped back and gave Darcienna an accusing look, but she didn't seem to notice.

"Well, it seems the bottle is not organic, so that is not going to work. So, I guess it needs to be organic. All we need to do is find some way to catch the wine," Darcienna said as if stating the most obvious fact.

"I suppose that would work," Kade said as he looked around the area.

"Good," Darcienna said, happy with how this was going.

Kade watched as her eyes stopped on something on the other side of the dragon. He turned to see what she had found as she got to her feet. Darcienna walked around Rayden to a torok tree. It was perfect. Its leaves were cone shaped and made for catching rainwater. It was a survival skill of the tree, but tonight, it would be used to catch wine.

"This should work," Darcienna said with a smile. "I will hold it under your hands while you perform the calling."

Kade, begrudgingly, had to admit that her ability to look at things differently helped them find a solution. Even with hands that were becoming sticky with the drying wine, he was grateful for her creative thinking. He smiled at the thought of tasting the sweet drink and was eager to try again.

"Okay, let's make some wine," Kade said as he started the Food Calling. He felt the wine splash past his hands just as it did the first time. He opened his eyes and saw Darcienna proudly displaying the cup of liquid. He could not help but to smile at her pure innocence. There was nothing but the honest intent to help. She was not trying to show him that she was superior because of her creative way of thinking, nor was she gloating about finding a solution. It was just pure altruism.

Kade held his breath as she lifted the makeshift cup to her lips, afraid she would cough and sputter at what was supposed to be wine. He recalled his failed attempts when he first tried to make meat and dreaded the same outcome. Darcienna took a sip and nodded her head in approval. Kade breathed a sigh of relief. Darcienna lifted the cup to her lips again, and took two deep swallows with her eyes closed, savoring the taste. She handed it back to Kade, who did the same. He handed the cup back to her and she took the last drink. He filled the leaf several times, giving them both more than their fair share.

Darcienna wiped her mouth with the back of her hand. How she was able to do this and still look proper was beyond him, but he was sure if he had done the same, it would have earned him a disapproving look. But, then again, she could do almost anything, and it would be fine with him.

"That was a good idea," Kade said, feeling the effects of the wine.

"I can't believe I drank that much," Darcienna said, barely able to form her words.

Feeling the ground start to rock, Kade held onto Rayden to keep from falling. He turned his back to the dragon and slid down to the ground. He put his hands on his stomach as he leaned back.

"You know, you look a little familiar," Kade said as he studied her for a moment.

"Of course I do. You know me," Darcienna said with a giggle.

"I do?" Kade asked, almost grasping something. It was right there.

"Yes silly. We have been traveling together for about two or three days now," Darcienna said with anther giggle.

"Oh," Kade said, but he was still studying her as if that answer was not good enough.

"Kade, don't you think we should be getting some sleep?" Darcienna asked, trying to change the subject.

"Yes, we should," Kade said, enjoying the feeling he was experiencing from the drink.

Getting to his feet a little clumsily, Kade turned to find that Rayden was already in the world of dreams. He looked around for a soft spot to sleep for the night and saw a clump of moss beneath the torok tree. With a little coxing, he convinced Darcienna to lie down on the soft patch. She patted the very small spot of moss next to her, and seeing no reason why he should not, he did as she bid. They talked for a while, until Darcienna no longer answered his questions. He leaned over to see her eyes closed and watched her breathing deeply. For a moment, he considered moving away, but he did not want to leave her alone, and what better way to make sure she was safe than to be right there with her. He lay on his back as he looked up at the stars, feeling at peace. Soon, he drifted off to sleep. Darcienna snuggled into him, and he draped his arm around her. They would stay like that for most of the night.

The sun broke through the leaves of the torok tree to arouse Kade from his slumber. He rubbed the sleep from his eyes and looked around the clearing. He found that he was off the moss and Darcienna was sprawled over the entire patch. He stretched his back to work out a few knots and looked over to see the dragon had not moved. He was taking in the calm air as he watched Rayden and did not even notice as Darcienna reached over for him.

"Good morning," she said as she laid a hand on his arm.

Kade flinched hard, spraying dirt into the air as his hand came up out of reflex. When he saw it was her, he studied her to see if she was trying to repay him for his little prank back in the kitchen of his parent's cabin. He shook his head at his foolishness and took a steadying breath. Was that a smirk on her face?

He worked his way to his feet and checked for the sack of books. Satisfied everything was as it should be, he returned to look at

Darcienna. She looked beautiful, even in the early hours.

"Good morning yourself," Kade said as he offered her his hand. "It sure felt good to sleep," he said as he tried to recall the night.

"We should get going as soon as possible. Half of the day is already gone," Darcienna said.

"Well, let's have something to eat first, and then we can get moving."

Kade made a full three course meal of cheese, bread and meat. He sat down next to Darcienna, eagerly looked forward to the food. After checking to make sure the dragon was still asleep so he could eat in peace, he enjoyed his morning meal. They ate without saying much as they enjoyed the calm of the land.

Kade finished his food while Darcienna still had half of hers left. He climbed to his feet and proceeded to make a pile of meat for the dragon. He had placed eight steaming pieces of juicy meat right in front of Rayden's nose, wondering when the dragon was going to wake. As Kade laid the ninth one down, the dragon's nose started to work feverishly. It was not long before its eyes popped open, and it tore into the pile of meat with huge bites. Kade laughed and looked at Darcienna to see how she would regard the dragon's eating habits.

"Rayden is a dragon," Darcienna said simply, as if that was all that needed to be said. Kade shook his head, not knowing where to go with that.

It took no time for the dragon to finish. As a matter of fact, Darcienna was still eating when the dragon inhaled the tenth piece. Kade made a mental note to see how big a piece of meat he could create. Cooking like this was really starting to turn into work.

"Time to go, my friend," Kade said as he patted Rayden on the neck.

The dragon, reluctantly, bent down for the riders to mount. Kade got the feeling that the dragon would have preferred to lie back down and spend the day doing nothing. He knew exactly how his friend felt.

Kade helped Darcienna to her feet as she shoved the last of the bread into her mouth. He boosted her onto the dragon and then easily vaulted onto Rayden's back. Kade flexed his hands, feeling the stickiness of the wine and wiped them on his pants. It did not do much to help so he decided to stop at the first stream or lake they could find. For that matter, a full cleaning was in order.

He tied the books into place and signaled the dragon to go. Instead of the lazy lope as Kade expected, the dragon merely walked. He considered coaxing it into a run but decided that it was probably best if they started the day out slowly. He found that this slower pace helped his mind relax.

After the sun had traveled across most of the sky, Kade realized they were just barely halfway to Valdry's place. He considered once more asking the dragon to pick up the pace, but the warm sun made him feel just as lazy as the dragon. He let it go, dreading rushing into more danger. His nerves needed a break, and he did not need to hold on so tightly to the dragon.

Many hours later, night threatened to creep across the land when they came upon a lake. Kade could picture the water washing over him, removing the many days of travel. The sun was starting to set, and it cast a long reflection across the lake, causing Kade to have to shield his eyes. It was beautiful, and he stared for a while, soaking up the view.

"This looks like a good place to stop for the night. We will see the Chosen, Valdry, in the morning," Kade said.

"I thought this was going to be half a day's ride," Darcienna commented.

"If we would have pushed Rayden, then it would have been, but it felt good to take it slowly for once. Besides, I needed rest before we meet this Valdry. I need to be prepared for anything. He is a Chosen, and from talking to Zayle, I have to be cautious," Kade said as he slid down from the dragon.

"Why cautious?" Darcienna asked, confused. She swung her leg over and slid down to land in Kade's arms. He regretted, momentarily, not losing his balance and then stepped back as he turned toward the water. Before taking one step, he turned back to the dragon and untied the books. He gently laid them on the ground and headed for the water.

"Because...," Kade started to say, struggling with how best to explain it for her to fully understand. "Because we have secrets... even from each other. Zayle says that each Chosen works a lifetime compiling knowledge but does not share it. It is a status thing, and of course, power. For example, Zayle is the only one that knows the Lightning Calling. He is not even sure if any of the other Chosen know the Divine Fire Calling. He has more knowledge compiled than any other Chosen. Many have tried to steal these very books," Kade said as he patted the sack. "It's these secrets that keep us from interacting with one another, unless we have a common interest where we must work together."

"But, that is crazy," Darcienna said, stunned at his words.

"Why?" Kade asked, surprised at her reaction.

"Because you should work together like we do."

"You work together?" Kade asked in surprise. After a moment, it made sense. "Wait. Just think about it. You cannot gain power until it is given to you," he said as he watched her to make sure she was following his logic. "If you were able to travel great distance at the blink of an eye, would you want that?" he asked as he turned to face her.

"I believe anyone would," Darcienna said as she tried to see where he was going with this.

"Okay, so let's say that your kind, who uses Nature's Gift, can share these abilities. Let's also say that you find just one person who has this knowledge but won't share it. What would you do?"

"I would respect their wish to be left alone," Darcienna said, still not understanding how this was supporting his argument.

"But you are willing to share?"

"Of course," Darcienna said quickly.

"And what if you were willing to share but that one who knew

38

the travel ability would not share with you? Would you share with that person?"

"I...but that is not how it is."

"Isn't it? If just one person decided they did not want to share their ability, that would start a chain reaction of others not wanting to share or one person might become too powerful. And then, pretty soon, you would have people guarding their secrets closely. But you don't have to worry about that. You get your abilities given to you, and you don't need to fear another of your kind lusting after that knowledge. Do you understand what I am saying?" Kade asked as he smiled easily at her.

"I still think it should be okay to share the knowledge, though," Darcienna said, trying to salvage a bit of her point of view.

"In a perfect world, I would agree. But, this is not a perfect world. Zayle used to say that it had to be this way. He told me hundreds, no, thousands of times that power corrupts and absolute power corrupts absolutely. He would preach over and over that the more knowledge and power one person held, the more temptation there would be to use that power. And, that person would be tempted to shape things into the way they wanted. He would say that even if you start out with good in your heart, sooner or later your actions would infringe upon others. He would lecture me over and over that as soon as this line was crossed, one would be well on their way to self-destruction. With the knowledge spread between several Chosen, they would keep each other in check. Morg wants to eliminate us all so there is no one to challenge him. At least, that is all I can figure out until I can learn more."

Darcienna sat there in dismay. She had never seen so much drama. Her simple world of how things worked was quickly changing as her mind actually started to grasp what Kade was explaining. For just a moment, she saw the world, not as the beautiful place she believed it to be, but as intricate plots and subterfuge while people jockeyed for positions that would give them advantage. It made her sick to think that the basic nature of man could be reduced to such selfish motives that might hurt others. She could not recall a time when she wanted something for herself that might harm another. The more she contemplated this line of thinking, the more she was sure she could never accept someone suffering for her betterment. It just was not acceptable.

"You stay here while the dragon and I go get cleaned up," Kade said. "On second thought, come with me. I want to make sure I can keep you safe."

The dragon was eager to launch itself into the water. Kade patted it on the side and pointed to the lake. Rayden tore off like he was hunting prey. He leapt high in the air and hit the water with a splash that sent a wave in all direction. Kade charged after the dragon without taking his clothes off, splashing through the water until it was too deep and then dove. The lake was just too inviting to take the time to undress, and the clothes needed washing anyway.

Kade shot to the surface, eyes wide with shock at the frigid temperature of the water. He waded back toward shore until the water was at his waist and then stopped. Darcienna was watching him, obviously entertained.

"You mind turning around," Kade said as he started to work at removing his clothes. He struggled as the wet fabric clung tightly to his body. He heard a thread tear as he put his strength into it. He eased his grip and worked the clothes up one side and then another until he had his shirt off. He tossed it to shore and went to work at his pants until he saw that she was still watching.

"Maybe I confused you when I used the words turn around. That means, face the other way," Kade said, scolding her.

"That's no fun," Darcienna said with a wink. She was relieved that they were back to where she could tease him again. She loved to watch him blush, as he was doing right at that moment.

"Darcienna," Kade said sternly.

"Okay," Darcienna said, her hands up in surrender. "You have only to the count of ten, and then I turn back around again," she added.

"Darcienna," Kade warned, but she started to count. Kade huffed as he started to wrestle with his pants.

"One. Two. Three. Four," Darcienna called over her shoulder. Kade gritted his teeth and worked to pull his pants off, but like his shirt, it clung to his body with tenacity as if it were alive. "Five. Six. Seven," she said as she prepared to turn. Kade hopped on one leg as he struggled to pull the other leg out. "Eight. Nine. Ten," she said as she spun around. Kade sank down into the water as he fought with the last leg.

"Kade!" Darcienna screamed as she watching him thrash violently as he fought with something unseen. She had her hands up, ready to project a shield around him when he finally subdued his foe. He stood with his vicious pants in his hands and glared at her. Her eyes widened in surprise, and then she let out a laugh that she could not stifle.

"I am happy you find this so entertaining," Kade said, irritated. He balled up his wet pants, wound up and threw, hitting her square in the face. She stumbled under the weight of the water in the cloth but did not fall. She shook her head and wiped her eyes clear. Kade was afraid he had gone too far, but she quirked a smile at him as she ran her fingers through her hair, straightening it.

"Nice throw," Darcienna said with a twinkle in her eye.

How can I fight my feelings for her? Kade asked himself. *She is perfect. How many women would accept a ball of wet pants in the face and not come unhinged? She takes as well as she gives. Bah. I am only torturing myself,* he finished as he turned to find the dragon.

Rayden was galloping around the lake just as he had done at the hot spring. Kade found himself laughing as he watched this fierce dragon look like the goofiest thing he had seen with the way its head would bob up and down with each stride. This lake was ten times the size of the hot spring. As Rayden ran around the far side, he was barely recognizable.

The water was freezing and Kade found it difficult to

completely immerse himself, even after his short wrestling match with his pants. He slowly edged deeper, sucking in his gut as the cold crept up his torso. He held his arms above the water, waiting until he had to duck under.

"You need to wash everything. Your hair looks like a rat's nest, and I am not sure what your true skin color is," Darcienna chided.

"I am going as fast as I can. This lake is so cold, it should already be turned to ice," Kade said as he sank his arms into the water and wrapped them around his sides.

"Okay, then I shall have to come in and dunk you myself," Darcienna said with a glint in her eye.

"You can't," Kade said as he looked down at his unclothed body and then back up at her.

"Why not? The dragon seems to like it, so I am sure you will survive," Darcienna said as she feigned ignorance to the reason for his concern and edged closer to the water.

Taking a deep breath, Kade turned and dove, vowing to make her pay. He felt the icy, cold water rush over his body, causing a dull hum to echo in his ears. He could feel his heart pounding as he came back to the surface. He wanted to get out of the water, but Darcienna still stood at the edge, watching.

"I will get you for this," Kade said between teeth that started to chatter.

"Well, feel free to come get me," Darcienna said as she cocked an eyebrow in challenge and held her arms out to her side with her palms upward.

Her taunts were almost enough for him to overcome his modesty and charge out of the water…almost. She knew he was not going to come out, and she used it for everything it was worth. She reached down and picked up his pants, dangling them by one crooked finger. She eyed him deviously as she swung them back and forth. That was the last straw. His mind started working feverishly as he struggled to devise a plan of revenge. He glanced around for something, anything when he saw that Rayden was climbing back on shore just down a ways from Darcienna. He fought to hide his grin as he formulated his plan.

I might not come out of the water, Kade thought to himself, *but the dragon will. Rayden,* Kade sent, *sneak up on Darcienna. You must be as careful and quiet as possible. Pretend she is the most deadly prey you have ever hunted. She must not know you are there.* Rayden instantly dropped to such a low crouch that his belly was just barely off the ground. Kade had to fight a laugh at the comical way the dragon exaggerated such stealth. It moved so smoothly that even the Silence Calling was no better. The dragon's deliberate movement with every step had Kade in awe.

"I will get you somehow," Kade threatened as she started to turn. He moved through the water to keep her attention on him so she would not see the massive predator closing in on her from the side. One glance at Rayden, and the game would be up. Kade steadied his heart, eagerly wanting this to go as planned.

"Well, you are there, and I am here," Darcienna continued to taunt.

Just a little closer. Almost there. Just keep her busy a little longer, Kade thought as he fought the urge to smirk. Rayden was focused and did not even so much as blink as he stalked his victim. Kade took another step, and she turned just ever so slightly to follow him with her eyes.

"Oh, trust me. You will learn, and unfortunately, it has to be the hard way," Kade said as he casually looked down to study the dirt on his arms. He fought hard to keep from grinning but lost control as the edge of his mouth tweaked up into a grin. He pursed his lips hard to hide the smile as he looked up at her. She was studying him with her eyes narrowed.

"I doubt that," Darcienna said but there was no confidence in her voice.

Kade locked eyes with her. He was so eager to see the look on her face when he sprang his attack that he could hardly contain

43

himself. *Just a little bit more.* Rayden was virtually a statue with how slow he crept while moving into position directly behind her. The dragon just needed to move forward ten more feet, and it would be ready to pounce.

"Well, I must admit that you do have me at a disadvantage," Kade said as he smiled easily and spread his hands out to his side. He used the smile to hide his grin, but she was studying him now.

Darcienna opened her mouth to give some sort of retort but stopped. Kade felt his heart thumping, knowing that she was sensing that he was up to something, but the question was…would she figure it out in time. Just five more feet and he would have his revenge. Kade could swear the dragon was not even breathing as it crept toward its target. He tried hard not to look past her as even just a shift of his eyes would give it away. Darcienna was feigning casualness, but she was watching him as sharply as a hawk, and he knew it. One slip and this would end in her favor.

His clothes still dangling from her finger, the smile slipped from her face. Four feet. She turned her head to look at him sideways. Three feet. Her wrist went slack as she looked around the lake, sensing something was not right. There was something missing, but she could not quite place what it was. Two feet. Kade was sure that any moment she would feel or sense the massive, hulking dragon just barely out of her peripheral view. One foot. Darcienna's eyes came open wide as she scanned the lake. Her eyes locked with his. She inhaled sharply and then she spun.

"Now," Kade commanded and the dragon attacked.

Darcienna moved like lightning but it was not fast enough. The dragon hit her in the backend with his snout and lifted all in one smooth motion. She was propelled well into the air with such a look of dismay that Kade burst out in laughter instantly. He was laughing so hard that he no longer noticed the cold of the lake. It was all so very worth it.

Darcienna landed with a splash a good fifteen feet from shore. She went under and came up sputtering. For a moment, Kade stopped laughing and watched closely to make sure she was okay. When she got to her feet with her hair stuck to the side of her face, he relaxed and immersed himself in his victory. The look of disbelief was still strong in her eyes, and it made this so much sweeter. Kade grinned and sent Rayden a thanks. The dragon was lying down on the beach with its front legs crossed as it sat, its mouth hanging open in a relaxed way, watching.

"Wow is that cold," Darcienna said as she hugged herself.

"I told you. But, you made me get in, so I thought it only fair to share this amazing experience with you," Kade said as he chuckled again. "It's not bad once you get used to it."

"Then you enjoy your swim," Darcienna said as she worked her way back to shore. "You could not get me back in here if your life depended on it." Kade watched as she walked out of the water, seeing the wet clothes cling tightly to her shapely body.

It was definitely worth it, Kade thought with a grin.

He laughed again as he took a deep breath, dunked his head under water and came back up again. He scrubbed his hair with his hands to loosen the dirt and then ducked back under the surface. He swished back and forth and then stood.

"Just to show you I am a good sport, I will lay your clothes out for you to dry," Darcienna said in as sweet a voice as she could muster. She sat down on a log and ignored the cool night air as she made it clear she was not going to turn her back or close her eyes. The sun was down and the sounds of night animals drifted through the air.

"Can't you just admit that I won and let this go?" Kade asked with a grin.

"Of course I can," Darcienna said innocently but there was no sincerity in her voice.

"I'll tell you what. If you leave my clothes alone and turn your back, I won't drown myself," Kade said as he formulated his next plan.

"Come get dressed," Darcienna said, curious what Kade was

up to now? She might not admit it to him, but she did enjoy seeing his humorous side.

"Okay," Kade said as he turned toward the deeper water. For this to succeed, he had to be in up to his neck or she would discover his ruse.

"Last chance," Kade yelled over his shoulder, but she did not reply.

Darcienna moved to the edge of the water, watching him curiously. Kade grinned to himself as he started the moves for the Transparency Calling. Just as he finished, he ducked under the water. The timing had to be perfect or she would see his head disappear and she would know his plan.

Kade swam at an angle to shore and surfaced as quietly as possible, struggling not to take a deep breath. The night was too quiet so he knew any sound would give him away. His only chance was for the insects and water sounds to mask any noise he made. With concerted effort, he was able to get his breathing under control.

Darcienna put her hands on her hips as she continued to stare, a grin on her face. She was enjoying these little games. She turned and walked toward him. He was sure he was discovered until he realized that she had not taken her eyes off the water where he had been. She paced back the other way and gave a gasp of frustration. Kade almost let out a laugh at this.

"He will come up any second," Darcienna said to herself. Kade stifled another laugh and her head whipped around to look in his direction. After a moment, she returned to watching the water. Another thirty seconds passed. "Okay, time for you to come make a fire," she said as she studied the water. She yelled his name but still no response. She turned to walk away from the lake as if to ignore him, but after just three steps, she came back to the edge of the water.

He felt a twinge of guilt as he saw the worried look on her face. Just a twinge, and then he stifled another laugh. She could no longer take it. She waded in to the spot where he had been.

Kade hurried onto shore and dressed as quickly as possible.

Darcienna was too busy looking into the water to see the clothes lift into the air like a leaf caught by the wind. Kade struggled into his outfit that clung just as tightly going on as they did coming off. He grinned to himself as he adjusted his shirt and sat down on the log.

"What are you looking for?" Kade asked Darcienna casually as he let the Transparency Calling go. When she looked up, she jumped as if she were stuck by a pin.

"What the…," Darcienna started to say.

"I am a Chosen," Kade said as if that answered it all.

"How did…wait. Uggg. You used the Divine," Darcienna said as if she was handing down a guilty verdict and accusing him of cheating.

"Was that against the rules?" Kade asked with an innocent look.

"Make a fire," was all Darcienna said to that.

Kade quickly pulled some wood over into a pile as he watched Darcienna shiver. He started to feel guilty and worried that the cold might even cause more problems than he realized. He motioned her to move back and then set the wood on fire with an explosion. Darcienna flinched and looked at him. Kade gave her a sheepish look that did for an apology. The medallion on his chest cooled ever so slightly. He was conscious of it any time it changed now. She sat by the fire, shivering for some time.

"That was a cute trick," Darcienna said with a smile. She looked at him sideways and the smile reached her eyes. Again, Kade could not believe how perfect she was.

They both huddled next to the fire and enjoyed the warmth as it soaked into their bones. Darcienna slid next to Kade and held onto his arm for comfort. He leaned into her slightly, enjoying the closeness. After a while, they turned to face away from the fire to give their backs a chance to dry. They sat looking over the water well after the wetness had left their clothes and talked for quite some time until Rayden started to huff. Kade did not even need to look at the dragon to know why. He glanced at Darcienna, who unwrapped

47

herself from his arms. Wearily, he rose and moved away from the fire. Rayden started to dance from foot to foot, eager to be fed.

Kade forced himself to focus as he worked his way through the calling over and over again. He found it very difficult to stay on task as his mind threatened to wander. Feeding the dragon was becoming monotonous and routine. This made it dangerous, and he knew, sooner or later, he might make a mistake that was permanent. After feeding the dragon his standard ten pieces, he decided to try an experiment. He thought back on his battle with Morg and how much of the Divine Power surged through his body during the fight.

I wonder if I can channel the Divine like that again, Kade thought. *Maybe it can be used to affect the size of the meat that I can conjure.* The problem was that he had never called on that much of the Divine intentionally. It had always come through anger and of its own accord.

Kade closed his eyes and reached deep for the Divine. It was there, as usual, and came to him like it always did, but this time he tried to grab more of it. There was no discernible change. He felt for the power swirling in him, and it was nothing more than a gentle tide, not the raging flood he had experienced previously. He performed the Food Calling and visualized the piece of meat, trying to see it as twice the normal size. The calling fizzled and crackled, but nothing materialized. He tried making the normal size piece of meat, and it materialized just as it always had.

"Kade?" Darcienna asked. "Are we going to eat?"

Kade looked down and realized she had been waiting patiently for their meal. He quickly handed the meat to her and continued to make cheese and bread. He looked around for a torok tree, but seeing none, decided to pass on making the wine.

"I was trying to figure out a way to feed the dragon without having to make so many little pieces. It barely keeps him satisfied," Kade said, glancing at Rayden.

"I can see the problem," Darcienna said and then took a bite of meat. Her hands were greasy from the hot, juicy food, and yet, she still looked elegant where he would have looked like a brute.

"You do?" Kade asked, curious.

"Maybe. Explain more to me," Darcienna said between bites.

"This calling seems to only be able to create a certain amount of food each time. I am trying to make a larger piece so I am not always making so much. I want to perform one or two callings and be done with feeding him," Kade said.

"And what were you trying that you thought might be different?" Darcienna asked as her mind digested every possible clue.

"Well, I was trying to call on more of the Divine to make a larger piece, but I can't seem to draw in enough of the power."

"But, how would you know if you had drawn in more, if it always feels the same?"

"Oh, I have channeled ten times that amount before?"

"You have?" Darcienna said as she stopped chewing, her eyes going wide. "When?"

"When I was fighting Morg," Kade said as he watched her contemplate this information.

"I think I may know what the issue is," Darcienna said.

"What then?" Kade asked, eager to hear her discovery.

"It's not that you can't draw on more of it, if I understand this correctly, it's that you are not letting yourself draw on as much as you want. I am guessing the block is in you."

"So...if I can remove the block, I should be able to call on more," Kade said a bit more excited, seeing her point. He looked at her, but she was not looking back with the enthusiasm he expected. He narrowed his eyes and watched her, waiting for her to respond. He could see there was more and started to get the same uncomfortable feeling he had when he last spoke with his father. She sighed and slowly looked up at him.

"Kade, the only time you have called on more is when you have been so enraged that you were beyond reason," Darcienna said. "If that is the only way, then...," she started to say, but let the thought trail off.

"Then I cannot do it," Kade finished. "I cannot channel that much power unless I can ensure I am in control. I am starting to understand," Kade said as he looked out over the lake. Darcienna got the distinct impression that he was talking about something else completely. She raised an eyebrow in question, but he waved it away.

He stood with a sigh and walked over to the sack of books, looking down on them without really seeing them. After a few seconds, he shook his head slightly to dismiss his thoughts and returned to the fire with the sack. He laid on the ground and put his head on the books. He stared into the fire as he mulled over what Darcienna had said. More of the puzzle came together, and he was not liking what he was seeing.

"How can you just go to sleep when Morg could ambush us?" Darcienna asked, still sitting in the same spot.

"You weren't worried last night. How come all the worry now?" Kade asked as he rolled onto his back and looked up at her.

"Last night I was too tired to think straight, and we had a little too much to drink, don't you think?"

"You did not seem to worry during the day," Kade said, as he watched her.

"That is because we were all awake," Darcienna said, exasperated. "No matter what Morg does, I don't think he can kill us that easily. I can sense if he is going to try, and the dragon can deal with almost anything he sends. And your callings are formidable. But, if we are asleep, he could sneak right up on us," she said as if he were a child.

"You would not wake up?" Kade asked in shock, ignoring her condescending tone. "You would sleep right through the warning?"

"I am not sure it works while I am asleep," Darcienna said grimly. "And, I do not want to find out the hard way."

"Well, I am sure that Rayden would sense if someone got close," Kade said as he leaned on his elbow and looked over at the dragon.

Rayden was out completely. Darcienna got up and walked

over to the dragon. She shoved Rayden and stepped back. His eyelids fluttered slightly, his breathing faltered just barely, and then he returned back to his rhythmic breathing. Darcienna gave Kade a look, and he held up his hands in surrender.

"What do you want to do? Take turns staying awake?" Kade asked, dearly wanting to relax and close his eyes.

"No. Don't you have any callings you can use to warn us if someone comes while we are sleeping?"

"I don't know any callings like that," Kade said as he mentally scrolled through his limited repertoire. "But, I could look and see if I can find a simple one. A very simple one," he said, putting heavy emphasis on the word simple. He was not in the mood to try to stumble through a new calling while this tired. This felt like a bad idea, but just going to sleep was a bad idea, also.

"I'd feel much better if we tried instead of just leaving it to chance," Darcienna said, full of confidence in him. He cringed. She just did not understand the full depth of the danger of the situation. Learning a calling should take days. Learning a calling while this tired? Foolish! He would make a good show of it and then put the book back away where it belonged.

Kade sat up and opened the sack carefully, as if it contained a venomous snake. He pulled out the pile of prized knowledge and sat it on the ground gently. Anytime he contemplated untying the strap, he handled them like they were going to explode at any moment. They were cinched so tightly that the pile of books felt like a brick. He undid the leather strap, handling them as if a calling was going to trigger at the lightest touch. He gently took out the main book of callings and then cinched the remaining ones tightly. He performed the Disarm Calling and laid his hand on the cover. As casually as he could, he pulled the book open. He relaxed, grateful that he was able to hide his anxiety from Darcienna.

Darcienna had her hand on Kade's shoulder as he placed his hand on the cover of the book. His body was tense. As if his muscles were not already tight enough, they turned to iron as he flipped the book open. As Kade laid the cover on his lap, she felt his arm quiver slightly as the muscles fought to unwind. She looked at the side of his face, watching as the muscle that ran along his jaw unclenched. He turned toward her, and she smiled sweetly. He smiled back. He was trying hard to keep her from worrying, but unless she were a corpse, she could not miss all those signs.

Kade turned page after page, looking for something that would fit the situation. Darcienna sat, looking over his shoulder, feeling privileged as if she were looking at some ancient secret knowledge. She thought back on their conversation about how each Chosen guards his callings with his life, and here she was, looking at his as if it was nothing.

"Would I be able to perform any of these?" Darcienna asked.

"If you had the ability, and that is a big if, it would most likely take you years and years just to sense the Divine. I had to meditate every day for hours at a time to even feel it. It's like reaching into a pool of water. At first, it all feels the same. But, the more you do this, the more you start to feel the subtle differences. It took me so long that my master almost gave up on me," Kade said as he glanced at her. "It took me more than five years to sense it and then another four to really make any progress."

"How did you know you had the ability in the first place?"

"I didn't. I would have never known I could do what I can if it were not for Zayle. He could see it in me. He had a way of seeing things about people. All Chosen have something that develops in them. It's said to be a gift from the Divine. Zayle explained it to me once. He told me that he could look into a flame and see things," Kade said, recalling his father's story about those five words Zayle spoke. "And, some can do other things like communicate with others without calling on the Divine," Kade said as he recalled the voice in his head.

"Oh," Darcienna said. "Would you be willing to teach me…if I can call on the Divine?" she asked a bit timidly. She was unsure if there was a secret to becoming one of the Chosen. *Maybe there was some initiation or there was an approval process,* she thought.

"I don't know if there is more involved to being allowed to channel the Divine, but I would not be against it if it was allowed," Kade said as he glanced up from the book. "But, don't forget, it could take five years or even ten just to sense it if you can even sense it at all. And, it might not work due to your Nature's Gift. There is a lot that is unknown. You must never forget that it is extremely dangerous. You must never take it lightly," he said gravely. He could hear the very same words said to him, but in the voice of his master.

"I understand," Darcienna said. "I don't have anything else planned after this if we are...," she was saying when Kade firmly interrupted her.

"When," Kade said quickly, correcting her. "When we are successful," he repeated, leaving no room for doubt. She smiled and loved him for his confidence. It made her feel safe. It was definitely one of the things she admired about him.

"When we finish this," Darcienna repeated with a smile. "That's what I like about you, Kade. You are always optimistic, and you never give up," she said as she laid her hand on his cheek.

He enjoyed the way her hand gave him a warm feeling inside. There was a struggle raging in him as the feel of her touch lingered on his cheek. His heart was at war with the common sense part of his mind. He wanted to keep his head clear, and yet, when he built up that wall, she was able to make it evaporate.

Why am I so weak? he asked himself

"Kade?" Darcienna asked.

"I'm sorry. I was off in thought. Did you say something?" Kade asked.

"I was just asking if you thought there might be something you can use," Darcienna said as she indicated the book.

"I am not sure. I am still looking," Kade said as he closely scrutinized each calling.

He had looked at over thirty one callings when he came to the thirty second. Darcienna squeezed his shoulder as he read. He stopped and turned to look at her.

"This looks like what we want," Kade said as he returned to reading the page. "Yes, this looks like what we need."

Detection Calling:

This will allow the user to place a calling on the area approximately sixty feet in diameter. While creating the calling, it is important to pay close attention to how much of the Divine Power is used. The more Divine Power used, the more sensitive the calling will be. If too much power is used, then one who is strong in the use of the Divine Power will be able to sense the calling.

There were six moves to the calling. Kade studied them for several long minutes. At the end of the calling, he was to say the word surround in the ancient language, and the calling would be cast.

"Why are you taking so long?" she asked.

"Darcienna, there is no room for mistakes," Kade said, exasperated. "If I do the calling wrong, there will be no undoing the damage I cause. If I do the calling incorrectly, I might change you into a tree or make myself float off the ground and never come back. If I had Zayle here, I could do the calling over and over until I got it right. Zayle could do something that would snuff out the Divine Power before I could kill myself with it. Now, I do not have that protection. I absolutely must get it right the first time. There is no room for mistakes," Kade said as Darcienna stared at him in awe.

"You mean…every time you do a calling of any kind…you could have that happen?" Darcienna asked as she considered how many times he must have used the Divine in the last few days.

"Yes," Kade said firmly, driving the point home. He thought about reminding her of the damage done to his arm from the Lightning Calling, but the look on her face said she understood.

"Take all the time you want," Darcienna said, sitting back a little, glancing at the arm that she had healed. "When you said dangerous, I didn't know you meant dangerous like that. I thought that," she said, indicating his arm, "was just a careless mistake." She realized her insult a little too late but Kade waved her away. It was a careless mistake and Zayle would have made sure Kade knew it, too.

He returned to studying the calling. He read for twenty more minutes before he started the small hand movements. Hours slid by as the moon crawled across the sky. He finished his last practice movements with the calling and decided it was time to focus on actually performing the calling. He did his best to ignore the knot in his stomach and tried to clear his mind of all distraction. He was weary and wanted sleep badly, but he knew Darcienna was right about not letting down their guard.

"You had better stand back a little," Kade said as he put his hand up to her and ushered her to move.

"Kade, maybe I pushed you a little too much. Maybe we can do this next time," Darcienna said with concern thick in her voice.

Kade gave her a look that said he appreciated the thought, but this was going to happen. He closed his eyes and visualized the moves over and over in his head. He had to reference the book many times but better that than guess. He returned to his stance with his hands down at his side as he went through the motions in his mind. He was not aware that he had been standing for almost an hour, practicing. And then, the time came.

Clearing all thoughts and focusing, as his teacher taught him, Kade reached for the Divine Power, drawing it into himself. He molded it with the first move and then slid into the next. He was committed now. A part of him felt a sense of panic as there was no turning back. He knew as soon as he actually started to mold the Divine, he had crossed the point of no return. Unlike the Lightning Calling that was safe up until the tenth move, this one was dangerous right at the start.

Kade forced himself to focus, just as his master had taught him. Zayle used to roar at him at the top of his lungs for allowing distractions, and now they seemed to come at him from every part of his mind. He wished dearly that Zayle were here to watch over him, but it was not to be. For just a brief moment, his mind compared this to diving to the bottom of a lake and swimming through a tunnel. He was not sure if he could make it to the end. He feared panicking half way through that tunnel and drowning. It was time for the fourth move. The memory of almost losing control of the Lightning Calling flashed through his mind, and it was all he could do to suppress the terror of what could happen. There was no room for thinking like this. His mind reeled for a moment as he focused hard on the next step. He completed it and then moved onto the fifth. His stomach was twisted in knots, and he struggled to focus. He breathed deeply as he felt the Divine Power responding to his graceful shaping. The end of the tunnel was coming as he completed the sixth move. He blurted out the word surround in the ancient language and felt like he wanted to collapse to the ground in exhaustion.

There was a momentary flash as a pattern of script, symbols and figures glowed along the ground only to fade out of sight. Kade felt himself breathing hard. Sweat was sliding down his back, and his head was pounding. He was not sure if it was from his heart or from the thrum of power. He started to move when he felt an odd tingling in his outstretched hand. The Divine was still flowing through him. He felt panic start to well up. His mind raced to figure out why when he recalled the passage about the amount of Divine Power that was to be used.

It must still be active and under my control, Kade thought to himself. He breathed a small sigh of relief, hoping he had this right.

"Darcienna," Kade tried to say, but his voice cracked. He cleared his throat and tried again with better success. "Darcienna, go over there. Wait there until I say," he said, pointing to a spot by a tree, as he focused on the Divine Power. Without understanding how, he was able to feed more of the Divine into the calling. "Okay, walk toward me," he said while still focusing on the flow. "Not strong enough. Go back, and try again."

Darcienna walked to the far side and paused. Just as she reached the starting point, Kade doubled the amount of Power flowing into the calling. She started back toward him at a nod of his head. He felt a type of jolt to some part of his brain that he knew nothing about, but it felt right. He was satisfied with the results and cut off the flow. The pattern on the ground flashed once brightly and then faded. Kade could feel the dull thrum of the calling as it stood ready to warn of approaching danger.

"Okay, that should do it. Let's try one more time, and then I am going to sleep," Kade said so wearily that Darcienna's heart went out to him.

She was not sure if it was the dim light, or if she was seeing right, but she could swear that his face was as pale as the moon. *Was that from using the Divine?* she asked herself. *Maybe I will stick to using Nature's Gift.*

With a sigh, Darcienna walked to the far edge until he indicated for her to turn and start back. As she walked, Kade could feel a strong vibration in his head with every step she took. When he looked down, it was as if she were setting the ground on fire as she walked. Her footprints shone brightly for her to see, also.

"Is this supposed to happen," Darcienna said in awe as she looked back the way she had come.

"This is the first time I have ever done this so I could not say," Kade said as he studied the ground.

Closing his eyes and using the Reveal Calling, the ground lit up like it was on fire. Kade flinched and clenched his jaw. He knew he had to either leave the calling like it was, expecting Morg to see it if he looked for it, or he had to allow this calling to fade and create another one that was not detectable. He knew the right answer was to do the calling again. He could just hear Zayle's voice in his head now. "If you are going to perform a calling, you need to do it right, otherwise, you have wasted your time." Zayle was right, as he always was. Kade laughed once, giving in to his master and his master was not even there. The calling faded.

"Kade, what happened?" Darcienna asked as she tried to make the ground glow with her footsteps once more.

"Go stand over there by that tree," Kade said with his eyes closed and his head tilted back in frustration. Darcienna complied, but what she really wanted to do was tell him no more for the night and to lie down and go to sleep. But, she could not because she knew it was important to support this decision. She knew that Kade was not one to allow failure to stand, and for some reason she could not understand, he had to do the calling again. She regretted pushing him now as she watched him suffering.

Kade stood still as he worked the calling in his mind over and over until he thought he could do it again as he had the first time. He referred to the book once more, making sure his weary brain was understanding and nodded his head in satisfaction. Taking a deep breath, he closed his eyes and dove into that deep lake and headed for that tunnel. He forced his mind to see the moves on the page. His breathing was far from smooth, but he stayed focused. Thoughts threatened to invade his mind as they did during the first time, but he vanquished them with the fact that he had completed this calling once, and he was going to complete it again. Finally, the sixth move and he held out his hand, but the Divine Power did not activate the calling as it had previously. The pattern did not form. His mind reeled, and then it hit him what he had done wrong. He spat out the word for surround so fast he was unsure if it was recognizable.

The pattern blazed into view. Kade breathed a deep sigh of relief while holding his hand out with the Divine flowing through it. He looked at Darcienna and nodded for her to walk forward. As she entered the pattern, he could feel a tingle in his mind that was feather light. He focused on how it felt to make sure he would know it, even while asleep. It was not going to demand his attention, but it should do what he needed, as long as he slept lightly enough.

"It didn't work," Darcienna said with a frown as she looked at the ground. There were no glowing footprints.

"Yes it did," Kade said with a weak smile. "I felt a vibration run through my mind, indicating that someone, or something, had entered the area," he said triumphantly, as he looked at the ground longingly.

Kade closed his eyes and completed the Reveal Calling. He

tilted his head this way and that way as he scanned the area. If he looked closely, real closely, he could just barely make out a symbol here and a shape there, but it could easily have been mistaken for the reflection of the moon off a rock or moisture on a leaf. Kade nodded to himself, satisfied and relieved beyond words that he did not have to complete the calling again.

"There, that should make you happy," Kade said, as if he were talking to Zayle.

"So, you are able to know if someone is coming without them knowing that you know," Darcienna said to herself as she nodded her head in approval.

Kade did not hear Darcienna as his mind returned to almost a month prior when he was struggling with the Drift Calling. *A simple calling, and I could not perform it,* Kade thought. *Now, it makes perfect sense why Zayle used to get so angry when I failed. It was not that I did not have the ability, but that I did not put my best effort into every calling I performed.* Master Zayle hammered Kade for a decade saying, "Using the Divine required complete dedication every time." *How could I not see something that was so blatantly obvious? It was just so easy to not try with Zayle there to save me if it went wrong.*

"Kade, is everything okay?" Darcienna asked gently.

"Yes. I was just thinking about my lessons with Master Zayle," Kade said, feeling the sadness in him threatening to grow.

"You will be able to get revenge for your master," Darcienna said, trying to cheer him up.

"Justice," Kade corrected. "We will get justice," he said, feeling right about what he had said.

Darcienna chewed on that for a bit and then nodded her head in approval. She gently put her hand on his arm and smiled. His eyes focused on hers, and he relaxed as the knots in his stomach began to untie. His shoulders slumped slightly as he took a deep, long breath and let it out slowly. Darcienna thought he was going to deflate to the ground right before her eyes. Once again, her heart went out to him.

"I think it's time we get some sleep," Darcienna said as she coaxed him to lie down next to the fire. "So, you can detect someone or something from about thirty feet away?" she asked as she contemplated the ground.

"About that, yes," Kade said, feeling his muscles start to turn to water.

"And you think that is enough warning?" Darcienna asked, doubt in her voice.

"As soon as I sense something, I'll signal Rayden. That should give us enough time, and you can have your shield up immediately. And besides, I'm still wearing the amulet, so Morg is unable to track us," Kade said as he feebly reached up for the protective necklace. He was about to pull his hand away when he felt a tremor run through it. He became a little more alert as he focused on the feeling. The amulet warmed slightly.

"What is it?" Darcienna asked, seeing the concern in his eyes.

"The amulet felt warm for a few seconds. I think it does that when someone is trying to find me."

"Did it keep us from being detected?"

"I believe so," Kade said with a sigh. "I am afraid that Morg may break through sometime, though. It seems that I am feeling the vibrations more and more, and the amulet feels warmer every time," he said as he put his chin to his chest, trying to look at the protective jewelry. "This might mean that the amulet has to use more power to keep us cloaked. If this is true, then there might be a limit to its power. But, I am sure we have a while before we have to worry about that," Kade said as his hand fell to his side.

"I hope you're right," Darcienna said as she laid down on the other side of the fire.

"I am. Now go to sleep. We need to have our rest," Kade said as he started to slur his words.

It took only seconds, and Kade was out cold. His mind fell into a dream where he and Master Zayle had gone for a walk in the forest. Zayle would patiently tell him about this flower or that

60

creature as they strolled along the path. Kade enjoyed listening to his master on these walks, but he never really absorbed much of what Zayle said. But, there was one thing that he did recall, and now it was making more sense than ever. Zayle used to preach that the more knowledge one had of his surroundings, the less one needed to depend on the Divine. The way Zayle used to comment about the Divine made Kade feel that his master considered it a bad thing. Kade never agreed with Zayle's thinking and looked forward to using the Divine for everything possible. *Why would anyone not want to use the Divine?* he used to wonder, but now he was seeing things differently. Zayle had said, "Those that became too dependent on the Divine, would end up losing themselves because of the Divine." Something about it being a two-edged sword that, sooner or later, would cut both ways.

Kade was breathing deeply and almost completely in the world of dreams when the amulet vibrated stronger than it ever had, warming considerably. Kade tried to clear his head as his hand reflexively moved up to the necklace, but he slipped deeper into the world of dreams. Out of nowhere, he felt something kick him in the ribs hard enough to roll him onto his back. Kade was afraid that several of his ribs were broken as his mind raced. He gasped for breath, struggling to drag his weary mind to wakefulness. He looked up and his vision cleared. He was looking into the face of the one person he hated, feared, dreaded more than any other living thing on the planet. Morg.

CH3

"How did you get past my Detection Calling?" Kade wheezed, his mind struggling to grasp what was happening.

"Your puny calling is no match for me. You are just a child playing at being a man," Morg said as he sneered.

Kade spared a quick glance at the other side of the fire and found it empty. Darcienna was nowhere to be found. He turned quickly to call for his dragon, but Rayden was also mysteriously missing. Something was more wrong here than what he could see. Morg glanced in the direction Kade was looking and narrowed his eyes.

"Hoping for help? Don't expect any," Morg said, taking immense satisfaction in Kade's confusion. Morg was the type that would skin a cat alive just to hear it howl. "The only thing you need to consider is do you want to die quickly or long and torturously?"

"What did you do with them?" Kade asked with venom in his voice. He felt anger growing in him like an avalanche. The Divine Power rushed to embrace him like a long lost lover. Kade reveled in it and let it sink into every part of his being. The rage filled him and became him. He became the rage. They were one and the same. Hate was power and he filled his heart with it. The pain from his injury faded.

"Them," Morg said as he peered at Kade. It was more a contemplative response but Kade was too far gone to see this, too far gone to think clearly.

The pain in his side was distant as the power surged through him. *Revenge*, he thought. He needed revenge, craved it more than anything. His lips curled and he let out a growl as he lunged like a snake striking its prey and caught Morg in the knee with a boot. The evil Chosen let out a howl as he stumbled backward a step and then recovered immediately. In one swift movement, he stepped forward while raising a heavy, ornate staff, and then brought it down on Kade's head with a heavy crack. The world spun dangerously under that blow. Kade focused on his hate for Morg and kept himself from collapsing to the ground. He threw himself clumsily to the side, rolled to his knees and then stumbled to his feet as he tried to clear his head enough to cast a calling. Every move to the Lightning Calling beckoned for him to empower it.

"You would not get even the first move completed before I was able to blast you into a thousand pieces," Morg said as he leveled the staff at Kade's face. It was so close that Kade almost went cross-eyed to look at it. There were symbols carved in almost every inch of the wood, and it even seemed as if they were alive with power, but that could not be. His hate waivered just slightly and a sliver of logic slipped into his consciousness. Somewhere inside, he realized that if he were to survive this, he needed to think his way through it. He pushed the blackness back from his heart with effort. He watched the staff retreat until Morg held it vertical with the butt end of it on the ground. It was approximately five feet tall. It was three inches thick

63

at the base and grew to four inches thick at the head.

"How did you get here?" Morg asked as he looked around. The way he asked the question was…odd. Just a sliver more logic and the rage eased a little.

"What does it matter? You are here now. You won. But…," Kade started to say and then hesitated. Something nagged at him, but it was hard to think. He wanted desperately to destroy this man utterly and completely. *No,* he told himself. *Think.* Something was odd about the way Morg was watching him. "Why do you hesitate?" Kade asked, trying to buy time.

Kade felt his chest start to burn as the amulet heated up. He looked down, but it wasn't hanging around his neck as it should have been. Something was not right. He had to think. He felt he was on the verge of understanding when Morg's boot slammed into his gut, knocking the wind out of him. He doubled over, and Morg brought his knee into Kade's face, splitting his lip, sending blood spraying across the ground. Kade landed hard on his back.

"I find it difficult to believe that something as pathetic as you could kill my pets," Morg said with contempt.

"You mean that thing you used to call Kroden?" Kade said, emphasizing the past tense of the comment as he let out an antagonizing laugh. Blood shot out as a cough took the place of his laugh. That earned him another boot to the other side of his ribs. He tried to speak but had to clear the copper tasting liquid from his mouth. He spat and then continued. "And, that cat thing was not much of a challenge, either," Kade said in gasps as he waited for another blow that never came. He reached out with his mind to find his dragon but there was nothing. Rayden was nowhere to be found. Or…was he? Something…was there but it was not right. The burning on his chest drew his attention again. He looked down and still…nothing.

"I might let you live for just a little while longer if you answer my question. I might even let you join me. Think of all the things we could do together," Morg said nonchalantly as he bent down to look

Kade in the eyes. "How did you get here?" Morg asked as he traced the patterns in his staff with his finger as though the answer really did not matter.

"Why do you keep asking that? Why don't you just do what you came to do? Or, is there a reason you can't?" Kade asked, taking a gamble as just a sliver more of his logical mind worked.

"Like I said, I might let you live if you just answer my questions," Morg said as he delivered another sharp blow to Kade's head. His ears rang furiously and he was certain his left ear was already starting to swell. His stomach lurched, and he felt the sand on the back of his head for just a moment. The amulet burned his chest now. He wearily reached up to lift it away from his skin, but his hands found nothing

"You...keep asking that as if...as if you don't know. You are trying to figure something out," Kade said as he laughed through the pain. "Why not just kill me?" he asked and then stopped. He could have sworn he heard a distant roar, a panicked roar. Was Rayden trying to find him? Kade reached out with his mind and could have sworn that his dragon should be answering but...there was a wall.

"You think this is a game!" Morg screamed as he bent to within inches of Kade's face, spittle flying from him. "The pain is real and so will your death be if you keep this up," he said as he put his right hand around Kade's neck and started to squeeze. "Now, where are we?" Morg roared as he looked around. He was shaking with fury. Kade felt his air being cut off.

"A days walk," Kade rasped, trying to buy time. "A days walk from town."

Morg let Kade fall to the ground and stood while laughing lightly. After a moment, he leveled his malicious gaze at the Apprentice Chosen, making his skin crawl. Morg sneered.

"And Zayle thought you were a challenge for me," Morg said as he laughed in contempt.

The burning feeling on Kade's chest was almost more than he could bear. Glancing up, he was sure he saw the evil Chosen shimmer slightly. The burning in his chest drew his attention again. He reached down, trying to find the source of the heat, but his hand came up empty once again. Morg watched Kade's actions with curiosity. He narrowed his eyes and leaned closely to look at Kade's chest. He jumped back, and his eyes came wide open with understanding.

"It burns," Morg said, feigning uncaring again. "If it burns, then take it off," Morg said as if talking to a simpleton. "That Zayle sure is a clever one," he added with genuine admiration.

"What are you doing?" Kade asked as he clawed at the spot. The burning felt so intense he was sure his skin was blistering, but there was nothing to grab. It was just bare skin.

"Well, why don't you take off the amulet?" Morg asked casually.

"You already have it," Kade said as he looked down to find the amulet hanging around his neck. Morg took a breath and waited. Kade's hand shot to the amulet, but just as he was about to rip it from his neck and throw it, another sliver of logic worked its way into his mind. The burning was too intense for him to ignore, so he lifted it away from his skin. Morg stood so still with his eyes on Kade, he could have passed for a statue.

No sooner had Kade lifted the amulet away from his skin when he would feel an unseen force push it back down. The burning amulet started to glow slightly as heat radiated from it. It was too intense. Kade felt sweat start to bead on his forehead as he fought to control the pain. His jaw was clenched tightly. Another sliver of logic worked its way into his mind. Something was very wrong here. Morg wanted the amulet off, but why if he had already found him?

The amulet heated just a little more. Kade could not take the pain. He put his strength into lifting the protective necklace and it slowly rose. Far off in the distance, Kade heard a voice. Was it Darcienna's? That caused him to pause as more things fell into place. And then, he heard a violent roar that shook the ground, but the ground did not shake so why did he think he felt it?

Kade twisted and the counter pressure that had been pressing down on the amulet was gone instantly. He let it dangle from his neck as he panted while on his hands and knees. He looked at Morg and saw that the man was shaking with immense effort, but why? What was he doing? And again, there was another sliver of logic. His anger faded and then things clicked into place. He slowly stood, and after spitting a good amount of blood, laughed.

"This is not real, is it?" Kade asked, taunting the evil Chosen. "This is my dream, or a trance, or something other than the real world, isn't it?" He was very conscious of the amulet, but now he knew he needed to keep it around his neck. "You are not really here. That is why you keep asking where I am and how I got here," Kade said, filled with confidence as he walked up to Morg, looking him in the eye. The Master Chosen shook with rage as he glared back. "You have no idea," Kade said as he threw his head back and laughed in Morg's face. Kade knew he might regret it, but he just could not help himself. He had figured out Morg's game, and he wanted him to feel the sting of being defeated in this battle of wits. The pain might feel real, but he won this round.

"Oh, I can still make you suffer," Morg said as he snarled and swung the staff. The pain was excruciating. The last thing Kade saw was the twisted smile on Morg's face that was mixed with rage and hate. The man was beaten this round but not before he inflicted his fair share of suffering.

Kade ground his teeth, trying to withstand the agony. It racked his body for what seemed like forever but was closer to mere seconds. It slowly faded to be replaced by the sound of Darcienna's voice. His vision returned, and with that, she came into focus. She had tears streaming down her face. Her eyes were blazing bright blue but rimmed in red. He looked up at her weakly and gave a slight smile. She hugged him fiercely and sobbed.

"Kade," Darcienna cried as she held him tightly. There was fear and terror in her voice. He winced at the pain that should have been in his ribs. But, there was none. The more he awoke, the further the pain faded. "Can you hear me?" she asked as she moved back only far enough to look him in the eyes.

"Yes," Kade said as he took a deep breath and reached up, putting his arms around her. He needed to feel her, to know she was there, to know this was the real world. Her eyes started to quickly fade to their natural color.

The dragon shoved between them with his nose and huffed at Kade worriedly. Rayden was not going to be put off a second longer. The connection between him and the dragon slammed into place and everything was back to normal. Deep concern flooded through the link. Kade let go of Darcienna and patted Rayden on the muzzle to reassure him. Darcienna wiped the sweat from his brow with her sleeve as she checked him over for injuries.

"What happened?" Darcienna asked through the tears as her sobs started to slow.

"I am not really sure," Kade said as he sat up and looked around. "I was lying here next to the fire, or I thought I was," he said as he scratched his head, "when Morg appeared out of…," Kade was saying when Darcienna cut him off.

"You saw him?" she asked in a rush.

"Yes. He appeared out of nowhere and started to question me as to where we were. He hit me several times, and it hurt. It hurt badly. It felt so real. The pain was so intense," Kade said as he ran his hand over his head to feel for lumps. There weren't any. "I thought that Morg had taken you."

"I thought you said that amulet would keep him from finding us."

"It did. He still has no idea where we are. As a matter of fact, I think he was barely able to be in my dreams because of the amulet. I believe he was fighting its power," Kade said as his hand went to his chest, expecting to find nothing. There was a huge blister forming where the amulet hung. He furrowed his brow as he ran his finger gently over the spot. "He still does not know where we are."

"He tried to get you to take off the amulet, didn't he?" Darcienna asked as she bent to inspect the burn. She placed her hands over the spot and the blister melted away.

"Not at first. I don't think he was even aware of it until I told him I had it. He was only trying to get me to tell him where we are," Kade said and then paused. "You…were trying to stop me from taking it off, weren't you?" he asked as he recalled the counter pressure he felt in the dream.

"Yes. You almost had it off until I stopped you. Even then, it was close."

"How did you know something was wrong?" Kade asked as he stood.

"It wasn't me. Your dragon figured it out. From out of nowhere, he roared so loudly it almost stopped my heart. It was enough to wake the dead. When I saw that you did not even flinch, I knew something was wrong. I tried to wake you, but it was no use," Darcienna said as her eyes threatened to spill over again. "That's when I noticed that the amulet was scalding hot."

"Yes, I noticed that, too. That's why I tried to take it off. Morg knows why he has not been able to track us now," Kade said with regret.

"How did the dragon know that you were in trouble?" Darcienna asked, her composure returning.

"I suspect it was when I tried to call to it with my mind."

"Well, I am glad it worked," Darcienna said as she looked at the dragon. Rayden was still watching Kade intently. The apprentice hugged the dragon tightly around the neck.

"We have to leave now," Kade said. "Morg does not know exactly where we are, but he does have an idea," Kade said as he felt a slight vibration in the amulet. His hand shot to it and held it tightly, as if suppressing the vibrations might keep them hidden.

"I think that would be best," Darcienna said as she looked around the site, preparing to leave.

Kade felt the feather-light touch in his mind and recognized it for the Detection Calling. Just for a moment, he felt as if he wanted to give up and fall to his knees. And then, he looked into Darcienna's blazing eyes. The Divine raced in, ready for Kade to meet whatever it was that was stalking them in the night.

"Darcienna," Kade whispered fiercely. She turned toward him, her eyes showing like bright flashes of lightning.

"I can sense it," Darcienna said, trying her best to keep her voice low. "Does it ever stop?" she asked in exasperation.

"I can feel it on all sides," Kade hissed as he quickly scanned the dark, struggling against his exhaustion. Before he knew what was happening, he felt a pair of hands lock onto his head. Out of reflex, he tried to jerk away and prepared to deliver a crushing blow. Just as he was turning to attack, his mind cleared of the fatigue. "Thanks," Kade said with a glance, grateful for her help once more.

Rayden, be alert. I am sensing danger on all sides, Kade thought to the dragon.

Natures best hunter spun around, sniffed the air rapidly several times and then tensed, ready for battle. Kade quickly worked the Silence Calling while trying to keep an eye on all directions at once. He got ready for the Transparency Calling when he saw something drift through the shadows as silent as the wind. It was gone before he could see any details, but it was not small. He raised his hands, ready to fly through the calling when, out of reflex, he fell to the ground and rolled as something fell toward him from the sky.

Jumping to his feet and tensing, ready to execute the Divine Fire Calling, Kade scanned the area quickly only to find nothing. His heart was racing wildly. Sometimes the unknown was much worse than the known, and right now, there was a lot of unknown setting off the Detection Calling.

Rayden lunged at Kade with whip-like speed and snatched something out of the air just above his head. The Apprentice Chosen felt the wisp of something on his hair as the dragon's teeth crashed down on the attacker. When the dragon stepped back, it had what appeared to be a spider that was approximately six feet long hanging out of its mouth. Kade shivered hard and stepped back. He hated spiders with a passion.

The creature was twisting, trying to get at least one bite on the dragon before its life was crushed out of it, as Rayden bit down hard. There was a sickly green ooze coming from its mouth as it let out such a high pitched scream that Kade felt the hairs on the back of his neck stand on end. Rayden took a deep breath with the spider still struggling and exhaled a blast of fire that cooked the wriggling creature. The smell of burnt hair filled the area. Rayden twisted his head and tossed the spider aside with a flick.

"Darcienna!" Kade yelled, trying to prompt her into action. It was clear that it was too much too quickly. She was still reeling from so much danger as she stood rooted to the spot. "Darcienna!" Kade said in a voice of command, "Your shield! Now!" Kade exclaimed as he sent the Divine Fire at a shadow that was skittering through the treetops.

Two spiders screeched in pain as they lit up and fell to their deaths. Kade did not have a chance to revel in any sort of victory as the scene before him unfolded. He felt his chest constrict as the Divine Fire lit up the tops of the trees, revealing hundreds of the black creatures.

"Darcienna!" Kade yelled as he roughly grabbed her by the arms and spun her around to face him. "Your shield!" he said harshly, breaking through to her.

Darcienna slowly raised her hands as if she were waking from a trance. The green energy shot forth to surround them. Two spiders bounced off the shield as it formed. Kade jumped back as one hit the ground directly in front of him. The dragon lunged. Its teeth came together in a crash, but the spider was no longer in the same place. It bounded into the air and landed gracefully on the dragon's back. In a fraction of a second, Kade realized that this fierce dragon may find an end at those poisonous fangs.

Rayden swung back and forth trying for the spider, but it was out of his reach and it was not going to be dislodged. The spider reared slightly as its fangs extended. Kade flew into action and performed the Lightning Calling faster than he had ever thought

71

possible. His hands were a blur and his movements were as fluid as water. The spider lunged but missed as the dragon bucked. The spider gripped the dragon tighter and reared, again. It was not going to be denied in its second attempt. It was just barely enough time. The lightning shot forth to catch the spider just a mere hairs-breath away from the dragon's hide. How the Divine could interpret such a blur of movement was beyond Kade's understanding, but it had.

The bolt caught the spider and ripped through it, blasting it off the dragon's back to tumble through the air as it and the lightning bolt slammed violently into the side of the shield. Darcienna screamed in agony as the shield shimmered. She fell to her knees and Kade saw she was clenching her teeth so tightly that she shook. Her arms trembled dangerously but the shield stabilized. Unfortunately, Darcienna did not appear to be recovering as well. She was able to get to her feet, but her eyes were slammed shut in concentration. To make a shield large enough to encompass the dragon had to be pushing her to her very limits. To withstand a blast of Divine Power, virtually impossible.

Rayden roared his challenge, but even he realized they were in trouble. Kade could feel what most closely resembled concern coming through the link. He was not sure if the dragon even knew how to fear, but if it could, this was the closest he had seen it get to it. And then, the spiders started to drop onto the lifesaving barrier. With each one that landed, Kade could see Darcienna struggle just a little more.

His mind worked feverishly. He considered the Transparency Calling but Darcienna's shield definitely gave away their position. And, with the number of spiders covering the barrier, if she let it go, the arachnids would fall on them in droves.

"Dacienna, are you able to hold?" Kade asked, but he was afraid that he already knew the answer. It was not looking good. She could not even spare the effort to answer his question.

The spiders started to vibrate while emitting an ear splitting, high-pitched buzz. Kade covered his ears as his mind felt like it was reeling out of control.   If he was doing this badly, he knew that Darcienna was doing worse.

"No," Darcienna said through clenched teeth.   "That... Lightning Calling...was too much...for my...shield," Darcienna said through gasps.

"I had no choice. I had to do something to save Rayden," Kade yelled over the deafening buzz that was increasing by the moment.

Rayden let out a roar as he shook his head back and forth, trying to escape the mental assault. Kade pressed his hands tightly to his head and realized that Darcienna did not even have that small reprieve. He had to do something. It would be mere moments before the spiders would have them in their grasp, and he dreaded the suffering that would follow. He planted his feet firmly, ready to set them all on fire, even if it meant that they themselves were to die. If he had to go down, he was going to go down fighting.

"Darcienna!" Kade yelled. "Can you open a window in the shield?"

"No. It's...all or...nothing," she grunted through clenched teeth.   There was a slight trickle of blood coming from her nose, running over her lips. "Kade...," was all she could get out in an effort to warn him that the shield was going to give way.

He felt like everything was spinning wildly out of control. Where was the clever solution to this? How could this end in anything other than tragedy? He did the only thing he could think of. He did his best to confuse them by making them appear to disappear by using the Transparency Calling. This was only a short reprieve as the shield still showed their position. But, were the spiders smart enough to figure this out?

You will die today servants of Morg, a voice boomed in Kade's head. He looked up, and at the edge of the shield, stood a spider of the most pure white he had ever seen. It appeared to be covered in snow white fur that flowed with the wind. It was magnificent. The only other thing that showed besides the majestic, white, feather-light

73

hair was its fiery, green eyes. For a fraction of a second, he thought it was one of the most beautiful creatures he had ever seen. The irony that he detested spiders was not lost on him.

I can still sense your presence, the voice said in his head so loudly that it hurt. *You shall not escape us. As soon as this one who is gifted in the use of Nature fails, we will devour you and you will suffer.*

Kade looked up at the spiders as they blocked out the stars. He was out of options. Darcienna gasped and the shield shimmered. Time was up. He had to do something now.

Would they listen to reason? Kade asked himself, fighting the panic that gripped his heart.

"We are no servants of Morg," Kade said, deactivating the Silence Calling as he moved to stand just feet from the white spider. He let the Transparency Calling go and locked eyes with the majestic creature. Was there just a tiny bit of hesitation? The voice that echoed in his head showed no signs of doubt.

Do not try to deceive me, the voice exploded, sending Kade reeling. The voice was already mind-numbing, but this sent him down to one knee under the crushing weight of it. Kade clenched his jaws, and with all his will, forced himself to stand, looking the spider in the eye once more.

"I am not one of Morg's servants!" Kade screamed in rage. The blackness started to cover his heart and the Divine begged to fill him. He was on the verge of embracing the sweet taste of power when he heard Darcienna groan. No. He must keep his wits about him. Anger has only caused him problems. He had to think. "I can prove it," Kade said, trying to buy time.

You can tell your lies in the world of the dead, for soon you will be there, the voice said, but it was not as strong, and now there was doubt. Kade was sure of it. He forged on, praying in the next few moments he could deliver them from certain death with his words alone. The Divine was not going to save him here. As powerful as it was, Kade understood Zayle's sage advice that to count solely on the

74

Divine was to assure failure.

"We are enemies of Morg ourselves. We were on our way to see another Chosen," Kade said. He waited as the moments ticked by, but still, there was no reply.

Was there no getting them to see? What had they done that made these spiders believe him to be allied with that absolutely corrupt being? Kade asked himself as he tried to force his logical mind to work quickly.

The shield waivered and then reformed. One of the spiders fell to the ground and charged. Kade knew that if they were to survive, it was going to be by facing the white spider. The majestic creature buzzed once at the black spider just when it was about to spring on Darcienna. It turned to look at the white spider and then shrank back in agitation.

"Why do you think I would ally myself with such an evil man?" Kade asked as he stepped to the very edge of the shield to look deep into the green eyes. He vowed he was not going to flinch, even if the shield gave way.

This was his only chance, and he knew he had to do this carefully. The more he thought on this, the more he was certain how this must be handled. Something of what the white spider was thinking slipped through when it had communicated with him. No fear, for he had nothing to fear. If they saw fear, then it was as much an admittance of guilt in their eyes as if he had confessed. If he was not guilty, then he should have nothing to fear. However, there was something else. What could it be?

"You have not answered my question. If you plan on taking our lives, then admit to yourself that you do so without knowing the truth. You say you are going to kill us because we are servants of Morg. Are you ready to turn your back on those that might be allies instead?"

The black spider chittered furiously and moved toward Darcienna, venom dripping from its fangs. The white spider let out an ear-splitting, high-pitched sound that made Kade's head hurt furiously

75

as it lunged right to the edge of the shield. But it was not for Kade that it threatened. The black spider recoiled as if it had been struck. The glowing, green eyes refocused on Kade as they moved back slightly.

Darcienna was panting as her nose continued to bleed from the exertion. The blood was coming in drips as it hit the ground. Kade spared her a glance and then locked his gaze with the white spider once again. The shield faded and then returned but a few more spiders had fallen in. Kade turned quickly toward the dragon.

"Do not harm them. Not even one," Kade sent to the dragon as he yelled. The white spider was clearly in charge but no society, spiders or humans, would follow a leader that allowed its kind to be killed. No, the dragon had to stand down.

Rayden froze as the link between him and Kade exploded with confusion. The dragon's desire to rend these spiders into pieces tore at him furiously. Kade forced the dragon to understand trust as best he could. Rayden had to trust him if they had any hopes of surviving. Their lives depended on this killing machine fighting its natural instinct.

"Again, you have not answered my question," Kade said firmly, fighting the panic as the image of Darcienna blazed in his mind. No fear.

Besides sensing the presence of Morg? the spider communicated in disgust. *The dragon,* it added a bit more cautiously and curiously at the same time. The spiders were still poised to attack, eager to feed, craved to sink their fangs into flesh and bring death. The only reason the three of them were not dead already was because of the one white spider that was face to face with Kade, and he knew it.

He realized that he had missed the obvious. Morg and his minions were probably the only humans that commanded creatures as powerful and dangerous as dragons. Now, he had the final piece of the puzzle. It was so clear and he had thought nothing of it.

"Darcienna, drop the shield," Kade said.

It was obvious the barrier was going to fail, but being the one to bring it down had to count for something. No fear. There was no reason to fear so there was no reason to have the shield. No fear.

Darcienna collapsed to the ground. Her eyes rolled back in her head as she breathed in ragged gasps. The blood that ran from her nose came in a trickle now. The shield evaporated. He was not sure if she dropped the shield because he told her to, or if she dropped it because she could not hold it for even one more second, but he was willing to bet on the latter.

The spiders fell like death from above. Kade fought his instinct to cringe from these hairy eight-legged creatures. They were spiders and that was all that needed to be said. He could not react to them no matter his distaste for their kind. If he did, it would appear to be fear and fear was not acceptable; not if he wanted to save Darcienna and the dragon, much less himself.

The dragon was covered with spiders to the point that Kade thought the sheer weight of them alone would drive it to the ground. In an act of defiance, the dragon stood. Kade, once again, asked the dragon for trust. Rayden quivered, but he did not attack. His lips pulled back hard, showing every inch of his fangs. He continuously emitted a deep rumble as heat wafted from his nostrils. The battle the dragon fought within itself to keep from tearing the spiders to pieces was fierce, but the dragon held…for now.

Explain, the leader communicated. For the moment, they were surviving, but it was still very clear that any misstep would mean a swift end. Kade forced his mind to calm as Zayle had taught him during his lessons. It helped build confidence, also. No fear.

"I came across the dragon after one of Morg's monsters tried to kill it," Kade said as he watched the spider sway slightly while it considered his words. The wind caught its foot-long fur and it looked like it was floating in the air. "The dragon was injured when I found it and I decided to help it. Rayden is not under my command," Kade said as he leveled his gaze at the spider. No reason to fear. No reason to look away.

Rayden? the white spider asked.

"Yes. His name is Rayden. At least, that is what I call him. He follows my instructions only because he trusts me. He has become attached to me and I to him," Kade said calmly and confidently, but never once did he look away. Not even for an instant did he break eye contact. Not challenging but not submissive either. No fear.

Where did you come from? the white spider asked.

"A town called Dresben."

A loud buzzing sound started as the spiders readied for the massacre. The white spider reared up instantly and emitted that ear splitting sound once more. The mass of poison-fanged creatures seemed to quell their eagerness but only for the moment. One of the black spiders screeched and it was clearly a sign of defiance. It leapt at the dragon, and in one smooth move, the white spider launched over Kade's head to grab it in its fangs. It tore the smaller black one off the dragon and slammed it to the ground while landing gracefully. The buzzing ceased and there was a silence that was so profound that Kade rubbed his ears to ensure he could still hear.

The black spider tried to hold its ground, but it was not long before it was emitting a pitiful wailing that was hardly audible. The white spider hissed violently as it slowly lowered its blazing green eyes to stare directly into the black eyes of its prey. If there was ever any question of who the leader was, there was none now, and there was none for the spider on its back, either. Kade did not need to know what was being said to understand that to act again as it had would mean death for the black spider. Without moving its body even one inch, the white spider turned to look at Kade as it communicated.

Dresben? the white spider asked again, cautiously. Kade knew he was still walking on ice that could crack beneath his feet at any moment.

"My parents...," he said and then regretted bringing his mother and father into this. He desperately did not want to drag his parents into another dangerous situation, but it was too late. Kade mentally sighed. To change his story now would appear as though he were trying to hide something, which, of course, he would be, but unfortunately, it would also make him look guilty of whatever it was they suspected. He knew more than anything that the white spider was locked onto him, waiting for the next words to be spoken. "My parents live in a cabin just north of Dresben. We were on our way to see the Chosen, Valdry."

"Valdry? What do you know of the Chosen, Valdry?" the white spider hissed audibly. Kade flinched, expecting all communication with this creature to continue in his mind.

Kade took a moment to compose his thoughts as he studied the beautiful creature that stood only one short stride from him. It was four feet high and a little over seven feet long. When it spoke in a hiss, it reminded Kade of silk rubbing against silk. When it would buzz at the other spiders, the sound was more like that of a cat purring than an insect as he might expect.

"I was on my way to see him in hopes that he would help me fight this Morg that you so desperately hate," Kade said, hiding his shock that this creature could actually communicate with words.

The white spider seemed to be considering something as it stood regarding him. It turned to look back at the spider still pinned to the ground. The black spider started its ever so subtle wailing again. With a violent hiss directly into the face of the black spider, the white spider rose majestically and stalked around to glare at all the other spiders. They shrank back and put their faces to the ground as they swayed their heads back and forth. Yes, clearly this spider was their royalty.

"Valdry was killed. We attempted to help him for all he has done for us, but we were handed a crushing defeat. I lost almost half my clutch before we had to retreat," the white spider hissed.

Kade felt anger explode in him, and with a deep breath, screamed his rage at the sky, needing to vent his frustration. At every turn, Morg was there, always one step ahead of him. Kade clenched his fists in fury and the Divine rushed in. He raised his fists in anger,

79

and without thinking, allowed the Divine to flow forth from his hands, creating light. The spiders shrank back. Fear came at him in waves. Hate and anger swirled in him, and the area lit up like it was day. The spiders keened in terror and fell from the dragon as if stunned. None could look on the blazing light that pulsed from Kade's hand. The dragon added its rage to Kade's and roared viciously as it swung its head back and forth, shrugging off any of the remaining spiders.

"How?" Kade demanded as he stalked up to the white spider and leaned forward to peer into its eyes as it had done to the black spider. Kade did not notice the slight flinch. "How did Morg find him?" he demanded, forgetting that he was the hunted.

"I don't know. The Chosen Valdry called to us for help, but by the time we got to his mansion, he was under attack from beasts of long lost times. But, even without the creatures, Morg wielded so much power that he alone could have wiped us out if we had stayed," the white spider said as it spared a glance at Kade's glowing hand.

"The time has come to decide," Kade said dangerously. He saw his opening and he knew to take it. "Either you are truly against Morg and with me, or you stand in my way to bringing Morg to justice, and that is not a safe place to be. Decide," Kade said ominously as he fed the light with more of the raging Divine. He turned to Darcienna as if he had nothing to fear from the white spider.

Kneeling down, Kade felt for her breath. It was very shallow, but it was there. There was a fair amount of blood in a small pool around her face. Kade used his free hand and brought the Healing Calling forth, sending it into her. Her breathing steadied. With the next healing, her eyes fluttered opened. She looked into his eyes and smiled at him. A mere moment later, she shrieked at the glowing, green eyes of the white spider that was looking over his shoulder.

"For the love of the Divine, woman, please don't do that again," Kade said, trying to regain some of the hearing he had just lost.

"But…," Darcienna said as she fought the urge to scoot back.

"You are safe," Kade said as he looked at the white spider.

"They are on our side," he added as he turned to look questioningly at the arachnid.

"We are with you," it responded. And with that, Kade let the light fade considerably.

"Human, we need to talk," the white spider said and then turned to find itself nose to nose with Rayden. The shift in power was overwhelming. Rayden's lips were twitching as he fought the urge to rend this creature to pieces. Kade could feel it through the link so strongly that he found it hard to think.

"Rayden, no. He is an ally. Peace, my friend," Kade said as he placed his hand on the dragon's head and pushed it to the side while caressing it.

Morg does not heal, the spider communicated as it contemplated the woman. *He brings only chaos, suffering, death and destruction,* the voice said in his head. "Yes human, we are allies in this fight against evil," it said as it gave a graceful bow. "I need to hear more of what is happening, but first, I believe introductions are in order. My name is Rakna. I am the queen of my clutch. At least... as long as the king lives."

"The king?" Kade asked, feeling all anger fade from him. *A queen?* he questioned in surprise, expecting the spider to be male.

"My mate is sick. If he dies, I will die, also."

"I don't understand. Are you tied to him in a way that you will parish if he dies?" Kade asked, looking her over. You don't look the least bit ill."

"That has nothing to do with it. If the king dies, I will be put to death. It is the way of my kind. Until then, my clutch will continue to follow my orders," the queen hissed.

"I think it is fortunate for both of us that you found me. If you take me to your king, I might be able to heal him," Kade said as he turned for the dragon. "Take us to him," Kade said as he prepared to boost Darcienna onto Rayden's back. After just a moment's hesitation, the white spider hissed several times to the clutch, and then they turned and took off into the woods.

81

Just as Kade was readying himself to boost Darcienna up, he recalled the books. He turned quickly, raced over to recover the sack and then returned to tie them to the dragon's back. Next, he lifted Darcienna up and then leapt up to sit in front of her. The dragon was clearly not keen on staying with the spiders, but with a little prompting, it accepted Kade's direction and followed their new-found allies. If not for the white spider, it would have been nearly impossible to follow the black, ghost-like shapes as they moved like shadows flowing over the ground. After twenty minutes at a modest pace, they came to stop in front of two of the largest trees Kade had ever seen. They were just on the edge of a massive forest. Kade look up in awe. The trees were so tall they appeared to go on forever.

In here, Rakna communicated as she disappeared into the base of the tree. The other spiders stopped at the opening.

Kade signaled for the dragon to wait for him and turned for the entrance. Rayden complained, as he always did when left behind, but did as was requested. Kade and Darcienna followed after the white spider. It was a short walk up a spiral staircase to a large open room that had been hollowed out of the trunk of the tree. There was a straw nest in an upraised bed at the back of the room with a spider lying motionless in it. He was easily as large as the queen, if not larger. He had thick, flowing fur that was as black as coal. There was a stark white patch on his chest in the shape of a diamond.

"This is Crayken," Rakna said as she stopped next to the bed and gazed at the spider.

The king slowly opened his eyes and weakly reached out to touch his queen. There was love in that gentle touch. Kade was looking at the spiders, and for the first time in his life, he felt something other than revulsion. He was feeling compassion so strong that he had to help.

"Let me try," Kade said as he approached the bed. Crayken's eyes opened wide as Kade stepped into view.

"Who?" the black spider asked weakly.

"They are friends. They may be able to help," Rakna said as

she stroked his leg. He settled back, too weak to do much more.

Kade moved to the edge of the bed and completed the Healing Calling. He reached down and placed his hands on the spider, letting the Divine flow into the king. A glow formed around the dying creature for just a moment then faded. Kade furrowed his brow as he contemplated what he had just seen.

"Did it work?" Rakna asked.

"I'm not sure," Kade said in confusion, not taking his eyes off the king. "I have never seen the Healing Calling react like that."

"Kade?" Darcienna whispered, hesitant to interrupt.

"Yes?" Kade asked as he turned toward her. He narrowed his gaze as he looked intently at her eyes. Were they showing just a little of the blue glow?

"I think I am sensing something within the king," Darcienna said slowly, as if she were listening hard for a distant voice.

"What is it?" Kade asked, watching her closely. He had learned never to ignore her warnings, and now he was so focused, he noticed nothing else in the room.

"I am not sure. But, it seems to be attached to the king," Darcienna said as she moved her hand over Crayken.

Kade closed his eyes and looked at the ailing king with the Reveal Calling. He sucked in his breath as he studied a sickly, yellowish aura that surrounded Crayken. Kade opened his eyes and slowly turned to the queen, letting out a long breath. She was not going to like what he had to tell her.

"When did he get sick?" Kade asked.

"Just yesterday after we got back from the battle," Rakna said.

"That makes sense," Kade said as he scratched his chin thoughtfully. "There is a powerful calling placed on him that is keeping me from healing him. It was, most likely, placed on him because of your support for Valdry."

"I am not sure I understand," Rakna said as she slid closer to Crayken.

"Morg put a calling on him that is acting like a poison. It is sapping the life out of him."

"But, Morg never got close to the king. Crayken stayed back to direct the battle. The king never left my side," Rakna said, confused. "Why kill him slowly? Unless he was unable to get close enough, and this was his only way," she said thoughtfully.

"I cannot say, but it is more important that we focus on finding a way to save him," Kade said as he looked Crayken over again.

Kade had only one idea left, and it had to work. He turned to Darcienna and held his hand out to her. He cringed at the thought of asking her to help so soon after her last ordeal, but it was that, or the king was going to die in the next few hours. She looked at his hand but did not move from where she stood.

"Can you try?" Kade asked quietly. Instead of taking his outstretched hand, she slowly shook her head.

"I am too weak. I am so sorry, but I have no energy," Darcienna said as she held her hands out to her side, palms up as if to say, "I am sorry but I am helpless here?" Something about the way she held her hands sparked a memory.

"When you healed me at the cabin, you did something to re-energize your ability. Maybe you could do that?" Kade asked hopefully.

"It would take some time, Kade," Darcienna said as she closed her eyes and shook her head in exhaustion.

"It is either that or the king dies. We have no choice," Kade said as he gently put his hand on her shoulder.

"I know," Darcienna replied as she leaned back against the wall and slid down into a sitting position. She crossed her legs and placed an arm across each knee with her palms up.

"This is our only chance," Kade whispered to the queen. "Darcienna has the Gift of Nature. She may be able to heal the king where I cannot. We have different ways of healing. Where mine fails, hers may succeed."

The king slipped into a coma as the queen looked on in concern. Several times a black spider or two would duck into the room only to be chased out by the queen. Something in their manner, however, indicated resistance.

Kade paced for an hour, watching for Darcienna to show any sign of coming out of her trance. Moment by moment, the king slipped away. The queen sat by Crayken's bed, dreading that his body would just give out at any moment. Kade walked over to Darcienna, ready to wake her. As he started to reach a hand toward her, black spiders started to file into the room too numerous to be repelled. It was now or never as many of the clutch lined the far wall. The queen charged at the group and hissed as she walked up and down the line. They were not going to be denied the next few moments. The best the queen could do was herd them out of the way before returning to the king's side.

"Darcienna," Kade said gently as he crouched down on his haunches. "Darcienna, we must try now," he said as he laid a hand on her arm.

"Then now we shall try," Darcienna said as her eyes fluttered open. There was definitely a spark back in those rivers of blue. She grinned at him and held out her hand. Kade stood and pulled her to her feet.

"See if your healing can cure him," Kade said as he motioned for the queen to give them room.

Darcienna placed her hand on the king and smiled, but soon, that smile turned into a frown. She shook her head as if trying to work through something that did not make sense. She gritted her teeth and concentrated harder, but again, the look of disappointment was strong on her face. The glow was there as it had been before, but this time there was a pulse to it. Kade realized in horror that it was fighting her. It was still firmly in place, showing no signs of weakening. Or, was the fact that it was glowing brighter an indication that it took more strength to fend off the healing?

"Darcienna," Kade said as he pulled her away from the king. He was afraid she was going to expend all her healing with nothing to show for it. She gasped as if she had been holding her breath.

"I don't know what that is, but I can't break it," Darcienna said as she glanced at the queen.

"I have an idea," Kade said as he moved to the other side of the bed.

Kade looked at Darcienna as he raised his hands. She nodded and he started. He performed the Healing Calling and let the Divine flow. Darcienna laid her hands on the king and worked Nature's Gift. The yellow glow was becoming much brighter by the second. He signaled Darcienna to step back and watched as the glow faded. He knew what he must do.

The entire room was quiet and every eye was riveted on him. He scanned the small crowd and met each and every gaze until he got to the queen. She looked back at him, waiting anxiously for him to speak.

"The poison is still there," Kade said as he broke eye contact with the queen to look at the king. "But, I have an idea," he said as he caught Darcienna's eye. "Okay, let's try it again, but this time, you keep healing," Kade said as he stepped up to the king. "You may be able to hold the progress we make. If I heal and you continue to heal, maybe, just maybe, we can break the calling. Yes," Kade said, brightening. "Have hope yet, Rakna."

Kade used the Reveal Calling, and then with his eyes closed, started the healing. The yellow glow was alive as before, but this time, Darcienna grabbed ahold of it with a vengeance. She held out her hands and the Poison Calling fought back.

"I think this might work," Kade said as he studied the poison with his eyes closed.

He performed the healing again and watched as the yellow became slightly more vibrant. He smiled to himself, sure he was on to something. Now, he put his heart into it. He performed the healing again and again. Each time, the Poison Calling would change hues. As he completed the tenth healing, the Poison Calling flashed to a bright red, making it appear as though the king were on fire. It was almost too bright to watch. Kade opened his eyes and stopped, seeing sweat forming on Darcienna's brow.

"Darcienna, are you okay?" Kade asked.

"Just keep going," Darcienna said as though she had the wind knocked out of her. She was barely breathing. Kade realized in alarm what was happening. She was fighting to keep the calling from adding her to its list of victims. He closed his eyes and the colorful lights were starting to creep up her arm.

"Hold on," Kade said in panic.

He worked the calling over and over. There were bubbles forming in the red glow. If he had to compare it to something, he would have compared it to molten lava as it prepared to erupt.

"Hurry," Darcienna urged in a forced voice.

Kade worked the calling constantly. He had lost count after twenty. As much as he tried to keep his eyes closed, he was too worried about Darcienna not to check on her. She had her chin on her chest as she clenched her jaw in sheer determination. She was starting to shake. Her knees were buckling, and she was beginning to sink toward the floor ever so slowly. She was no longer breathing. If he was to break this calling, it had to be now. It was only moments before she passed out.

Kade performed the Healing Calling, but at the last second, he lunged at Darcienna and let it flow into her. She gasped. It seemed to be a small reprieve. She stabilized momentarily as he returned to healing the king. The Poison Calling was hissing and popping violently as it struggled to hold on. The king appeared to be a boiling inferno of fire.

It had to end at any moment, Kade thought, but still, it held on. Once more he let the healing flow into Darcienna, but this time, it had very little affect if any.

Wiping the sweat from his own forehead, he continued to work the calling as fast as possible. Darcienna was sinking to the floor once again, holding her breath. The king was moaning under the strain. His eyes flew open wide as he inhaled sharply and held it. This had to work now or they had lost. Crayken was motionless as though trying to decide what to do next. Kade poured his heart into the Healing Calling, willing it to work as Darcienna's arms waivered. Her right knee touched the ground. Rakna came up behind Darcienna and held her from falling any further or her hands would have pulled free of the king.

Kade recalled the determination he had while saving the dragon after the targoth attempted to rip the life from it. He called on that very same determination for the king. He was not going to let Crayken die. Not today.

There was a high-pitched keening sound that started to echo throughout the room. The black spiders began to back out of the chamber in terror. Darcienna's arms were slowly dropping as she gritted her teeth, straining to keep them on the king. Kade put his hands on Crayken for what had to be the thirtieth time or fortieth time, fighting exhaustion himself. It was all a blur. It could have been sixty times for all he knew. Darcienna screamed as she fell to the floor, her arms collapsing to her side. There was a deafening snap as the room exploded in a mix of colors. The tree shook under the explosion. Kade stumbled against the far wall and then immediately returned to place his hands on the king once more. Crayken let out the breath he was holding and then…took in another.

Kade knelt down next to Darcienna and put a supportive hand on her shoulder as she took several ragged breaths. He put his arms around her to give her support, and she leaned into his embrace. He would hold her as long as she needed.

"Are you okay?" Kade asked, trying to catch his breath.

"I…think…so," Darcienna said in between pants.

"Rakna?" Kade asked.

"I'm fine, Chosen."

Kade turned toward the king as his vision cleared little by little. He looked down and saw that the bed was empty. Just as he was about to say something, there was a deep, commanding voice to his right.

"What has been happening?" Crayken demanded as he glared

at the black spiders.

"My king, you are okay," Rakna said with intense joy as she moved over to stand next to him.

"I am a little sore, but that will pass." Crayken said as he turned to face Kade, who was helping Darcienna to her feet. "You saved my life. And, by doing that, you saved my queen. She is more precious to me than life itself. I am at your service," the king said while bowing gracefully. The queen joined him in the bow.

"Thank you. Any enemy of Morg is an ally of ours," Kade said, smiling at the regal couple. There was not a king or queen in all the lands that could surpass the presence of royalty he was seeing. Their personalities alone justified their right to leadership. He inclined his head in deep respect. "It was my honor to save such a noble and deserving life," Kade said as pride welled up in him.

"And who do I have the pleasure of meeting?" the king asked as he walked up to Kade, every step exuding confidence. His stride was confidence as his fur swayed with each step. He presented a magnificent image.

"Yes, you never did introduce yourself," the queen added.

"My name is Kade, and this is Darcienna," he said, indicating the beautiful blue-eyed woman standing at his side, who smiled weakly, still trying to catch her breath.

"Did you say…Kade?" Rakna asked in surprise.

"Yes," he responded, sensing that she knew the name already.

"If I had only known when we first met," Rakna said with a look of awe in her eyes. I would have helped you immediately."

"Well, I find it hard to trust those who attack me in the middle of the night," Kade said with a grin.

"You do have a good point," the queen said.

"Enough talk for now. I need to address our clutch and let them know all is well," the king said as he headed for the exit. "We will have food brought for you shortly," Crayken called over his shoulder as he exited the room.

"You will have to forgive the king. He is very loyal to his

people," Rakna said.

"There is no need for apologies," Darcienna added, recovering quickly.

"What did you mean when you said I should have told you my name sooner?" Kade asked.

"We heard that Morg was looking for a Chosen by the name of Kade. It has become known that the evil man is removing anyone who can be a threat to him. If he was looking for you, then that means you are a threat to him."

"I would have introduced myself right away, but I must be cautious of almost everyone I meet," Kade said.

"It's getting late," the queen said. "And you humans probably need to get some sleep; after you eat, of course."

"That's a good idea. We do need to get some sleep," Kade said, feeling himself crashing after his adrenalin rush. "Tomorrow we will figure out what we are going to do," he added, feeling the fatigue start to set in every part of his body. He motioned for Rakna to lead the way.

Kade felt honored to have the queen of this society acting as his personal guide. Darcienna slid up next to Kade and smiled. He offered her his arm and she gladly took it.

Exiting the tree, Kade could see hundreds of spiders that had come from all around to watch the newcomers. Rayden was a serious curiosity for them. They circled the massive killing machine, touching his tail here and a wing there.

No longer a threat, Rayden considered the spiders mostly a nuisance. Kade could feel indecision through the link. The dragon was torn between preferring them as a nuisance or as a threat. A threat it could do something about. A nuisance it had to tolerate. Kade let out a laugh and the dragon's head swung around to watch him.

Was that a glare? Kade asked himself and then laughed again.

He was looking very forward to getting some food, enjoying the fact that he did not have to be the one to make it. Doing all the cooking was definitely starting to wear on him. For once, he wanted someone else to take care of preparing the meal, even if just for one night.

"Stay here," Kade said to Rayden as they approached a tree just as large as the one they had just left. He conjured a piece of meat and tossed it to the dragon as a reward. He started to turn but felt something from the dragon. "Fine," Kade said, rolling his eyes dramatically. After conjuring ten more pieces of meat, Kade turned to go, happy to be done cooking. He stopped before taking two steps, retrieved the sack of books from Rayden's back and slung them over his shoulder. He patted the dragon affectionately on the side and followed after the queen.

After entering the large tree, they traveled down instead of up as they had in the previous tree. They descended a spiral stairway that was wide enough for five broad chested men to walk shoulder to shoulder. The steps were hard packed dirt until about ten feet down where the walls and steps turned into stone. There was a strong earthy smell as they continued to descend. A glow came from the walls but Kade did not take the time to examine the source. They continued to spiral down, making eight full turns around the middle until exiting into a grand cave that echoed with their footsteps. It was a massive cavern that could have held at least fifteen dragons with room to spare.

Darcienna and Kade sat with the king and queen at a table that barely came up to Kade's knees. He looked around and noticed that not even one spider was within ten feet of them, even though there had to be hundreds in the room. This was obviously meant for royalty as the table was the nicest one.

It was not long before one of the spiders brought a large bowl of vegetables and fruits. It set the food on the table in front of the travelers and quickly retreated. Kade looked the assortment over skeptically and wondered if he should have done the cooking.

Meat, cheese and bread sounds much better than carrots, nuts and berries, Kade thought. Glancing at Darcienna, he could tell that she was thinking the same thing. But, to reject this offering would be taken as an insult, so they both grabbed some of the food and started to eat. Kade was pleasantly surprised and pleased to find that it was actually very tasty. Darcienna returned his smile as they savored the exotic fruits. Juice dripped down his chin. Darcienna reached over and wiped away the mess as though she had been taking care of him this way for years. He felt his heart fill with joy at the simple gesture. He had no idea why it had such an effect on him, but it did.

The king finished his meal quickly. Soon, Crayken was on his feet and addressing the clutch. They cheered him for his words, and they cheered him for his good health. They loved their king and queen and it showed. To Kade and Darcienna, it was nothing but clicks, hisses and buzzing. But it did not matter. The queen easily translated for them. Several times the king made a reference to Kade, having him stand for the congregation to see. It was inspirational to hear the king speak, and it was clear that this clutch would follow their king, regardless where he led them.

"How is it that you have come to be involved where Morg is concerned?" Rakna asked as the king walked off to speak with his subjects.

"He killed my mentor," Kade said, hiding his anger as much as possible. "He killed her teacher, also," Kade said, indicating Darcienna. The queen's eyes widened in shock, and then she gave a nod.

"I am sorry. My heart goes out to you. If we can help in any way, we will. I am sure that goes for the king, also," the queen said. "What do you plan on doing now?"

"I am not sure. I only have two options," Kade said. Darcienna turned and watched him closely. "I can continue to search for Morg and try to deal with him myself, or I can try to find another Chosen to help me," he said as he noticed a look on Darcienna's face while she was deep in thought.

"Did you have something you wanted to add?" Kade asked.

"Didn't you say that your father told you about a doorway to the land of the dead; the very doorway that Morg is trying to find, also?" Darcienna asked.

"Yes," Kade said hesitantly, not sure where she was going with this.

"What if we were to try to find this doorway? If it matters to Morg, then maybe if we find it first, we can stop him. It is worth a try, don't you think?" Darcienna asked.

"I have heard Valdry speak of such a doorway," the white queen said. Kade and Darcienna both froze and then turned to stare in awe at the queen.

"You have?" Kade asked in surprise. "What did he say?"

"He had information indicating that the Morphites were in possession of this doorway. He never had a chance to find out if it was true, though," Rakna said.

"Maybe we can find out," Darcienna said.

"That is as far as the good news goes," the queen said. "We have been at war with those creatures for as long as time itself. If we were able to get to the caves, I believe I could lead you to the doorway, but I do not know how we are going to get past the Morphites. Valdry did explain where it was, hoping I would assist him in his search. There is a positive side to this," Rakna added. "Valdry does not believe that the creatures know of the door."

"It looks like we have some planning to do," Kade said.

"Yes, we do," Darcienna said, emphasizing we. "But first, we need a decent night of rest."

"I will take you to your chamber," the queen said.

"Thank you," Kade said, looking very forward to sleep.

Even though there was plenty of night left, Kade was certain that he could sleep well into the day if left to it. He sent the dragon a message letting it know the plans. He could almost picture Rayden running circles around the tree, waiting for him to emerge.

What a faithful friend, Kade thought as he smiled.

The king bade them goodnight and assured them that they would talk when they arose in the morning. Kade made what he felt were the appropriate responses about looking forward to the talk and how gracious they were for the hospitality. He followed the queen out of the room, eager to fall into a bed and let his mind go.

They walked up a flight of stairs and down a hall, stopping in front of the only room with a door. When he opened it, he was very pleased to see what could almost pass for a mattress on the floor.

It was definitely better than the hard ground, he thought.

"Valdry would come on occasion," the queen said by way of explanation. "These are your quarters. I will look forward to seeing you in the morning," she said as she turned to go. Before she could leave, Kade put a hand on her to hold her in place.

"Valdry," Kade said, hesitant to continue. "He was attacked two days ago?"

"Yes," Rakna responded.

"Then, it was him," Kade said to himself, recalling the plea for help. The queen, not understanding, waited for Kade to explain. "He called for help when Morg attacked him. I was not sure who it was as the message was cut off, but I suspected it might have been him," he added, feeling Darcienna stiffen. "Thank you. Good night."

"Good night, Kade," Rakna said and then disappeared down the hall. He watched her go, feeling the guilt due to his night of drinking with Darcienna and the swim in the lake.

"Kade…," Darcienna said as she laid a hand gently on his arm.

"You were right," he said, holding up a hand to forestall her apology. "We can't race to everyone's rescue, and we did need rest. And, we did not know it was he who called. It does us no good to dwell on this. I just wish I could have done something," he said as he let out a sigh. He was too mentally fatigued to be angry.

Kade walked into the small room and glanced around, taking in every little detail. It was very modest with virtually nothing besides the bed, window and door. However, it was not the room size that mattered but the comfort of the bed that had his interest. His eyes wanted to close even before he lay down, but he was not to have his sleep just yet.

"Why have you stopped?" Darcienna asked, almost walking into him.

"There is only one bed," Kade said, as he stepped aside to let her see the room. Darcienna smiled as she pushed past him and fell onto the mattress.

"Don't worry. I don't bite," Darcienna said as she snuggled into the bed. Kade stood still as he watched her. "What?" she asked.

"What makes you think there is something wrong?" Kade asked casually. But, there was a slight bit of red creeping into his cheeks.

"Because you are still standing there instead of lying down to sleep," Darcienna said as she propped herself up on one elbow.

"It's that obvious is it?" Kade asked.

"To me, it is," Darcienna said casually.

"It's just that there is something very familiar about this. It's like I have been here before," Kade said, his eyes losing focus as his mind worked.

"We should go to sleep," Darcienna said, as she hid her face in a yawn. "I have a bad feeling that tomorrow is going to be a very busy day for us."

Kade watched Darcienna for a few moments, still trying to grasp that elusive thought. Was it a memory? What was it? It was right there, but again, it just would not come to him. With a sigh, he looked down to see her blue eyes begin to glaze over slowly as he watched. She stifled another yawn. The edges of her mouth quirked up into a smile.

What was she thinking? he pondered. He was not going to get the chance to ask as her eyelids started to close.

"You may be correct about tomorrow," Kade said as he dismissed his elusive thoughts. He dropped his sack of books by the bed and laid down next to her. Her eyes opened just a crack as she grabbed ahold of his arm. Her smile faded as she slowly drifted off. Minutes passed and her breathing became deep and regular.

Kade watched her for a long time, noticing the pure innocence as she slept. He thought about how brave she was and how much she suffered by staying at his side. She followed his lead because she trusted him, and she paid for it dearly. Not only did she not run from him, but she continued to fight to stay with him. It reminded him of his dragon. He knew he was lucky to have such loyalty at his side.

Propping himself up, Kade watched her breathing peacefully. He noticed the way her eyes fluttered slightly as she drifted deeper and deeper into her dreams. Watching her sleep made him love her even more. Without thinking, he let his heart guide him and he leaned over, kissing her ever so lightly on the lips. It was a kiss that says, "I love you" in the most gentle but meaningful way. He smiled as he lay down and put his arm across her. Kade closed his eyes and missed the smile that crept across her face. Her eyes came open ever so slightly, and then she fell asleep for the night.

CH4

Kade awoke with a jolt to the sound of loud buzzing coming from outside the tree. He heard the dragon roar and recognized it for what it was immediately. It was Rayden's battle cry.

"Darcienna, wake up! Something is wrong!" Kade exclaimed excitedly as he shook her.

"Mmmmm. Kade, let me sleep just a little longer, please," Darcienna said with barely formed words.

"Darcienna!" Kade said roughly as he shook her.

"What?" Darcienna asked with a fair share of irritation in her tone. She would have glared at Kade, but she was not able to keep her eyes open. She rubbed them, trying to work the sleep out.

"Don't you hear all that buzzing?" Kade asked, his pulse starting to race.

"Yes. So there is buzzing. Let me go back to sleep," Darcienna said as she started to lie back down in the makeshift bed. Kade grabbed her by the shoulders and held her sitting upright.

"When was the last time you heard buzzing like that?" Kade asked more forcefully.

"When the spiders were attacking us," Darcienna said, still clearing the cobwebs out of her head.

"But why did they attack us?"

"Because they thought we were their enemy," Darcienna said, still not following where he was going with this. She looked back at her pillow longingly.

"Don't you get it?" Kade asked, exasperated.

"Get what? There…" Darcienna started to say when her eyes came wide open. "We are under attack," she said, now awake.

"Yes," Kade said as he turned and looked out the window.

The opening in the wall was barely a slit. It was too narrow for him to use both eyes. Several spiders raced past the window buzzing wildly, and then the sound decreased as they moved off.

"Kade," Darcienna said, her face starting to turn white. "We need to get out of here," she finished, and as if to make her point, her eyes exploded into the bright blue that Kade was all too familiar with. Not quite blazing, but bright enough to say that the danger could be fatal for them. Kade swallowed hard.

"We can't just leave the spiders. They are our allies. Wait here until I get back," Kade said as he quickly rose from the bed and headed for the door.

"You are not leaving without me," Darcienna said as she grabbed Kade by the arm and spun him around. He could see the fierce determination in her eyes and decided not to even try to fight this battle.

"Okay, but you must be careful."

Rayden let out a deafening roar that shook the tree. It was clear that the call was aimed at them as a warm gust of sulfurous air wafted into the room through the window crack. Kade ran to the opening and was met by the huge, golden disc of an eye.

"We are on our way," Kade said to the eye. He spun and headed toward the door with Darcienna close on his heels.

"He is trying to warn us of something," Darcienna said as her eyes darted from the entrance of the room to the back of the tree as if to find escape.

"I know. Let's get going," Kade said, dragging Darcienna through the tree to the exit.

Kade burst forth through the opening as Rayden rounded the corner. The dragon spun as something tried to attack it from behind. Kade raced through the moves of the Lightning Calling as a black mass came at them from around the other side of the tree. The calling exploded from his outstretched hand, causing the creature to disintegrate. It didn't even have a chance to cry out before spraying the area with the black ooze that must have done for blood and guts. Darcienna's green shield sprang to life, encompassing the three of them. Kade heard a dull thud as one of the attackers bounced off the shield to his left. It hit the ground, stunned from the impact.

"Blood and ashes!" Kade swore. "What in the great Divine are these things?" he yelled.

"I don't know, but I really think we should get away from here," Darcienna yelled back. "It may be us that are putting the spiders in danger, Kade."

"No. First, we must find out what is happening and why. I will not abandon them!" Kade exclaimed, leaving no room for argument.

Bending down to get a closer look at the creature, Kade studied it as it started to recover. It raised its head and looked directly into his eyes. It was not more than a foot away when it locked eyes with him. Black drool was coming from its mouth as an evil smile crossed its face. Kade shivered as he looked into those eyes. Not only did this thing want to kill him, but he was sure it wanted devour his very soul and more if it was possible. The creature looked past Kade and focused on Darcienna while it licked its lips hungrily.

Kade might have felt some form of fear as it looked at him, but as soon as it looked at Darcienna, all fear evaporated, and he drew the Divine into himself so fast his head spun. The thought of this foul creature sinking those fangs into his Darcienna was more than he could take. He snarled in reply.

The creatures had skin that looked like it was made of shiny, sticky tar. It was as black as a moonless night. Even its eyes were black. The only things that had any color were its white nails and its pink mouth when it opened it to show its white fangs. It was humanoid in its stance, but it moved in a hunched manner. Even hunched, it moved with grace.

"Drop the shield," Kade growled. Darcienna looked at him as if he were crazy, and maybe he was, but she knew not to argue.

Kade flew into motion. He was almost a blur as he danced a dance of death for this creature. Darcienna was just barely quick enough in removing the barrier before he acted. As soon as the shield was gone, the creature lunged at Darcienna with such speed that Kade was caught off guard. He recovered instantly and let the Divine Fire engulf the filthy thing. It stumbled back about twenty feet, but it did not stop moving right away. It screeched and screamed as it looked at him with pure hatred. As Kade watched, he realized that it was not screaming because of pain or even because it was dying. It was screaming from the pure hatred it felt, and more importantly, it was screaming because it was being denied its kill. More precious than life was its desire to rend and destroy. If it was not firmly impaled by the dragon's fangs as it hung half out of Rayden's mouth, fire or not, it would have continued its attack until it could no longer move.

"Those things don't care whether they are on fire or not. It's as if they don't feel the pain," Kade said in shock and awe, not taking his eyes off the creature.

"Kade," Darcienna said, her eyes blazing fiercely. "The feeling of danger is so strong," she continued as she fought to keep from hyperventilating. Terror was showing on her face as she turned pale. She swallowed hard as she locked frightened eyes on him. "It's

100

as if there is an army of these things."

"I guessed as much," Kade said as he quickly scanned the area for more of the evil creatures. "We need to find the king and queen," Kade said, as he approached Rayden, who was acting as their guard. "Let's go," Kade said, cupping his hands for her. "Rayden, we need to find the white spider."

Kade surveyed the area and was disheartened at how many of the black creatures were overrunning it. Spiders everywhere were fighting for their lives, and it was not looking good. Kade had a sickening feeling in his gut that this attack was because of him. It was too strong a coincidence that this attack came one day after his arrival. Guilt hit him hard. This entire colony could be wiped out, and it was all going to be his fault.

Glancing off to his right, Kade caught sight of the white spider as Rayden let out a deafening roar that shook the ground. He gasped as he watched four of the deadly black things surrounding the majestic white spider in their attempt to bring her down. When one would move in, she would dodge nimbly as she tried to catch it with her deadly bite, but it was just as agile and would dive back out of the way.

Rayden exploded with power as he forced his way through several small skirmishes. Even though it took everything Kade had to hang on, it still felt like the dragon was moving in slow motion as he watched the queen. At any moment, he expected her to be dragged down and devoured. To say she may be killed was just not enough. These things wanted to completely consume anything living, mind, body and soul. The hunger in their eyes could not be missed. But, the queen was holding her own, dancing in and out with grace. Kade was amazed at Rakna's ability to transform from a regal creature to an agile fighter that commanded respect, even from the black creatures.

Rayden charged in just as one of the Morphites found an opening. Rakna was focused on the three in front of her and could not see the one behind her as it leapt with a crazed look in its eyes, eager to tear the life from the regal, white spider. Kade's head rocked back hard when Rayden stopped, crouched and then launched to grab the thing in midair with his claws. As the dragon landed, it proceeded to slam the creature into the ground hard enough to cause the black mass to mix with the dirt. All that was left was a black, sticky, tar-like spot that never looked like it was ever alive.

"Thank you...Kade," Rakna said as she sidestepped another black creature. "I...don't think I could...have held out...another second," the queen said breathlessly.

Kade turned to see that Darcienna had fallen off the dragon when Rayden had attacked. She was lying on her side, clearly dazed as she struggled to stand. He jumped down and charged just as one of the creatures turned and leapt on her. It drew its head back, ready to bite down as Kade slid to a stop behind it. All in one motion, he reached around to grab its upper jaw with his right hand and the lower jaw with his left just as the creature was ready to tear her throat out. It was so close that the back of his hand brushed her neck. Rage fueled his muscles as he pulled with all his might. The creature screamed, but its fate was sealed. There was a sickening snap as the jaw separated from its head. Kade grabbed it by the neck, and with one mighty hurl, spun around to get momentum and then threw it as he let out a yell. It flipped through the air like a ragdoll to land in a heap.

Working the Healing Calling quickly, Kade placed his hands on Darcienna's head and let the Divine flow. She inhaled sharply, and then her eyes cleared. She looked up at Kade and then wrapped her arms around him. He tried to dislodge her but she would not be denied.

"Stay still you oaf," Darcienna commanded. "Unless you want those on your back."

Kade turned to see her shield holding three of them at bay. Without even a word to Darcienna, he slid out from under her arms and flew gracefully through the moves for the Lightning Calling, letting it fly. He did not even need to say a word to Darcienna. She knew to let the shield go for him to do his work. The lightning bolt tore through the closest as Kade raced to grab the next one. He spun hard while holding it by the arm to throw it into the third. They collided with a thud and hit the ground in a twitching mass. Before they could get their bearings, Kade leapt as high as he could into the air and then came down on one of their heads with the heel of his boot, smashing it like a grape. The next, he kicked so hard its head separated from its body and landed in the weeds.

Rayden was in his glory as he tore and rent. Kade was sure the dragon was going to regret when the creatures were no more. It lived for this. Rayden was a fighting machine and it showed. The black creatures did not seem to understand as they continued to come, but they would learn the hard way, and it would be the last lesson they would ever have.

"Where is the king?" Kade asked as he tried to catch his breath. He was grateful that Zayle kept him in shape or this would have surely been exhausting, to say the least.

"I am not sure. We were separated almost immediately. You need to find him, Kade. This is no coincidence that this happened the day after the king was expected to be dead," Rakna said as she sank her fangs into the eye sockets of one of the creatures. Kade cringed at what that must taste like as she drew her fangs back out of the creatures head.

"You saw the look in their eyes?" Rakna asked as she dispatched yet another one.

"Yes," Kade said, noticing the queen was limping when she used one of her right legs. "Let me heal your injury."

"We don't have time," the queen started to say when Kade finished the calling and placed his hand on her leg. "We need to find the king," she said as she flexed the healed appendage. "One thing you must know," she added as she stopped him to emphasize her point. "Kade, no matter what you do, it is imperative that you do not let them get their hands on you. They have a grip that is beyond breaking. Do not let them get ahold of you," she said again for emphasis. Kade nodded his understanding.

"Rayden, can you find the king?" Kade asked the dragon out loud along with his mind. It had black slime dripping from its mouth as it spat out one of the creatures. Kade thought of how the white spider had done something similar and cringed again at how those creatures must taste. The dragon knelt down quickly for them to mount. "I take that as a yes," he said as he spun around and grabbed Darcienna.

"Get on," Kade said as he looked at the queen. Rakna hesitated and then leapt up gracefully. "Darcienna, can you use your shield while we ride?"

"It's complicated. Not in this situation is all I can say," Darcienna responded. "The shield is stronger as I stay still. The more I move, the more effort it takes to keep it active. I have my guesses as to why, but for now, no."

"Okay, but be ready to use it," Kade yelled over the fighting. He turned back to the queen, who was firmly attached thanks to nature's natural gift given to spider allowing them to cling tenaciously to almost any surface. "Here we go," Kade said as he gave the dragon the mental command to go.

Rayden took off with a burst of speed, causing two of Rakna's legs to come loose, almost sending the white spider into a crowd of black creatures that now occupied the space where the dragon had just been. Rayden raced down a path into the forest, rounding a mound of boulders larger than himself and ground to a stop as a wall of black creatures came at them. Kade felt the dragon expand like a balloon and smiled, knowing what was coming. He did not know if it was wrong or right to enjoy this, but he was very much looking forward to watching the carnage. Rayden opened his mouth and lit up the sky, setting at least twenty of the creatures on fire as he swept his head back and forth. How the dragon was able to let out a deafening roar along with the blast of dragon fire was beyond Kade's understanding, but it was glorious nonetheless. The dragon deflated and the creatures fell screaming. It did not take long for the way to be clear.

A movement off to his right caught Kade's attention. Turning, he saw the king and six of his guards surrounded by a black hoard. Kade could see that the king was trying to work his way to several large trees so they could climb out of danger, but if left to their own, they were not going to make it. As he watched, two of the guards went down in a boiling mass of black ooze. It was as if these things were endless. But, there had to be an end to them. There just had to be.

"My turn," Kade said as he let the hate and anger surge through his body. The Divine rushed in and made his head swim. It was intoxicating. Kade was drunk with power, and he gave himself over to it. At this moment, his greatest desire was to kill. He leapt off the dragon and landed in a crouch, as though he were a lion hunting prey. The look of pure malevolence alone should have scared these creatures into running for their lives, but intelligence was obviously not their strong suit. He stood and flowed from move to move in a blur. Lightning flashed from his hand in a deafening roar to race along the ground, destroying anything in its path. Rayden was not to be denied his fun as he filled the area with his deadly dragon's breath.

Kade heard Darcienna say something from behind him, but it did not matter because there were still black creatures to destroy. Combining his rage along with Rayden's killing frenzy coming through the link, he was the destroyer. Somewhere in him, he dreaded the end of the black creatures as he would no longer be the bringer of death.

"When he is like this, it is imperative we stay out of his way, and let him do what he must," Darcienna said to the white spider as they watched in horror.

Kade finished another Lightning Calling and sent more of the mass of creatures to their graves. The air was thick with a black, pungent smoke as the Morphites went up in flames or exploded under the power of the Divine. Just as he finished the last calling, he spun to catch a creature by the neck and used its own momentum to slam it into the ground. Kade came out of this spin to send Divine Fire to wreak more havoc. The Divine flashed through him as bright as the sun. Kade opened himself up completely as he became death incarnate. He was unstoppable and the creatures knew it. Kade no longer brought callings to his bidding as he craved the feeling of ripping the life right out of these creatures with his bare hands. He used his strength to rend them limb from limb as if they were weeds being plucked from a garden. The blackness that surrounded his heart was filled with hate and rage. Whether the Divine fueled his strength or not was unknown, but they died in his grasp over and over. Every life he crushed out of existence brought pure pleasure.

The king and his remaining guards made it to the trees and quickly ascended. The queen joined the king as Kade continued his frenzied rage. She watched in horror as one of the creatures came at Kade from behind, and just when she was sure it was going to strike a deadly blow, Kade spun around to grab the creature with both hands, took a step and vaulted high into the air. With the creature held over his head in both hands, he started back down, and then with all his might he slammed it into the ground with a sickening thud that made the ground shake from the impact. It exploded and covered him in ooze. He spat, gagging on the black slime. Something about that sparked a dim memory.

"Thanks for the warning, Rayden" Kade said through ragged breaths.

Kade searched for his next victim and noticed that the area was filled with dead and dying creatures. There was smoke so thick in the air that he coughed a few times and his eyes stung. The power was starting to ebb as he came down from his anger. He looked up, seeing the king and queen safely watching from their perch, but only two of the six guards were with them.

The dragon roared and lunged, its jaws crashing together just behind Kade. He did not even need to look back to know what had happened. Kade smiled, knowing that his faithful companion was always watching over him. He glanced to his right and saw Darcienna with her back to the boulders and her shield barely surrounding her. It was the safest place for her at the moment.

Thank you, Crayken said with his mind. *I fear I would have perished if it were not for your timely intervention. My clutch owes you debt of gratitude.*

"I only helped," Kade said, feeling himself crashing as his energy left with the Divine.

Again, we owe you our lives, the queen said, her voice echoing in his mind. Kade inclined his head in what he believed to be a show of respect, as he accepted the praise. He turned and surveyed the area, looking for any other spiders that may need help.

"Where is your clutch?" Kade asked. He looked around the area and realized for the first time that there were very few dead spiders.

"You're looking for them in the wrong place," Rakna hissed as she raised her front legs to indicate the trees. "They are all up here where we have the advantage."

Darcienna dropped her shield and moved to stand next to Kade. Before he had a chance to respond to the queen, Darcienna's shield sprang back to life, startling him. He turned quickly to see her eyes were blazing. He spun around and looked for anything that was a threat but there was nothing. He looked back at her and noticed she was tilting her head as if trying to hear something but not quite getting it.

"Where is the danger?" Kade asked.

"Something…is happening. I am not sure what it is, but I got a very strong feeling that we were just about to be attacked," Darcienna said as her eyes dimmed considerably. "Come close," she said as she let the shield go and placed a hand on his head. She closed her eyes for a moment and then nodded in satisfaction. Kade stood tall again, ready to do battle.

"Kade, we need to get to the Great Hall," Rakna hissed.

"I've got a plan that may help," Kade said. "Let the dragon and me worry about making a path for you," he added, feeling the urge to massacre more of these vile creatures begin to grow once more. For just a moment, he wondered if he was enjoying the killing, or the killing of these evil monstrosities.

Kade opened himself up and the Divine Power eagerly embraced him. He found it hard to think again, but he focused on his plan. "When we get into the hall, Darcienna will use her shield to keep the creatures out, and I'll heal any of the wounded," Kade said, eagerly watching as scores of the creatures rushed toward them.

"How will we take care of these wrenched things once we are in the tree?" Crayken asked as he surveyed the enemy.

"I think the dragon would love to play with our guests," Kade said as he patted it on the shoulder. Rayden roared, eager to return to the battle. The dragon took in a deep, long breath and then, with an immense amount of force, roared again so loudly that Kade was sure it could be heard across the continent. It shook with the effort as its lips flared, showing those deadly fangs. The black mass hesitated momentarily at the dragon's promise of slaughter. Maybe there was a shred of intelligence in those black heads.

"I think I like your plan," the king responded boldly. He turned and started the odd buzzing sound as he addressed the spiders in the trees. Kade was not positive, but it seemed as if the queen amplified his words. Was there a synergy working here?

Kade turned on the black mass as they unwisely started forward again and worked his Divine Flame Calling, visualizing the flame as large as he could. He sent it into the creatures as though he were throwing a javelin. It exploded with such a backlash that Kade was certain he had singed off some of his own hair. It was glorious. They died in droves as he and the dragon basked in the violence. He performed the Lightning Calling and sent it ripping along the ground to destroy anything in its path. Kade held his hand out, willing the bolt to continue.

Before he could flow into his next move, something grabbed him by the neck from behind with a grip like iron and started to squeeze, cutting off his air. Kade fell back hard, trying to crush the foul creature, expecting it to be dislodged easily, but it only tightened its hold to the point where Kade thought it might break his neck. The warning from the queen flashed through his mind and he felt panic. He started to see spots as he furiously grappled with the creature's hand. It was slick and impossible to get a hold on it.

"I'll have that pretty little thing of yours as soon as I am done with you," it whispered in his ear.

If Kade was not feeling hate before, he was feeling the full effects of it now. But, there was also fear for her life causing him to feel panic. *What if I fail and the creature is able to kill me? What would happen to her?* he thought frantically. Kade looked over and saw that Darcienna was holding her shield over her head with the queen, king and maybe as many as fifty spiders around her. The creatures were piling on the barrier. The last glimpse Kade saw of Darcienna was her holding firm, but the strain was there.

She was supposed to stay on the dragon where it was safe, Kade thought for just a brief instant, and then his mind was reeling out of control.

Kade tried to call to Rayden with his mind, but it was hard to think, and Rayden was in a killing frenzy as he leapt and slashed. Kade knew it was up to him to save his life and Darcienna's, not to mention the spiders. The clutch could not come to his aid because of the shield, and Darcienna could not afford to let the barrier go or they would surely all be slaughtered. His plan was failing.

Furious, Kade rolled to his side, but the creature would not loosen its grip. It hissed and laughed in his ear, taunting him. Kade got to his feet and threw himself back again but to no avail. He was starting to see more spots as he struggled desperately to get air into his burning lungs. Its grip was tightening as it worked to snap his neck.

Kade scratched at the hands violently, but the creature acted as if it felt no pain. His fingernails were clogged with the tar-like substance, and yet, it did not even flinch. It let out a laugh, anticipating its kill at any moment. It started to twist his neck. Kade tried to work his fingers underneath the iron clamp that was constricting around his neck, but it had too tight a grip. His neck was wrenched even further, and he felt his spine start to creak under the force. The creature twisted just a bit further, and as things started to fade, Kade saw its elbow out of the corner of his eye. He reached out and hooked his hand under that joint, pulling hard. He pulled for all he was worth. The creature was forced to slide more to Kade's side as he pulled. He was able to get both hands in the crook of the creature's elbow now. With all his strength, he pushed and extended his arms. This was just enough for him to get a breath before the clamp tightened again. The sweet taste of air filled his lungs once but once was all he needed. The blackness faded.

Along with the air came hate. Hate so intense Kade could feel it. Hate so strong he could taste it. He not only wanted to kill, but he wanted this thing to suffer horribly. How dare it threaten him! How dare it try to take his life and the life of the one he loved! The creature grunted hard, and for just a fraction of a moment, it thought it might have a chance to gain the upper hand again, but then something happened to the man holding its arm. The man became infused with the Divine. Kade resituated his grip, and the arm snapped at its shoulder, separating from the body. The creature fell back hard and its arm fell to the ground.

Kade climbed to his feet and slowly turned to look at the creature while tasting the clean air. He was pure malevolence. It tried to scramble away, but Kade grabbed it by the ankle and twisted. The leg snapped with a sickening pop. He let it go, and again, it tried to scramble away. Kade grabbed the other leg and twisted until it, too, snapped with a sickening pop. It fell onto its back and put its remaining hand up to fend off the man, but Kade just grabbed it by the wrist, put his foot on its chest and pulled. The arm snapped free of the body, and black blood oozed everywhere.

Kade reached down, picked up the creature by the neck with one hand and lifted it into the air. He brought it to within inches of his face as he looked deep into its wide eyes and started to squeeze. Was that fear he was seeing? If not, it was the closest thing these creatures could feel, and it was good enough. Kade squeezed, and squeezed, while the creature squirmed furiously. His fingers sank into the flesh, if it could be called that, and kept going until he felt what had to pass for a skeletal structure, and then he squeezed even harder. Kade shook under the effort, and his teeth shown as his lips curled into a snarl. With a yell, he put everything into that grip and the neck snapped as the head popped to the side. The body jerked spasmodically as it fell into death. Kade held it for several long moments, watching the life fade from its eyes.

"Rayden, here, now!" Kade yelled as he threw the quivering body to the ground. The dragon flinched hard under the mental command that accompanied the voice.

Kade raced to the mound of black mass and tore into it. The dragon raced up and joined him in his killing rage. The shield was failing quickly. Kade knew what he had to do, but Darcienna was not going to like it.

"Darcienna, hold on. This is going to hurt," Kade yelled over the noise. He performed the Divine Fire Calling and let it engulf the pile of writhing, black bodies that were still covering the barrier. They fell away from the shield screaming just as it failed. He could have sworn he heard Darcienna's scream mixed with the creatures', but he was not sure. She was down on one knee, panting hard.

Kade rushed to her side and quickly performed the Healing Calling. Her breathing eased, and she wearily looked up into Kade's eyes. She smiled weakly and nodded her head in approval. Kade let out a long breath, grateful she was okay.

"Rakna, how are you doing?" Kade asked, but he was met with silence. Fearing the worst, he yelled again. "Crayken! Rakna!"

"Over here," the king responded from a nearby tree. "We made it back to safety. We are much better fighters up here. We should be able to hold our own for a while."

Kade and the dragon returned to clearing the path to the Great Hall. The spiders dropped back to the ground and stayed close to formidable pair. The Apprentice Chosen focused on keeping the right side clear while the dragon burned the left side with its breath. The area reeked of burnt tar. They moved quickly and made it to the Great Hall with only two spiders going down, but they were not mortally wounded.

"Everyone in," Kade yelled. The queen buzzed, and the spiders poured into the tree. Kade scanned the clutch, looking for the king, but he was not among them. He watched for Crayken to pass, but the black spider was nowhere to be seen. Kade was certain the king was bringing up the rear.

"Rayden, keep the king safe until he gets in," Kade said.

Rayden quickly moved to the back and smashed several of the creatures into the dirt. All of the Morphites around the clutch were either killed or mortally wounded. Soon, the spiders were all in the tree and Rayden turned, eager to find more of the creatures.

Kade froze as he heard a loud screech of anger that caused his scalp to tighten. He watched in surprise as a winged monster about half the size of the dragon faded into view. It was just like the creatures with the exception of its size, the wings and the huge talons that hung at the end of each hand. It was only visible for a few seconds, and then it disappeared from sight again.

"That is the leader of the Morphites," the queen said. "He won't attack. He never enters the battle. If things get too dangerous, he will retreat," she said in disgust. "What kind of leader lets his people be slaughtered while he stands by and watches? He will only strike if he is sure not to take injury. He is a coward. My only worry is those things overrunning us."

"We will do everything possible to keep them from taking your home from you," Kade vowed as he rubbed his neck. "I am sure we can handle whatever they throw at us," he said with a malicious grin. "I think Rayden is enjoying this," he added as the link brought him the feeling of what could only be called pleasure.

Kade turned to the dragon that was guarding the entrance and gave it the signal to attack. Rayden roared excitedly. The tree shook with the vibrations as the dragon tore into several of the black creatures that were trying to slide around the entrance. Rayden obviously considered himself immune as he charged in with teeth and claws slashing, tearing into anything he could reach.

"Your dragon seems to be a little more effective than we were," Crayken commented as he limped over to stand next to Kade.

The dragon chased a group of the creatures into a clearing that was two hundred feet from the tree. Kade watched and narrowed his eyes, sensing something odd about the way the creatures were acting. These things fear nothing, so why are they running? If Rayden were not easily seen, Kade might have been more concerned, but as it was, there were only a few large trees between him and his dragon. He watched for a moment more as his companion raced around to snatch a creature and bite down hard. Rayden quickly turned to look for the next victim as it spat the black mass to the ground.

Just as Kade was about to turn away, he saw something strike Rayden, causing the dragon to stumble as a slash about three feet long opened up on its side. He understood immediately why the creatures' actions did not make sense. They were not smart enough to know to run. They had led the dragon into a trap. Kade gasped, and the king and queen buzzed furiously. Darcienna grabbed Kade by the arm and squeezed.

"I'm shocked!" the queen exclaimed in disbelief. "There has to be some reason he is doing this. There is more going on here than we know. There must be."

"Us," Kade said as if that was all that was needed.

Rayden lunged in the direction from whence the attack had come. His teeth came together on empty space. Several of the creatures screamed in delight at the sight of their leader turning things in their favor. Rayden expelled a blast of fire, but it dissipated without finding its target.

"I've got to help Rayden," Kade said as he moved for the exit. Another gash opened in the dragon's other side. Rayden made another attempt to catch the invisible creature, but again, came up empty.

"You can't go out there. You will never see him coming. One

strike and you could be dead," Rakna hissed desperately as she wrapped her legs around him and held him fast.

"The dragon may be our only chance to keep these creatures from defeating us," Kade said as another slash opened up just behind the dragon's right wing. "I don't know if I can keep all these creatures at bay for long if the dragon dies. Besides, I would rather give my life defending Rayden than stand here and watch him be torn to shreds. I will not let that thing kill him without hearing from me first!" Kade vowed as another slash opened on the dragon's leg, causing blood to run. Rayden stumbled and almost fell but then righted himself.

The dragon regained his footing and lunged for the air again only to come up empty once more. Kade felt the call in his mind from his friend, the call for help. His throat closed up, afraid that at any moment the creature would strike the dragon in a vital area. Rayden spared a glance toward the tree and mentally called out for Kade again. The dragon knew without a shadow of doubt that Kade would come. Kade would never abandon him.

"I am not going to just wait here and watch!" Kade screamed, preparing to use his strength to pry off the queen's legs. The dragon started to back away from where it expected the next attack to come from. Kade watched as another long slash appeared down the center of its back. Rayden was covered in blood and glanced back at the tree once more. "Darcienna, prepare your shield," Kade called to her. She did not answer. He turned to look at her and saw despair in her eyes.

"Kade, I am too exhausted," Darcienna said as she tried to raise her arms.

"NOOOOOO!" Kade screamed as he forced his arms free of Rakna's grip and conjured a lightning bolt. He sent the calling racing the two hundred feet through the air just over the dragon's back in hopes of catching the creature making another run. The bolt passed over the dragon without making contact. Kade quickly called on the Divine Fire and sent that over the dragon, and again, it made no contact, but at this distance, the flame was almost useless.

Kade realized that there had been no attacks while he was

throwing blasts of fire so he conjured them as fast as he could. The calling was quicker to perform so he conjured fire over and over in hopes of keeping the dragon safe until he could get to it and perform his healing. Just as he threw another calling of the Divine Fire, the creature struck the dragon in the tail hard enough to spin it around, but it did not get away without taking its own injuries. The Divine Fire had connected. Even though the distance diminished its effectiveness, the Divine Fire still made the difference.

The bushes to the dragon's left were smashed to the ground as something unseen flattened them. Kade immediately sent another blast of Divine Fire at the spot, but the fire consumed only the bush. The dragon was moving sluggishly as its life drained from it. It was losing so much blood that Kade had doubts about it being alive by the time he got to it.

"Wait," Kade said as he quickly closed his eyes and performed the Reveal Calling. The leader popped into view fifty feet to the right of the dragon and twenty feet up as it flapped its massive leather-like wings. It looked like an oversized bat, but it was pure black like the creatures on the ground.

The leader of the Morphites oriented for another strike at the dragon. Kade worked his Lightning Calling just as it started its run. Kade finished the calling and it exploded from his hand. It raced to intercept the creature. Kade felt his pulse pound at the anticipation of the contact, but at the very last second the creature swerved. It banked much sharper than Kade thought possible, but not enough to avoid being clipped by the calling. The lightning bolt spun the creature around as it crashed into several small trees. It let out a loud screech as it oriented on Kade.

"I'm coming, Rayden," Kade yelled. He also sent the thought to the dragon and felt something back through the link. Was it hope?

"I need to get to the dragon," Kade said forcefully. Rakna was still holding him around the waist. "I hit the leader with the last bolt. He won't be able to attack again without me seeing him," Kade said as he half pleaded. He did not want to hurt the queen, but he was not going to stand and watch his dragon die. If he had to use force to dislodge her, so be it.

"Then we go together," Rakna said. Kade opened his mouth to argue when the king weighed in. "There are still too many of those black creatures out there to make it to the dragon safely," Crayken said with all the authority of a king. He turned and issued several short buzzes of command. Thirty spiders leapt to their feet and raced to follow.

"It's now or never," Kade said as he surged forward. Rakna released her hold.

As Kade worked his way toward Rayden, he could see the dragon was quickly losing strength. He was not even sure that Rayden could fend off another attack, even if he knew from where it was coming. Darcienna's eyes blazed bright blue. She screamed as her shield popped into existence for just a fraction of a second. Something large thudded off it and the shield was gone. He looked back, shocked and surprised that she was with them.

Kade closed his eyes, performed the Reveal Calling and saw the flying creature wheeling away. It flew directly toward the dragon and circled overhead. Its wing was injured, causing it to fly awkwardly. *No*, Kade started to think in panic when an idea so obvious came to him that he kicked himself mentally for not thinking of it sooner. He only hoped the dragon was not out of his range. He planted his feet and performed the calling. The dragon faded for a moment and then materialized again. The calling had failed. Kade opened himself up to his hate for the creature and rage filled him. The Divine crashed through him like an avalanche. His special gift was alive. Kade performed the calling again, and the dragon faded from view.

Working the Divine Fire Calling as fast as he could, Kade held it in his hand, ready to throw. As he approached, no less than ten of the creatures dropped out of a tree. He threw the Divine Fire up out of reflex, setting them ablaze. Kade and the spiders had to dodge the burning creatures as they fell to their death.

"That explains why they were not attacking us. They were waiting for us to come out so they could ambush us," the white spider said.

"I thought it was because they were trying to concentrate on the dragon," Kade said as he kicked one of the smoldering creatures hard, sending it flipping end over end through the air. "I will need to be guided to the dragon. I must keep my eyes closed to use this calling that allows me to see their leader," Kade said as he started toward the dragon once more.

"I will lead you," Crayken said as he came up behind Kade and put his front legs on his waist to guide him.

With his eyes closed, Kade saw that the leader had landed. Kade quickly conjured the Divine Fire Calling and launched it at the creature just as it started to charge. It danced to the side easily avoiding the attack. Kade quickly called on another Divine Fire Calling and held it up as a threat. Right now, the most important thing was to get to the dragon. Killing that thing had to be second. If just the threat was enough to accomplish that goal, then that was good enough for Kade…for the moment.

The leader charged and Kade threw. The Fire Calling flew and missed as the leader anticipated the move and dodged easily as it sprang into the air. Kade had another Fire Calling ready and held it up once more. The leader veered off but came back to the ground quickly. Its wing was too badly damaged for it to stay aloft.

"Blood and ashes, that thing is fast!" Kade swore as his heart beat like a drum. "This should confuse it," Kade said as an idea came to him. He threw the Divine Fire and prepared his next calling. "You will like this," Kade said over his shoulder.

"What is your plan, Chosen?" the king asked. The use of the word Chosen was meant as a title of respect, but Kade would not be able to appreciate that until later.

"Watch and see. I am going to even the odds," Kade said as he performed the calling.

"Amazing," Crayken said as they faded from view. "You are

truly powerful," the king said with more confidence than Kade was feeling. He was only hoping the king's confidence was not misplaced.

"Let's move before we lose this advantage," Kade said as he started forward.

I am almost to you, Rayden, Kade thought to his friend. The dragon was so weak that Kade almost could not sense its response. Just a little more and the dragon would live. The distance was closing, but not fast enough for him.

The group of spiders dispatched the creatures easily now that they were cloaked in the Divine. Kade kept his eyes closed as he headed toward the dragon. The leader was not fooled for more than a moment. It used this same tactic and recovered almost instantly. It started to move toward the dragon. Unknown to Kade, this was the one creature that could see through the Transparency Calling.

"We must hurry," Kade said as he moved as fast as he could while the king's legs still held his waist.

"The clutch will get disorganized," the king said into Kade's ear.

"If we wait, we lose the dragon, and we cannot afford that," Kade yelled.

He saw the creature's head jerk in the direction of his voice. He paused only long enough to flow through the moves for the Lightning Calling and sent it racing through the air only to explode in a thunderous crash where the creature no longer was. Kade knew their only hope of defeating this thing was for him and the dragon to work together. He had to get to Rayden.

Now only twenty feet from the dragon, Kade prepared the Healing Calling. His heart raced as he could just about reach out to his friend. Just as he felt real hope, all Holy Divine broke loose. Without warning, hoards of the black creatures came from every hiding spot imaginable.

"Another ambush!" Kade yelled.

A line of the creatures barred their way and more were rushing to fortify that blockade. *Too many,* Kade thought as he prepared to let the Healing Calling go to bring the Divine Fire back to life. Just as he was on the verge of doing so, he felt the king's powerful legs lift and propel him over the sea of black creatures to land on the invisible dragon. Kade crashed face first into the knee of his friend, but he still had the sense to get his hands on Rayden to let the healing flow before falling to the ground. He felt his lip split as blood flowed but he did not care. He leapt to his feet and soothed Rayden as he felt his way to every injury. He worked quickly, racing to each wound and healing. Each one closed up smoothly as he let the Divine do its work.

"Stay still," Kade said as the dragon became eager to join the battle. *I have an idea. We need to set a trap for that thing, and you are going to be the bait,* Kade sent through the mental link. *I will make you visible. When it attacks, I will tell you when and where to strike. Together, we will kill it!*

For the second time in a short span, Kade felt eagerness and the urge to hunt and kill flow through the link so strongly that it was hard to think. *He is off to your left,* Kade sent. *Get ready.*

Kade moved back, eager to bring this thing to an end, eager for revenge, eager to bask in the glory of its suffering. As he watched, he realized the leader was considering retreating. He let the Transparency Calling fade and the dragon shimmered into view. Kade checked the dragon quickly for its appearance. If the leader saw that the wounds were healed, it might know that the dragon was lying in wait. He scanned Rayden and breathed a mental sigh of relief. There was so much blood that the beautiful silver dragon was almost completely covered in red. He felt sick as he looked at all that crimson liquid. His beautiful dragon had taken so much torture while calling out to him. He vowed never to let that happen again. For now, he would be grateful that the blood hid the fact that it was healed.

Kade warned his faithful companion to be ready as he watched the leader close in slowly, studying what it thought was easy prey.

Afraid that the leader might not attack, thinking it had already achieved its goal, Kade instructed the dragon to move a claw here and a tail there but not to overdo it. His lungs were starting to burn as he held his breath, hoping their plan would work. The leader crouched and Kade could feel it coming. His pulse raced, and then it happened. The leader charged with a speed almost too fast for Kade to follow.

"Now!" Kade yelled without thinking.

The leader was clearly smarter than Kade hoped. It realized what was happening and skidded to a stop, its claws working furiously to grip the ground and send it in another direction. As fast as the creature was, Rayden was speed and power incarnate. The dragon craved revenge more than anything at that moment, and it was not going to be denied. The leader scrambled desperately as it changed direction. Kade watched in horror as it looked like it might get away. The best way to describe what happened next was to say that the dragon and Kade linked. Without having to say a word, the dragon knew what Kade was seeing and lunged, barely catching the leader of the Morphites by the wing and spun it to the ground.

Kade brought the Divine Fire Calling to life and held it ready, waiting. Rayden lunged again, but the leader ducked and scrambled back, just barely avoiding the crashing jaws. It turned and jumped into the air, but another violent swipe from the dragon's claws sent it reeling. And then, Kade saw his opening. With careful aim, he let the Divine Fire shoot forth from his hand to envelope the leader. It screamed, but the fire was not going to be enough to end its life. But…that was not Kade's goal. It lit up like a beacon. Rayden pounced on it with all his weight and might. The creature fought furiously, but the dragon now had the advantage. The leader screamed in fury and fear. The black creatures surrounding the spiders were frantic as they watched their leader being torn to shreds right before their eyes.

"Now we shall see who has the advantage," Kade said as he turned to look at the two fierce combatants in their fight to the death. It was more accurate to say their fight to the leader's death. The

120

dragon fought and rent as if it were trying to dig a tunnel through to the other side of the world. Clearly, one of them was not going to leave this fight alive. And with the ferocity of the dragon, Kade knew it was going to be the leader that never moved from that spot ever again.

Kade, a voice boomed in his head. *The king is in dire need of your help.*

"Where?" Kade yelled. Before the queen could reply, Kade saw at least ten black creatures fighting furiously with something they had surrounded, and he immediately knew where. He closed his eyes and the Reveal Calling showed him three glowing forms lying on the ground, motionless, and three more fighting for their lives.

"I'm coming, Crayken. Just hold on," Kade said as he charged into the mob of black creatures. While keeping the king and spiders cloaked, he let the Transparency Calling go. He wanted to draw them to him, hoping they would prefer a target they could see. And then he swung, tore and crushed for all he was worth. At one point he put his fist right through the skull of one of the creatures, and when he pulled it back, the skull was still attached. He swung it at the next and both skulls split apart.

"Careful, Chosen. You are close to us with those mighty blows," the king hissed.

Kade let the Transparency Calling vanish completely. The king and all of his fighters shimmered into view. Two of the spiders on the ground were still alive but not moving. The king and the two remaining spiders were fighting to protect them. Crayken had broken his front right and front left legs when he had propelled Kade through the air as he had come in contact with the hoard. How he was still alive was beyond Kade's understanding, but he was and that was all that mattered.

"We need to get you back to the tree," Kade said as he threw several more of the creatures away to land in crumpled heaps.

"Lead the way," the king said in exhaustion.

As they made their way to the Great Hall, Crayken made

several short buzzing sounds. The other spiders that were now visible came to the king immediately and made sure the path to the Great Hall was clear. There was not much resistance as it appeared that there was, indeed, a limit to how many of these creatures there were.

Darcienna's shield was fading in and out as she struggled with every last bit of energy she had left, valiantly trying to protect the spiders in the tree. Kade could not recall when she had returned, but it appeared that she was needed there since there were several of the creatures screaming at her, furiously trying to get through the shield. Kade quickly ran up to the Morphites and violently tore them apart. He soaked up the pleasure of the kill.

Am I happy for killing or am I happy for killing these things? He vanquished the thought immediately.

"I thought you would never return," Darcienna said as she let her arms fall to her sides. She was breathing heavily as the shield blinked out of sight. She leaned against the wall and then slid down with her head back. She was definitely out of the fight.

"I started to think the same," Kade said as he performed the Healing Calling and placed his hands on her head. She breathed a deep sigh of relief.

Kade stood off to the side to let the spiders enter. Darcienna rose up and reach for his face. He tried to dodge her, but she grabbed his head in both her hands and held firmly. He felt his split lip mend and waited for her to finish.

"That is the extent of the healing I can do until I am able to meditate," Darcienna said as she patted him on the face affectionately, twice. She was still exhausted, but her sense of who she was, was still firmly in place.

"Rakna?" Kade asked, as Darcienna stepped back.

"Yes, Chosen?" the white queen responded.

"Why do they not just storm the trees and crush you? There are so many of them," Kade said as he watched the dragon.

"There is something about the trees that repels them, or we would be dead. All we needed to do was stay close to the trees and we were fine. Even in the branches they seem weaker, but inside, they lose their strength almost completely."

"So, I have been wasting my time," Darcienna said, annoyed.

"No. It's not to say they won't try. It's just that they are not as dangerous," the queen said, ignoring the tone.

"The strong danger you sensed when we were out there had to have been the leader of the Morphites," Kade said as he watched the dragon tear every piece of it apart. Its wings were easily twenty feet from its body. It was past dead, and Rayden showed no signs of stopping. The black minions frantically tried to save their leader, but the dragon did not even acknowledge their presence.

"Crayken?" Kade called out as he turned to survey the spiders in the room. They were up the wall and a few were even on the ceiling. Kade shivered slightly, remembering his old dislike of spiders.

"Over here," the king said.

"I will heal you first, and then I'll heal the rest of the wounded," Kade said as he placed his hands on one of the broken legs. It straightened out immediately. The king winced from the discomfort while it mended. Kade reached for the other leg and got the impression that the king was gritting his teeth. The leg straightened out. Kade worked his way around to all the wounded and then came back to the entrance to stand next to Darcienna.

He mentally called the dragon to return so he could check it for injuries. It was still covered with blood, and it made him cringe. So much blood meant so much damage. He shook off his unease and worked his way around his friend. Rayden's belly had deep, serious gashes, but the dragon was too excited for battle to notice. It started to fidget, eager to continue the hunt. The wounds closed and soon the dragon was off again. It roared enthusiastically as it raced after its prey. Several of the creatures tried to attack the dragon from behind. Rayden spun, and with a few powerful swipes of his claws, sent both of them flying in many different pieces. Kade just shook his head at the sheer stupidity and turned to go back into the tree.

"I think it is time to tell the clutch that your life long nemesis are no more," Kade said as he stepped up to the king.

"Your dragon was truly formidable," Rakna said in deep admiration. "You were correct in saving it."

"Rayden definitely was the key," Kade said with a grin.

"No my friend," the king said as he turned to face Kade, giving him his full attention to emphasize his point. "Not just the dragon, but both of you. All three of you," Crayken added while glancing in Darcienna's direction. "Without you, the dragon would have perished, and we would have taken heavy casualties."

"Yes, we did need each other," Kade said. "All it took was for the dragon to get ahold of the leader and the tide of battle changed," he added, shifting the attention back to Rayden.

Kade started to turn his attention toward Darcienna when something black flying through the air caught his attention out of the corner of his eye. He turned in time to see another black thing flying through the air, only this time, he realized it was one of the Morphites. Kade stepped into the doorway and watched in awe. There were three black creatures furiously trying to scramble away from the dragon. But, every time one would get more than the length of the dragon away, Rayden would pounce and grab the creature in his mouth. Next, Rayden would flip it high into the air. As soon as he flipped one in the air, he would charge for the next one and do the same to it and then he would be onto the third. It almost appeared that the dragon was juggling with how he constantly kept the creatures flipping end over end. Kade stared, wide-eyed.

"What?" Darcienna asked, seeing the look on his face.

"It would appear that Rayden has found a use for the creatures," Kade said, chuckling as he pointed out the door.

Darcienna looked out and her jaw hit the floor. Over and over the dragon would pounce on the creatures only to flip them into the air to land back where they started. Around and around Rayden would go as he galloped from one to the next. Darcienna shook her head, speechless, as she watched the dragon play. The king and queen

124

looked on in wonder as the dragon continued to pounce and twist and turn, enjoying its game.

"Let us descend to the Great Hall," the king said as he and the queen turned from the dragon and led the group down to the massive cavern.

Crayken and Rakna walked toward their thrones as they buzzed to a spider here or another there. After walking over and climbing the five steps to the royal chairs, they sat, buzzing back and forth between themselves. Kade and Darcienna climbed the steps to join them. The room fell completely silent as Crayken and Rakna spoke for quite some time. Not one spider moved or hardly even breathed. Kade was distracted slightly as something came through the link from the dragon. He focused on it momentarily and recognized it for amusement. Kade felt as if he wanted to chuckle at this, but he knew that this was not the right time for levity. He was certain something profound was happening, and he needed to show respect. He glanced at Darcienna, who shrugged slightly, and then went back to watching the royal couple. He looked around the room and noticed that no other spiders had ascended the stairs. For a moment, he wondered if he had blundered by joining the king and queen without being invited.

Crayken looked around the room slowly, making eye contact with the spiders to ensure he had their attention. He started a slow but deliberate buzzing, and the clutch hung on his every word. Soon, even the king stood silently, waiting. For what, Kade could not even guess. Moments passed and not even one spider moved. Kade knew that something very important was happening but he had not even a clue as to what it could be.

Several of the spiders glanced at Kade with what had to be a stunned look and then back to the king. Shortly after, they started a slow buzz which seemed to pick up in intensity by the moment. They were all on their feet. The buzzing seemed to take on a rhythmic chant to it as it increased in pitch. Kade looked at Darcienna, and again, all she could do was shrug.

125

"I think we are being honored. At least, that is my best guess," Kade said as he watched the clutch.

"They honor both of you for what you have done," Crayken said. "You have helped us fight what was not just a battle but the final war. The black leader has been trying to drive us to extinction for as far back as we can recall."

"The king told the clutch that they are to honor you as though you were a king and that your word is to be as if it had come from Crayken himself," Rakna said.

"I am much honored, but I did only what was right. You are my friends, and I could not leave you to those things," Kade said as he motioned toward the outside.

"Regardless, without you, we would have sustained heavy losses, if not the destruction of our clutch. The best we could have hoped for was to escape with our lives. Never before has their entire race attacked us like this. Again, we owe you our lives. If we can ever be of any assistance at any time, you only need ask," Crayken said in a very serious tone, as he looked Kade in the eye.

The Apprentice Chosen knew that the king meant every word he spoke. All eyes were on him. The king and queen waited patiently for him to respond. Kade felt self-conscious as his mind tried to take in all that had transpired.

What if I say the wrong thing and make a fool of myself, or even worse, offend the king and queen? Kade pondered. *Is there some customary response expected?*

He took a breath and worked up his most regal posture. He tried to stand tall and proud. If he was to be looked upon as a king, he should act like a king. Or at least, act like what he thought a king should act like.

"This day is a day that will live forever in my heart," Kade said as the queen buzzed his words to the clutch. "I am honored and privileged to fight alongside such brave warriors. I would have proudly given my life to defend you and your home," he added with what he hoped was as serious a tone as Crayken's. "To be raised to

126

the level of king in your eyes is more than I deserve," Kade continued. Several of the spiders stood taller and moved a little closer as they listened intently. "I can only hope to bring half as much honor to my title as your king and queen have to theirs," he said as he turned to the royal couple, ending his speech. He paused for a moment as he pondered something that had been on his mind since the first time he met the queen. He feared he may be pressing his welcome with what he wanted to ask, but he took a deep breath and forged on.

CH5

"May I speak with you in private for a moment, Crayken?" Kade asked as he glanced at the queen. The king gave a nod. "Crayken, what would happen if you were to fall in battle or if you were to have perished last night?" Kade asked, already knowing the answer.

"I am not sure what you are asking," The king said, confused by Kade's question. Kade hoped and prayed to the Divine that he was not committing a grave offence by the spider's standards.

"Specifically, what would happen to the queen and the clutch?"

"The queen would be put to death, as our custom calls for, and the clutch would split up to find a new king and queen. It is the way of our kind," Crayken answered, confused.

"Is there any way that Rakna could be spared? Would it be possible to tell the clutch that if something were to happen to you, she would continue on as queen?" Kade asked.

Crayken flinched. Clearly this was one of the most absurd things he had ever heard. The king slowly looked at the queen and then back to Kade. Rakna also seemed to be surprised by this question. Were they looking at him as if he were a simpleton? Did he instantly reduce his standings with them by asking these ridiculous questions?

The room went completely silent at the king's reaction. They did not need to hear what was said to understand that Crayken had been taken aback by Kade's words. Kade could feel his heart pounding in his chest as he waited for the king to respond. Crayken and Rakna once again locked eyes, and Kade was sure they were communicating. It was not more than a few moments when they both turned back toward him, but their moods had not changed.

"That would be impossible for me to ask of the clutch," Crayken said gravely.

"I don't understand," Kade said, still fearing he was on the verge of offending. He got the strong impression that the king had sighed, but it was a sigh a forlorn person would give and not one of frustration. With a bit of sadness, the king continued.

"We are designed by the Great Divine to follow a king. The clutch can follow the queen as long as there is a king. A queen is not allowed to rule by herself. It is in our genetic makeup," the king said. Kade could see this was an emotional topic for Crayken and tried hard to choose his words carefully.

"But, could not the queen be spared?" Kade asked gently.

The king turned toward Rakna, and Kade could see the love that passed between them. This was a painful issue for Crayken, and Kade was starting to regret bringing it up. This had to be the king's worst fear. Something told Kade that it was a topic that was never brought up due to the heartfelt pain it caused, and here he was, blindly stumbling through it.

"No, Chosen. There is only one king born for every one thousand of our kind, and the same goes for the queen. We are born to lead. When we find each other, we imprint on each other. When that happens, the queen can never again imprint on another. The clutch must have a king. No other king will be able to imprint on her after I pass," Crayken explained patiently, as if he were talking to a child. He was not talking down to Kade, but he was talking as if explaining that the sun will come up day after day.

Kade felt himself sink inside at the thought of all his new allies separated and the white spider being killed in the unfortunate event of the king's death. *Crayken could have died today, and this all would be for nothing,* Kade thought. *There just has to be a way.* Just then, Darcienna whispered in Kade's ear while the king and queen waited patiently. Kade looked at Darcienna for several long moments, uncertainty filling him. She nodded once in encouragement and he continued.

"Crayken, you said that I was to be honored as if I were a king, correct?" Kade asked, holding his breath as he waited for the king to respond.

"Correct," the king said, sensing where Kade was going with this.

"And you said that my word was to be treated as if it came directly from you?"

"I did," Crayken said, as the spider king took a step toward Kade, starting to see more depth to this line of questioning.

"Then, can the clutch be instructed to follow me, in the event that you should fall in battle?" Kade asked. The irony of the situation hit Kade hard. Here he was fighting for the queen's life, and it was her own clutch that was the threat. Was there a solution to this dilemma? Something deep inside said he was onto something, but it had to be done perfectly. Kade took a deep breath and jumped right to the point. "Can I be king so as to keep the queen from being killed and to keep the clutch from separating if something were to happen to you?" Kade asked as he felt his palms start to sweat.

Darcienna put her hand on his arm and squeezed in encouragement. His heart pounded heavily in his chest. Why was this so difficult to ask? Were they ready to shun him for asking such a bold thing? His head spun slightly as he tried to stay calm. After a moment, the king and queen locked eyes again. The queen flinched and looked at Kade. He feared he may have gone too far but there was no turning back now.

"You did lead most of the war, even if I was the one giving the orders," the king said slowly. Kade swallowed hard as he processed the king's words. "And you were instrumental in defeating our most feared and hated enemy," Crayken said as he thought back on the battle. Kade was not fooled for one moment. He knew immediately where this was going. Darcienna squeezed his arm hard in excitement. "And I don't think there is a spider in here that does not respect your judgment or fighting skills," the king continued methodically. "And, you are a Chosen, so they would have that protection, also," the king finished thoughtfully.

"So then it is possible?" Kade asked hopefully.

"It would be impossible to change tradition but to bend it, maybe," Crayken said as he performed what appeared to be a nod. "There is nothing that says the king must be a spider," he added. Kade knew the argument was its weakest with this fact. "It would be up to the clutch. If they accepted this, then it would be binding and the queen would rule with you if I were to meet an unfortunate end. But, it must be unanimous amongst the elders or it will not be binding."

Kade looked at Rakna and saw her staring straight ahead, as if hearing none of this. Crayken and Rakna exchanged a glance as the king turned to address the clutch. Kade got the impression that Crayken had taken a deep breath as he prepared to speak. Kade worried he may be asking for something that would cause the spiders to revolt against the king? Or worse, would these spiders look on the king as a buffoon for even suggesting it?

Crayken started to address the congregation and instantly there were gasps from all corners of the great hall. He continued on, confidently. "Confidence was half the battle," Zayle used to say, and here it really showed. Kade watched intently for any indication of acceptance or rejection. Again, he drew the attention of many of the spiders as they took in what was being asked of them. He could not tell if this was good or bad, but he continued to hope. He tried to appear confident, but inside, his stomach felt as if he had hundreds of bats fluttering wildly.

The spiders started to buzz excitedly for several long moments until the queen quickly shot to her feet. The king and queen both said something in their language that caused all the spiders to quiet. It took a short time for the excitement to die down, but eventually, calm was restored to the Great Hall. The queen slowly sat down and held such a regal pose that Kade felt his admiration for her grow immensely. The king buzzed a few short words, and one of the older spiders with grey on its legs buzzed back.

They aren't sure about your proposal, Rakna said in his mind. Kade almost jumped. He was not aware that she had moved to stand close to him. But, even if she were across the room, he still would have jumped due to the fact that he was so focused on the interaction between the king and what appeared to be one of the elders. *They give you a lot of credit for vanquishing our enemy, but not all are comfortable with you as their king. They say it is ludicrous to consider such a thing.*

"So they have rejected my proposal?" Kade asked, disheartened. The queen swept the clutch with her gaze as she analyzed their reactions.

I cannot say just yet. They understand why you are asking, so they are not concerned with your motive, and you are a Chosen, so they credit you with the right to lead. And your feat today showed that you would make the most formidable leader this clutch could ever hope for; after Crayken, of course.

"Of course," Kade said, quickly agreeing. He was wise enough to understand that leading a society was much more than wielding great power. But, he did not expect to be leading. He was doing it for the queen. That was not lost on the clutch.

"But…," the queen added and did not need to speak anymore.

There were too many buts for this to be accepted easily.

Kade looked out over the crowd of spiders and noticed several of them looking at him, analyzing him as they contemplated the request. He tried to give what he thought was a look of confidence and hoped it was not one of arrogance. He was careful not to look too long at one spider, as it might be seen as a challenge, so he made sure to keep his eyes moving. One of the spiders that had been studying Kade turned to the king and started to speak.

It would appear you have some support, the queen whispered in his mind. *This is more than I expected,* she thought in controlled surprise, but Kade could feel the intensity in her tone. It was only because of years of practice at remaining calm that she was able to hide her emotions as well as she did. Kade was sure that she, too, had dozens of bats flapping around in her stomach. The king turned and confidently made his way back to them. The Apprentice Chosen felt his stomach clench as he dreaded the news. It had to be good. He hoped more than anything it would be, but the doubt in his heart was there, and he could not ignore it.

"They argue for your proposal and against your proposal," the king said calmly, but Kade could sense the tension in his voice. "Raksin says that even though you are indeed an excellent leader and would make one of the greatest kings ever, there should be no talk of their king dying. He says we should deal with that situation when and if it arises," Crayken said while pointing out the spider.

"Raksin is one of the king's most loyal supporters," Rakna added.

"Archon says that your intentions are honorable, and that if I endorse you, we should accept the proposal. Archon was very impressed with your prowess in battle and your ability to command during the fight. He says that the clutch would be assured to live on forever with you as a leader," the king said while indicating the second spider. "They seem to think you Chosen can live forever," Crayken said as he leaned forward and whispered, almost chuckling. Crayken stood back up. "I cannot just tell them to accept you. If all of the elders were to agree, with no coercion, then it would be law, and they would follow you loyally to the end of time. But, if just one of the elders disagrees, it cannot be accepted. This is our law and it must be followed"

Kade took one step forward as he looked out over the spiders. Some of the clutch met his gaze as he swept the room with his eyes, while others glanced away. It was close, but it appeared that the key to this were the two elder spiders. Kade turned confidently, moving in a way he thought a king would move and approached the royal couple.

"May I address them?" Kade asked. He sounded much calmer than he felt. His nerves were on edge, and the bats in his stomach had multiplied.

"They are not able to understand your words," Crayken said. "If you would like me to translate, I do not think it would be an issue," the king said as he waited for Kade to respond. Kade was shocked to see he had missed something so obvious. Never at any time had he interacted with any of the spiders except through the king or queen. None had tried to talk directly to him, even one time. Rakna must have realized what was going through his mind and explained.

"Only royalty are born with the gift to talk with our minds. All spiders do have the ability to learn to speak your language, but kings and queens are the only ones who do. It is the mark of royalty," Rakna said.

"Would you like me to translate for you?" the king asked.

"I appreciate your offer," Kade said as an idea came to him. "But with your permission, I would like the queen to translate for me."

The king looked at Rakna for a moment as he pondered Kade's request. Not seeing a reason to deny it, he nodded once in approval. Crayken bowed slightly as he stepped back to give Kade the floor.

"You can speak directly to the spider you would like to address, and I will translate," Rakna said.

Kade reached for Darcienna's hand that was still holding his arm and squeezed it once. He locked eyes with the queen for a moment as he readied himself. *It was all going to come down to this,* Kade thought. He hoped and prayed to the Divine that this would succeed. The king and queen looked at him, showing no emotion. He patted Darcienna's hand once as if to indicate that he was on his own for this one. With a last glance at the queen, he turned and stepped forward, displaying much more confidence than he felt.

"Raksin," Kade said as he locked eyes with the elder spider. "Your loyalty to your king is commendable and one of the most important traits a king could ever hope for. I respect your judgment greatly and hope that I can have someone with your strength of character to support me when the time comes. I have proposed what I have because I have fought side by side with your clutch and would have died with your clutch if needed," he said, feeling his confidence grow as he spoke. "I would be saddened to see it disbanded if the king, who has worked hard to keep it together, was to experience an untimely death. I would give my life for such a noble king, as I know you would," Kade said as he stepped up to the spider with the queen in tow. Raksin swelled with pride the more Kade spoke.

Kade was surprised at how the queen was able to translate at the same time he spoke. It was so perfectly timed that it was as if he were the one making the buzzing sound. It occurred to him that she was not translating his words but translating his thoughts as he felt a feather light touch caressing his mind continuously. He smiled at the queen briefly and turned to Archon.

Kade could see that Archon was staring at the ground. Was the spider ashamed of what he had said? Kade hoped this was not the case or he might not be able to gain the support he needed. For this to work, he needed both to see what he wanted them to see.

"Archon, I am greatly honored that you are willing to speak for me. I appreciate and respect you for your loyalty you are willing to give. Your words are filled with wisdom. You care for this clutch and it shows. I know that you, too, would give your life for your king and queen, as your love for them both is very clear. But, we all must make hard choices at times, and you have made a decision based on what is best for the clutch. I have also made my request for the good of the clutch, as any good leader who cares about his people would," Kade said as Archon lifted his gaze to look into Kade's eyes. The spider was starting to stand taller and even appeared to be puffing out its chest. "It takes a brave spider to speak as you have. Your faith in me is very admirable and it is something I will never forget. It is what I ask of this clutch," Kade said as he turned and addressed the entire congregation. "It is for this clutch, for your king and for your queen that I offer my life to preserve what stands before me," Kade said as he raised his voice. "It is for you that I offer to lead, if ever you should need," Kade said, feeling the emotions in the room building.

Kade walked back to stand by the king. Archon was beaming with pride. Raksin was starting to fidget. Archon turned and buzzed something at Raksin. Raksin in-turn buzzed something back, but it seemed to lack conviction. Was there hope? Kade forced himself to remain calm.

"They argue about which of them is more correct. They are using your words to judge each other," Rakna said while Kade still had his back to the spiders. He turned and held his head up high.

"Both of you have honorable intentions. You are both trying to do what is best for the clutch, except, you are doing it differently. I value both of your opinions and always will," Kade said as he studied each one at a time, gauging their reactions to his words. "Raksin is correct to say you should honor your king, and Archon is correct to want what is best for the clutch."

Archon and Raksin both looked at each other thoughtfully and then back to Kade. They both relaxed and listened closely to what he had to say. The elder spiders started to buzz back to Kade, and the queen translated.

"I believe we would follow you, if it came to that," Raksin said. "But, tradition says that we are to…," Raksin started to stay but then hesitated, hating the taste of the word he did not say. It was clear that no one wanted to see the queen put to death. "We are to find a new king if our current king dies. It has been that way for as long as any spider has lived. I, myself, have been in two other clutches before this one. If you had a queen, we would follow her," he said as he glanced at Darcienna.

"You could not follow me at all if you followed my queen. You would have no way to communicate with me," Kade said…and then it happened. All eyes shifted to the white queen. He hid his smile as he continued on. "Rakna has been doing all the communicating for us," Kade said as he stood with pride.

He spared a glance back and saw understanding in the king's eyes. He nodded ever so slightly at Kade, and then stood still, letting the clutch decide. He was a good king and an honorable one. Kade was proud to be thought of in such high esteem by such a great leader. Kade turned back to the clutch to put the final touch on this, and then it would be out of his hand.

"And I do not think I would accept any other queen for this clutch. You have all followed her for a long time, and you all know that she would die to protect you."

Kade looked around the room as he tried to guess how this was going to end. His eyes found Raksin, and he watched as the old spider looked from the queen to the king and then back to him as he considered Kade's words. Raksin then locked eyes with the king and stepped forward. The king stood tall, showing no emotions as he watched the old spider approach.

Raksin stopped at the bottom step and buzzed several short words at the king. Crayken nodded his head slightly and then buzzed something back. The queen did not translate. Kade looked at her and his heart beat wildly. Why did this matter so much? He tried to find the moment when he decided that this civilization's survival meant more to him than his own life and could not pinpoint it. It just was. It took everything he had to wait for the queen to translate. She slowly turned to look at Kade.

Raksin has just asked if the king is in favor of this proposal,

Rakna translated. Kade held his breath as he hung on her every word. It seemed to take forever for her to answer. It was driving Kade crazy, waiting to hear what had transpired. *The king has indicated that he is.*

Kade watched as the old spider considered hard what was being proposed. The room was buzzing with talk. It began to increase more and more as individual arguments broke out as to which elder was more correct. Kade looked to Darcienna for her reaction and read only uncertainty in her eyes. Raksin buzzed several times, and the room fell silent. He moved over to stand face to face with Archon and then turned to face the clutch. Everyone in the room waited with baited breath. It was so quiet you would have thought the room was empty.

"I think that Kade's words have merit," the spider buzzed to the rest of the clutch. "If the king wishes us to honor Kade as though he were a king, then I say we honor him as a king. If the king names him as his successor, then I find no reason to stand in the way of this. I am loyal to my king to the end, and if this is my king's wish, then I support it," Raksin said, and the room erupted in a deafening buzzing. Raksin held up his front legs again for silence. The room quieted down quickly. "Also," the spider added, "I do not see where we have the right to decide who our king chooses for his queen. If Kade were to become our king, then it would not be right to kill the one he would choose to be queen," Raksin finished, and this time the room really exploded. There was no calming them anytime soon.

Kade had to resist the urge to cover his ears, afraid that he would not look too kingly. He glanced up at Crayken and saw that he and the queen were face to face. The love they felt for each other came off them in waves. Kade's heart filled with warmth. He always believed crying was for babies and women, but at that moment, he actually felt choked up.

"They love each other so much," Darcienna said as she watched the interaction.

"It would seem that you were able to convince them," Crayken

138

said as he walked over to stand in front of Kade. "You have fought two battles today and won them both. I am not sure which was more formidable, but victory was yours."

"I hope I have not offended you. I wish no harm...," Kade was saying when Crayken cut him off.

"On the contrary. You have accomplished something that I could never have done. My queen, along with my clutch are the most important things to me. To know she will not only live, if I am to parish, but continue on as the queen makes me happier than you will ever know. You have done me a great service this day, and I will never be able to repay you, but I will try. You have also managed to keep the clutch together. A king works his entire life to hold his clutch together only to know that when he dies, everything he has worked for will unravel.

Kade smiled as he reveled in his victory. It was a good victory, and now he could relax. The clutch was to stay together, and he had kept the queen safe. He looked at Darcienna and saw her regarding him with a smile. It was more than a smile. She was beaming as she looked at him with pride.

"What is it they are chanting?" Kade asked, turning back to the king.

"It is a ritual that indicates their loyalty and praise for you. It is a great honor. This has never been done for an outsider before," Rakna said as she looked on in wonder.

Just as Kade was starting to unwind completely, a deafening roar echoed through the tree. He jumped as the room shook. The chanting stopped, and the spiders froze. The king jumped up, ready for battle.

"What is it?" Crayken asked, ready to face any challenge. Kade had solved the mystery almost immediately.

"It would be a mighty battle indeed," Kade said as he readied himself. "You would need to battle my dragon's appetite," he said as he shook his head. The king laughed for the first time that Kade could recall. Rakna buzzed something to the spiders and the room erupted in good cheer and laughter. They settled back down and began to mingle.

"We should celebrate and have something to eat. Unfortunately, I am not sure we can feed your dragon. It is a shame. After all he has done for us, I would feed him until he was stuffed, but something tells me he is not partial to nuts and fruits," Crayken said.

"Don't worry about him. I'll take care of feeding that bottomless pit," Kade said.

The king turned to the mass of spiders and buzzed several times. The clutch buzzed eagerly and set off doing chores to get ready for the celebration. The festivities were going to be something that would be talked about for decades.

Kade exited the Great Hall and climbed the stairs, but before exiting the tree, he held Darcienna by the arm to stop her. She turned toward him, and before she could ask why, he pulled her into a tight embrace. She breathed a sigh, enjoying his strong arms around her. As they started to separate, he stopped and kissed her on the forehead.

"What was that for?" Darcienna asked.

"For your support," Kade said as he stepped back, still holding her by the arms.

"All I did was stand next to you."

"Exactly," Kade said as he smiled again. "You stood by me. Your support meant a lot. Knowing I was not out there alone made the difference." Darcienna grew a huge smile and hugged him again.

"Now, let's make some food," Kade said as he turned and almost walked into the dragon's big head.

He had to put his hands on the dragon's chest and push. Rayden was blocking the doorway, eagerly awaiting his feeding. He backed up but stayed close, already starting to drool in anticipation of the tasty meat. As soon as the doorway was clear, spiders started filing in and out as they prepared for the feast. Kade stopped to survey the area and saw black bodies that had to count into the hundreds if not closing in on a thousand.

"That is quite a fighting machine," Rakna said as she exited the tree to stand next to him. Kade sensed that there was more on her mind as she stood looking out over the carnage. "Why did you do that?" she asked without looking at him.

"I could not stand to think of what would happen to you," Kade said. Like Raksin, he too could not bring himself to speak in a way that referred to her death. "I think you are an excellent leader, and it would be a great loss if you were to be...," Kade said, not finishing the statement. "You showed us that when we first met. All the spiders where willing to follow you without question. Well, one did need a bit of encouragement to follow your direction," Kade said with a sidelong glance. "I would not want to see a clutch that I was willing to give my life for lose an excellent leader like you," he said as he turned to look at the white spider. And right then, he realized why the spiders meant so much to him in such a short time. He had put his life on the line to save them, and because of that, their survival meant everything to him. But, there was more to it than that. They were a good-hearted civilization that he was proud to be a part of. The fact that he very well may have brought the danger to them was not lost on him, but regardless, in the end, it worked out in their favor considerably.

"Thank you, Chosen. You have given me my life. I will never forget that. Now, it is time for celebration. You are our honored guest for the night."

"Thank you," Kade said as he smiled a genuine smile. The queen turned to leave and prepare for the night.

"Rakna," Darcienna said, halting the queen in her tracks.

"Something troubles you?" Rakna asked, seeing a confused look on Darcienna's face.

"I am having a hard time understanding something. You have known us no more than a day, and yet, Kade is second in line for the throne. Not only that, but he is to be king if Crayken falls in battle?" Darcienna asked.

"This confuses you?" Rakna asked. Kade understood where she was going with this and found that he agreed with Darcienna's thinking. He listened eagerly, curious.

"It just does not make sense why the clutch would be willing to follow Kade after just one day. As much as I wanted this for you and us, I never expected it to actually be possible. We are human, and you are spiders. But one day…and they accept him as their leader?"

"I see," Rakna said as she let out a small laugh of amusement. "You judge us by human standards. As much as this is not possible among humans, it is easily accepted by spiders. To be honest, I am shocked that not only was Kade willing to take on the mantle of leadership, but that he offered."

This caught Darcienna off guard and she stood, gaping like a fish. Kade found it amusing as he watched the interaction. He could see where this was going, and it made more sense by the moment. Rakna also found it amusing as she continued to explain.

"You say it is the fact that it was only one day? Consider this; if Crayken were to die, the clutch would put me to death and then go out in search of another clutch to join. You have a firm understanding of this, yes?"

"Yes, but…," Darcienna said and stopped, waiting for the queen to help her understand.

"If the clutch were to join another king and queen, they would know them not at all. It may be a day, but in that day, Kade proved himself to be a worthy leader that allows this clutch to stay together. Also, the clutch would feel the loss of two leaders; one they lost through the act of fate, and the other they brought about by their own actions. They would put me to death because it must be, not because they wanted it. Kade has offered them a way to spare me. So, yes, they were not only accepting of the idea, they were deeply grateful for it. Kade, being a Chosen and vanquishing a feared enemy, has easily proven that he has the right to lead. The only issue I felt might cause a problem is the fact that he is not a spider. But, his character overcame that obstacle."

"I see," Darcienna said slowly as she absorbed all that Rakna had explained. "I see," she said more confidently as she focused on the queen. "When you put it like that, it makes sense."

"As I previously said, I am honored to offer myself for this clutch," Kade said, feeling genuine affection for the queen. "I understand why they cherish you so," he said with a smile.

"Once again, you honor me with your words, second in line for the throne. Now, I must go and make ready for the celebration," Rakna said with a slight bow. And with that, she moved off gracefully.

The dragon started to huff impatiently, eager for a feeding. Kade worked the Food Calling, and by the twelfth piece of meat, he decided that he had made enough. This was getting monotonous. He needed to find a way to feed the dragon more efficiently.

The food smelled so good that he decided to make some for him and Darcienna, also. He hoped it would not be taken as offensive that he was not waiting for the feast, but his stomach was growling now. They quickly ate their food and went in to see how preparations were coming along. They gladly offered their assistance, starting to feel like one of the clutch.

Kade and Darcienna were approaching the king and queen to offer their help when, suddenly, there was a commotion behind them that caused the spiders to buzz excitedly. Kade turned to see several of them advancing on a black shape that had glided into the room. Four spiders tried to corner the animal, but it was able to dodge them with ease. If he did not recognize the animal right away, he would have definitely recognized the familiar sack of books it dragged across the floor.

"Kade!" Darcienna exclaimed.

"I know," Kade said as he moved to intercept the creature. "Don't hurt him. He is mine," Kade called out as he knelt down. Chance ran up to him and dropped the books, waiting for his reward. It was hungrily licking its lips as it sat back on its haunches, waiting. Its paws were together as though it were praying, ready to catch any tasty morsel Kade was willing to throw.

"I don't know how you always manage to find my books, even

when I don't know they are missing," Kade said, chastising his silky, black friend. "But, taking them from my room does not count," he finished with a chuckle.

"That's a Mordra," Rakna said. "They are said to be able to sense the Divine itself. I have never seen one before, but from the descriptions I have been given by Valdry, I would have to say that that is exactly what we have here."

"It can sense the Divine, eh?" Darcienna asked while Kade affectionately stroked the silky fur. "Maybe that's why it is drawn to the books. You did say there are some powerful callings placed on them," she said as she tilted her head thoughtfully.

"How did you get it to bring you the books?" Crayken asked as he moved closer to look at the creature.

"He feeds it," Darcienna said simply.

"You may be right," Kade said as Chance looked at him eagerly.

The creature's eyes quickly went from Kade's hands to his face and back again, eagerly waiting for Kade to go through the motions that would conjure fresh meat. The Chosen stood and quickly conjured the food, causing Chance's nose to start twitching furiously. Kade laughed as he tossed it its undeserved reward. The Mordra caught it in its hand-like paws and began to hungrily devour the food. It curled up protectively around its meal with a wary eye on anyone that strayed too close.

"I have been meaning to ask something of you, if I may?" Kade said.

"Anything. If it is within my power, consider it done," Crayken promised.

"The queen says there is something in the caves where the black creatures live that I am looking for. Is it possible to have her take me there?"

"If it is the queen's wish, then let it be so. I will not stand in your way," Crayken said.

"Thank you," Kade said as he bowed his head slightly, feeling

144

it was the appropriate response. The king responded with a slight nod of his head.

"Rakna?" Kade asked.

"I would be honored to assist you. We will take two guards with us," Rakna said as she signaled two of the spiders to join them. "We leave now," she said, surprising Kade. He was not expecting such and expeditious departure. Maybe tomorrow, but this very instant? With a shrug of his shoulder and a glance at Darcienna, he accepted the plan. "The caves are close enough that if we hurry, we can be back well before the feast begins," she said as she headed for the stairs.

The small group exited the tree and quickly mounted the dragon. The queen and her two subjects joined together and covered the dragon like a net just behind the wings. The dragon looked back at the spiders, and Kade got the distinct impression that Rayden had to fight to keep from shivering. Rayden craned his neck just a little further to look at Kade, and then with a mental sigh, turned and started out at a slow lope. Kade could not help but to chuckle. Rakna gave Kade a set of directions who, in turn gave them to the dragon. Rayden altered course slightly as he ran over the open plains. Kade relaxed, enjoying the wind flowing through his hair while he watched the land whisk by.

Just as the queen promised, they were at the caves in just over twenty minutes. Kade felt excitement surge through the connection from Rayden and looked around for what had the dragon's attention. It started to dance eagerly as it impatiently waited for the riders to dismount. Kade started to question Rayden when he saw something black shifting in the shadows. There were several of the black creatures attempting to sneak up on them.

Morphites, Kade thought as he laughed and shook his head at the sheer stupidity of the race. *Sneak up on a dragon? Soon they are going to see that they should have been running in terror.*

The riders dismounted in seconds, but even this was too long for the eager dragon. The spiders had barely hit the ground when

Rayden leapt after the closest of the creatures, and had it before it knew what hit it. Kade marveled at the height that Rayden was able to get that thing. The dragon pounced and leapt as he grabbed and flipped, getting as many as three of them in the air at a time. Pure entertainment came through the bond between him and the dragon. Rayden leapt and twisted as though he had not a care in the world while he played his little game. Kade shook his head again and turned back to the queen, who was watching the dragon in awe.

"He has an interesting idea of what is fun," Rakna said as she watched, unable to take her eyes off the dragon for several long moments. She looked up and shielded her eyes from the sun as she watched them flip end over end. As difficult as it was for her to turn away from this amazing display, she forced herself to focus on Kade. "I believe the cave we are looking for is this one," Rakna said as she indicated a large opening in the mountain.

The queen glanced once more at the dragon and then headed toward the cave with the two guards in tow. Kade fell in behind with Darcienna close at his side. The queen stopped at the back of the cave as she studied a pile of rubble.

"Valdry said there was a tunnel here that was concealed by rocks, and from what I can see, this fits the description," Rakna said.

Kade stepped close and analyzed the boulders. At first, it looked like nothing more than rocks that had been piled along the back of a cave, but the closer he examined the area, the more he could see that there was, indeed, an opening. He felt excitement growing in him as he reached down to grab the first of the boulders. He strained, but because of the size of the rocks, the best he could do was to roll it out of the way. They were a little less than half his size but more weight than he was able to lift. Rolling was good enough. The queen and her two guards joined in and helped clear the way. An hour later there was enough of an opening to enter the tunnel.

"We will need light," Rakna said as she looked at him, waiting.

She expects me to have unlimited powers, Kade thought.

When he had time, he would tell her just how misinformed she was... maybe.

Kade started to draw on the Divine to produce light when he changed his mind. He completed the Divine Fire Calling and held the seething flame up to guide them. It did not light the way as well and the Light Calling, but he was good with the tradeoff. This allowed him to be ready for attack in the event that they encountered resistance. He was pleased with himself and confidently led the way as the light from the blue flame flickered off the walls.

"Your skill in the Divine never ceases to amaze me. How do you hold the fire without it burning you?" Rakna asked as they worked their way down the tunnel.

"The Divine does not allow it to burn until I cast it. It's like a formula. The last ingredient to activate the calling fully is for me to cast it," Kade said as he moved it closer to show her it held no heat. Rakna flinched back but then slowly waved a leg over fire. She nodded, impressed. "If I was to throw the Divine Fire at a wall directly in front of me, I would feel the backlash of the heat," Kade said casually as he turned and started to work his way down the tunnel once more.

It was damp and musty, making it uncomfortable to breathe. But, there was more than just that. There was something else in the air that Kade could not quite figure out. It was a combination of how the air tasted and how it smelled. He tried to decide if it was good or bad, or if it just was.

"I am very grateful that you were gracious enough to talk with us the day our paths crossed. I can see now that you could have destroyed us if you chose," Rakna said easily, as if it were the most obvious fact. "At first, your lack of fear had me confused. But now, I understand why," the queen finished.

Kade stopped, his mouth hanging open but no words coming out. She had it so wrong. The dragon had so many spiders on him that he most certainly would have died a horrible death from the venom, and Darcienna was no longer able to protect herself. He might have survived between his strength and the Divine, but what good would that be, with his most faithful friend and the one he loved lying dead?

Kade's mind drifted back to a memory during one of his lessons with Zayle. So much of what had been said did not make sense, but once more, it all seemed to fit like a piece to a puzzle. How could he have been so stupid not to listen to wisdom so profound?

"Sometimes it is not your abilities that will win you the war but how your enemies perceive your abilities," Zayle would say. "Sometimes it can be as simple as how you portray yourself. If you show confidence and display the correct attitude, then that alone may end a war without even one calling being cast. The most successful Chosen will never have to use a calling even once in battle to emerge the victor."

Kade recalled thinking that his teacher was seriously confused at the time. To never use a calling and still win a war was just complete and utter nonsense. Everyone knew the Chosen were to be feared and respected, but to not use callings? Absurd! Now, as Kade thought about it, he saw what his master was trying to teach him. If only he had not been so thickheaded and actually listened. *If only,* Kade thought as he fought off the sadness. He turned to go and stopped, almost walking into Darcienna. She reached up gently to remove the tear from the corner of his eye with a gentle caress of her hand. Kade clenched his jaw, angry that his emotions were showing so easily.

This is not the time to morn or feel pity for myself, Kade thought roughly, angry that this weakness in him had shown for all to see. The sadness dried up and his face turned to stone.

"I think your opinion of us is a bit inflated," Kade said, showing no sign of the emotions he was feeling just seconds ago.

"I can sense that you think you are telling the truth, Chosen, but I find it hard to believe, after witnessing all I have in the past few days. Kade, we are just one clutch. We would have been a minor inconvenience at best. Nonetheless, I do appreciate what you are trying to say," Rakna said as she bowed her head slightly. Kade returned the gesture.

The apprentice relaxed a little as he smiled and slid by her to light the way. Darcienna wrapped her hand around his arm as they moved into the darkness. The air grew cooler but not uncomfortable. Kade started to get an odd feeling that was somehow familiar, but he couldn't quite put his finger on why he felt as if he should know it.

"Darcienna, can you sense anything?" Kade asked as he glanced at her. He stopped and looked closely at her eyes. They were starting to glow ever so slightly. It was a bit eerie in the darkness.

"I'm not sure. I can sense something, but it's not the normal feeling I get when there is danger. It's as if my abilities are confused and don't know what to make of it," Darcienna said. She tilted her head as if trying to hear a distant voice.

"Maybe it wasn't meant to be danger but something else," Rakna added.

"That may be," Darcienna said as she focused hard.

"How much further?" Kade asked.

"Valdry did not include that information when he informed me of this tunnel," Rakna said.

Kade did not respond as he stared into the dark. There was something going on, but he was not sure if it was danger or not. The hairs on the back of his neck started to rise up in warning. Something was not right here.

"Is it just me, or is it getting darker in here? I mean…is it darker than it should be?" Kade asked as he tried to focus on the blackness that seemed to hang in the air. "Maybe if I use more of the Divine to feed the fire, it will help," he said as he opened himself up and let more of the Divine flow into the flame. He could still feel the block within himself, but it did not keep him from drawing on a little more for the fire. It flared, but there was not as much difference in what he could see as he had expected. He pulled as hard as he could on the Divine and fed it into the fire, and yet, the dark seemed to swallow up every bit of the light.

"Kade, I am getting an uncomfortable feeling. It's as if I am sensing danger one second, and in the next instant, it is gone," Darcienna said as she dragged him to a stop.

"I am sensing it too," Kade said as he stopped to look at his companions.

Rakna showed no sign of fear. Her confidence in him was overwhelming. He just hoped it was not misplaced. He took a deep breath to steady his nerves and continued on with what he was saying.

"I can't quite figure it out. I think it has something to do with what is past this darkness," Kade said as he took a cautious step forward.

"It appears as if your light will not penetrate," Rakna said as she moved to stand next to him. The blue light made her look eerie in the darkness.

"Let's see what this will do," Kade said as he launched the Divine Fire down the tunnel.

Kade was shocked to see that the dark seemed to swallow up the fire immediately. It disappeared as if it never was, and with that, they were plunged into absolute darkness. None could even see the hand before their faces. Kade drew the Divine up instantly and set his hand ablaze with light so bright that everyone had to shield their eyes. The pain of too much light so quickly was much more desirable than the intense dark. Everyone let out a sigh of relief.

"And you say we spared you," Rakna said as she looked on in awe. Kade knew it was useless to argue and realized it may even be seen as patronizing to disagree, so he made no comment. She believed and nothing he said was going to change her opinion. He smiled as he recalled feeling exactly the same way while in the presence of Zayle.

Kade turned toward the darkness and stood in shock. The increase in light actually seemed to make the darkness appear more solid. It was almost as if there was a wall. He spared a glance at his hand and looked into the dark again. Clearly he should have lit up the entire tunnel for a hundred feet, and yet, it was pitch black in front but well lit behind. Kade reached out but froze as Darcienna's eyes blazed instantly. He pulled his hand back and her eyes dimmed.

"I don't understand. The...," Kade started to say when the odd feeling that had been with him intensified for just a moment. He stopped, listening with his ears and mind. Was his dragon trying to contact him? He reached out to Rayden only to get the sense of amusement as the dragon played its game. He turned to look at Darcienna to see if she was sensing the same thing only to find her and the queen patiently watching him. For a moment, he sensed it was actually a living presence trying to get into his mind. He panicked slightly and pushed it away. Or...was he just imagining things? The next instant, there was nothing.

Kade noticed both the queen and Darcienna were studying him as they waited for him to pronounce his findings. It was more than that, though. They were waiting for him to explain exactly what it was they were facing, what it was that they should do next, and how. They expected him to have all the answers. He was not sure if he liked the confidence they put in him, but there was nothing he could do about it now. They were depending on him. He understood how Zayle felt.

"Did either of you just sense that?" Kade asked.

"I felt nothing but the warning of danger," Darcienna said, her eyes a faint glow.

"What is it you are feeling?" Rakna asked.

"I'm not sure. It almost feels as if something is trying to reach out to me, trying to get into my head. It's like a pressure in my mind, but then it goes away," Kade said. "You feel nothing at all?" he pressed Darcienna again.

"Like I said, it's as if my ability can't make up its mind. It's like we are causing the danger to ourselves," Darcienna said as she tilted her head again. "One thing I am certain about," she continued as she narrowed her eyes, peering intently ahead, "this darkness has something to do with it. I received a strong warning as you reached out, but as you pulled your hand back, it disappeared."

Kade slowly reached out and Darcienna's eyes lit up the closer his hand got to the darkness. Darcienna gripped his arm tightly. Kade watched her, certain she had taken in a sharp breath and was holding it. He pulled his arm back, and she relaxed as her eyes dimmed.

"This must be the doorway that Valdry spoke of," Rakna hissed.

"This?" Kade asked as he studied the space just one long stride away. "But, there is nothing."

"A doorway is just an opening into another place. Maybe passing through this takes you somewhere," Rakna offered.

"Maybe...," Kade was saying when his eyes caught something on the far wall. He moved to the side of the tunnel and ran his hand along what had gotten his attention. He studied the markings that were partially covered by dirt. He rubbed at the wall, exposing more of the image. "Maybe these explain what this is," Kade said as he studied the drawing. He looked back at the queen and Darcienna, waiting for their input. Just then, a crushing presence descended on him. It was so strong that he sank to his knees and gritted his teeth, doing everything he could to fight it off. Now Kade was more certain than ever that something was trying to get inside his head. Darcienna and the queen raced to his side. "I know this does not make sense, but I get the strong feeling of urgency," he hissed through clenched teeth.

"Urgency?" Darcienna asked in concern. "Are we supposed to do something?"

"I'm...not sure," Kade said, every muscle in his body was as tense as iron while he waited for the feeling to pass. "It's gone now," Kade said as he gasped and fell forward onto all fours, panting. "I think it has something to do with that," Kade said as he pointed weakly to the darkness, breathing heavily. Darcienna bent down and placed her hands on him. He breathed a sigh of relief and shakily got to his feet. He took another deep breath and let it out slowly, steadying himself. Darcienna gave him a disapproving look, but he waved her concern away. She ground her teeth at his stubbornness.

"I think we need to try to figure this out before we do

anything," Darcienna said as she scraped dirt from one of the symbols. "Kade, can you make anything of this?"

He moved closer to the image and leaned over as he studied it. He realized it was not just a symbol, but a drawing. It was of a man standing several feet off the ground with his body arched and his head titled back. The man's feet were together and his arms were just barely away from the body with the palms up. Kade cleaned off more of the wall and saw what looked like an arch around the floating figure. He stood up and turned toward Darcienna as his mind worked.

"It looks like a man floating in the air through some kind of arch," Kade said as his mind grappled with what he was seeing. The pieces of this puzzle were falling into place.

"What does it mean?" Darcienna asked.

"The arch in the drawing could stand for the darkness. If this is really a doorway to another place, then this would make sense," Rakna said.

"That has to be it," Darcienna said as she cleared more of the wall off.

Kade walked over and stood studying the darkness. After several long moments, he moved back to the drawing. Darcienna watched him with furrowed brows. She could sense he was onto something and knew when to stay quiet. Kade quickly turned and moved back to the darkness. Her eyes flashed momentarily as he got too close. He stopped, and her eyes faded. She opened her mouth to chastise him when he looked up at the ceiling. His eyes seemed to follow something along the rock as he called on more light.

"It's not figurative. It's a literal drawing. Look here," Kade said as he pointed to the ceiling. There, barely in the rock was what looked like an iron structure. It was embedded into the rock so far that it was easy to miss. His eyes followed it around to the ground.

"Can you make anything out of this?" Darcienna asked as she cleaned more dirt off the wall. Kade moved over to stand just behind her. He leaned forward, looking over her shoulder.

"There appears to be some kind language carved in the

153

structure," Rakna said as she peered closely at the arch. The darkness seemed to come alive as though it were mist. It was pure blackness that swirled just inches from Rakna's face. The spider queen leapt back just as a wisp of blackness drifted out only to evaporate and drift away when the queen retreated.

Rakna glanced at Kade and Darcienna. They were both watching her with concern. Darcienna had her hand on her chest after inhaling sharply. Kade looked to be as tense as a rock. He gasped loudly. He did not even want to think what would have happened if the queen had been in that spot just a moment longer. Kade and Darcienna looked at each other and then at the arch.

"It's obvious we need to learn more before we go through there," Kade said.

Darcienna's head whipped around to stare at Kade. He showed no signs of noticing her reaction, but she was certain he knew she was going to protest. After a moment longer, she glanced at the queen and then back to the drawing on the wall. She cleaned off more of the image and then stood back. She turned to study Kade, waiting to see if the uncovered image made sense.

"This has got to be as old as the ancients," Kade said, peering closely at the faded drawing.

"Then you can read it?" Darcienna asked.

"I did not say I could…," Kade was saying when he paused, his eyes opening wide. "Give me a moment," he said excitedly as he licked his finger and then ran it over the drawing. "It says death."

"Death?" Darcienna asked, echoing Kade's confusion.

"Perhaps this is the gateway to the land of the dead that Valdry spoke of," Rakna said evenly. Kade and Darcienna turned to see that she had approached the arch, again.

Kade moved to stand next to the queen. He held up his hand to the darkness and peered as closely as he dared. The image of the black wisp coming out at the queen was emblazoned in his mind. He was careful not to get too close, but he could swear, the longer he stared into the blackness, the more he thought he could see something taking shape. He was straining his eyes when he flinched hard. The faint image of a face faded in and out, and at the same time, the pressure exploded in his head. The world spun and Kade felt himself falling forward. He fought with every bit of his will to keep the presence from invading his mind. It was overwhelming. He lost all sense of what was up and down. Something enveloped him and pulled. He hit the ground hard, but he was too far gone to feel the pain. Kade felt a pair of small hands grip his head tightly. The presence faded. His vision cleared enough for him to see a pair of concerned, green eyes peering down at him.

"Chosen, you had us scared with that one," Rakna said, fear and concern thick in her voice.

"Kade," Darcienna said as she did her best to control her emotions. "We almost lost you. I don't know what got ahold of you, but something in the darkness latched onto you, and it took everything I had to free you from it," she said as she breathed a sigh of relief. "It drained me instantly. And, if not for the queen, you surely would have been lost," she said as she spared a glance for Rakna.

"Thank you," Kade said as he struggled to recover. "I think it would be best if we all stayed away from that," he said as he nodded his head in the direction of the arch.

"Wise words if ever I did hear," Rakna added.

Kade was looking at Darcienna when something on the wall behind her drew his attention. He stopped for a moment, understanding making him alert. He struggled to his feet and worked his way to the wall. He ran his hand over the image as another piece of the puzzle fell into place.

"Zayle, what have you been preparing me for?" Kade asked out loud.

"What is it?" Darcienna asked, eager to learn what he had discovered.

"Perhaps you recognize this?" Rakna asked.

"Yes. The word written in the ancient language next to the image is just one word. Drift," Kade said in awe as he recalled

Zayle's rage when he failed to perform this simple calling just a little over a month ago. Now it made sense. Zayle needed him to be able to drift, and the reason it was so important was unfolding right before his eyes.

"I don't understand," Darcienna said.

"It is a calling that allows your awareness to leave your body," Kade said as he ran his hand over the image. "I believe it may be a way into the world of the dead," he said as he looked from the queen to Darcienna. "Or, a way to talk to the dead, but either way, the Drift Calling is meant to be used here."

"Then, that means this was meant for one versed in the use of the Divine," Rakna said.

"I believe so," Kade replied as he studied the drawings again.

"So, you are meant to go through?" Darcienna asked, desperately afraid of the answer she was sure he was going to give. If ever she wanted to hear a no, it was now.

"I think so," Kade said. Darcienna felt as if she wanted to cry. "But, it wouldn't be a good idea right now. I don't know what is in there. If I did…," Kade started to say when the pressure began to build in his head again. He fought it as he had the previous times but something about it felt too familiar. This was not the same as the last. He was readying himself to fight it, but then at the last second, he allowed it in. Kade could not stop the gasp that escaped from him as the feel of Zayle embraced him. He could smell the scent of old, leather books and hear his teacher's voice in his head. The way his master would look at him filled his very being, and he knew who it was that was trying to reach out to him. It was then that he recognized the face that had floated before him in the darkness. His heart ached furiously. Kade's reaction was so strong that Rayden roared in concern. It was overwhelming, but now was not the time to allow himself to fall apart. There was something his grandfather was trying to tell him, and he knew he needed to hear it.

"Morg is only a pawn," the voice said and then paused as if it were trying to gain strength to continue. "He uses the Staff of the

156

Ancients."

"Master," Kade cried out. "What must I do?"

"Doren." It was as if the voice used its last remaining strength,

"Kade, are you okay?" Darcienna asked as she helped him to a sitting position.

"Did you hear it?" Kade asked.

"Hear what?" Darcienna asked.

"A...voice," Kade said as if coming out of a trance. "It said the name Doren." He paused as he considered what he had just heard. He searched his memory for anytime Zayle may have mentioned the name Doren and recalled the thief that had been turned to stone. The thief had been sent by Doren to steal Zayle's book. "Darcienna, it was Zayle," Kade said as the presence disappeared completely from his mind. "It's gone," he said with a heavy heart. The queen and Darcienna glanced at each other and then back to him. "We need to leave right away," he said regretfully, noticing that Darcienna was watching him closely. He firmed his resolve, forcing back any tears that threatened to come. He slowly stood and shook his head as if to clear the remaining fog that still hung in his mind.

"Any idea who Doren is?" Darcienna asked, pretending not to see the hurt in his eyes.

"Valdry used to refer to another Chosen by that name," Rakna said. Kade and Darcienna both turned to stare at her, stunned that she had an answer for the question. "Valdry said that if anything happened to him, we were to get to Doren at all cost and inform him of what has come to pass."

"Did you send word?" Kade asked. "And, do you know where this Doren is?"

"Unfortunately, I must answer no to both questions. As you saw, we had issues of our own that we needed to deal with."

"Of course," Kade said. "I think I may be able to find him," he responded as he thought on the small black book back at his parents place.

"Then you have no time to waste. When we return, I will inform the king of what has transpired," Rakna said.

"Thank you," Kade said as he started up the tunnel. They emerged from the cave, but the dragon was nowhere to be found.

Rayden, come. We need you. We must leave quickly, Kade sent. He heard a roar far off in the distance. He watched as the dragon charged over a hilltop and raced directly at them, tearing at the ground so furiously that it left a dust trail. It was not long before Rayden skidded to a stop, spraying them with dirt. Rakna wiped the soil from her flowing, white fur while still appearing every bit the regal queen she was. Kade mentally chastised the dragon, certain there was a bit of playfulness in its actions.

The group quickly mounted, and the dragon raced back to the spider's home. They came to a stop in front of the tree, and the king met them out front. They dismounted, and Rakna quickly approached the king while buzzing excitedly.

"Kade, my heart goes out to you," Crayken said as he came to stand in front of him.

"My king, there is more," Rakna said as she hissed her words for Kade to hear. "Kade has received some insight as to the purpose of the cave. They have to go see Doren," Rakna explained.

"Doren?" Crayken asked in surprise. "The same Doren that Valdry informed us to seek out?"

"The same," the white spider said.

"Then, by all means, we shall not stand in your way, but first, is there anything we can get for you to help with your journey?" Crayken asked.

"No," Kade said as he prepared to depart. "I will just need my books, and I will be on my way.

"May I ask one small boon?" Rakna asked as she rose up as much as possible to look him in the eyes.

"You may ask anything of me," Kade responded.

"May we join you in your fight when the time comes?" Crayken asked, finishing his queen's thoughts.

"I would be honored to have a fighting force such as yours at my side. Thank you for your willingness to help me with my battle," Kade said as he placed a hand on each of the royal couple's shoulder. The king and queen both looked at the hand on their shoulder, then to each other and finally to Kade.

"This has meaning to your kind?" the king asked.

"It is something we do with those that matter to us," Kade said as he smiled.

"Then it is appropriate," Rakna responded. "I hope you will always honor us with this gesture."

"And I, also, hope you will honor me as you have done. I know I could not have found a more worthy ally for my cause," Kade said as he felt the press of time. "I have one more request. It is very important, but unfortunately, it will also be dangerous. Please do not feel you must do this."

"Ask," Crayken said.

"The caves are extremely important. If you are willing, I would ask you to keep them safe, but it may be very dangerous. The queen can explain why, but for now, I am unable to guard them. My path leads elsewhere," Kade said.

"We shall keep them safe until your return," the king said. The queen nodded, also.

"Give me a moment," Kade said as he ducked into the opening. He was back out quickly, strapping the books to the dragon. He looked longingly at the tree and regretted missing the celebration. Darcienna put her hand on his arm, and he could see she mirrored his thoughts. With a sigh, he turned toward the king and queen and gave them both his most regal bow. The spiders started their buzz-chant. Kade looked up to see the trees filled with the clutch. He looked at the queen and then back up at the spiders.

"They are disheartened that you are not staying for your own celebration," Crayken said evenly.

Darcienna gave Kade a look, and he took a deep breath then let it out slowly. He looked up at the spiders and then came to a decision. He was not sure he was making the right decision, but it was the one he was going to make.

"We shall stay for a short while, but we must leave tonight," Kade said as reached up and untied the books.

The king and queen buzzed excitedly as they addressed the spiders in the trees. The clutch erupted, making Kade's head swim. They dropped out of the trees in droves. Kade could not recall seeing so many spiders before. Now, it seemed as if there were hundreds or maybe even a thousand, and they were all excited for him. They buzzed constantly as every one of them crowded him, trying to get a leg on him. It took Kade a moment to realize what was going on. They were mimicking his gesture. They were putting their "hands" on his shoulder in a show of affection. He smiled as the last of them touched him. The spiders filed into the tree to start the feast.

Kade stood by the dragon until he was the only one outside the tree. The night was just starting to descend. He thought back on his experience in the cave, and his heart ached to see his grandfather again.

"I am sorry I was not what you tried to make me into, Grandfather," Kade said as he looked off in the distance toward the cave. "But, I vow to become what you need, and I will make you proud," he said as he turned to join the celebration. Before taking one step, he froze. The amulet was starting to heat up. Kade placed his hand on it and closed his eyes. It was continuing to heat more and more by the moment.

Morg is trying to find me again, Kade thought with trepidation. The memory of Morg in his dream made him cringe. For just a moment, he considered grabbing Darcienna and riding off. He shook his head, afraid he had made the wrong decision to stay, and reluctantly, joined the celebration.

CH6

"We should not have stayed the night," Kade said as he pulled his boots on, the room growing brighter as the sun rose.

"It was that drink the spiders made out of the fruit. It had to be their version of ale," Darcienna said as she winced at the bright light coming through the window.

"Just stop talking so loud," Kade said as he held his head.

"This is going to be a fun day," Darcienna said with sarcasm.

"Let's try to deal with it the best we can," Kade said as he slowly got to his feet.

He walked to the door and turned, waiting for Darcienna to get out of bed. He was trying to be patient, but his head ached terribly, and he was not in the mood for any more delays. Darcienna glanced at him, and even though he had not said a word, the tight lipped expression told her of his irritation. She sighed as she rose from the bed. Unlike Kade, her patience was infinite. She smiled sweetly at him and wrapped her hand around his arm to lead him out. He melted inside and even felt a bit of a fool for his rudeness.

The king and queen met Kade outside as they prepared to see them off. Rayden was calm as he lay by the tree, waiting for his passengers. Kade turned to the royal couple and felt a warm spot grow in his heart. The pounding in his head eased a bit. Spiders or not, these two had souls that even the Divine would be honored to have.

"Thank you for your hospitality," Kade said as held his hand up to block the light from the sun. He squinted, barely able to see at all.

"We will celebrate in your honor for a week, Chosen," Rakna said.

The wind was blowing gently and the queen's fur floated on the wind. Kade watched the way her foot-long hair shifted in the breeze, making it appear as though she were swimming through the air. The king's silky, jet black fur mimicked hers. They were the only spiders to have this majestic fur. The rest of the clutch had hair that was short, course and bristly. The royal couple did indeed look amazing as they stood side by side.

"This day every year will forevermore be deemed a celebration day in your honor for ending our life long feud. You must come back often, friend and second in line to the throne," the king said with such pride that Kade forgot his pounding head and smiled widely.

"Again, I am honored. I will never be able to find the words to convey the joy my heart feels. Thank you. We must be on our way. I fear we may have lost time that was not ours to lose," Kade said as he turned to Darcienna.

"We shall keep you no longer," Rakna said.

Kade readied himself to mount the dragon when he caught a movement out of the corner of his eye. He looked up into the massive tree and saw hundreds of eyes looking back at him. There, covering the tree and every branch was the entire clutch. He smiled and turned to the queen for one more translation. He smiled broadly at her and

162

then turned back to the tree.

"This is not goodbye, but only, until we meet again my soul brothers and sisters," Kade said as the queen buzzed away. "I will miss you dearly and look forward to the day I can return. In some ways, I feel I belong here with you more than I do my own kind. You have welcomed me into your home and into your hearts. I shall not soon forget. Stay safe and may the Divine watch over you," Kade said, trying to emulate how a king might speak these words. The spiders cheered loudly. Kade smiled widely to hide the pain in his head as the buzzing set his nerves on fire.

He put his hand on Darcienna's shoulder and turned her toward the dragon, wanting to be underway. Rayden was already lying down. Cupping his hands, Kade boosted Darcienna onto the dragon's back. He picked up the sack containing the books and leaped up smoothly. He turned and tied them securely between the wings. The dragon rose majestically. The spiders hissed and buzzed excitedly. Kade grinned, enjoying the feeling as so many looked upon him in awe as he sat proudly on the magnificent dragon.

"Thank you again, and if you are ever in need, find me and I will come. I will be back sometime for the arch. It is my destiny. Thank you Rakna, Crayken. Stay safe," Kade said as he urged the dragon to move out.

"I shall remember our talk," Darcienna said while grinning at the queen. Kade glanced at her to ask what he had missed, but she avoided his eyes. His suspicions about some type of female conspiracy sparked. He watched her a little longer, waiting for something. "The queen and I had a nice chat. Not for you to worry about," she said as she waved to the king, queen and all the spiders. It was clear this was all he was going to get so he faced forward and signaled the dragon to go.

Rayden started at a slow, rolling lope. Kade cast a last glance over his shoulder and then settled in for the ride. Darcienna watched the black and white spider until they were just specks in the distance. The king and queen did not move from that spot until the dragon was well out of sight.

"Did we have to leave before having something to eat?" Darcienna asked.

"Yes. If we stayed for morning food, we would have stayed for half the day. Then, it would be time for dinner, and we would have been there for another night. Darcienna, we really did need to get moving. I shall feed us shortly, but for now, we just needed to cover some ground," Kade said, not gently but not too firmly. Darcienna sighed, knowing he was right and let the subject drop, even though her stomach rumbled.

Time passed slowly as both riders sank into their own thoughts. Kade worried deeply about what Zayle was trying to tell him. He knew he needed to stop soon, but he was already worried he had lost too much precious time. The black book flashed in his mind, and then something occurred to him.

What if Doren is not in the book? How will we find him? Maybe he would need more information from the king. With this last concern, Kade decided this line of thinking was going to do him no good and decided to focus on food. His stomach was rumbling and hunger flowed through the link from the dragon continuously.

"What are we doing?" Darcienna asked as the dragon came to a stop.

"I thought it would be a good time to stop for food," Kade said as he reached back, untied the sack of books and then slid down.

"I was hoping you would say that," Darcienna said as she swung her leg over the dragon's neck and slid down on her belly. Kade caught her as she landed.

"Maybe a three course meal?" Darcienna asked.

"Sure, but first I have to feed this eating machine," Kade said as he looked at Rayden, who was wide-eyed and eager to eat. "I am surprised you were able to wait this long," he chided while patting the dragon on the neck.

Kade cleared his head, ignoring the throbbing and focused on the calling. *Even a simple conjuring like this needs attention*, he told himself. He was starting to get complacent about the callings and reminded himself he needed to be vigilant; even with the easy ones. Zayle's warning that complacency has brought many Chosen to an early grave, rang through his head. He focused as best as he could, but after five times of creating meat, his mind started to wander back to the image that had formed in the arch. He was performing the calling for the eighth time, not remembering the sixth or seventh, when he forced himself to focus. He had too much on his mind, and it was definitely very distracting.

With the dragon finally fed, it was time to cook for himself and Darcienna. Creating the cheese and bread was a good break from making the meat. Changing things up made it easier for him to focus. Unfortunately, once again, he had forgotten to bring something to drink. He shook his head at his forgetfulness and swore he would get a canteen at the first possible chance. He paused, seeming to recall having already made that declaration.

"May I ask you something?" Darcienna inquired in a quiet voice, afraid she may be touching on a sensitive area. Kade took a breath and then let it out in a long sigh.

"You may ask."

"Back in the cave," Darcienna began as she watched his reaction closely. Kade winced slightly but then did his best to hide it by taking a bite of meat. "What…what happened?"

Kade stopped chewing as he looked out over the horizon. He thought back on the face that had drifted toward him from the darkness and the sound of the voice he had heard in his head. The memory of the smell of old, leather-bound books came to him.

"I'm sorry," Darcienna said, interpreting his silence as a refusal to answer. "I should not have asked."

"It was Zayle," Kade said as he swallowed his bite while still looking off into the distance. "It was he who gave me the message." Darcienna sat quietly, not knowing what to say. "He was the one who was trying to communicate with me the whole time."

"He was the one that I pushed out of you?" Darcienna asked in shock.

"Oh no," Kade said as he turned to look at her. "No. That was something else. You did well with that. I have a guess as to what was going on, but it would only be a guess."

"I don't even have a guess so feel free to give me yours," Darcienna said, the food in her hand completely forgotten.

"I think that arch is a doorway. Or maybe it is just a thinning of the veil between the world of the dead and the living. But, my guess is that something on the other side tried to get out through me. It got inside me, and I could feel it pushing me to the back of my mind. It was as if it was pushing me out of the way. You saved me," Kade said, offering her a smile. She smiled back, pleased at the praise.

"See. You do need me," Darcienna said. Kade expected to see the playful look in her eyes, or that, I-told-you-so look, but it was not there. It was just a statement of fact. She was right. He had needed her many times already, and he had no doubt he would need her many more times to come before this was over.

"Yes," Kade said simply and then took a bite of his food. It was more than Darcienna could have hoped for. That one simple word meant more to her than he could know. He needed her.

They continued to eat the rest of their food in silent thought. Kade could not get the image of the face in the dark out of his mind. Over and over again it would float toward him, and then it would be gone. Several times it had tried to reach out to him only to have him reject it. He was grateful that he had finally realized what it was.

"Any idea where Doren lives?" Darcienna asked, rescuing him from his mind.

"I am hoping that information is in the black book," Kade said as he finished his last bite and looked at the sack of books. Darcienna saw the look and cringed. If she had not insisted he leave it behind, he would not have to retrieve it.

They finished their meal in relative silence, each retreating to their own thoughts. Kade closed his eyes several times as he studied

166

the image in the dark as though it were right before his face. He opened his eyes to vanquish the image before his heart could ache too much. He desperately wished he could hear his master's voice, even if it was to chastise him hotly.

The two finished their food and quickly mounted. Darcienna rubbed her backside to try to keep from getting sores but she feared it was not going to do any good. Kade just sat and stared straight ahead, trying his best not to fear the worst. Doren just had to be in that book.

Kade could sense the dragon's desire to stop and rest but he urged it on with the promise of more food shortly. There was still much daylight left when they came to a stop in front of his parents' cabin. Judeen came out the front door with a look of shock and dismay on her face. She was holding Marcole in her arms. She quickly descended the steps, handed the boy to Darcienna and gathered her son into her arms, hugging him tightly for several long moments. When she stepped back, she looked him all over, checking for injuries. Seeing none, she looked into his eyes and then narrowed her vision at the new look she saw there.

"You are different," Judeen said in as neutral a voice as she could muster.

"Much has happened in the few days we have been gone. I do not have time to explain. I have come back for the black book. It has information that I need. At least, I am hoping it does."

"I am certain it is still where you left it."

"I do not mean to rush things mother but I must do this quickly. I will explain when I have time," Kade said as he disengaged from his mother and headed for the entrance. "Sorry, I almost forgot," he said by way of apology for the dragon, who was watching him with anticipation.

Kade stretched and worked out the kinks in his muscles before performing the calling. He did his best to calm his mind as he found it spinning from the race to retrieve the book. He stood and closed his eyes, trying desperately to focus on the calling, but with the knowledge he needed so close, it was almost impossible. He had to know if the information he desperately sought was in the book. It was torture but he finished the calling ten times and then turned for the house. He scooped up the sack of books and walked straight to the kitchen, plunking them on the table. He probably should have been more cautious but the knot in his stomach would not go away until he had what he came for. The girls both waited for him in the kitchen, knowing he was going to return to the same seat where he had sat when he previously opened the book.

Kade quickly walked to his room and pulled the bed away from the wall. He pulled the board free and leaned down to look in the hole. He called on the Divine Power and let light shine into the open space. There sat his precious black book, waiting for him to claim it once more. Kade carefully reached in, making sure to keep it closed. He placed the book on the floor next to himself and then put the board back in place. He slid the bed against the wall and then firmly picked up the book. When he returned to the kitchen, both women were waiting, both glaring at the small book in his hand as if it were something evil. Kade dismissed their looks and sat in his chair.

He took a deep breath, knowing what was coming and flipped the book open. The blue spark leapt from finger to finger and traveled across the backs of his knuckles. His hand twitched spasmodically as the charge verified his identity. Both women reflexively had covered their mouths with their hands, holding their breaths as they waited for the spark to vanish.

"Does that hurt?" Darcienna asked as she tried to unclench her jaw.

"It is uncomfortable but not really that painful," Kade said as he flexed his hand after the blue spark disappeared.

Kade turned to the first page and found it blank. He ran his hand over the empty sheet, wondering if it would impart its knowledge about the Chosen Valdry for a second time, but there was nothing. It was just a piece of paper. He turned the next page and ran his hand over it. This time, the tingling sensation ran along his scalp, and his eyes glazed over as the knowledge settled into his mind. Darcienna looked at him hopefully, seeing that something had happened.

"That was the Chosen, Meril," Kade said as he shook his head.

"How many more Chosen are there in the book?" Darcienna asked as she shifted the boy in her arms.

"Two," Kade said, trying to ignore his anxiety. He turned another page, and again, he was imbued with the knowledge as he placed his hand on the blank sheet. "That one was Hydel," Kade said as he turned to the last page and looked down, worried it would not have the knowledge he desperately needed.

If this does not work, I will need to go to Meril or Hydel or go to Valdry's place to see what I can find there, Kade thought, discarding the idea of going back to the king. Maybe there were answers at Valdry's home, but he did not look forward to finding out. He was sure that Valdry's place was just as riddled with traps as any Chosen's place would be. The image of himself lying paralyzed on the floor while his cabin burnt around him flashed through his mind. He swallowed hard. Maybe someday he would go to Valdry's and try to recover anything worth saving, but at this time, it was not something he wanted to risk. He looked down at the last page and steadied his nerves.

"Kade?" Darcienna asked as she watched him sit as still as a statue. Without answering, he reached down and placed his hand on the book. Kade's eyes lost focus as he analyzed the information from the page. After a moment, he let out the breath he had been holding.

"Doren," Kade said as he breathed a sigh of relief.

"Good," Darcienna said, mirroring his reaction.

"That is all the book has to offer," Kade said as he sat staring at the page, grateful it had what he needed.

"Then you have no more need of it," Darcienna said as she plucked it out of his hand and marched purposefully toward the fireplace, ready to throw it in. Kade winced as he if it were a bomb about to go off.

"Darcienna, please do not ever grab one of the books like that," Kade said roughly, angry at her carelessness. She froze just before tossing it in.

"It has no more knowledge, so why keep it? And you have just deactivated the trap set on it so it's safe. It is just another book that can cause us problems. We are better off without it," Darcienna said. After a moment, she added, "Right?"

"We may have use for this," Kade said as he carefully took the book out of her hand, afraid that the blue spark was going to appear at any moment and destroy her. "I may keep it as a journal. It is still protected for just my hand, so anything I put in here should stay safe," he said as he breathed a deep sigh of relief.

"I should have thought of that. It is just that…I would love to be rid of those books. The way you handle them scares me. I would just like them gone. I look forward to when we do not have to keep them with us," Darcienna said, not the least bit regretful for her attempt to get rid of it. Kade was surprised at her emotional response. He had no idea she felt that way, but it did make sense.

"I am sorry, but I have no choice. I am keeping the books. You just have to deal with it for a while longer until I have a place I can store them to keep them safe. Besides, right now, I must still learn from them as we go."

"But you rarely open them," Darcienna said.

"I open them when the situation requires it. You will just have to accept that every time I open them to learn a new calling, I am putting my life in grave danger. Learning callings is extremely dangerous, Darcienna, but it is our kinds' way. It just is."

"I understand. You have made that clear," Darcienna said, giving in. "But they still scare me to the bone," she said firmly.

"Soon, Darcienna, soon we will be safe," Kade said as opened the sack and pulled the pile of books out. He loosened the straps, placed the black book back in the pile and then cinched the straps tightly again. "We should get moving," Kade said as he slowly stood. "We have a long ride ahead of us. It will take us well into the night,"

Kade said.

"That long?" Darcienna asked, absentmindedly rubbing her back end.

"That long," Kade said simply.

"Kade, you cannot leave without seeing your father," Judeen said. Kade was so focused on retrieving the book that he neglected to realize that his father was nowhere to be seen.

"Where is father?" Kade asked, unsure his father would want to see him.

"He is in town getting supplies. It is not that far. You need to rest for a short while before going after this other Master Chosen. Just a short time until you have had something to eat and drink." Judeen hesitated a moment before continuing on. "I know what you father told you but he does love you, Son. He just does not understand the Divine Power. As a matter of fact, it scares him to death. He always dreaded my father being around."

"I can understand," Kade said, still feeling the sting of the words that rang in his mind.

"Why don't you let me take you into town so we can buy you a few things for your travel and then you can leave from there," Judeen said, making every bit of effort to hide her emotions. For the second time in days, she felt she was saying goodbye for good. She fought to keep the sadness and worry from her voice. She never was one for letting others see feelings like these so openly. She despised pity, and she was not going to accept it now. It ran in the family. "You could also use some clothes," Judeen said, as she turned and glided up to him. She grabbed his shirt and stabbed a finger through a hole to make her point.

She turned away just as Kade was looking deep into her eyes. Her shoulders were squared in defiance but there was something to her tone that made Kade's heart ache. He stepped around her just as she wiped away a tear. She looked down at her dress and pretended to straighten it as she fought to regain her composure. After a moment she looked up at him to await his decision.

Kade would have never known that just seconds before she had been crying if he had not seen it himself. He was even starting to doubt whether he had seen it at all until he looked in her eyes. Her mannerisms did a great job of hiding her feelings, but when he looked into the windows of her sole, it was as plain as if she were crying with tears streaming down her cheeks. Kade felt his chest ache horribly for her, but he knew that he needed to act as though he saw nothing. He had to for her.

"I don't know if that is such a good idea," Kade was saying when he caught a look from Darcienna. After several long seconds of silence, he finally gave in to her request. "I would like that," Kade said as he stepped up and wrapped his arms around his mother, hugging her tightly. She sighed out a breath and melted into her son's arms as she laid her head on his chest. Kade held her for a while and stayed like that for as long as she needed. When she stepped back, the sadness had genuinely been replaced by something more peaceful.

"I could use a new pair of pants and maybe some boots," Kade said with a smile. "And, I am sure Darcienna could use some new clothes, also," Kade said as he looked her up and down.

"We go north to get to Dresben. That is the closest town, now. We won't be going to Arden for a very long time, if ever again," Judeen said.

"We should leave on our journey from there," Darcienna said gently. Kade wanted to be gone even sooner, but if this helped his mother find at least a small measure of peace, then it was worth the risk.

"We leave shortly," Judeen said. "And I am certain your father will be pleased to see you," she said, attempting to dispel any remaining concerns Kade may be feeling.

"Well, I will enjoy spending time with him, also," Kade said, thinking it might be the last chance to really talk with his father. "How far is it?"

"It's about half a day's walk."

"The dragon can cut that time down to just an hour or two,"

Kade said.

"Well, let's get going. I don't want Father to come back and miss us," Kade said, ushering his mother out of the room to prepare for the journey.

"That was good thinking," Kade said to Darcienna as he watched his mother go from room to room, gathering things to get ready for the ride into town. Darcienna smiled a knowing smile.

Kade wanted to take one last look at the comfortable bed in his room as he waited for his mother to prepare for the ride. He walked down the hall and made the left turn into his room, smiling as he looked upon the bed. He walked over and turned, sitting on the plush mattress, unable to put words to the memory that eluded him. When he came out of his thoughts, he noticed Darcienna staring at him from the doorway. He stopped, certain he recognized the mischievous glint in her eye and cocked his head as if to ask, "What?" She just smiled and laughed playfully as she avoided eye contact while pretending to straighten her son's hair.

"What?" Kade pressed, seeing her redden just a bit.

"It's nothing. We should get ready to go," Darcienna said, obviously changing the subject.

"That's a good idea," Kade said as he studied her suspiciously.

He dismissed her actions as more mysteries of the female species that he was never going to understand. He looked at the bed one last time, already missing the comfortable sleep and turned for the kitchen. He grabbed the sack of books and gently put them over his shoulder as he waited for his mother to return.

Mentally communicating the plans to the dragon, Kade worked his way out front. Rayden came around the corner, eager to go. Shortly after, Judeen and Darcienna came out. Judeen handed Darcienna a hat to wear that did a good job covering much of her face. Darcienna had her son firmly strapped to her back. Kade realized that he had not made one sound and recalled how he wailed like an alarm when they were trying to rescue his parents. Dismissing the thought, he helped his mother and Darcienna mount. Next, he vaulted up and they were on their way.

Kade felt his stomach growl and realized he had not eaten, even though he had fed the dragon. He tried to ignore the hunger, but the more he tried to pretend it was not there, the more he noticed it. Exasperated that they had only traveled for thirty minutes at best, he signaled the dragon to stop. Rayden could sense Kade preparing to cook and started to fidget eagerly. Kade tried to ignore the frustration of having to perform the calling so many times but failed. He was hoping to cook for just himself, Darcienna and his mother, but it was not to be. Feeding the dragon was turning into a considerable chore, but he could not eat without feeding it, even though it just had its fair share. It was just the price he had to pay.

"Why are we stopping?" Darcienna asked.

"I need something to eat," Kade said as he leapt to the ground and planted his feet, preparing to make the dozen or so pieces of meat that the dragon would want.

"Son, we can eat in town."

"I can't say if we will be staying long enough to eat, besides, I am hungry now," Kade said as his stomach growled loudly.

"I do hope you are planning on making some extra," Darcienna said playfully.

"Of course," Kade said, his mood improving marginally. He quickly made a chunk of steaming, hot meat and handed it to Darcienna, who passed it off to Judeen. Darcienna smiled sweetly at Kade, as she waited for the next piece. "Here," he said as he handed her the food. "Does the boy need any?" Kade asked, looking fondly at Marcole.

"I shall share mine with him," Darcienna said as she tore off a piece for Marcole.

The dragon was now huffing loudly at him as it waited impatiently. He glanced at it and shook his head, seeing the slimy, wet liquid pooling at the edges of its mouth. Kade was careful not to get anywhere near that mouth. He was learning.

Soon, Kade was making and tossing meat to the dragon, who

174

would quickly snap it up. On the eighth time of calling on the food, Kade yelped and jerked his hand out from under the meat as it materialized in his hand. He had started to lose focus and had made the meat too hot. He shot his mother a quick glance, afraid she was going to become upset, but she had not noticed. Darcienna cast a glance at Judeen and quickly healed Kade before his mother could see. Judeen was surprisingly interested in something in the dirt. Kade breathed a sigh of relief as soon as Darcienna finished.

Kade made a few more pieces of meat for the dragon. He was sure that it was not enough, but he could only do this for so long. Finally, he made one for himself and eagerly sat down, tearing into the food. He closed his eyes, enjoying the strong flavor of the meat as the juices ran down his throat.

"I wish I would have thought to make this before we left the cabin," Kade said through a mouth full of food. He had taken several more large bites and was wolfing them down when he noticed that the women were staring at him. He stopped in mid chew to stare back.

"What?" Kade asked around the food, not understanding what he was doing wrong. He was starting to realize that men could never do anything right where women were concerned.

"You eat like you are starving," Darcienna said.

Kade sat looking at her, waiting for her to explain further. Why she would state the obvious when he already knew this was beyond his understanding. The only thing he was certain of was that the comment was made to make a point. To this he responded by swallowing and then taking an even larger bite. Darcienna shook her head in disgust and turned her back on him, blatantly ignoring his gesture. Why, he would never know, but he was grateful for the chance to eat in peace. They finished their meal and stood, preparing to leave. As Kade readied to help Judeen mount, she grabbed his hand firmly and studied his palm. With a twist of her mouth and a shake of her head, she tossed it away and waited for him to boost her onto the dragon's back. Kade ground his teeth in frustration at his incompetence and vowed to do better at hiding his foolishness.

The four of them had been traveling for just short of an hour when Darcienna's hand shot out to latch onto Kade's leg without warning. Kade, being deep in his own thoughts, jumped hard. He could have sworn his heart stopped beating for just a moment. His hand went to hers, but before he was able to dislodge it, he understood what the grip meant. He quickly turned to look at her and saw her eyes were starting to indicate danger. He got a sinking feeling as he studied her face, hoping to find a clue there as to what the threat might be. He immediately brought the dragon to a stop.

"What?" Kade asked, trying to stay calm.

"There is danger ahead!" Darcienna exclaimed with a gasp.

"What danger?" Kade asked, letting all his senses become as sharp as possible.

"I'm not sure. It seems to be coming from there," Darcienna said as she pointed in the direction of town. "The longer we travel, the stronger the feeling gets."

"The town is just in the distance," Judeen said as she watched the couple closely.

"Do you think the danger is in Dresben?" Kade asked as he focused intently on her. "My father is there," Kade said, fighting not to panic. His mind flashed back to the scene of his father being bound to the tower.

"Yes," Darcienna responded. "It doesn't seem to be as strong as when we ran into Morg, but it is definitely there."

Kade eyed the town as he mentally warned Rayden of the approaching danger. He performed the Transparency Calling and the Silence Calling. Judeen gasped but he ignored her and urged the dragon to move forward cautiously. He hoped it was not needed, but Darcienna had not been wrong yet. Rayden seemed to pick up the pace with the promise of battle. Kade wished he could feel the same way, but his mind was full of worry for his father. He brought the dragon to a stop just on the edge of town.

"Rayden, stay here while I go check this out. Mother, Darcienna, stay here until I return. I should not be long," Kade said as he prepared to slide off the dragon. Darcienna grabbed his arm and held on, not liking this plan one bit.

"I am coming with you," Darcienna said as she prepared to dismount.

"No, you are not," Kade said firmly, leaving no room for argument. Kade felt Darcienna tense and knew she was ready to argue. "If something goes wrong, I will need you to keep my mother and Marcole safe." After a moment, he softened and added, "Please."

"For you," Darcienna said with a sigh. "But you cannot keep making me stay back. You need me with you," she scolded.

"I know," Kade said, and felt her relax considerably. "Keep my mother safe," he said as he slid to the ground.

Kade started toward the edge of town when Rayden growled deeply and long. It was a guttural rumble that reverberated from deep within the dragon. Rayden was obviously not pleased with being told to stay behind either. Kade reassured his friend that he would stay in contact and call on him if needed. The deep rumble ceased, but he could still feel the displeasure through the link.

Does everyone have to question my decisions? Kade mentally grumbled to himself.

Making his way into town and down the street, Kade made sure to keep clear of everyone. His mind saw the image of Darcienna's blue eyes. He could not help but to watch for a tall man holding a staff, hiding around every corner. He looked at the ground a time or two to ensure he was not leaving prints. Relieved that he was completely undetectable, he relaxed and started toward the tavern to search for his father. That was as good a place to start as any.

Stopping just outside, Kade peered in and immediately found Garig sitting at the bar, talking to a stranger. Garig tipped his head back and drained a mug. The stranger ordered him another and placed it in his hand. Kade slid into the room and worked his way across the tavern. He had to dodge a few patrons, but seeing as the place was virtually empty, it was not too difficult.

Garig laughed at something the stranger said, and Kade felt a considerable amount of relief that his father was safe, but something seemed odd here. He moved just a few feet away from the men as they spoke, careful not to get blocked in if someone were to come toward him. He studied the stranger and instantly did not like him but could not put his finger on why. He was a deadly man that looked like he had seen lots of action. He had a look in his eye that said he would take a life in between drinks without even caring, as long as he did not spill his ale.

"You'll be able to meet my son sometime. I will have to introduce you," Kade heard his father say, and then Garig laughed as though he had told the most hysterical joke. The man laughed just as hard. Obviously Kade was missing the funny part of the jest, but he figured it was an inside joke and gave it no mind. For just a moment, Kade swore the stranger's eyes were a touch more narrow and his nose a bit sharper, but then just as quickly, Kade was sure the light was playing tricks on him.

He considered letting the callings go and surprising his father but thought better of it. It would not go over well here, and it would not help him keep his secret. As much fun as it would be to see the shocked look on their faces, it was much better to be conservative in his actions. *And besides, father hates the Divine*, he reminded himself.

He turned and headed for the door. Just before he ducked out the exit, he glanced back at his father and paused, seeing the old man looking around as if trying to find something. Kade could swear he was trying to find him as he stood and narrowed his eyes, studying everyone and everything that moved. After a moment, he shook his head and slid back onto the bar stool.

Kade quickly returned to the dragon and the women. He could sense Rayden's impatience and did his best to calm his friend. He called out to Darcienna and followed her voice until he bumped into Rayden.

"I found Father. He is in the tavern talking to one of the other patrons. We should go now," Kade said as he let the callings dissipate while keeping the dragon cloaked.

I know you are not going to like this, but you must remain here, Kade thought to Rayden. The dragon responded with a quick snort directly in his face. Kade gagged and coughed as he backed away.

"Not funny," Kade said as he glared at the empty space in front of himself. "Just wait here."

"Kade, are you sure it's okay? I still sense danger," Darcienna said, unsure.

"I did not see anything out of place," Kade said as he found himself staring into her glowing blue eyes. For a moment, he wondered what she saw when her eyes changed.

"It's not real strong, but it is definitely there. We need to be careful," Darcienna said gravely.

"Trust me. If father sensed any danger, he wouldn't have been talking to a stranger about me. Anyway, he looked like he was having a good time," Kade said.

"He was talking about you?" Judeen asked. Kade could swear he caught a tone in her voice, but when he looked at her, there was nothing out of the ordinary.

"Yes," Kade said as he watched her for a reaction.

"Well, let's go find him," Judeen said casually, but there was something about the way her eyes turned to daggers that put him on edge.

Rayden fussed over and over, protesting at being left behind. Kade would have enjoyed traipsing into town with a dragon in tow, but again, it would do nothing for keeping a low profile. Rayden had to stay. He soothed the dragon several times with the promise to call for help if needed.

Kade led the small party right to the tavern. As he walked, he reassured the dragon several more times that he would be fine, but Rayden's agitation did not lessen. At a loss as to what he could do to placate the dragon, Kade sighed and just let it go as he worked his way to where he had last seen his father. He started to go in when his mother grabbed him by the arm and squeezed while turning him.

"Kade, are you sure he is in here?" Judeen asked, suspicion heavy in her voice.

"Yes. I saw him talking to a man right over there at the bar," Kade said as he pointed at the tavern. He turned to go, eager to see his father. Kade glanced up and down the street and then back to his mother. Judeen reluctantly let her grip go and followed after him. Darcienna hesitated as the sense of danger grew ever so slightly. She told herself that the feelings were not really that much stronger, so it had to be ok.

Besides, between Kade and me, we should be able to handle anything this slight danger can offer, she thought.

Kade walked in and saw his father sitting at a table in the back of the room with a mug of ale in his hands. He had his back to the wall in a way that allowed him to watch both the front and back entrance. Kade smiled at his father as he walked up to the table. Garig looked up at him and opened his mouth as if confused and then smiled. Kade saw the look in his father's eye for just a moment, and then it was replaced with a look of recognition. Kade smiled at the empty mug sitting in front of his father and wondered how many empty cups had already left the table.

Motioning for Judeen and Darcienna to sit, Kade pulled up a chair next to his father. Darcienna took her place next to Kade while sitting Marcole on her lap. Judeen sat next to Garig. She studied her husband for a brief moment before relaxing.

"You could at least say hello," Judeen said tersely.

"I am sorry. I just did not know what to say," Garig said, still not looking at her. He never seemed to take his eyes off Kade. "Don't you have your dragon with you?" Garig continued.

"Father!" Kade hissed. He made a motion with his hand that was meant to convey for his father to keep it quiet. "He is just outside of town, in the woods. I didn't think it would be a good idea to bring him," he said as he gave a quiet chuckle while glancing around the room. "As much fun as it would be to see everyone's reaction, I am sure he would attract too much attention, and right now, I want to avoid that at all cost."

"You should have him come to the back of the tavern so we can give him some spiced meat. He would love it," Garig said with a smile.

"I've fed him already," Kade said, starting to get thirsty as he looked at the empty mug.

"I am sure he would like this meat. It's like none other that I have ever tasted. Why don't you call him to the back, and I will have one of the men put a huge bucket of it out behind the bar. Then we can take care of that thirst of yours," Garig said, noticing the way Kade was eyeing his cup.

"If you are certain it is ok," Kade said, knowing his dragon could never have too much.

"Oh, I am more than certain," Garig said with a broad grin. Kade decided he did not like when his father drank, but so far, he was harmless. It seemed to change who he was, but then again, ale or wine appeared to do that to everyone.

Kade reached out with his mind and found the dragon. He could almost see its head pop up with his mental caress and promise of more food. The dragon was more than eager to follow Kade's directions. He felt for the Transparency Calling that was surrounding the dragon and let it melt away. He gave directions to be careful to stay in the woods until reaching the rear of the tavern and then turned his attention back to his father.

"Garig, are you okay?" Judeen asked.

"Maybe I have had too much to drink. I'm sorry," Garig said, still not looking at her. He turned his attention back to the bar and flagged one of the men over. Within seconds, a man came skidding to a stop next to the table. "Give him one of your special drinks, and leave a bucket of spiced meat out back for his pet. Kade will be going to get his pet any moment," Garig said as he cocked an eyebrow as if to prompt Kade into action.

"He is on his way," Kade said, casually watching people as

they mulled around the tavern. He did not see the confused look on his father's face.

The man hastily returned to the bar. On the way, he stopped one of the other workers and pointed at the table where the small party was sitting while talking very animatedly. Kade tried to hear what was being said, but there was too much other noise in the bar. Shortly after, the first man, who had come to the table, disappeared out a back door, and the second man went to the bar.

"Now that that is taken care of, we can enjoy something to drink. You will have some wine in a moment," Garig said as he smiled at the young man.

Darcienna kicked Kade under the table, trying to get his attention. He ignored her as he focused on his father. She continued to kick him harder and harder until he could no longer pretend she was not bruising his shins black and blue. He turned toward her, exasperated and ready to scold her when she looked up at him. Her eyes were blazing. He did not need to hear the next words out of her mouth to know what she was going to say.

"Danger?" Kade asked quickly in a whisper.

"It is very close," Darcienna said in a hiss.

"It has to be that stranger my father was talking to," Kade said as he quickly scanned the area. "Father," Kade said as he leaned close and spoke. "Where is that man you were talking to earlier; the one that was asking about me?"

Garig seemed taken aback for a moment as he studied Kade. Then, he nodded his head as though something just made sense. He gave a chuckle as he leaned toward Kade to whisper back.

"He left a short while ago. Said something about having to change," Garig said and then laughed as though he had told a joke.

"You have had enough of this," Kade said as he slid the mug away from him. "Keep an eye out for the old man," Kade said and then leaned toward Darcienna. "If anything comes up, I'll be able to handle it," Kade said in an attempt to sooth her. "And besides, if I can't, we can always count on the dragon and your shield to help us, right?"

"I'm not sure," Darcienna said cautiously, checking to see if anyone was paying too much attention to them. No one appeared to be. Not one person in the bar was looking at them...not directly.

"I'll tell you what. We will leave shortly. How does that sound?"

"The sooner the better," Darcienna said as she hid her eyes by pulling her hat down further.

The server came to the table with three mugs of wine. He set them in front of Kade, Darcienna and Judeen. Before the server could leave, Judeen grabbed him by the arm and held him fast.

"There must be some mistake. I did not order any wine. Please take this back," Judeen said as she plunked the mug down on his tray roughly. The server seemed slightly nervous as he shot Garig a glance. Garig gave a slight, almost imperceptible nod, and the man hurried away to disappear back into the kitchen with the mug.

"You know I don't drink," Judeen said, scolding Garig as she studied him. She looked at his mug, wondering how many he had downed already and shook her head in agitation, intending on giving him the scolding of his life.

"I only ordered for him," Garig said defensively, indicating Kade. "I am sure it was just a simple mistake," he said as he glanced at her and then quickly back to smile at Kade.

Judeen seemed mollified and turned her attention back to her son. He looked down at his mug and licked his lips eagerly. The last time he had had wine was on the rare occasion when Zayle had let him go into Corbin almost two years ago. He had enjoyed much more than he should have. He smiled to himself as he played the memory through his mind. He recalled drinking too much while he and a few strangers played at the game of dice. The night became hazy the more he drank, but he could swear he met a very beautiful woman. Too much wine had erased what he was sure was a great memory. He sighed as he returned to the present and smiled down at his drink, eager to savor the sweet taste of the liquid.

"So, why did this man want to meet me?" Kade asked as he lifted the mug to his lips. He closed his eyes and tasted the wine as it flowed down his throat. After several long pulls, he placed the mug on the table and wiped his mouth with the back of his hand. He glanced at his mother and thought he could see disapproval in her eyes for just a moment. The look was soon replaced by one of acceptance. Garig seemed to relax. Kade paused, seeing an odd look in his father's eyes that disappeared so quickly that Kade wondered if he were seeing things.

"Father? Why did the old man want to meet me?" Kade asked again, pressing for an answer.

"I could not say," Garig said with a small laugh.

Kade turned to Darcienna and noticed she had not touched her drink. Marcole was not sitting on the bench next to her. Garig noticed, also, and sighed. They both watched as she stared down at the mug, as though she were trying to figure out what she was seeing.

"Go ahead and take a drink," Garig urged as a smile slid across his face.

"Yes Darcienna, take a drink. Don't you like wine?" Kade asked.

Darcienna had her arm lying on the table with her hand out as though she were going to reach for the mug. Kade watched, his curiosity growing. Slowly, she moved her hand toward the cup, as though she were going to grab it, but just when she was about to wrap her fingers around it, she paused.

Were her eyes a shade brighter as she moved her hand toward the mug? Kade wondered as he watched. She narrowed her eyes and then shot Kade a glance.

"Darcienna, what…" Kade was starting to ask when something feather-light brushed his mind. He stopped and tilted his head to listen. He tried to clear his mind, sensing it was important but could not find what had reached out to him. Darcienna grabbed Kade's leg under the table and squeezed so hard he was sure her nails were drawing blood. He could not seem to understand why it

184

mattered as he glanced at her.

"So, Kade, when do you plan on leaving?" Garig asked with a mischievous glint in his eye.

The apprentice saw the devious look, and this time, it stayed to be joined by a sneer. Something was wrong but Kade was having trouble reasoning out what it could be. He looked at Darcienna to warn her but was having a tough time organizing his thoughts. He felt his heart start to race and reached out for the dragon, but it was not there. He put everything into calling to Rayden but found only emptiness. Kade looked back at his father and noticed his mother was no longer sitting in her seat.

He struggled to keep his thoughts from turning into one big blur. He tilted his head, trying to grasp something. His mind drifted back to when he had first heard his father talking to the stranger. Something his father said. He almost lost it but then it became like a beacon in his mind.

"Father," Kade said a bit slowly. "How did you know I was coming to town? We did not decide that until after you had left."

And then...everything made sense in a rush. It had been so obvious. The way his father had acted like he did not recognize them at first. The way he would not look directly at Judeen. The way he had ordered his wife wine when he should have known she did not drink. The danger signs Darcienna had sensed. The lack of response from Rayden. Kade turned back to Darcienna to warn her.

"Darthenna, thith ith a tap," Kade slurred, but she was no longer sitting next to him. When had she gotten up from the table?

Trying hard to keep his wits about him, Kade looked at the man sitting across from him. Garig was no longer trying to be coy. Kade closed his eyes and performed the Reveal Calling. He did not see the use of the Divine, but he did see that there was some sort of distortion around the man. He tried to formulate a plan, but the scream off in the distance that must have only been several feet away, distracted him just as his head hit the table with a loud thud.

Was that Mother's voice? He pondered. And then he recalled the look his father had had when he had first walked up to the table. It wasn't a look that said he recognized who it was, but rather, a look saying he realized who it was. The last feeling Kade had was that of falling off a cliff.

CH7

Darcienna was standing now. She tried to think back on when Judeen had left the table, but she was too focused on the mug to have noticed. Her eyes were blazing bright blue as she looked around the tavern. Kade was trying to speak, but his words came out all wrong as his head hit the table with a thud. She reached out quickly and the sense of danger became overwhelming. She quickly threw up a shield, not caring what anyone thought. Three men leapt over the bar and raced at her. They were no match for the shield, and after some effort, stopped and stared. But, it was not her that had their attention.

"Garig!" Darcienna screamed. "Do something!"

"As you wish." He reached up and pulled her hands down, causing the shield to vanish. She struggled violently, but his grip was like iron.

"What are you doing?" Darcienna screamed in panic. No matter how hard she struggled, it was useless. The men had her in seconds. They were trying to wrestle her to the ground, but she fought like the fiercest wild animal. She lunged for Kade and grabbed his hand. He never moved. She gripped him for all she was worth as the men pinned her to the ground. Darcienna left deep gouges on

Kade's hand as the men jerked her free of him. They had her hands tied behind her back and roughly yanked her to her feet.

"You may call me, Vell," the man said as his form shifted. When he was done, he looked like a greasy man with a touch of crazy in his eyes. He exuded strength and stood a good hand taller than Kade. He had enough arrogance for ten men. There was no mistaking that this man, or whatever he was, was very deadly.

Vell was holding her son as he cooed at him. He turned and smiled at Darcienna, mocking her. She looked at her boy, and her heart froze in terror.

"If you hurt one hair on his head, I swear by all that is sacred that I will make you pay!" Darcienna said vehemently.

"Oh I would not dream of it," Vell said, pretending fear. "You. Come here," he said as he thrust the child into an old woman's arms. "Take care of that. I may need it for leverage later," he said, not trying to conceal his malicious intent. The old woman took the child without a word and turned toward a flight of stairs.

"On second thought, take it to the cell where that one went," Vell said, pointing to the chair Judeen was sitting in just minutes ago. "Tell her to behave and be quiet or that thing will suffer." She nodded once and left the room.

Vell looked at the men and nodded toward the back of the tavern. They shoved Darcienna roughly toward the door behind the bar. She stumbled but kept her balance as she glared at the men from beneath her hat. One of them squinted, trying to understand what he was seeing beneath the brim.

Vell grabbed Kade by the arm and dragged him from the chair, heading toward the back door. He pulled Kade along as if he weighed virtually nothing. Vell took no care to keep Kade from hitting his head as he rounded the corner of the bar.

"Oops," Vell said, pretending concern and then laughed as though he had heard the best joke ever.

The men shoved Darcienna roughly out the back door. They were making a game of this, seeing how hard the shove would need to be to send her sprawling. This shove was enough. She landed on her stomach, knocking the wind out of her and sent the hat flying off her head. She quickly turned and glared hard at the men. They instantly stopped laughing, their mouths gaping open in fear. They swallowed hard and looked nervously at Vell as he exited the tavern.

"She cannot hurt you," Vell said in disgust.

"But...her eyes," one of the men stammered, avoiding looking at her at all cost. With that, she glared even harder. She could have sworn he was on the verge of wetting himself.

Darcienna looked over in horror to see Rayden lying on his side, secured with chains. She screamed for the dragon but the special kind of spice in the meat would keep it out for a week. She turned and glared at the men again and every one of them, with the exception of Vell, immediately found anything other than her to look at.

"Bring her," Vell said as he headed toward another building a little ways into the woods. The men stood looking at each other, waiting for the others to follow the order. It was obvious they feared those blazing blue eyes. Vell walked up to her and said one word in a deep, threatening tone. "Move."

Darcienna started toward the building, if for no other reason than to be close to Kade. If not for him, Vell could have beat her senseless and she still would not have complied. She heard a sigh of relief from two of the men as they moved. Vell spat on the ground in disgust as he started toward the hidden structure.

"Okay you scared little chickens. Do you think you can handle this one?" Vell asked as he dropped the arm of the unconscious man.

Vell grabbed Darcienna roughly and propelled her through the door into an unlit interior. She stumbled as she found stairs just inside. Her eyes were far from adjusted to the dark and she paid for it. She tripped down the steps and hit her head against something solid, almost knocking herself out. She fought to keep hold of the waking world and succeeded, barely. Her vision cleared with effort.

189

"You four will pay for this. I swear this by all that is sacred!" Darcienna promised as her eyes blazed in the dark. She looked up the stairs and two of the men wilted and started to whimper. "Oh you will pay!" said the glowing eyes from the dark.

Darcienna fought to ignore the frustration, anger and helplessness. Her vision cleared a little more as her eyes adjusted to the dark. She had stumbled down the seven steps to hit her head against the wall. She would have gone further if not for the landing that had stopped her fall. The stairs took a sharp, right turn at the landing and continued down another fifteen steps. The men started to drag Kade down further into the dark, not caring that he hit his head on every step until Vell exploded.

"Do not kill him!" Vell raged. "Do you have any idea what will happen to you if he comes and finds him dead?" he screamed. Darcienna was shocked to see this fearless man, or whatever he was, reacting so strongly. The men instantly handled Kade as if he were a delicate flower that could lose all its petals at any moment.

They struggled with their unconscious prisoner, trying to get a better hold on him as they reached the landing. While trying to get by Darcienna, she lashed out with her foot and sent the lead man sprawling down the stairs to hit something with a crack. Vell hit her in the head so hard her vision swam. She felt like she was going to empty her stomach but fought it off. The darkness threatened to overwhelm her, but through sheer force of will alone, she held on. She found a light at the bottom of the stairs and stared at it, bringing it into focus. It took a moment, but for the second time, she was able to keep herself from passing out.

"Behave or there will be more of that," Vell said right into her face. His breath was like a swamp and she gagged. He laughed at that and grabbed her by the arm, dragging her down the stairs.

Darcienna had to step around the unconscious man. Vell pushed her roughly against the wall and shoved past her. He stuck a key in a lock, and with a loud clank of metal on metal, he opened a wooden door.

"I don't know if he is going to live," one of the men said nervously as he looked down at the Apprentice Chosen.

"You had better hope he does or you will pray to the Divine for a quick death," Vell said with a snarl.

The men backed away from Kade, as if to make sure they did not hurt him any further. They began to argue amongst themselves as to who was at fault. Vell rounded on them.

"Find something else to talk about. I am not going to listen to this. You sound like old women bickering."

They continued to glare at each other accusingly, but soon, the conversation turned to how much gold each was going to be paid for this when Morg arrived. This was clearly a much better topic for them. Darcienna was seriously considering kicking another one when she heard the name Morg and stopped to listen.

"When will we get paid?" one of them asked.

"As soon as I can get word to Morg that we have found the Chosen," Vell said.

"What do you mean, as soon as you get word to him? How long will it take?" a sniveling, young man asked.

"I have no way of communicating with him. I will need to go get him," Vell said slowly as if talking to a child. "It should not take more than a day, maybe a day and a half at the most. Don't worry. You will get paid," Vell said as he propelled Darcienna into an open cell and slammed the door shut. It locked with a loud click as the latch caught.

"Open that door," Vell said, indicating a cell across form Darcienna.

"Wait," the younger of the two said shakily. "You expect us to watch them while you are gone?" he asked nervously.

"Only if you enjoy being alive," Vell said as he stepped up to within inches of the man and glared directly into his eyes. The young man held his breath and turned a few shades of green. "Just keep them both tied up, and above all else, do not let them have the use of their hands."

191

"But, what happens if they get loose?" the young man asked. He was scrawny and could not be much past twenty years old. He had very little, if any, hair growing on his face, making him look like a kid. He was the type that was afraid of his own shadow but did his best to hide it. He would talk tough just to convince himself he was not the coward he knew himself to be. Some would even say he had himself mostly convinced that he was brave, but in the end, he would run for his life if things started to fall apart. He was not frail, but he was not far from it either. One might even describe him as gangly. He took a step back to put some distance between himself and Vell.

The man-boy shook with fear. He watched as Vell closed the distance as if he were a panther stalking its prey. The man-boy tried to lift his chin to be brave, but at the same time, he found the exit and firmly planned his route to it, if needed. Vell passed in front of the light and seemed to shimmer slightly. By the time he was standing in front of the young man, he had grown long fangs and dagger-like fingers. He slowly pressed them against the man-boy's cheek and worked his way down to his throat.

"Are you telling me that you are not going to make sure the Chosen stays tied up and in this cell?" Vell asked in a menacing hiss.

Man-boy tried his best to sound calm and confident, but the sweat that had started to coat his forehead was betraying the bravery he was trying to pretend. He glanced down at the daggers and tried to take a step back. Vell easily matched him step for step. As a matter of fact, you would not have even realized that Man-boy had taken a step away with how easily the shapeshifter matched his pace. Man-boy appeared to be on the verge of whimpering.

"He will be kept tied up," the old man said gruffly from nearby.

The old man was in his middle years and very much used to violence. He did not flinch as Vell turned on him. The old man had seen much in his life and this little trick from the shapeshifter was enough to cause him to hesitate, but to feel fear? Not anything like he felt when he looked into those bright, glowing, blue eyes he was avoiding at all cost. He had faced death almost every day of his life, but those blue eyes were like nothing he had ever seen and the unknown shook him. Yes, he was afraid of her.

"I am sure he was only asking as a precaution. He is a Chosen," the old man said as he matched Vell glare for glare. The shapeshifter considered ripping the man's throat out just to make a point, but he knew he needed him. Out of the three, this one was the most competent and he could not afford to lose him. But, that did not mean he could not rip his throat out the next time they met. He very much looked forward to their next meeting.

"Just make sure he is tied up at all times. I don't think he can do anything that would cause us any problems. He got enough of that stuff to keep him out for a week," the shapeshifter said as he turned to head for the stairs. He paused in front of the quivering man-boy and considered ripping his throat out just for fun. Man-boy wilted as the warm fluid ran down his leg. After a moment, Vell continued toward the exit. Without another word, he ascended the stairs and the door slammed with a loud echo.

"He is lucky he did not try anything," Man-boy said, but his voice waivered.

The old man smacked Man-boy in the back of the head so hard he sent him sprawling. Man-boy hit the ground and whimpered. When he looked up, the old man could see a touch of blood on his lip. The old man moved closer to lean over him.

"Shut up you sniveling little girl," he snarled. "Or I will shut you up permanently. I don't know where they found you, but I don't like you and I will send you back in a box. Your pants reek of the coward you are," he said as he wrinkled his nose in disgust.

The old man raised his hand as if to back hand the coward. He decided against hitting him only because he did not want to hurt his hand on this worthless, sniveling, pathetic excuse of a man. He shook his head instead and spat in disgust. He pointed at the cage Darcienna was in as he spoke.

"Keep an eye on her. If she does anything, kill her," the old man said. Man-boy turned white as a sheet as he glanced at those blue eyes. But, as he watched, they started to fade. Right then, the other man, who now had a broken nose after his fall, stumbled over to stand in front of her cage.

Darcienna focused on Kade to see if there was any movement. His form still showed no signs of coming to any time soon. It would take time, but if she was right, it would not take the week that Vell expected. Time might just be on her side, but that was yet to be seen.

"Darcienna," said a voice further down the row of cells. The familiar voice shocked her out of her own thoughts.

"Judeen?" Darcienna asked, not expecting to see her again.

"Yes. Are you okay?" Judeen asked.

"I am. Do you know what they did with my boy?" Darcienna asked, almost pleading.

"I have him. They believe you will behave, knowing he is still alive and knowing they could take him from you at any time."

"Don't forget it," the old man said in a threatening voice.

Darcienna glided to the edge of the cage as if he were the one behind bars. She locked eyes with him. He blinked first.

"You ain't worth it," he said as he swallowed hard and moved away.

"How are you, Judeen?" Darcienna asked.

"About as good as I can be, under the circumstances. How is Kade? Is he going to be alright?" she asked, trying to hide her fear.

"I'm not sure. They gave him some kind of drug that is supposed to keep him unconscious until Morg gets here," Darcienna said.

"Who's there?" a weak voice called from the end of the hall.

"Garig?" Judeen asked as she raced to the front of the cell.

"Yes," he said as he struggled to stand. "Is that you, Judeen?"

"Yes," she said with such relief that she almost cried. "We fell into a trap set by one of Morg's men. What happened to you? Are you alright?" Judeen asked in a rush.

"Yes. Apparently Morg has agents in every town in all

194

directions for days," Garig said as he pressed against the bars to look down the row toward his wife. "I did not know you were coming to town."

"We were not, until we decided to buy Kade some clothes."

"Kade? He is here? Why?"

"He needed to come back to the house for something he left," Judeen said, praying he would not ask what. He was sure to become enraged if he knew that a book empowered by the Divine was left under his roof.

"I see," Garig said, breathing deeply and stretching. "How is everyone else?"

"I am okay," Darcienna said. "They hit me a few times, but it is going to take more than that to keep me down," she said as she raised her voice. "And wait until you see how I make them suffer," she said for their captor's benefit. There was frantic talk at the end of the hall until the old man could be heard telling Man-boy to shut up. Darcienna smiled to herself, satisfied that she had hit home with her comment.

"My son sure can pick them," Garig said.

"Who says he was the one doing the picking?" Darcienna added sweetly.

"Well, it's good to see you still have your sense of humor," Garig said.

They continued to talk for several hours, careful with what they said, as they were certain there was always a chance of being overheard. Darcienna steadfastly watched Kade for any movement. She started to have her doubts about her plan working.

None of the men wanted to stay in the cell area for fear of those blue eyes. They took turns coming in and checking on them but would quickly retreat to slam the door shut and lock it. Broke-nose came in first and would not even so much as glance in Darcienna's direction, then Man-boy for the next hour followed by the old man. They all seemed most concerned with Kade, but none forgot about Darcienna and her threat.

195

After some serious deliberations, the men decided to slit Darcienna's throat. However, after they agreed it was a good idea, none of them wanted to complete the task. Finally, the old man looked on Man-boy and Broke-nose with disgust and headed for the dungeon. He opened the heavy, wooden door, walked through and stopped in front of her cell. Darcienna stood defiant, glaring. She moved closer to him, and he flinched. He swallowed hard as he looked into those eyes that were so bright now he would swear they were pure lightning. He swallowed hard again, turned and quickly retreated up the stairs.

"You didn't do it," Broke-nose said accusingly, confronting the old man. He got a solid hit directly in the nose for that comment and Broke-nose started to bleed again.

"You bastard," Broke-nose screamed. "I should kill you," he said, drawing his boot knife.

"You go ahead and try," the old man said, sitting down on a log by a fire while turning his back to Broke-nose. The old man was a grizzled veteran and he knew that Broke-nose would not even consider following through on his threat, even with his back turned to him. "You think it's so easy? Then you go do it. I ain't touchin' her. I ain't doin' a bloody thing with her. She can rot for all I care, but I ain't going near her again," he said with such finality that both men knew it to be true. Man-boy even thought that maybe the threat of Morg might not be enough to get him in a cell with her. Broke-nose walked to the other side of the fire and plopped down on a log while jamming his knife back into his boot. He grabbed a cloth from his pocket and pressed it to his nose to stop the bleeding.

"You did not have to hit me," he scolded.

"Well now you know I am serious," the old man grumped.

"What do we do if that Chosen wakes up?" Man-boy asked.

"We will decide that if and when it happens," the old man said, trying to sound unconcerned, but clearly it had him on pins and needles. What the other two did not know was that the old man was considering dropping this entire operation and running as fast and far

196

as he could. He did not get to be as old as he was by not knowing when to fold his cards and retreat, no matter the amount of money involved…even if he thought he had a winning hand.

"We could just slit his throat," Broke-nose said while dragging his finger across his neck and making a sound to match. Broke nose was clearly the least intelligent of the group.

The old man looked at Broke-nose as though he were looking at a child. The level of ignorance, and a clear lack of understanding of the consequence of such an act left him speechless. It was one thing to leave, but it was very much another thing to kill the person that Morg wanted above all else. Without this Chosen to occupy Morg, they would, most likely, be the next target for his revenge. No. Killing this man was not an option.

"If you ever utter that again, I will end you where you sit!" the old man raged as he shot to his feet. Spittle was flying from his mouth as he spoke. The two men sank in their seats. "I do not know where they found you two bumbling little children, but if you want to live, you will stop thinking. If I don't kill you, then Vell will, and if he does not, I dread to think of how much Morg is going to make you suffer. Now shut up, and don't even say another word," the old man said as his hand moved to his knife at his side in a practiced move that said he could have it out and bloody in the blink of an eye.

Both men looked at each other, but neither dared say a word. Man-boy considered holding his ground as he was not a coward, or at least, he told himself this. He decided it was his idea to stay quiet and let it go.

Knife or no knife, he better watch his tongue, or he will lose it, Man-boy thought to himself as he looked into the fire. He stole glances at the grizzled fighter and flinched when the old man tossed something into the flames.

Back in the cell, Judeen breathed a sigh of relief. She quickly moved to the entrance, watching the door at the end of the row. Satisfied they were alone, she hissed to Darcienna.

"What was that?" Judeen asked in concern.

"They decided to kill me but could not follow through. I make them too uncomfortable," Darcienna whispered.

"How did you know?" Judeen asked.

"It's my gift," Darcienna said as if that was all that was needed. She was not about to tell them that her gift fired off strongly because of their intent to take her life. Ironically, their attempt to take her life is what saved her. The glowing blue eyes were too much for them to take. She was not willing to explain any more in the event that the men could overhear.

Kade heard the voice of Darcienna drift into his thoughts. He tried to focus on her words but found it difficult. He struggled to figure out where he was but came up blank. He lay still, listening to the sweet sound of Darcienna and felt himself drifting toward her. The closer he got, the more things he could sense and feel. His hands were tied behind his back. He could smell dirt from the floor, and it made it hard for him to breathe. He rolled onto his back as he listened to other voices that also seemed familiar. He pried his eyes open and saw he was in a cell. He looked through the bars and saw a pair of bright, glowing eyes looking down the row of cells. It took a moment for him to realize what he was seeing. Relief flooded through him as he looked upon those beautiful, blazing, rivers of blue and listened to her.

"Darcienna," Kade said in a dry, hoarse voice. Almost no sound came out so he cleared his throat and swallowed to get some moisture worked up so he could talk. "Darcienna," Kade said. She was already looking at him.

"Kade. Keep your voice very, very quiet. They think you are going to be out for a week. We must let them think that," Darcienna hissed. "Are you ok?"

"No," Kade said through tight lips. "My head is pounding and my whole body hurts. What happened?"

"We fell into a trap. That was not your father we were talking to in the tavern. It was a shapeshifter. He calls himself Vell," Darcienna whispered.

"I figured something like that just before I passed out," Kade said as he recalled the last few moments just before the drugs took full effect.

"Kade, we need to get you out of here. Morg will be here by tomorrow. The shapeshifter is going to get him as we speak," Darcienna said as she struggled to be as quiet as possible.

"Do you have any ideas? My hands are tied behind my back," Kade said as his muscles cramped.

"What about the dragon?" Garig asked.

"Father," Kade said in surprise, speaking a bit more loudly than he intended.

"Kade," Darcienna hissed. "Quiet!"

"Father. I am so glad you are okay," Kade said, barely a whisper, praying he was not still the object of his disgust.

"Yes, Son. I am okay. They did hit me a few times, trying to get information about you, but I'll survive."

"We will have to return the favor as soon as we get out of here," Kade said roughly. Darcienna hissed again for him to be quiet. He turned toward her cell. "Are you okay? Did they do anything to you?" Kade asked, afraid of what men might do with a beautiful woman.

"They hit me a few times but nothing beyond that. I am fine, Kade."

He gritted his teeth as the anger started to flow through him. Every second that passed cleaned the cobwebs out of his head. He forgot about his pain and pulled as hard as he could against the ropes. They strained and loosened. In time, they would give way, but for now, they held. Kade could feel a trickle of blood flow down from his wrist onto the back of his hand.

"Can your dragon help us?" Garig asked again.

"I will get us out of this," Kade promised, not hearing his father through his rage. "And, I will make Morg pay. If there is one thing I am going to do, it is make that man pay," he vowed.

"Kade, can your dragon help us?" Garig asked more

insistently.

Just then, the door slammed open. Broke-nose came in and looked around cautiously. He slowly moved closer to Kade's cage, ready to jump and run, as if he was expecting something to leap out at him. He crept over to the door and found Kade the way he had left him. With a huge sigh of relief, he turned to look at Garig and Judeen.

"I heard talking," he said accusingly.

"You did not say we could not talk. And, even if you had, we still would not do as you say," Judeen said rebelliously.

The man drew his knife and advanced on the cell. Kade opened his eye just a sliver. It was clear she was trying to distract him and get his mind off the line of questioning. Make him mad. That was all she was trying to do, but Kade feared it was going to backfire. He was trying to formulate a plan when his mother continued.

"Yes, that is a great idea," Judeen said, indicating the knife. "I am sure Morg would not mind you killing us. I am sure he kept us alive when he had us captive in town for no reason. Oh, wait. There was a reason. Because he wanted us alive," she said as she glared hard at the man. "So, if you want to kill us, know that your death won't be far behind," Judeen said without so much as a touch of fear.

"Bah. You are not worth it," Broke-nose said as he slammed the dagger back home in its sheath and stormed out.

"You might want to have that nose looked at," Judeen called after the man. Kade mentally shook his head. He was sure that there might be a time when his mother was going to push things a little too far. But, not this time. The man slammed the door so hard it echoed like thunder.

"My dear, you do have a way with words," Garig said. "That could have gone wrong."

"My dear," she echoed. "It went as I wanted," she said simply.

"Kade," Garig said, turning his attention back to his son. "Can your dragon help?

"They have him drugged and tied down with chains," Darcienna said.

Kade rolled toward the door. The cells were made of iron bars that were spaced six inches apart, allowing him to look and see his parents. After two complete rolls, he was at the door. He lifted his head and found himself staring into Darcienna's faintly glowing eyes just five feet away.

"We will get out of here," Kade said as he felt his strength coming back to him. He pulled hard on his ropes and felt just a slight little more give, but they still held him fast.

"You should save your strength," Darcienna said as she watched him strain against his bindings.

"Kade, how were you able to fight off the poison? The men said you would be out for at least a week." Judeen commented.

"I am not sure," Kade said.

"See. What would you do without me," Darcienna said.

"You had something to do with purging the poison out of me," Kade started to ask, but then realized as he spoke that she must have healed him and ended it as a statement.

"I was able to touch him just before we were captured. I tried to heal the poison out of his body, but they broke the contact between us before I could get all of it out. It looks like it was enough, though," she said as she looked at him.

"I did feel your hand on me for just a moment," Kade said, thinking back. "Yes, I do recall."

Right then the door at the end of the hall opened, and Man-boy stalked in to stop in front of Kade's cell. His eyes went wide with fear as he looked down at the Chosen, who was looking back at him in defiance. Kade saw the look of fear in the man's eyes and decided to bluff.

"I'll give you one chance to live," Kade said as he watched the man's jaw hit the floor. "If you open this door and help my friends now, I will spare you. If not, I will destroy you, this place, and all those who were involved with this," he said in his most intimidating voice. Kade could see the sweat start to bead on Man-boy's forehead. His composure was quickly crumbling. He tried to swallow several times, but his throat had closed up in fear.

"Morg will have me killed if I let you out," Man-boy pleaded.

"Morg is not here right now, but I am," Kade said in a snarl as he slowly rose to his feet while keeping eye contact. His captor quivered visibly. The fear was wracking him, and Kade could see he was having the effect he wanted. Man-boy was looking anywhere but at him. "NOW!" Kade yelled into his face as he took a step right up to the bars.

Man-boy seemed to snap as his eyes whipped around to lock with Kade's. They were no longer the eyes of a sane man. It was too much for Man-boy. His eyes went wild.

"I'll do something," he said as he frantically reached for the keys on his belt. A lifetime of being afraid while keeping it hidden had finally pushed him too far. He was going to prove once and for all that he had nothing to fear, and what better way to do it than to kill a Chosen.

Kade took a step away from the door while looking behind himself. He swallowed hard as his mind worked feverishly to find a solution to this problem. This was not quite the way he had pictured this going in his head.

"Leave him alone," Darcienna screamed. Her eyes blazed bright blue instantly. He turned and locked eyes with her, which was a first for him.

"You will be next," he hissed as spittle flew from his mouth.

"If you come into this cell, I will make you suffer beyond your worst fears," Kade threatened, trying to regain control of the situation.

It only hastened the man to find the right key. Soon, he jammed the jagged piece of metal into the lock, and with a violent turn, the door was unlocked. He flung it open as he glared at the source of his fear. Man-boy leered at Kade, feeling brave for the first time in his life. He felt like he was the one in control and the one with power. The feeling of not being afraid filled him with strength, and this time when he looked at Kade, his intent was clear. Nothing meant more to him than killing this Chosen. With Kade's death would come the death of his cowardice.

Man-boy took one step into the room, and Kade heard a sickening thunk. The coward, who had turned brave, stumbled as his head twisted at an odd angle. He hunched his shoulders and clenched his fists, his face screwed up in pain. At first, Kade was just as confused as Man-boy, and then he saw the reason why his captor had stumbled. He recognized the hilt of the knife sticking out of Man-boy's neck. The point had gone all the way through and was sticking out several inches on the other side. Man-boy's hand went to his neck as he tried to pull the knife out, but the life was already ebbing from his body. For just an instant, Kade could see sanity return to him. A look flashed in Man-boy's eyes. Was it understanding? Was it the look someone gets when they finally realize something they were not able to figure out for an entire lifetime? Kade would never know, but at that moment, it was very clear to Man-boy that it was his cowardice and his fears that had kept him alive all these years. He was now going to die because he had overcome those fears. He gurgled a laugh and then fell to the floor, never to fear again.

Kade moved to the open door and looked down the hall from where the knife came. There was a shadow closing the wooden door slowly, obviously trying to be quiet. It slipped down the hall toward the cell where Kade was waiting. He looked back at the knife in the man's neck and knew who was going to step into the light.

"I knew you were going to be needing me sometime," Dran said matter-of-factly.

"You could not have timed that better," Kade said as he breathed a sigh of relief. "Quickly, untie me."

"First, let me get my knife back from the man who borrowed it," Dran said, as he smiled at his own joke. He put his foot against the man's head for leverage and pulled the knife free.

"You know this person," Darcienna said, more as a statement than a question.

"Yes. I ran across him in the woods just before I came upon you. He was leaving the town where my parents were captured," Kade said and then turned back to Dran. "How did you find us?"

"I saw that black animal of yours heading toward this dungeon. From there it was only a guess but a good one I see," Dran said with a smirk.

"Yes, but how did you come to this town?" Kade asked, suspicious. He was not ready to trust anyone to be who they say they are with a shapeshifter around.

"Who do you think helped your parents build that beautiful cabin? And of course, it did not take a genius to know they would come here. It is the closest town. Once I got here, I kept seeing a silky, black creature with a bent ear. At first, I could not place it, but then it hit me; I saw him when we first met and knew it was not just a coincidence. I realized it was trying to lead me to you, so here I am."

"I didn't know it was here," Kade said, turning his back to Dran, waiting for the man to cut his ropes.

"Dran, is that you?" Garig asked.

"Garig?" Dran responded, surprised at the voice he heard coming from the dark cell at the end.

"Yes, it's me," Garig said. "Why are you here?"

"I ran into your son. He told me what he was doing, and I decided I was going to help," Dran said as he cut the ropes binding Kade. "So, I was right when I told Kade you were too stubborn to leave town?" Dran asked.

"Someone had to stay and try to get rid of that monster," Garig growled.

"You two can talk later. Right now we have to get out of here," Kade said as he reached for the ring of keys.

Kade pried them from the dead man's grip and quickly opened Darcienna's cell. Dran cut the ropes from her wrists. She breathed a sigh of relief as she rubbed her arms to help the circulation. Dran eyed her with deep appreciation at that intake of breath. Next, they freed Garig and Judeen. Darcienna raced over to her son and took him into her arms, looking him over for any injuries.

Kade stopped and looked at the knife in Dran's hand, grateful it never left its sheath when they first met. The man knew how to use a blade almost too well. He had to remind himself that any man could still be deadly, even those that did not use the Divine.

"You're pretty good with that thing," Kade said, motioning to the knife. "That was at least a fifty foot throw."

"Well, a man has to be good at something," Dran said as he flipped the blade over and over in his hands. It was almost as if he was doing this without having to think about it. It was as if it was an extension of his body.

"Well, who is this?" Dran asked while staring at Darcienna. She slid closer to Kade and put her hand on his arm, not liking the attention she was getting.

Kade longed to introduce her as his intended but instead said, "This is Darcienna. I met her the same day I left you. Look, we need to get out of here before the other men come back," Kade said, not liking the way Dran was looking at Darcienna. Without thinking, he put his arm around her protectively. Dran shrugged his shoulders casually and pretended to check over his knife for any damage.

"You're right," Judeen said as she smiled a hello to Dran. She made a point to ask him later if he and Tracella were split up again as she took in the way he eyed Darcienna.

"There should have been two others," Darcienna said. "How did you get by?" she asked of Dran as she glanced at Kade with worry.

Dran started to laugh as he said, "they took off after your little pet."

"Well, we should have no trouble getting out," Kade said as he flowed through the moves for the Transparency Calling. Everyone disappeared from view. Just before they faded out, Kade saw a look of awe on his father's face. He could not help but enjoy seeing his father impressed with his ability instead of the disgust he expected. At least, he hoped that was what it was he was seeing. Next, Kade quickly completed the Silence Calling and breathed a sigh of relief. "Okay, we can leave now," Kade said, happy with himself.

"What just happened?" Dran asked in awe.

"I am a Chosen," Kade said, feeling that that was all the explanation needed. He neglected to use the word apprentice. "I just made everyone invisible. We need to stay close or we could lose contact. I also have a calling in place that will allow us to hear each other, but no one else can hear us. We still need to be careful. Someone could see us disturbing the ground, so keep that in mind."

"Well, Chosen, it looks like you have found what you're good at. My knife is nothing compared to this. This is incredible," Dran said, overly impressed.

"Kade," Darcienna said, trying to get his attention.

"Yes?" Kade responded, hearing worry in her voice.

Just then the door at the end of the hall opened, and Vell entered. Kade felt a cold chill run down his back as he noticed that there were two others with him. He closed his eyes as his heart started to pound. He completed the Reveal Calling and inhaled sharply at what he saw.

"Three shapeshifters," Kade hissed.

Vell was, once again, in the shape of Garig. This was obviously a game to him. Kade could not wait to see his reaction when he saw the empty cell with the dead man lying on the floor. Vell sent the other two shapeshifters forward with instructions to retrieve the Chosen. Kade felt the urge to blast them with his lightning but decided that caution was a more prudent course. Getting them all out safely was much more important than revenge…barely.

"Kade," Darcienna whispered in panic.

"I know," Kade responded roughly. "Everyone get behind me. Stand next to the wall at the end of the hall. If we are lucky, they will not sense us."

Just as Kade finished speaking, the first shapeshifter came upon the dead man. The second shapeshifter ran into the cell formerly occupied by Darcienna. The first shapeshifter ran back into the hall in a panic.

"There is a dead man here."

"This cell is empty," the second shapeshifter said in a hurry.

"No! It can't be!" Vell screamed in outrage. He changed into the form with the long daggers for fingers.

Kade went through the moves of the Lightning Calling in his head just in case they were discovered. He was not sure if the three could sense him or not, but he was going to be ready. He planted his feet firmly as he locked onto Vell. A part of him wanted this so badly he could taste it. He could feel the Divine Power swirling within him, promising him ecstasy, urging him to use it, to destroy with it, to enact his revenge. He felt the power calling to him and his eyes closed slightly as the sweet feel of the Divine filled him. Kade shook off the desire to let the Divine guide his hand.

"Check the other cells!" Vell commanded roughly.

"Darcienna, be ready to use your shield when I say but not until then. If I can take out Vell, then maybe the other two will make a run for it," Kade said.

"I thought they were not supposed to be here till tomorrow," Judeen said. "Does that mean Morg is here?"

"I am not sure. Right now we can't worry about that," Kade said as he watched the two subordinates check the cells one by one.

Kade watched as the two shapeshifters moved closer and closer. He was certain that his small group was not going to stay undiscovered. The shapeshifters were going to be too close when they got to the last two cells at the end of the hall. Kade smiled, grateful for the excuse to fulfill his urge to exact his revenge.

"Stay behind me and watch," Kade said as he grinned eagerly.

He planted his feet squarely and started through the moves. He was the wind moving gracefully through the trees. He was the water swirling easily through a winding river. He was grace and beauty as he performed the moves flawlessly. The closer of the two shapeshifters stopped just two paces in front of him as it smelled the air. Kade let the Lightning Calling explode from his hand to slam into the shapeshifter. The sound was deafening as it echoed off the walls. The building shook to its very core as dust sifted down from the ceiling. Although the shapeshifters heard nothing because of the Silence Calling, everyone else's ears rang furiously. Everyone panicked at the sound of the explosion and quickly pressed their hands tightly to their head. The creature was caught directly in the center of its chest. It exploded messily, spraying the small party, making them visible once more.

"We are under attack," the second shapeshifter said as he dove into a cell.

Kade could see him changing shape even before he hit the ground. He looked down the hall to see Vell grow to three times his size. Kade smiled at the challenge. Larger was not better, and Vell was about to learn that the hard way. He recalled Darcienna telling him of how this creature had hit her in the head and stepped forward to meet the challenge, eager to make this creature pay.

Kade was covered with the blood of the shapeshifter. He could be seen. It did not matter. He let the power fill him and he reveled in it.

He brought the Lightning Calling to life, again causing an explosion that rocked the very building. The calling raced down the hall toward its target. Vell dodged, but just barely, as the bolt slammed into the wooden door, causing it to disintegrate. The shapeshifter recovered quickly, changed into something else just as big, but much faster, and charged down the hall at an all-out run. For just a moment, Kade felt the urge to step back but quickly dismissed the idea. He raced through the moves for the Divine Fire Calling and sent the fiery blast to envelope the creature. Kade smiled in satisfaction as he saw the blast explode against the beast's chest, causing it to scream out in pain. When the smoke cleared, there was no sign of Vell.

"Kade, should I use my shield?" Darcienna asked, not seeing a trace of their captor.

"Not until it is absolutely necessary. If they get too close, they can surround us. I must keep distance between them and us," Kade said as the flames died down. He looked around and started to get a bad feeling. The seconds ticked by. Kade started to get nervous, knowing that Vell could be sneaking up on them this very moment. He was about to tell Darcienna to use her shield when he got an idea. He closed his eyes and used the Reveal Calling.

"Just as I thought," Kade said under his breath as he watched a slight distortion move along the ceiling toward them. He imagined that Vell had taken the shape of a spider and shivered. He hated spiders…or…he used to. He started through the moves for the Lightning Calling once more as the spot closed to within twenty feet. It got to fifteen feet and started to expand when Kade let the calling explode from his hand. Vell screamed as the ceiling crumbled under the impact of the calling.

"Now, Darcienna!" Kade yelled as the building started to fall down on them. The shield materialized just as the first heavy chunk of brick fell toward them. Kade ducked out of reflex. Every piece of debris that hit the shield caused Darcienna to grunt and her arms to jolt as if she were being hit, but she held. She fell to one knee and her hands had sank to the level of her shoulders, but the shield stayed intact. Darcienna was panting by the time the building stopped falling.

Kade closed his eyes and searched for Vell but found nothing. *There was no way he could have survived that,* Kade thought. *It was a direct hit.* Just as he was about to open his eyes, he looked to his left for the other shapeshifter. There, in the far corner, was just a speck of distortion. He would have easily missed it, but knowing what to look for, he had seen what he was seeking.

"Holy Mother of the Divine, Kade. What was that?" Garig said too loudly, trying to stop the ringing in his ears.

"Just a simple little calling I learned recently," Kade said with mock modesty.

"That is one bloody calling that I would not consider simple," Garig said as he swore, feeling his heart hammer at the inside of his chest. "And maybe a warning next time?" he scolded, letting another string of profanity fly.

"Kade. Are you okay?" Darcienna asked. He did not answer at first as he watched the spec in the cell. He was certain that this one was fairly weak in its abilities. It was, most likely, afraid for its life. "Kade," Darcienna said more insistently.

"I am okay. I am watching something," Kade said.

"Would you like to see if he likes the taste of my knife?" Dran asked, picking up on what was happening.

"No. I have an idea, though. I don't think this one is as strong, or as dangerous as the other ones. I am going to try something," Kade said as he kept watch out of the corner of his eye. "Can you keep the shield up while we work our way past the hole in the ceiling?"

"Yes," Darcienna said. Kade was certain he could hear a fair share of strain in her voice but, he trusted her. If she said she could do it, then he knew she could.

"Good. I am going to let both callings go that are cloaking us," Kade said.

"But, that will mean that the shapeshifter will be able to follow us and hear us," Judeen said, alarmed.

"I'm counting on that. If you don't want to be forced to move from that beautiful home of yours, then just follow my lead. It should also keep Morg from finding us if he doesn't show up before we get out of here. Father, play along," Kade said as he let both callings dissipate.

Kade led the way by the cell while watching for the shapeshifter out of the corner of his eye. They passed the gaping hole in the ceiling without incident. Darcienna let the shield go with an audible gasp. They stepped through the exit where the door had been and started to work their way up the stairs. Kade stood against the wall to allow the others to ascend as he closed his eyes and casually glanced down the hall. As he expected, there was a shimmer working its way toward them along the edge of the wall.

"Father, how much further south must we travel to get to your cabin?" Kade asked with a sly smile.

"Oh we are not even close. Its days if not weeks till we get there," Garig said.

"I will travel with you until you are home and then I will go on my way. We should be safe until then," Kade said as he glanced back down the corridor. He saw a small field mouse wedged up against the wall not more than ten feet from them. Pretending not to see, Kade turned back to the party as they all continued their climb. Soon, they were outside the dungeon. Kade could see the dragon through the trees.

"What about Rayden?" Garig asked.

"I don't know if we have time to set him free," Kade said, feigning regret. He must have done a convincing job as Darcienna looked at him slack jawed. "It has served its purpose."

"What do you mean the dragon has served its purpose?" Darcienna asked incredulously.

"Just that. Don't question me!" Kade said harshly as he leveled a glare at her. She was preparing to let Kade have it when Judeen laid a hand on her arm.

"The men have made their decision," she said as she looked into her eyes and raised her eyebrows, as if to say, "Let it go." Darcienna looked among the three of them, gaping like a fish. And then…she caught on.

"You're right," Darcienna said as she nodded. Judeen smiled slightly and nodded back. "It has served its purpose."

Kade breathed a sigh of relief. He looked back at his father and caught his eye. Almost done, but it could still fall apart. Everything had to be perfectly.

Now, to finish this up, Kade thought.

"Father, I almost forgot. I have to find the other shapeshifter. If he gets away, he can report where we are going," Kade said as he turned and hurried toward the dungeon. He had made it to within ten feet of the door when something shot into a bush and then flew out, flapping furiously off into the sky. Kade smiled to himself and relaxed.

"That should keep Morg busy for a while," Kade said as he watched the creature shrink to just a speck and then disappear completely. "That bat that just took off is now going to give Morg false information," he said with a grin. Darcienna nodded, understanding.

"Why do we care if Morg thinks we have the dragon?" Darcienna asked.

"Because he will not expect us to cover as much ground on foot as we can on Rayden, so he will look in the wrong place," Kade said.

He quickly returned to the group and performed the Transparency Calling and then the Silence Calling. He was not taking any chances until they were away from this town. He reached out for Darcienna's hand and felt her warm fingers curl into his, and then her nails dug into his hand.

"You should have trusted me enough to tell me what you were planning," Darcienna said with just a touch of heat in her voice.

"Well, it did help that you were so convincing," Kade chided, which earned him another hard squeeze of her hand. "We need to free the dragon," Kade said as he walked toward the slumbering form.

Rayden was breathing deeply as he slept. Kade felt his anger grow as his eyes followed the chains firmly holding the dragon pinned to the ground. He considered hunting the remaining two men but decided it was best not to waste the precious time they had. The safety of his family and their freedom was more important than his thirst for revenge. Was he craving the action or was he purely looking to right a wrong? Was it for revenge? He could not decide. Were his motives neutral, good or bad? He would think more on this later.

"I am going to heal the dragon and free it," Kade said.

He performed the Healing Calling and let it settle into the dragon. Nothing happened so he performed it again. Once more, nothing happened. The dragon continued to dream. Kade felt panic begin to grow. He never considered that he would not be able to free his friend, but if it would not wake up, might they have to leave it? Kade tried the healing once more, but yet again, nothing.

"Kade?" Judeen asked after hearing a frustrated huff from her son.

He sat silently for several long moments. He was so focused he did not even hear his mother call to him. Leaving the dragon was just not an option, but he knew he could not stay. He performed the Healing Calling again, knowing it was going to do no good, but he needed to try something. He willed the dragon to life as he cast the last calling, but still, nothing.

"Kade?" Judeen asked a bit more insistently. "What is wrong, Son?"

"I...can't seem to wake him up," Kade said hesitantly, not wanting to face the difficult decision. "Mother, I just can't leave him but if I stay..." he said and could not finish.

"Kade," Darcienna said.

"Darcienna, I am trying to think for a moment. Give me a minute," Kade said gently but firmly. He felt stress building by the moment.

"Kade," Darcienna tried again, but again, Kade was too focused on his own thoughts.

He felt Darcienna brush by him as she let out an exasperated gasp. *What could she be doing?* Kade started to ask himself, and then it occurred to him what she was trying to say. She was going to try Nature's Gift. It was more than he had so he waited eagerly. It was not long before the dragon's eyes fluttered open.

"The dragon was not injured you big ox. Your healing heals damage. The dragon is not injured. Mine works to purge the poisons as it did with you. Next time, you might want to listen to me," she said as she brushed past him again. Reminding himself to remember how her abilities worked, Kade stepped up to the dragon that was struggling to escape its dream.

Rayden, it's me, Kade thought to his friend. *I'm going to free you in just a moment, but I am going to need your help*. He recalled the Silence Calling he had placed on the dragon previously and let it go. He wanted to hear his dragon breathing, needed to hear its voice and know that it was ok.

Kade looked at the thick chains attached to the massive stakes that were driven into the ground. He had his doubts about the dragon's ability to break free. Moment by moment, Rayden became more alert. Within minutes, he was fully awake and furious. He roared loudly and strained against the chains. His muscles rippled as he struggled. His tail thrashed violently as he put everything into fighting for his freedom. The dragon pushed hard against the ground, its claws digging in deeply. Kade held his breath, praying for the chains to give. They strained and creaked, and the stakes in the ground shifted ever so slightly, but they held. The dragon huffed hard as it continued to put everything it had into gaining its freedom. Kade raced to the closest stake near the dragon's shoulders, and with all his might, he pulled. He put his strength to the test as he strained so hard he thought he might pass out. His hope started to fade ever so slightly, and then…he felt the stake shift just barely. This was all he needed to put absolutely everything into it. He urged Rayden to pull for all he was worth. It let out another roar even louder than the first and strained fiercely against its shackles, and then it happened; the stake shot out of the ground, sending Kade flying to land on his back side.

Kade breathed a huge sigh of relief as the dragon stood a little more. With better leverage, the chains started to come out of the ground one by one. It was not long before Rayden was free and flexing his wings.

"My friend, we need to get out of here," Kade said. Rayden sniffed the air several times where the voice had come from. Satisfied that he found what he was looking for, he relaxed just a little.

Several towns' people ducked around a corner only to race for their lives, screaming about the dragon. It was no surprise, with how loud it was. For that matter, he was surprised that more were not coming.

The entire town had to have heard, Kade thought. Two men came racing out of the woods. He recognized them instantly. Broke-nose skidded to a stop as his eyes went wide with fear. He turned and ran for his life. The dragon launched after him and had him before he could take four steps. Rayden bit down hard and then tore the man in half.

The old man grinned as he watched the fool run for his life. *Cowards never lived long*, he thought to himself as he planted his feet firmly. A planned retreat was one thing, but to run in fear was another thing altogether. He knew that there was something ingrained in animals that triggered them to chase after prey that ran, so he faced the dragon with an over-sized, two-handed ax in his hand. Maybe, just maybe, he could work his way out of this. It was an animal after all, and it had to be dumb like the rest. Not that he had ever seen a dragon before, but that did not change the fact that it was still an animal. For a fleeting moment, he considered making a break for the tavern while the dragon was distracted, but he quickly dismissed the idea.

Kade felt a blackness fill him inside, and the Divine Power thrummed through him like his own heartbeat. He snarled, savoring the sweet taste of revenge as he anticipated destroying this man. He grinned maliciously to himself, and he let the callings surrounding him melt away as he started forward. He wanted this man to see who was going to end his life.

The grizzled fighter visibly flinched hard when Kade appeared out of nowhere, marching purposefully toward him. Kade moved with confidence as he became the hand of death. He was focused intensely on the old man as he closed the distance. It might have even been more accurate to say he hunted his prey as he locked onto his victim. There was a vague sense of his name being called, but he tuned it out as his hate boiled to overflowing. He was focused, his bloodlust blinding him. He wanted this so badly he could taste it. The power in him swirled faster and faster as it built from a gentle

215

flow to a tsunami. The man glanced behind himself as if to look for a way out but then held his ground. He looked down in surprise to see that the ax had slipped from his weakened grip to land on the ground with a thud. He tried to get himself to pick it up again, but he could not move. He felt his heart racing wildly.

Is this what it's like to feel fear? A warmth ran down his leg.

Kade flew through the moves, and on the thirteenth, he let out a yell as the calling thundered from his outstretched hand to slam into the petrified man. The explosion was deafening and the blast caused his hair to blow back momentarily before settling back on his head. Kade barely heard a scream before the man was blown to pieces. For a second, Kade thought there were more screams than just the man's. As he thought back on the last few moments, he recalled hearing several voices calling his name.

The power slowly ebbed from him as the murderous rage faded. Kade turned to look for his small party, and seeing they were still invisible, let the calling fade. He was not sure why, but he needed to see them. When he did, all he saw were accusing eyes; eyes that looked at him in fear; eyes that looked at him as though they did not recognize who it was they were seeing.

"Kade," Darcienna said meekly. "He was unarmed," she said in almost a whisper.

Why did it sound like she was on the verge of tears? Kade thought. *The man had tried to kill her. Hadn't he?*

"Kade did what he had to do," Garig said, but even he sounded more like he was trying to convince himself than anything else.

Kade looked from face to face and found the same look in every one of them. It was as if they were looking at someone they did not recognize. He was breathing heavily as his eyes moved from person to person.

"It is done with," Judeen said as she glided up to Kade and wrapped her arms around him. "You have much to learn. I have faith that you will make the right choice in the end, my Son," Judeen said as she pulled his head down to lie on her shoulder. Kade was not sure why, but his heart felt heavy.

What did I do that I should feel this way? Kade asked himself. *That was a bad man who would have killed my friends and family if he had the chance, so why care? Was what I did even wrong? Wasn't the world a better place without him? Then, why does everyone act as though I had burned down a nursery full of babies?* Kade's head began to ache with the effort of trying to grasp something that was just barely out of his reach. Even Dran, the man who had just killed someone himself, was avoiding looking at him.

"I think it's time that we get you home," Kade said as he took a steadying breath and stepped back from his mother. He smiled, and she relaxed visibly, seeing the Kade that she knew.

"I hope you don't plan on eating there again, Father," Kade said halfheartedly, trying to lighten the mood.

"I never liked those places, anyway," Garig said. As much as he tried to hide it, Kade could see there was something still troubling his father. Was it what he had just done, or was there more to it? He sighed and decided that now was not the time to ask, so he let it go. "There is another town that is much nicer in the other direction. But, I am thinking your mother and I are going to be staying at home for quite a long time. That much I can promise."

"Why wasn't Morg here if the shapeshifter was back?" Dran asked.

"I don't think Vell went to get Morg. I believe he went to get some of his kind first, because he did not trust those men to do the job right. He was probably going to have his own kind watch over us. But, enough talk. It is time we get moving. We won't be safe until we are far from here," Kade said as the energy continued to drain out of him. He stopped a moment, feeling empty inside.

"My friend, are you able to carry so many?" Kade asked the dragon as he waved his hand to indicate the group. He let out a weak laugh at the unspoken response. It was not words exactly, but it clearly could be translated into something like, "This is supposed to be a challenge? Bah. Twice this would only help even out the load."

It was a trip that was made in total silence. Kade found himself replaying the last few moments of the old man's life over and over in his mind. He felt an uneasy feeling spread through his body. Every time he tried to think about something else, his mind would always return to the old man. When he looked back through his memory, he saw the man lose his grip on the ax, but at the time, he saw no such thing.

Why can I recall it now but not see it at the time? he asked *himself.*

Before they knew it, they were stopping in front of the cabin, and everyone was sliding down. Dran hit the ground and stumbled several steps before finding his footing. Kade landed gracefully and stood as he brushed off his clothes. Dran offered his hand to Darcienna, but she had her eyes on Kade. The apprentice turned to glare at Dran, and the man held up his hands in surrender, backing away with a smile on his face.

"I thought she was untaken," Dran said, feigning ignorance. Kade frowned hard. What could he say to that?

"Dran, you and I need to have a talk. Anyway, I am glad you came back with us," Judeen said.

"Someone needs to keep your fool husband from trying to fix every town he enters," Dran chided. Garig grunted as he ascended the porch but did not say a word.

Judeen started for the cabin but turned to look askance at her son, who had not left the dragon's side. Kade looked at Darcienna, who looked back at him and nodded. They had been talking and had come to a decision. Judeen narrowed her eyes as if to ask, "What?" but she already knew she was not going to like the answer.

"We feel it would be too dangerous for us to stay here," Kade said as he scratched a spot just below his neck. Judeen saw the move, and without taking her eyes off the spot, glided up to Kade. He tried to close his shirt tighter around his neck, but she roughly shoved his hand away and yanked the cloth back. There was a burn spot in the shape of the medallion. She looked at her son with the question in her eyes. Kade sighed, knowing that his mother was not going to be dissuaded.

"It's the medallion. It keeps Morg from finding me. Any Chosen that uses the Divine Power can be sensed by others who are connected to the Divine. I have yet to acquire this ability as I was not taught how, but Morg can. The more I use the Divine Power, the more this works to conceal the use of the power," Kade explained.

"But it's cool," Judeen commented.

"It was blistering cold earlier, Mother. For whatever reason, it gets colder and colder every time I use the Divine Power. It's like it is absorbing something. I don't really understand it, but regardless, I believe we should leave. I may have pushed its abilities too far. I am only putting you in danger by staying."

As Kade watched, her eyes started to fill. Judeen turned her head to hide the sadness that was plain to see. She squeezed her eyes shut in an attempt to hold back the flow of tears and failed. She was deathly afraid that this was going to be the last time that she ever saw her son alive. Kade wrapped his mother in his arms and whispered to her how much he loved her, and she openly cried. She held on tightly, as if to never let him go. Every moment she held on was a moment more her precious son was alive. It broke his heart, and once again, he cursed fate for putting him on this path in life. The path of the Divine was never a safe path to walk but he had no choice. It was his path.

"Mother," Kade said as gently as possible. "I will come back. This is not goodbye. It is just, I will see you later. No more tears," he said as he moved her back and looked upon her. He gently caressed a tear off her cheek with the back of his fingers and smiled at her like he used to when he was a child. A short laugh escaped her lips despite herself.

The tension faded from everyone. Kade walked up to his father, looked him in the eye, man to man, and then hugged him with every bit of love he felt. For just a moment, Kade thought that Garig was going to push him away. After a moment of being as solid as granite, he softened and hugged his son back. Kade felt as if he could cry at that simple gesture.

"Kade," Garig said as he searched for the right words to say. "The Divine Power tempts you Chosen into doing things that change who you are. It is wrong to kill just to kill," Garig said gently. "Revenge is only one step away from decisions that are made with no morality. Please, Son, be careful." Kade was stunned at his father's words. Why could he not see this before? After a moment, he looked his father in the eyes and nodded his understanding. Without saying a word, he stepped back and moved over to Dran.

"You made the difference at the right time, my friend. Thank you for saving my life," Kade said. Dran waved it away awkwardly. "Thanks," Kade said again to impress upon Dran that it was not something to be dismissed so easily. Dran nodded once and smiled a crooked smile while looking sideways at Kade.

The apprentice looked at the house and thought about that wonderfully comfortable bed. For whatever reason, his heart beat just a little faster, and then it passed. He felt sadness at having to leave. He stepped off the porch and walked toward the dragon. He looked at Darcienna and knew the response he would get, but still, he had to try.

"Darcienna, you can stay here if you want," Kade said as he looked at Marcole. Darcienna huffed in frustration.

"No! I am coming with you," Darcienna said tight-lipped with a focused glare.

She hugged Marcole tightly as she walked up the porch to stand in front of Kade's mother. Judeen did not reach out right away, giving Darcienna every last minute she wanted with her son. She understood fully what it meant to leave your son in the hands of another. Finally, Darcienna handed him to her and stepped back off the porch while wiping away a tear.

"Darcienna," Judeen called. Darcienna turned and gave a confident smile.

"I will keep him safe," she vowed, not needing to hear any

more to know what was going to be said. Judeen closed her mouth and nodded once.

"We should go," Darcienna said as she turned away from her boy who was starting to fuss.

"I will never be able to tell you how much I appreciate you looking after Marcole," Kade said to his parents.

"I can't watch you go, my Son," Judeen said as she gave him a hug and then retreated into the cabin. It reminded him of the previous time he had left. Kade was sure she was crying again, but he knew it was out of his hands to fix. His heart hurt for her. Dran gave Kade a smile, a nod of his head and then turned to go check on Judeen.

"Go look after mother," Kade said as his mind already started plotting out the path he must take to Master Chosen Doren's home. Kade turned to leave when a shimmer caught his eye. It was like when heat rises up off a dark rock in the middle of a hot, sunny day. When he focused on it, it was gone but there was a definite sense of urgency now that made his heart pound.

CH8

Kade tried to ignore the panic that threatened to well up in him. He could not race off every time something or someone told him to. His nerves were already on edge as it was. He did his best to ignore the knot in his stomach and mounted the dragon. He reached down and pulled Darcienna up to sit behind him. He gave the signal to the dragon to go and off they went.

The dragon started out and Kade gave it directions. Unfortunately, it was in the direction of the town they had just left. Kade could not help but to focus on the time he had wasted going back and forth between the town and his parents' home. *It was for a good reason,* he told himself. *I had to make sure my parents were safely home.*

Kade's mind returned to the old grizzled man. He kept seeing him holding the axe, ready to do battle, but at the same time, he would see him shaking in fear as the weapon fell from his grasp. If there was one thing his master preached almost incessantly, it was to never use the power for revenge. Once on the path of using the power for revenge, from there it was for using it for anything with no moral compass to guide your way. Kade knew this and so did anyone who knew anything about the Divine. It made sense to him why his mother and father reacted so strongly. Zayle had made it clear that Kade would be taught to use the power justly and that to do otherwise would be a step towards self-destruction. *But, it felt so good to destroy the man*, Kade thought and then gasped at his own thinking.

"Kade, what is it?" Darcienna asked.

"I just thought I saw something," Kade said, not wanting to give her something to worry about.

Kade let his mind wander as he considered what Doren was going to be like. Was he going to welcome Kade as a friend and ally, or was he going to treat him as an adversary who he had to guard his secrets from? With the way Zayle used to describe other Chosen, it could go either way. But, one thing Kade knew for certain; he needed to guard the secrets in his books.

Kade could see the town of Dresben off in the distance and turned north to give it a wide birth. He was not going to take the chance that Morg may be there. As the lights of the town faded behind him, he felt himself relax more and more.

"Kade?" Darcienna asked hesitantly after sitting quiet for almost an hour.

"Yes?" Kade asked casually.

"I'm not sure how to say this without sounding crazy."

"After the last few weeks, I doubt anything you say can surprise me."

"When we were back in the cave, it looked like there was a face in the darkness."

Kade stiffened momentarily and then relaxed. He took a deep breath, held it for a moment, and then let it out. He cast a glance over his shoulder and found her innocent blue eyes watching him.

"I...can't say for sure," Kade said, not wanting to discuss the issue. "I don't know what I believe," he said quietly as he turned forward. It was obvious he did not want to discuss this any further as the silence dragged on, so she let it drop.

"Do you know anything about where Doren lives?" Darcienna asked, purposefully changing the subject.

"Not really," Kade responded, somewhat relieved.

"I think it's time we move a bit faster," Kade said as he urged the dragon to increase speed. Rayden was more than okay with a faster pace now as he lowered his head and took off.

The sun had been down for hours as they came to the base of a small mountain. Kade looked up at the double moons as he pondered the information that he had received from the book. Yes, this was the perfect place to stop. They were getting close so it was a good time to rest and prepare. He wanted to be sharp when he met another Chosen for the first time.

Kade brought the dragon to a stop and slid to the ground. Not quite as graceful as he wanted, but he did not fall flat on his face, as he feared he might. Long rides like this tended to make his legs go numb. He turned, ready to catch Darcienna. She was more stable than he expected, needing only a little support, although she did not walk as upright as she normally did. He was sure she would need to work out some of the kinks in her back and deal with the bruises on her bottom.

"We should rest for a little while before we go," Kade said, squatting down to flex his legs.

"Agreed. And some food and warmth might be nice."

"The food I can do," Kade said as he felt the dragon focus on him. He had to figure out a way to feed the dragon more efficiently. Conjuring one piece at a time was getting to be too tedious.

"And the fire?" Darcienna asked.

"I don't want to take the chance that we may be seen. If he were to see the light…," Kade said and let the thought trail off.

"Well, as long as I have some way to keep warm," Darcienna said, giving him a smile.

"It's time for me to start making food," Kade said as he focused his mind and stood up slowly, still aching from the ride.

Kade went through the ritual, forcing himself to keep his mind on task at every step. He created ten pieces without issue so he decided to continue. He felt good that his mind had not wandered as he continued. Rayden was also very pleased with the extra pieces of meat. Kade patted the dragon on the neck and pushed him away, signaling that the feeding was finished. The dragon moved off a short distance and then dropped down heavily.

Kade made two pieces of meat and handed them both to Darcienna. Next, he made a loaf of bread and handed that to her, also. And finally, he made a chunk of cheese. He sat down next to her, and after several exchanges back and forth, they both had their three course meal. Kade enjoyed the flavors as he swallowed the juice from the meat.

"It is getting a little chilly out, don't you think?" Darcienna asked, hinting at him to share some of his body heat with her.

"Here, take this," Kade said as he pulled an extra shirt out of his sack. "This should help keep you warm."

"Thank you," Darcienna said, shaking her head and breathing a sigh. *Why do men have to be hit over the head with the obvious before they see it?* she asked herself. "I think I will look around for a torok tree. Some wine would be perfect with the rest of this bread and cheese," she said as she rose and turned to go.

"I think you should stay here with the dragon while I go," Kade said. She put her hand on his chest and held him still.

"You finish eating. I will be close. If I need anything, I will call to you. I won't be far," Darcienna said as she pushed him back to the log they were using as a seat. "And besides, I do need just a little time alone," Darcienna said as she turned to go. Her meaning was not lost on him.

"Just stay close," Kade called after her.

Darcienna moved off through the woods on what looked like a very lightly travelled path. She continued to walk, looking over her shoulder every now and then to ensure she had not gone too far. Although she could no longer see the dragon or Kade, she was certain she was within screaming distance. It could not have been more than ten minutes when she spotted the tree she was looking for. It was several strides off the path to the right. She felt herself start to salivate at the thought of wine as she walked up to the tree and reached for one of the lower leaves. She twisted and broke it free of its stem. A small shadow the size of a mouse drifted from a bush behind her to a similar bush just a little closer. Darcienna reached for another leaf and pulled, but it ripped. She huffed in frustration, and again, missed the shadow that was half her size as it moved just ten feet off to her side. It disappeared into another bush. Her eyes glowed softly. She glanced to her right at the bush for several seconds and then went back to reaching for another leaf.

So intent on removing the leaf from the tree, Darcienna missed the faint warning. She twisted and turned, trying to get a better position on the branch as it fought to keep its leaf. She gritted her teeth, trying her best not to tear this one and did not see as the shadow glided ghostlike behind her. It began to grow. She froze as her eyes began to blaze brighter and brighter by the moment. Her heart started to pound, and her eyes came open wide as she listened, hardly breathing. There was not a sound, and yet, the feeling of danger was increasing by the second.

The shadow was now her height and growing, still. Its arms were as thick as her waist and its legs were like tree trunks. She was torn between calling out and remaining silent. She listened hard but heard nothing. If she stayed quiet, the danger may pass, but if she called out, it would surely be on her instantly. She told herself to move as the leaves slipped from her hand, all but forgotten. The face formed and the eyes shown as it grinned down on its prey. Her eyes blazed. *Run!* She screamed at herself, but by this time, she was petrified with fear. Just call out, she begged herself, but she was hardly able to breath much less call for help. The fear of being alone and away from the dragon and Kade in the dark with this ever increasing danger paralyzed her. She was certain that if she took a step, her knees would buckle. A tear seeped out of the corner of her eye as she tried to call out, but it was no more than a whisper. She could feel its presence behind her as her warning of danger flared even brighter in her mind. The fear in her was so profound now that she almost welcomed death just to escape it. Almost.

"Darcienna, you are taking a long time," Kade said as he called out to her. Unfortunately, there was to be no response.

The creature was completely formed. It smoothly reached around her with both hands, clamping one over her mouth while smoothly lifting her off the ground with the other in a grip like granite. The more she struggled, the more she felt herself bruising. She was sure she was going to have a broken nose. She tried to press her head back away from such tremendous pressure, but her head was already against its chest. There was no getting away from the grip that felt as hard as rock.

"You are taking too long," Kade called out. There was no reply. Kade tried to put it off to her needing that private time, but it was not working. "Darcienna," Kade said as he got to his feet and started to walk in the direction she had gone. He stopped and looked further down the path as something caught his attention. His pulse started to increase as he studied the dark. He watched closely for any movement. "Darcienna," Kade called out again. He was looking forward to giving her a tongue lashing for making him worry like this.

Kade looked at the dragon to see if it was sensing anything, but Rayden showed no signs of concern as he was lying calmly, licking the juices off his front legs. The fact that Rayden was not acting as if there was any danger was comforting, but still, why was she taking so long? Kade went along the path she had walked, listening intently for any sound as he searched the dark.

Looking back and forth as he listened closely for any sound, Kade could not find even a hint of her. As he moved along the path, he spotted a torok tree off to his right. He listened carefully as he worked his way toward the tree, his gut instinct warning him over and over that something was not right. He approached the tree and stood completely still, scanning the area. He was barely breathing as he listened for any sound of her. There was nothing. His chest started to tighten as worry started to make his heart pound. He turned to go when he stepped on something that flexed slightly under his foot and then gave a soft pop. He lifted his foot and saw that he had crushed a leaf from the tree. There, next to it was another one. Two intact leaves and one ripped leaf.

Exactly two good leaves that could have been used to hold wine, Kade thought to himself and could no longer convince himself that everything was ok. He quickly returned to the dragon.

Rayden, Kade sent as his head started to spin. *Darcienna is missing. Can you sense her? Can you sense anything at all?*

Rayden inhaled deeply several times. He swung his head around to look at Kade, not sensing anything out of the ordinary. He sat back on his haunches and then stood up on his hind legs, using his tail for balance. Kade estimated that the dragon must have stood thirty feet at the top of its head. He looked up, surprised.

There was something in the link now. Rayden came back down with a thud as his head swung around to stare at Kade. There was now fire in its eyes and its muscles were tense as if ready for battle. Kade's heart pumped hard. Rayden turned and then headed toward the path. Kade was more than eager to follow, certain the dragon was on the trail of something.

"What do you see?" Kade asked.

He felt the dragon in his head and realized it was trying to show him something. He closed his eyes and did his best to open his mind. The image of a large, hulking creature lumbering toward the mountain with Darcienna held tightly to its chest flashed in his mind. He gasped.

"They have her!" Kade exclaimed.

He grabbed the sack of books and was about to swing them up onto the dragon when he stopped, setting the bag back down. Carefully reaching into the sack, he pulled the black book out and tucked it into the back of his pants. He signaled Rayden to kneel and pulled himself up, quickly tying the books into place. Kade performed the Silence Calling and then the Transparency Calling as his pulse started to race. Dragon and rider faded from view, and Kade signaled the dragon to go.

Rayden moved along the path, knocking branches out of the way as he traveled. The trail opened to a hillside where the landscape thinned. Kade could see the creature now with Darcienna held fast and yearned to send the Divine Power crashing into it.

Just put her down, Kade thought as he fought the urge to blast it in the back.

He watched closely, hoping to see Darcienna move. He focused on the limp form, desperate for a sign that would indicate she was still alive, but she hung limp in the creatures grasp as it moved methodically. It did not matter if it was up hill or downhill, it walked at the same steady pace as though gravity nor the steepness of the grade had any effect on it.

Kade rubbed his eyes, sure they were playing tricks on him. Or, maybe it was the lack of light, but he was sure there were two smaller creatures trailing the other one, now. Where had they come from? He turned away and rubbed his eyes once more, but when he looked back, sure enough, there were definitely three of them. Kade could feel the ground shake as their heavy footsteps thudded with each time their feet hit the ground. They marched in perfect step with each other as if something or someone were calling cadence. Kade could feel the vibrations, even from this distance.

He heard a sound so faint that he almost missed it. He paused, hoping he was wrong about what it might be. For just a moment, he could have sworn it was the sound of laughter.

Morg? But, if it was Morg, wouldn't he just come for me? He asked himself. His jaw hit the ground, and his eyes came open wide as the sound drifted to him once more.

One of the trailing creatures turned slowly to look back, and then just as slowly, turned to face forward. Something about the way it moved concerned him, but he was not able to say why. He continued on, watching for an opening, hoping he could swoop in and grab her, but they did not show any signs of stopping or releasing their grip on their captive. She was a ragdoll in their hands.

Kade kept his eyes on the creatures as they trudged up the

mountain…or maybe it was more accurate to call them huge, rolling hills. The creature in the back and to the right would look behind itself every few minutes. It gave Kade a bad feeling but he continued, regardless.

What could it be looking for? Kade questioned as he studied the three figures. *It cannot see or hear me, and I am too far back for them to catch my scent, so what could it be looking at?*

They gave no other indication that they knew they were being followed except for that glance back. *Maybe it was just their way of watching for me to make sure I was not following. Yes, that makes more sense*, Kade thought.

Rayden had to work his way around rocks here and there but nothing that hindered their travel. Kade continued to close the gap. Again, one would turn and look back, giving him the eerie feeling that they were looking right at him, watching him as if they knew exactly where he was.

The creatures crested the top of the hill and continued in their methodical march. As Kade closed the gap, he could see light in the distance. He came to a stop and listened. Sure enough, there was laughter again. He prepared to signal the dragon to continue when a movement off to his right caught his attention. His head whipped around, but there was absolutely nothing. If there had been something, he definitely would have seen it. Rocks, mounds of dirt and a few sparse shrubs here and there were all that littered the hillside. Something was nagging at him, but nothing seemed out of place. He closed his eyed and used the Reveal Calling, but yet again, nothing. He continued to stare for several long moments and then refocused his attention on the sound coming from over the hill.

"Let's keep moving," Kade said.

Rayden stalked forward carefully, as if hunting prey. Kade glanced back several times but never saw more than the empty field. The feeling of being watched crept over him and continued to grow, but after surveying the hillside closely one more time, he put it off to nerves. It was impossible for anyone to see him unless they were using the Divine, and if someone were using the Divine, he would know. He reached up and felt for the medallion. It was not warm or cool. It was just as it should be.

Kade worked his way over the hill and slowly peered around at the landscape. The area opened up into a vast valley with a mansion on the far side that could house twenty people comfortably. There were some large rocks and boulders he was able to use for cover. Kade was grateful for the cover as he watched the three creatures walk up the front steps and dropped Darcienna's body on the porch. She was still not moving. All three creatures turned to stare directly at him. Even at this distance, he was certain they were looking right at him. He did not need glowing eyes to know that something was just not right here.

Kade brought the dragon to a stop and slid down. He moved forward to crawl over a rock and then leaned on a boulder that came up to just past his waist. He watched. If he was able to see the dragon, he may have had a little warning of the danger as the dragon sniffed the ground several times, showing signs of agitation. Kade looked on as the laughter from the house erupted again. He recognized the sound of that voice instantly. He could not shake the distinct feeling that the laughter was aimed at him.

As he was searching for a way to approach the house, the front door flung open, and a man carrying a staff walked out with the most confident stride. Even if Kade had not recognized the voice, the arrogance that the man exuded would have easily identified who he was. The close-cut salt and pepper beard that was visible from where Kade hid. The man's presence alone made his six foot height seem more like nine feet tall. He walked as if he had absolutely nothing to fear and was now coming out to collect his prize. The man looked in Kade's direction and bellowed out a laugh that echoed down the mountain. Kade got the definite sense that he was fooling no one. He considered striking, hoping he still had some advantage he could use. Just as he was formulating his plan, he saw the moonlight glint off something spherical around the man with the staff. He realized in a

231

rush why his Lightning Calling did not finish off Morg back in Arden. The man was protected with a calling. Now, Kade felt fear, and it was as if a hand were wrapped around his heart, squeezing tighter and tighter by the moment.

The evil Chosen descended the steps as though he had not a care in the world. Kade wished more than anything that he could open the ground and have the man swallowed up, or call on the wind to sweep him away, but he had nothing. Nothing he could do would go through a shield that was made to protect from attack. His mind raced as he searched frantically for a plan. Morg took long strides directly toward him as if he had nothing to fear. He was a man that walked with purpose, a man who had nothing to fear. His arrogance made him an imposing figure that would have intimidated even the bravest of warriors. He exuded danger. The look in his eye was that of a killer through and through. This was not a man that ever found himself on the losing end of a battle.

Kade watched in horror as Morg marched directly at him with the larger creature in tow, stopping just fifty feet away. He raised his staff and Kade could see the muscles ripple in his forearms as he aimed the ancient artifact at him. Morg turned and half looked over his shoulder as he addressed the creatures. Kade could have sworn they were a solid lump in one instant, but in the next, they were humanoid in shape.

"Here?" Morg asked.

Kade looked around as a slight vibration came through the boulder he was leaning on. He quickly looked behind himself, but not a thing moved. Something made the ground shake, but what? Kade closed his eyes again and used the Reveal Calling. There was nothing except the man with the staff glowing with the Divine. His inner voice was screaming at him of danger, causing his mind to frantically search for what he was missing.

Kade glanced at the ground between himself and Morg, looking for a way to set it on fire, but there was nothing to sustain a flame. His mind started to race as he felt the vibration again. The creature spoke in a gravelly voice. Kade was not able to make out what was said, but Morg rolled his head back and laughed uproariously.

The dragon huffed several times, eager to attack, but Kade knew that his precious friend would not fare well against the power Morg was capable of wielding. He compelled Rayden to stand down. He thought back on their first encounter in Arden and shivered. Such power was unfathomable. Kade narrowed his eyes and tried to get a good look at the staff. Was that the reason Morg seemed to wield so much power? Kade felt he was onto something when a strong vibration ran through the boulder. He looked around at all the boulders and felt his heart start to pound. Just as he was about to stand up, the boulder he was leaning on shifted. He stumbled slightly as he pushed away. Something grabbed him from behind and lifted him into the air effortlessly.

Kade gritted his teeth under the pressure and twisted to look over his shoulder. At first, he was sure he was looking at nothing more than a rock until eyes appeared from slits, and a mouth formed from a crack. The creature squeezed, and Kade felt the air rush out of his lungs. He pounded at the arms, but all he got from it were bruised hands. An invisible force slammed into the creature, sending it sprawling. Kade was able to get a breath but then the pressure started again. The unseen dragon attacked mercilessly. Cracks formed in the arm holding Kade, and the creature let out a deep moan.

The dragon assailed the creature over and over to the point where Kade was sure he was going to take some of the brunt of the dragon's rage. Other creatures formed as if being made from the ground itself. Kade felt the dragon's breath in his face as it latched onto the creature's arm and violently pulled. The arm cracked and then shattered, dropping Kade to the ground. Fresh air raced in to fill his lungs. He lay on the ground, gasping for breath.

Kade felt his mind start to clear with every breath he took. The sound of laughter filled his ears. Kade looked up slowly and saw Morg laughing as if this were the most amusing thing ever.

Something in him snapped. A blackness so complete filled his heart that all semblance of rational thought evaporated. The Divine filled him so completely that nothing else existed except his target. Revenge burned in him like a wildfire. Justice be damned, he wanted revenge. He spun and launched into the thirteen moves, sending the lightning blazing over the ground. One of the earth creatures was caught in its path and exploded in a shower of rocks and dust.

Morg laughed a taunt at the invisible Chosen. Kade turned on him and sent a bolt ripping toward him with a thunderous crash that blackened the ground as it raced toward its target. The man staggered back, his eyes wide as the sphere shimmered and flashed but then stabilized. Kade hit him again with another thunderous blast and Morg was no longer laughing. He was knocked off his feet and down on all fours. He looked up and saw there was a trench ten feet long where the sphere had been pushed back as it dug in.

The earth creatures came at him in waves. He spun as the Divine coursed through him like a raging current. Nothing but hate filled him as he launched blast after blast at the creatures until the area was filled with debris. There was a constant shower of stone and dust as he continued to dance. All creatures between him and Morg destroyed, he snarled as he spun on the evil Chosen. Kade let the Divine blend with his fury. Again, he attacked over and over as he advanced on the evil Chosen. Morg barely had time to regain his balance before another violent assault from Kade would send him reeling. Kade felt power flowing through him beyond his wildest dreams as he danced and let fly his attacks. The shield shimmered and flashed. Kade opened himself up fully as he pulled the Divine into him and gave himself over to its unending power. The shield had to have its limits and Kade was determined to find what they were. Morg held the staff up in a death grip as he glanced behind himself. There was sweat on his forehead as he strained against the rage with which Kade was filled. Was he looking for retreat amidst the onslaught of this Divine Apprentice? Kade's gift was all consuming and unlimited power. His lips peeled back as he put every bit of sheer willpower into this next attack. The air crackled with power as the lightning bolt came to life, and he launched. But...for some reason his conscious mind could not grasp...he sent the bolt wide and it glanced off the shield, shooting up to disappear in the heavens. Kade stood, breathing hard as his mind struggled to understand what he was seeing.

He felt the blood drain from his face as he stood in shock. His gut twisted in such a tight knot that he thought he might get sick. The power slowly faded from him till he stood empty, his hand still outstretched from releasing his last calling. He looked at the limp form of Darcienna while she hung in the air between himself and Morg. The evil Chosen had his staff aimed forward, holding Darcienna in the air. Kade felt vile hatred for the man. He desperately wanted to make Morg suffer horribly for this evil trick. This was the most profound hate a man could feel. This was not a hate that was fueled by the rush of unthinking actions or emotions that sent him out of control. This was the most dangerous kind of hate. This was a hate that was felt during calm, a hate that comes from the heart, the kind of hate that can eat a man's soul.

Kade saw the blood trickling from her split lip. He ground his teeth, struggling to control his anger. He needed to think. He looked around and saw that there was a wall of walking rock quickly closing in on him.

"I knew you could be reasonable," Morg said in an overly exaggerated manner of civility. His voice was deep and commanding.

Kade wanted nothing more than to run to Darcienna and take her in his arms. He desperately wanted to save her and whisk her away to somewhere, anywhere that she did not have to be in danger. He yearned to heal her and see those beautiful eyes looking at him again. His heart ached for failing to protect her. It did not matter that she wanted to go off on her own. He knew better and should have made sure she was safe. It was his fault. The guilt was crushing. The despair was so thick he could taste it.

Kade knew that somehow he had to think his way through

this. "There is always a solution to every problem," Zayle used to say. *What is the solution to this one?* Kade asked himself. He thought back on Morg when he had first came out of the mansion. Morg was not able to see him but the earth creatures were. How? And then it hit him.

Rayden, they are closing in. They can sense movement. You need to stay clear of them and move as carefully as possible, as though you are on the hunt. You must make sure not to disturb the ground, Kade thought frantically. *You must go now! Don't argue! I will call to you when I need. Now! Go!*

Rayden turned and ran toward the advancing creatures. They braced, sensing his position as he moved. He leapt high over them to land on the other side. The creatures spun as one and moved toward the dragon.

If they sense you, then do your best to keep them busy while I figure this out, Kade sent to the dragon. Rayden roared a challenge, but Kade was the only one who heard. He turned back to Morg and continued to work on formulating a plan. There had to be a way out of this.

"Come now, Kade. It is Kade that I am speaking to, is it not?" Morg asked as he waited for a response. After several seconds, he sighed and continued. "You can't stay invisible forever. I know you are still there. You see, my earth creatures have told me you are still there, so you might as well come out. Come now. Show yourself so we can talk like normal, civilized men," Morg said. Kade even thought that Morg actually sounded sincere. He wondered if the man might actually be stark raving mad. He genuinely sounded like he believed what he was saying. "You do want to heal her, don't you?" Morg asked in all sincerity. He was incredibly convincing.

"You mean man to rat," Kade said as he released the Silence Calling. He knew Morg had him, and besides, he couldn't just leave Darcienna.

"At least we are making progress," Morg said as he smiled. "Oh, by the way, in case you did not notice, your woman is in need of healing. I suggest you comply with my requests or she may die of her injuries," he said as he looked at her with mock concern. It was so convincing that Kade had to remind himself of who it was he faced. This man cared for nothing but achieving his own goal, even if it meant her dying. Morg brought the staff to his side and let the butt end of it thud on the ground. Darcienna fell in a heap and moaned from the jarring impact. "She probably won't last much longer," Morg said as he looked down on her, feigning concern.

"I will trade myself for her."

"Oh, of course," Morg said in his most reassuring voice. He acted shocked that Kade would think he might do anything other than let her go.

"Move these creatures away and I will come out," Kade said.

"That is one option," Morg said, pretending to consider Kade's words. "But, I would rather have you remove your Transparency Calling first, then I will have them move out of your way," Morg said as if that was the most obvious course of action.

Just before letting the calling dissipate, he quickly removed the amulet and shoved it deep into his boot. He took a deep breath and then let the calling fade while making sure to keep the dragon cloaked. He looked back to see that many of the earth creatures appeared to be disorganized. They seemed to be wandering around aimlessly. What they were really doing was trying to get a sense of where the dragon was. Kade was grateful that at least something was going right.

Morg grinned. Kade saw the smile and felt like a mouse that had just been cornered by a cat. He swallowed hard as he tried his best to convince himself he was not scared, but he was failing miserably. He forced himself to breathe as Zayle had taught him. It was supposed to help him stay calm. He met Morg's gaze and made himself keep it. Morg slowly raised the staff and pointed the head of it at his target as a grin crept across his face. Kade felt a net of power descend on him. To his horror, he no longer had control of his body. He could barely breathe. He did his best to glare, but his mind was

237

struggling to stay in control as panic made his heart pound hard. Everything was falling apart. All he had left was the dragon and the few meager callings that could be done without the use of his hands. But, he was not about to call the dragon only to watch it die. Rayden might make the difference between if he could just figure out a way to use him at the right time.

"Now," Morg said, all pretenses of pleasantries gone. "I said come to me," he said with a hiss, anger in his voice. He was pure malevolence.

Kade felt his body lurch forward. He clenched his jaw as he fought the compulsion, but at best, he was only able to hesitate momentarily. His body stopped next to Darcienna. Morg was playing with him, teasing him, making him look down on her to make him suffer. Kade knew there was no chance that Morg was going to honor his word.

"Oh, when I said you could heal your little trollop, I lied. I changed my mind about something else, also. I believe I am going to keep you both for myself. I may even take that pretty little thing for my own…if she lives. She may not," Morg said as he feigned sadness while he studied her. His mood seemed to change with the wind.

Morg turned and headed toward the house with his captive stumbling along. Just as Kade started to move, he noticed that Darcienna's hands had fallen in such a way that both palms were facing upward. It was only a moment, and then his focus returned to the evil Chosen.

Morg whistled the entire time as he walked the distance to the mansion. He climbed the steps and marched over to the larger earth being, looking up at it. Kade was sure he could sense hatred from it, but that rock-face was hard to read.

"Now for that amulet," Morg said as he pulled Kade's shirt open. His eyes turned to steel as he bore into Kade's head. "Where...is...it?"

"I don't know what you are talking about," Kade feigned, knowing this was going to bring him pain. Morg opened his mouth, but before he could speak a word, his eyes whipped around to scan the field. "Where is the dragon?" Morg asked calmly but there was a danger underlying his tone.

Before Kade could offer another lie, Rock-face growled. Kade even got the impression that the creature wanted to take a threatening step forward but held its place. Rock-face said something that Kade could not make out. A vein started to pulse in Morg's neck. He glared at Rock-face and turned on Kade. The apprentice could see lines of anger creasing his face. Kade was afraid and there was no way he could convince himself otherwise. Morg walked up to stand nose to nose with the Apprentice Chosen. The evil Chosen looked Kade directly in the eye and enunciated each word as he spoke.

"Where…is…your…dragon?" Morg asked in anger, spittle flying in Kade's face.

Before Kade could offer his lie, the earth creatures found Rayden and were converging on him quickly. One of them went down as the dragon charged it. Morg's head whipped around and the staff came up. Morg snarled a word and the ancient piece of wood jumped. One of the earth creatures exploded. Morg fired wildly and several more of them went down. The large one on the porch roared as it charged the evil Chosen. Its footsteps echoed off the wood as it closed the distance. Kade waited for its feet to crash through the boards as it thundered toward Morg. Each step shook the entire mansion. Morg stopped his assault and turned to glare at Rock-face as it leaned down to glare into his eyes. There was obviously a contest of wills going on as they peered hard at each other.

"Just be glad it was not you," Morg said as he gripped the staff tighter.

Rock-face stood his ground for several long seconds. The air was thick with tension. Kade took pleasure in the nervous twitch that had developed in Morg's left eye. Kade was certain that the two were about to come to blows any second and prayed for it to happen. Before the creature could move any further, Kade could feel the Divine flowing strongly. He could almost see bands forming around the creature as the Chosen concentrated. Morg's grip on the staff tightened and the bands constricted, sinking into the creature. It snarled and then stood up slowly. It walked out into the field with the two smaller ones in tow. The three picked up the pieces of their fallen comrades and seemed to melt into the ground. After a few seconds, they all melted into the ground and the field was empty.

"Nifty little calling," Morg said with a chuckle. "Not quite the same as the one on you. Oh no. That one I used on them works on their will. It binds them to do my bidding," he said as his lip curled in contempt as another thought occurred to him. "They don't mind when they die in battle. But to die outside of battle is dishonorable," Morg said as though he and Kade were having a friendly chat. "Does that make any sense?" Morg asked as if he truly wanted an answer.

Kade, still paralyzed, was unable to answer. Morg seemed to take offense at Kade's refusal to answer and swung the heavy staff like a club, hitting him in the back of the head. Kade fell forward, his ears ringing furiously. His body stood up and waited. If it were up to him, he would still be on all fours, unable to think, let alone stand.

"That's right. You can't talk can you? How rude of me. Here," Morg said as he aimed the staff at Kade. The Apprentice Chosen's mouth went slack and his head sagged forward. "By the way, don't be surprised when your muscles start to hurt. This calling is not very good for the body," Morg said as he wrinkled his nose.

"They will turn on you," Kade said weakly, his head still spinning.

"That will be the first and last time that they ever do, then," Morg said as he considered the field, the dragon all but forgotten.

Morg turned toward the house to go in and stopped. He turned toward Kade as he narrowed his eyes. Kade trembled inside as Morg studied him.

"You're not one of those people, who like to talk nonstop, are you? Morg asked as if this was truly important. Kade stared, speechless, sure he was looking at a madman. "Okay, I take that as a no. Good," he said as he turned and went into the mansion.

240

"Why?" Kade asked as they walked into a den. There were hundreds of books on shelves that lined the walls.

"Why what?" Morg asked as he walked over to the most plush leather chair Kade had ever seen and turned as if ready to sit. He stood there on the verge of sitting and paused. He waited for Kade's answer while his eyes searched for something in one of the cabinets along the wall. "Why do I ask if you talk too much?" he asked, his eyebrows raised as he continued to scan.

"Why keep me alive?" Kade asked, his head much clearer now.

Morg turned toward him, unbelieving of what he was hearing. He watched Kade for several seconds, trying to figure out if the Apprentice Chosen was playing some practical joke on him. Realizing that Kade was being sincere, he started to laugh, and when he was about to stop, started to laugh all over again.

"Mind explaining?" Kade asked, still standing ridged just inside the doorway.

Morg found this incredibly amusing, and it was starting to grate on Kade's nerves. His fear was easing the more they talked. There was something important going on here and Kade intended to figure it out. If he could just keep Morg talking, then maybe, just maybe, he could learn something he could use. How he was going to get out of this was unknown, yet, but at least he was not dead, nor did it appear that Morg intended to kill him anytime soon.

"You really don't know. That's incredible. He never told you," Morg said as he put the staff in the crook of his arm. He pulled a bottle off a shelf and poured the liquid into two separate glasses. Kade was certain that Morg was talking more to himself than to him. "I guess it couldn't hurt," he said as he walked up to Kade with the glass held out for him.

Morg seemed confused for a moment and then it occurred to him why Kade was not taking the offered drink. He set the drink down on a table next to the only other chair in the room and put his hand on the staff. He motioned for Kade to sit. Kade's body lurched to the chair and sat. Morg waived the staff absentmindedly toward him. His right arm fell to his side. Kade flexed his fingers and tried to reach for the glass. His arm moved in a jerky motion. Kade flexed his muscles hard several times until they felt right and then tried again. He casually took the glass as though he had nothing to fear and lifted it to his lips, taking a sip. He was surprised at the smooth tasting spirits and felt it working its way down to his stomach.

"You will find out anyway," Morg said as he took a drink from his glass. He smiled, appreciating the potency of the ale. He closed his eyes as he savored the flavor and then exhaled as if preparing to tell a long story. "Have you ever wondered about the almighty Great Divine?" Morg asked as he tilted his head to the side in thought as he studied Kade. "You have," Morg said as though Kade had answered. "Good. I'll explain a few things. You see, a long time ago there were only a hand full of people, the original Ancients, who had learned the laws of the Divine and kept it all for themselves. It took them centuries to discover its secrets, but once they were able to tap into the Divine, they devoted themselves to learning everything about it. They learned the language, the gestures, they learned it all. Their thirst for knowledge was unequaled. They even made this," Morg said as he looked lovingly at the staff that he held in his right hand. "They had so much power it was incomprehensible."

Kade felt his mind reeling as he tried to absorb all that Morg was telling him. As crazy as Kade was sure this man was, he was just as certain that Morg believed everything he was saying. Kade was hanging on every word, eager to learn what part he played in this. He took another drink from his glass and closed his eyes to give himself time to think. Morg assumed he was savoring the drink as he, himself, had just done and smiled. But, what he did not know was that Kade was hiding the eager look in his eye as he soaked up every word. Kade was also grateful for the drink as it soothed his nerves.

"Many think that the Ancients invented the whole damn thing, but the fact is they only discovered it. Since they were the only ones who spoke it, they were known as the creators. But that part does not really matter," Morg said. He waived his glass through the air as if to dismiss the thought. "What does matter is that the Ancients knew some very powerful callings that have been lost in time," he said as he leaned forward to put emphasis on what he was saying.

"But, why all the talk about the Ancients? They have been dead for a long time," Kade said as he did his best to be casual while studying the staff.

"It has been rumored that they were able to create a link with the land of the dead," Morg explained as he rose from his seat excitedly. "I found something in a book in a Chosen's library that talked about how they were trying to live forever. It indicated that the only way to do this was to come back through an arch," Morg said as he recalled the book he had read.

If Morg had been paying closer attention, he may have seen Kade almost choke on his drink. Gripping the glass tightly in his hand, Kade forced himself to stay calm. Morg paced to the window as he formulated his thoughts. He was passionate and enthusiastic about this topic. Kade wondered momentarily if Morg had always been this evil, or if there was something that had triggered this behavior. For just a second, Kade could actually see Morg as a respected teacher, and then, he dismissed the thought. This was Morg. This was the most hated man on the planet. This was a man that Kade was going to make suffer.

"So, you think it is possible to communicate with the Ancients?" Kade asked, trying to sound casual. To his own ears, he sounded worried and nervous, so much so that he might as well have been screaming, "I know something," but Morg did not seem to notice.

"You do see!" Morg exclaimed excitedly as if Kade's question was a statement. "There is so much I could do with that knowledge," he said, smiling eagerly as if he were a child with a favorite toy. "But, they decided not teach what they know because they were worried that someone might use it for evil." He curled his lip in contempt. "Just think of all the evil I could rid from this world," he added as his eyes widened at the thought.

This time, Kade did choke on his drink. He gagged, trying to clear his airway of the alcohol. Morg flinched and looked at him with narrowed eyes. Kade wiped his mouth with the back of his hand and looked up at Morg.

"Too big a drink," Kade said quickly as he cleared his throat again.

"Of course," Morg said as he went back to pacing around the room while he lectured. "Anyway, there is supposed to be a passageway that allows the living to communicate with the dead. There is even speculation that the dead can cross over into the world of the living, if they can find a host. I believe they may even be waiting to cross back into our land, but they need something."

Kade, again, had to put every effort into hiding his shock. His mind raced as he recalled the presence that had tried to take over his body. Was that one of the ancients? Did he almost bring one of them back? Kade looked up to see Morg studying him and felt bats flutter dangerously in his stomach.

"You wouldn't happen to know where this doorway is would you?" Morg asked as he watched Kade closely.

"If I did, don't you think I would have talked with the Ancients already? And if I had, don't you think I would have used something against you?" Kade asked as he threw back the rest of his drink, trying to act casual.

"You do have a point," Morg said as he nodded his head. "The doorway is only part of the problem," he continued, satisfied with the answer. "The Ancients set it up so only they can pass from the land of the living to the land of the dead." He filled Kade's glass again. Kade felt as if everything was surrealistic. Morg was treating him as if they were good friends, but it was all an illusion. Sooner or later, Morg was going to turn back into the evil man Kade knew him to be.

"Then why do you need me?" Kade asked as he casually looked at Morg over his glass.

"I misspoke. Forgive me," Morg said as he tilted his head slightly while looking Kade in the eye. "What I meant to say," Morg said as he leaned forward to emphasize the point, "was... only the ancients and their...descendants are able to pass through the doorway," he said as he watched Kade for a reaction. Kade looked back, unsure where Morg was going with this. "You still don't get it?" Morg asked and then laughed.

"I understand that you are trying to talk to the Ancients," Kade said simply, his mind a little fuzzy from the drink. "And that you think I can help you with that. I am still at a loss as to why."

Kade stopped for a moment as he thought back on something Morg had said, something about ridding the world of evil. There had to be a reason why he had made that statement. Who did Morg think was evil, if not himself? Kade took a chance.

"Are you doing this for yourself or are you being given... direction?" Kade asked, trying to choose his words carefully.

In the short time he had known this man, Kade had rapidly come to the conclusion that Morg was easily enraged at the slightest insult and to imply he was taking orders from a higher power was sure to set him off. Morg was not one to accept being told what to do. Kade could see this as plainly as the staff that crashed into the table that had previously held his drink.

"They are not...," Morg started to say, red faced, and then paused.

Morg took a deep breath, let it out, and in the blink of an eye, was calm again as if he had never been angry. Yes, Morg was a very deadly man. The only thing that indicated that he had been angry at all was the slight color in his cheeks that was fading quickly.

"I think our chat has come to an end. It's time to take you to the one you came to see," Morg said as he swung the staff like a bat and smashed the glass from Kade's hand. The drink went flying. Kade felt his hand go numb and wondered if any of his fingers were broke. Any compassion he had started to feel evaporated instantly.

"Doren is still alive?" Kade asked, not reacting to Morg's

outburst. He also ignored his throbbing hand. Morg was watching him for a reaction, and when Kade showed none, he scoffed and continued.

"I thought I might need him as bait in the event that you discovered the Alluvium."

"Alluvium?" Kade asked.

"You met them in the field," Morg said, watching to see that Kade understood. "Looks like I gave you too much credit, didn't I? You were practically a fish waiting to jump into the barrel," he said with a smile.

"You weren't that difficult to beat back at Arden," Kade said, using Morg's own casual tone. Kade knew he should stop there but something in him just would not let it go. "And, your choice to use those shape shifters? An apprentice move if ever I saw one," Kade said casually as though he were the master and Morg were the student. He heard the sound of the staff being swung through the air for just an instant before feeling the crack on the back of his head. The world spun. Kade knew his comment was foolish but a part of him thoroughly felt it was well worth the clubbing he had just received. The floor seemed so much closer than he recalled. As his head cleared more and more, he realized he was on his hands and knees.

"I do hope you learn to control your tongue," Morg said, mocking the casual tone.

Morg sighed audibly as he reached down and gently helped Kade to his feet. He straightened Kade's shirt and even took the time to dust off his back. He smiled at the apprentice, pleased with himself and then guided his captive to the bookshelf. Morg waived his staff in front of it, and the bookshelf faded. Kade looked on in awe at the ghostly outline of the bookcase. Morg saw the look of awe on Kade's face and smiled.

"This way," Morg said as he motioned for Kade to follow.

Kade thought back on his master's study and the hidden bookcase there. He found it ironic that this Chosen, also, had something hidden behind his tomes of knowledge. He knew where not to hide his most sacred secrets when he became the master.

Following with jerky movements, Kade's body made its way down the stairs after Morg. His muscles started to ache. Kade was sure that at any moment he would plunge headlong down the fifty steps, but surprisingly, it never happened. The passage was ten feet wide with walls lined with large bricks. The steps were solid stone. Once at the bottom, Morg turned to face what appeared to be a blank wall.

"Doren was very clever with this one," Morg said. "I almost did not find it. If he had put just a little more thought into this, I would have never found him. But, who makes stairs that come all this way to end at a wall?" Morg asked as he pointed at the end of the long passageway. "So, all I needed to do was look for it," Morg said as he shook his head at the stupidity of the planning. Kade mentally shrugged and had to agree.

Kade noticed that there were some black scorch marks on the wall. There was also blood and hair where some unfortunate soul was caught at the wrong place and the wrong time. Kade took a breath and let it out, reminding himself that right now he needed to deal with his own issues. Morg saw the look on Kade's face and grinned.

"The Chosen had a few apprentices," Morg said in his casual tone. "That used to be one of them," he said and then chuckled.

Kade stood silently as Morg waited for a response. When he realized that Kade was not going to respond, he turned and walked straight through the wall. Kade stared, stunned. He knew he really should not be surprised, as it was basically the same thing he had seen with the bookcase. Kade's body started forward jerkily and walked right through the wall. He fought the instinct to hold his breath as his face approached the wall but he could not help but to squeeze his eyes shut. After taking two steps he opened his eyes to find himself in a lavish study.

Kade walked through, then let out his breath and sucked in another. There were several high-backed chairs that flared out to the

247

side near the head. They were facing away from the entrance with a low table in front of them. If someone were sitting in them, they would not be seen until someone was to walk around to the front. There was also a bookcase along the far wall. It was identical to the one upstairs, except, Kade was certain that this one held real books.

Morg casually walked around the corner of one of the high back chairs. He stopped and seemed to be studying something. Kade could feel his gut twist in a knot, certain of what to expect. Kade's body walked around the side of the chair and stopped. He looked down and saw a man that looked as old as Morg. He was not moving.

"If you are wondering whether he is alive or not, the answer is no," Morg said thoughtfully, as he studied the Chosen. Kade felt as if he were going to get sick. Exasperation spread through him and despair threatened to choke him.

"But, you said…" Kade started to say when Morg smoothly cut him off.

"I only said I was going to take you to him," Morg said as he considered. "I never said he was alive. I do wish I could take credit for killing him," he added as he sighed loudly. "But, I found him like this. He was too much of a coward to face me. I only wish he would have given me the chance to rip the life from his body." His temper flared and his face turned red as he snarled and shook. In the next instant, he was calm as if nothing had happened. "What I really needed was information that he had. It really does not matter since he was my last threat. I will just find that information elsewhere. I killed all the Chosen, including your master, Zayle," Morg said as he looked back at Kade. "I really did expect more from him. I thought he was going to be my toughest challenge," he said, studying Kade, waiting for a reaction.

Kade knew Morg was baiting him, but he could not hide his contempt. He felt hatred swirling in him like a whirlpool, and it was starting to spin faster and faster. He closed his eyes to control the rage that mixed with despair and failed miserably. He wanted to scream, but that would be giving Morg what he wanted. He opened his eyes and saw pleasure on the evil Chosen's face as he soaked up every last bit of Kade's misery. Kade took several deep breaths and forced his mind to let the anger fade. The calmer he became, the more the smile on Morg's face shrank. After just a minute, Morg shook his head in disappointment.

Kade felt his muscles move past discomfort as they started to throb. He was hoping it was because of the long walk down the stairs, but he recalled Morg's comment. The calling that was used on him was not good for the body and was most certainly the source of his pain. He did his best to ignore it, but it grew by the second. Morg was watching him, and a smile crept across his face.

"Might you be experiencing some of the side effects of the calling? Do your muscles hurt? All I need to do is let you go, and that would all disappear," Morg said. He lifted the staff as if he intended to use it and then paused in thought. "But, I don't think I can trust you," he continued, letting the staff thump back to the ground. "And don't think you are getting out of that calling anytime soon. As long as we are close to you, that calling will not fade," Morg said as he caressed the staff. The staff was the other half of the "we" that Morg was referring to. "I would suggest you not fight the compulsion. It speeds the process until the pain becomes excruciating. Soon after, your muscles will become damaged beyond repair. Shortly after that, you will beg me to kill you," he said with a grin.

For the first time in his life, Kade experienced a feeling that made him tremble inside. Helplessness. The mental anguish was almost too much to bear. Kade ground his teeth and squeezed his eyes shut tightly to hide his emotions. Morg fed on this. He knew that if he looked, Morg would be watching him with pleasure.

"I will not help you," Kade hissed.

"Now that is not very nice," Morg said as a devious smile crossed his face.

Morg aimed the staff at him. Kade's right arm was no longer his to control. The evil Chosen had ensnared Kade's entire body with the exception of his head. Kade's body lurched over to the table. He watched in horror as he placed his right hand flat on the surface while his left picked up a heavy, crystal decanter. He held it like a club high in the air. Just before he brought the club smashing down on his hand, Kade got an idea.

"So this is what it must feel like when you are told what to do like a dog," Kade said as the club started to descend. His arm jerked and the crystal decanter flew out of his grasp and shattered on the wall.

Kade could feel the rage coming off Morg in waves. The evil Chosen slowly circled him with his head tilted down while looking up at Kade through eyes that were almost squeezed shut in rage. His breathing was ragged as he leaned forward slowly. For the first time, Kade looked deep into his eyes. There was not even a hint of humanity in there. A fear so intense gripped him that his throat closed up tightly. A part of him wondered if it might not have been better to have a broken hand.

"If I thought I would not need you, I would rip your heart out and let you watch while it beat in my hands as your eyes glazed over in death," Morg hissed violently. "Oh how I do love to watch people suffer. For now, this should do," Morg said as he gripped his staff so tightly that his knuckles turned white. And then, he gripped it even harder.

Kade felt as if his entire body were being crushed in a massive grip. The air rushed out of his lungs. The force on his body was so intense that his vision blurred within seconds. He opened his mouth to scream, but all the air was already gone. Morg squeezed even harder, his arm shaking with the effort. The muscles on his forearm twitched rapidly. Morg clenched his teeth, and his lips parted as he shook. Kade felt his ribs creak. At any moment, they were going to start snapping one by one. Kade could not see, even though he knew his eyes were still open. And then, his body fell to the ground, air rushing in to fill his lungs.

Kade was breathing again, but it was not with a conscious

effort. His mind was numb, and it was almost impossible to think. The ground rocked as he struggled to hold his head up. A ringing sound echoed in his ears as the blood flowed through his brain again. The blackness started to fade, and the room came back into focus.

"Do we understand who the dog is now?" Morg hissed. He watched Kade for a response and was dumbfounded when the apprentice just stared at him. Such strength of character was just not possible. Somewhere deep in Morg, respect for this young man grew just a bit. He calmed down as he studied Kade. "You don't even know what I am going to ask of you. It can't hurt to listen, can it?" Morg asked. For a moment, Kade was certain that Morg was pleading with him.

Kade opened his mouth to make a sarcastic comment but immediately changed his mind. The crushing weight was still too fresh in his mind, and his ribs hurt furiously. He continued to stare at Morg without saying a word. Just as the evil Chosen was about to continue, something small and black winged its way into the room. Morg spun and raised the staff as if to blast the thing from the air.

"This had better be good," Morg growled. "I left explicit instructions not to be interrupted."

"They call you back, Master" the creature said in a rush as its eyes focused on the wavering staff.

Morg's head rocked back, and he took a deep breath as if he were about to scream in rage. Kade could see the veins in his neck start to bulge and pulse with every heartbeat. Morg turned and stalked away from the creature as he gripped the staff in both hands. He stopped, facing the far wall. Kade could see the muscles in his shoulders tense. He glanced at the creature that was still hovering in the air and cringed.

Too bad it was not smart enough to fly as fast as it could in any direction other than one where Morg was, Kade thought.

"I hate bad news!" Morg screamed as he spun with the staff held at his waist. He was holding it in both hands as if he were holding a battering ram. Morg spoke, the staff jumped, and the creature only had time to open its mouth before it exploded all over the room. Kade felt the slime of the creature splatter him and his stomach lurched. "Maybe, just maybe they will stop sending...," Morg started to say when he paused. He wiped a wet spot off his forehead as he clenched and unclenched his jaw over and over while he mulled something over. Morg's eyes regained their focus. He quickly turned, marched right up to Kade and glared at him.

"Remember that. I hate bad news," Morg said with force. Despite his effort not to, Kade felt himself shiver.

Morg paced the room, clearly at odds as an internal struggle raged. Kade was careful to stay neutral. He had had enough beatings for the day. Morg marched up to Kade, and looked down at him while trying to come to a decision. He turned, roaring his frustration as he swung the staff and shattered the table next to the high-back chair.

"As if they call me like I am their dog," Morg growled. His head whipped around to glare at Kade, and his lips parted in a snarl.

Kade cringed. He knew his beatings were not finished. Obviously, calling him a dog had struck home. The fact that he had just used Kade's own words without thinking enraged him. He charged Kade and swung his staff, hitting him in the back. Morg stepped back and then kicked him in the side so hard he actually lifted him off the ground. Kade wondered if that was two or three ribs he heard crack. He landed and spit up blood. Pain lanced through his body as his vision swam.

"Consider your options carefully," Morg said as he pounced on Kade and roughly pulled the apprentice's hands behind his back. "Let me rephrase that just in case you did not quite understand. You only have one option, and you had better decide to take it."

"And that option is to cooperate?" Kade gasped through the pain. He spit blood onto the floor to clear his mouth.

"See, you can learn," Morg said condescendingly.

Kade winced as his lungs protested painfully. Morg retrieved a rope from a sack on the floor and then returned to tie Kade's hands behind his back. Kade found a little relief in the fact that the bonds were not too tight. At least he did not have to worry that his hands might fall off from necrosis.

Morg stood and closed his eyes for several long moments while gripping the staff. There was a rumbling as something heavy came down the stairs. One of the Alluvium rounded the corner and came into the room.

"Watch him closely," Morg snarled. If anything happens to him, you will be dust," he threatened. The creature appeared to tense. Its fists come up slightly as if ready to fight. After a moment, they lowered. Morg sneered at the creature and then turned back to stand over Kade. "When I come back, you had better start making the right decisions," Morg said, glaring at the man on the floor. Kade definitely knew the threat was real. He did not think that Morg was going to have much more patience past what he had already had, if it could be called that.

The evil Chosen walked out of the room and was quickly gone. Kade lay on his side, trying to breathe, but it was difficult with the stabbing pain in his ribs. The Slave Calling started to fade almost immediately. He tried to reason his way out of this, but the agony made it almost impossible to think. His vision was blurry but not so much so that he would miss seeing another earth creature carry Darcienna into the room over its shoulder and drop her roughly onto the floor. It turned and both creatures walked through the wall. Kade cringed at the rough treatment.

Feeling too much pain to think clearly, he laid his head back down. A few seconds later he jumped at the touch of a hand on his side. The agony in his ribs melted away. The absence of pain was so profound that he felt like he could cry in relief. His vision slowly returned, and one of the most beautiful faces came into focus.

"Darcienna," Kade said, emotions choking his voice.

"Shhhhhh," she said as she put a finger to his lips. She whispered so quietly that he could barely hear. "I am sure they will be back shortly."

"You are not bound," Kade said incredulously.

"No," Darcienna said with a grin. Before Kade could ask, she answered his unspoken question. "They thought I was still out and they do not appear to be very bright. I am certain that Morg would have had me tied up if he did not race out of here so fast." *Another break*, Kade thought, mentally thanking fate for easing up on him. "And besides, they have no idea what I can do. They only see me as a helpless, little girl. How can they know any different?" she whispered with a grin.

"But, your eyes," Kade said.

"Not when they think I am out. My eyes were closed the entire time."

Darcienna worked at his bonds, and after just a small struggle, was able to finally remove them. Kade fell on his back. The memory of the damaged ribs was so vivid that he felt as if they were still broken. Darcienna leaned down and wrapped her arms around him, pulling him into her embrace. Kade melted at her touch. He looked over her shoulder at the dead Chosen and just stared until his eyes lost focus.

Kade let his mind wander as she continued to let her healing flow into him. The longer Morg was gone, the more his muscles became his again. His thinking cleared little by little and the pain in his body faded away. His focus returned, and he found himself looking at the Chosen once more. Kade narrowed his vision as he watched the man in the chair. He slowly pushed Darcienna away while keeping his eyes on the figure.

"Something about this is not right," Kade said as he spared a glance at Darcienna. She was watching him closely now.

"What is it?" Darcienna asked in a whisper.

"From what Zayle said about the Chosen, all the Chosen, I find it hard to believe that Doren would just give up," Kade said as he studied the lifeless body.

Kade got into a crouching position and then inched closer to the man in the chair. There was something out of place, but what was it? The more Kade studied the man, the more he was sure he was missing something.

"He can't be dead," Kade whispered to himself. "He just can't be," he added, shaking his head in confusion.

Darcienna moved closer as she, too, studied the Chosen. She looked at Kade as if trying to think, and then her head whipped back around to stare at the figure in the chair. Kade watched with excitement, waiting for her to reveal what she had just pieced together.

"Kade, do you see?" Darcienna asked as she stared at Doren.

"What?" Kade asked as he scanned the Chosen's face.

"He still has life in him," Darcienna responded, peering closely.

That is when it hit him. He could not be dead because he was not dead. His color was not quite the color of a living man, but it was not the ashen color of a dead man, either. Not that Kade really had much experience in seeing dead men, but this could not be what a dead man looked like. Kade glanced at Darcienna and smiled.

"I knew a Chosen would not just lie down and die," Kade said as he leaned a little closer to Darcienna.

Kade was certain he was onto something and closed his eyes. He used the Reveal Calling, but to his chagrin, he could see nothing. He tried again with similar results. Not willing to give up, he performed the Healing Calling and put his hands on the Chosen. The Divine sank in, but the man did not move. Kade tried again, and still, there was nothing.

"Can you bring him back?"

"I can try," Darcienna said as she laid her hands on him. After a few moments, she sat back with a look of exasperation.

"Darcienna?" Kade asked.

"I can't get to him, Kade. It's as if there is a wall in there. Maybe you can try something else. Kade, there has to be something. I can sense he is in there somewhere."

"I have an idea," Kade said as he quietly moved the table out of the way and laid down at the Chosen's feet.

"What are you doing?" Darcienna whispered.

"Going to find him," Kade said as he closed his eyes.

"Kade, I don't know what you are going to do, but whatever it is, be careful."

Kade closed his eyes and relaxed his body. He let every muscle melt, and then he called on the Divine to help carry his consciousness out. The Divine drifted in like a current and pulled him with it. He easily slid out of his body. He drifted over to the Chosen and merged with him. Kade sat in the chair as the Chosen had and felt contact.

"Doren, can you hear me?" Kade asked.

Kade watched as the room faded from view. He felt a momentary jolt of panic and considered breaking contact but then decided against it. This needed to work. He felt as if he were in a huge, empty space. There was nothing here, but somewhere off in the distance, he could feel a presence. He forced himself to go deeper, and it was as if he fell through the floor. Everything turned pitch black, and he plummeted. He got the uncomfortable feeling that this could be a one way ride as he continued to sink deeper and deeper. Kade called out but was met with silence as he continued to plunge downward. Falling in complete darkness was unnerving. He landed on what had to be the bottom and stood completely still, listening. There were no sounds of any kind. If not for hearing his own voice, he might have believed he was deaf.

"Doren!" Kade yelled. There was no response. "Dooorrrennnn!" he screamed again, but he was met with silence once more.

The emptiness was too unnerving. Kade decided that he had had enough of this dark pit and tried to climb back out. Nothing happened. Kade willed himself to ascend once more, but again, nothing happened. He started to get the feeling of being in a trap and cursed. A sound so faint echoed through the nothingness that Kade almost missed it. He froze, not even breathing, if that was what he was doing. There it was again. Kade moved toward the sound and it became louder.

"Who calls for the Great Master Chosen, Doren?" a voice demanded.

"My name is Kade," he said excitedly. After several long seconds of silence, he continued. "I was sent to find you by Master Chosen, Zayle."

"Zayle?" the voice asked cautiously.

"Yes. He was my teacher. He told me I needed to seek you out."

"I know who you are," the voice said with a sneer. "You are Morg. You cannot fool me, nor can you hurt me here," it said full of confidence.

"WAIT!" Kade screamed. "Why do you think me to be Morg?" Kade asked desperately.

"Why would I not? You can do almost anything with that bloody, cursed staff," the voice said.

The voice sounded as if it were directly in front of Kade. He was sure that if he reached out his hand, it would come in contact with a body. He strained to make out any shapes and failed. The darkness was getting to him. Kade felt claustrophobia setting in.

"Because, if I were Morg, I would be trying to kill you," Kade said in a rush.

"Morg could not resist the temptation to torture me for what I did to him," the voice countered.

"He really believes you are dead," Kade said, pleading.

"He would not leave me without making sure. I have information he needs," the voice said, but there was hesitancy in it.

"Well, he didn't check. He was too focused on me. For some reason, he needs me."

"Maybe. I know you have tried to escape from my little trap, and you may be saying anything to save yourself. If you are Morg, then there is no way out. You cannot leave my mind. I may have to sacrifice myself, but I will have beaten you again," the voice said in triumph.

"This is a trap?" Kade asked in panic.

"That depends," Doren said. Kade got the feeling he was being watched closely, even though he could see nothing.

"On what?"

"You still have not proven to me that you are not Morg."

"How can I do that?" Kade asked, trying to control his fear. This was a fully trained Master of the Divine. This was a Chosen. He was only an apprentice. If this man believed him to be Morg, his life was over.

"That is for you to figure out. I will not give you the answer."

"I'm not sure what I can do to convince you, so I am going to tell you what I know and some of what has happened recently," Kade said as he took a deep breath and prepared to tell the story. He paused for a moment, considering if it was air he had breathed in, or if he just thought it was air. He brushed aside the obscure thought and continued. "Before I start, I must tell you, Morg has been called back by something that seems to have a hold on him. He was furious, but he left."

Doren did not respond so Kade proceeded to tell the story from the first moment he met the dragon right up to this very instant. Doren only spoke to prompt him to continue. Kade intentionally left out the part about the arch in the tunnel in the event that this was a trick by Morg. He was fairly certain that Morg would not plan something this elaborate, but he had to be careful. Morg was too impulsive and irrational. This was too calculated.

"That was an interesting story. Too bad you will never get the chance to bow down before your master's feet like the dog you are," Doren said as he taunted him. "You were never any good at lying and you are still no good. You will die with me here, hound!" Doren raged. Kade panicked.

"NO! My name is Kade! You have to believe me!" he pleaded in desperation.

"I do,"

"I was sent by Zayle. You have to…," Kade was saying when

he stopped. His mind was spinning as he recalled those two words Doren had just spoken. "You do?" he asked, confused. "But I thought you just…," he started to say and then stopped.

"Morg could never stand to be told he was to answer to another as if he were a dog being called by his master. And, when you told me of that, it gave me an idea. Morg detested answering to anyone. If you were Morg, you would have been infuriated by me telling you to bow down before a master. That is his one true weakness. If you were Morg, you would have exploded with rage. And that, of course, would have ended your life," Doren said simply.

"You had me convinced," Kade said, wiping the imaginary sweat off his brow. "So, you can get us out of here? I left my friend, Darcienna, back in the room."

"Is she in danger right this moment? We need to talk, if possible."

"I think she is ok for the moment, but I would not want to leave her for long."

"Good. We have some things to discus, first. You did say that Morg was called away, correct?"

"Yes. He left."

"Excellent."

"Why is Morg so powerful?" Kade asked.

"You don't know?" Doren asked incredulously. "Have you seen a staff at all?"

"Yes."

"That staff allows him to perform any calling without having to mold the Divine with hand movements. The staff takes the place of that. It was created by the Ancients thousands of years ago. The symbols carved into the staff represent all the callings that that ancient artifact is imbued with. All one has to do to use the staff is be able to speak the Ancients' language. While holding the staff, you only need speak the ancient language, if it requires speech, picture the symbol for the calling, and the staff does the rest. It channels the Divine and does your bidding. We never knew this until recently. He always

259

kept the staff cloaked. He must be getting careless in his overconfidence," Doren said thoughtfully.

"He has reason to be overconfident," Kade said as he thought back on the crushing his body took. "How were you able to beat him the first time?"

"There were too many of us for him to fight at one time. We were not able to take that cursed staff from him, so we trapped him with it. We hoped our trap would hold him forever, but apparently he is stronger than we anticipated. Either that, or he had help, which is a strong possibility," Doren said thoughtfully.

"Why not kill him?"

"He was able to protect himself with a shield and a few other tricks. We were lucky to be able to trap him. We lost two Chosen in that fight, so we accepted what we could get," Doren said with a sigh.

"Is there no way to take the staff?"

"We have tried. Our only hope was to try to communicate with one of the Ancients and ask them how we could conquer such immense power. Enough talk about the staff," Doren said, waiving away the topic. "I need to think. Let me be for a moment while I figure out what we are going to do," Doren said as if talking to his own apprentices. Although Kade understood that Doren was the far more experienced one here, he found it difficult to return to the status of an apprentice who was ordered around as if he were a child.

"There is one other thing," Kade said, but Doren hushed him. Kade shook his head as he tried to wait patiently. "Doren, there is something else."

"Kade, did Zayle allow this kind of outburst from his apprentice?" Doren asked, irritation showing easily.

"No," Kade said meekly.

"Then please, do not shame him by doing so here. You are with me, now. Quiet until I say otherwise," Doren said as if there was clearly to be no arguing. Kade considered complying for a moment but only for a moment.

"I may not be a Master Chosen, but I will not be talked down to. You must listen to what I have to say," Kade said firmly.

Doren sat silently for quite some time. Kade was starting to think that Doren had left as the silence continued on. After what felt like forever, the Master Chosen finally spoke.

"I am listening," Doren said evenly, but Kade could hear the tone that said, "This better be important."

"There is one thing I neglected to tell you. I know where the doorway is that Morg seeks. I believe someone from the other side tried to communicate with me. Well, not tried, but did communicate with me. That is why I am here," Kade said as he did his best to remain calm.

"You know?" Doren asked, the darkness vanishing as the Chosen stepped forward. "Why didn't you tell me in the first place?"

"I thought you might be Morg trying to trick me."

"Wait a minute," Doren said as he digested Kade's words. "Did you say you had talked with the dead? Only the Ancients and their descendants can do that," Doren said in awe. "Kade, that means you are one of the descendants. We must hurry. If we went back to the doorway, do you think you could communicate with them again?"

"I'm not sure. I believe so, but things did not go that well the first time," Kade said, remembering the presence that tried to possess him. "And, I did not really talk to them. I just, more or less, was given a message to come see you."

"If that is all we have to work with, then it will have to do. You said there is only two earth creatures guarding the room?"

"Yes."

"Good. I can take care of them. I have lived here for many decades. I know them well," Doren said with confidence.

"Okay. I will do what I can. How are we going to get out of here?" Kade asked.

No sooner did he ask the question than he felt himself being propelled upwards at an amazing rate. Kade shot out of the Chosen's body and stopped at the ceiling. He looked down in shock to see the earth creature nudging him and then drawing its foot back to really kick him hard. He quickly descended into his body and opened his eyes.

"I don't think Morg is going to be very pleased if you do that," Kade said in a snarl. It froze, its foot still drawn back.

Kade looked past it and saw Doren open his eyes just a crack. The earth creature looked at Kade's hands and tensed. Seeing they were no longer bound, it reached for him. Kade scrambled back and the creature pursued. The second creature came from behind the chair and quickly cornered Kade. Doren stood smoothly without making a sound and completed several gestures with his hands. Both creatures fell to dust.

"What did you do to them?" Kade asked as he looked down at the pile of dust. He gave it a symbolic kick, sending dust floating into the air.

"I made them revert back to their natural form. They are part of the ground. They will recover but not until long after we are gone. They will suffer greatly when Morg returns," Doren said matter-of-factly. "I had lived in peace with them for decades, but I made certain that I could always defend against them thanks to Zayle's warnings."

"Zayle's warnings?" Kade asked in confusion.

"Another thing you do not know, eh?" Doren asked, looking at Kade as if he were a simpleton.

"It would appear that I was not told much of anything," Kade said in frustration.

"Zayle had an ability to see possible futures. He warned me that I should have a defense against this race if the day came when they turned on me. I could not believe it myself, but he was adamant. I had to divulge two of my callings to another Chosen to get this one, but enough of this talk. We need to plan," Doren said as if dismissing him. Kade immediately recalled that Zayle would dismiss him the same way. He almost bit back with a retort but resisted the urge to comment. It was almost impossible to accept being talked down to. He had been through too much recently to continue to be treated like an apprentice. Unfortunately, he was an apprentice and he knew it.

Kade quickly scanned the room for Darcienna and found her slumped against the wall. There was a huge bump on the side of her head. He raced over to her and felt for breath. Relief washed over him as he watched her chest rise and fall. He healed her, and in no time, she was awake and staring at him.

"What happened?" Darcienna asked as she sat up, rubbing her head.

"We found you knocked out," Kade said as he checked her over for more injuries.

"I am fine," Darcienna said as she gently pushed him away and got to her feet.

"This is Doren," Kade said.

"Master Chosen Doren," the Chosen corrected. Kade cringed at his misstep. He recalled how he had referred to Doren informally while in the master's mind and cringed again.

"Master Chosen Doren," Kade repeated.

"It is a pleasure to meet you," Darcienna said sweetly. Doren raised one eyebrow as he glanced at Kade. He nodded his head slightly in approval. Darcienna saw the look and added just a bit more charm with a tilt of her head and a flash of her eyes.

"We need to leave now," Doren said as he turned to head for the exit. "A dragon, eh?" he asked over his shoulder with a grin. He was impressed. He even gave a chuckle. "Zayle missed that one."

"What if Morg had not found this chamber?" Kade asked as they walked through the wall. Doren took a deep breath and sighed as if he was readying himself to speak slowly and clearly. Kade could swear it was a look of disappointment that he was seeing in Doren's eyes. Kade rankled at the slight, but again, kept his mouth closed. For just a fleeting moment, he wondered if he would prefer the beating he took from Morg over the condescending, judgmental attitude he was getting from Doren.

"The stairs lead down to this empty space," Doren said simply as if that was enough.

Doren turned to look at Kade and continued. It was as if he

was preparing to give a lecture. Kade recognized the posture instantly and mentally affirmed to himself that he was going to refrain from asking questions as much as possible. For now, he would do his best to hide his ire as he listened.

"Why would I build stairs that lead down to nowhere?" Doren asked the question rhetorically. "I wouldn't. But, Morg would not know that. He would know that I had to be here somewhere and look for me," he said in conclusion as he looked at Kade. "I could not make it too obvious or he might realize it was a trap."

Kade felt like a fool as he thought back on his initial impression of the Master Chosen, believing him to be the fool but now knowing different. He chastised himself for given a Master Chosen so little credit. Doren saw the look on his face and assumed it was all for the blood on the wall.

"That was unfortunate," Doren said in a sincere tone. He sounded like he meant it deeply. "Sometimes we must sacrifice a good for a greater good," he said, but there was sadness there that ran deep.

Kade saw the pain in his eyes, and his heart went out to the old man. If Doren and his apprentices were half as close as he was with his master, then he fully understood the loss. And now for the trap to have failed must have made the pain that much more profound. Kade decided that playing the part of the apprentice might not be so bad if it helped the Master Chosen. It filled a void, if only temporary, and the old man did have much he could teach.

"What about when Morg gets back? Won't he be able to track you?" Kade asked, wondering if Doren was going to pull out an amulet of his own.

"That won't be a problem," Doren said as some of his composure returned. "Follow me." He re-entered the den. "Watch this," he said with a devious smile.

The Master Chosen went back to the chair, and as he faced it, performed a calling. Kade looked on in shock as he recognized the moves. He was not able to perform the calling yet, but he had seen it enough times to know what it was. An exact replica of Doren appeared in the chair. Doren looked at Kade with a grin.

"I got that one from Zayle," Doren said, pleased with his work as he studied the image. "That was very good thinking," he added. Kade beamed at the praise. Yes, he felt like he was back to being an apprentice who soaked up his master's approval. He was not sure if he liked the idea or not, but he could not deny the pride he felt at the compliment. "It would appear that Zayle has taught you to use your mind as well as using the Divine," Doren said as he nodded his head in thoughtful approval. "But enough of this chat," Doren said, becoming intense. "We must leave." He purposefully strode for the exit.

For a moment, it reminded him of the way Morg would switch from a good mood in one instant, to a bad mood the next, and then he dismissed the thought completely. There was no comparison between the two men. He shook his head and fell in behind the Master Chosen as they exited the room and quickly ascended the stairs. Kade watched as the old man climbed the stairs as if he were half his age. He wondered if there was more going on than he could see. Was there an Illusion Calling hiding what he really looked like? With a Chosen, the possibilities were endless. Kade dismissed the thought and focused on the stairs. The closer they got to the main level of the mansion, the more Doren was careful not to make a sound.

"You must walk lightly and quietly," Doren whispered as he watched Kade to make sure he understood the instruction. Satisfied, he continued. "Is this dragon of yours close by?" he asked as he slowly crept through the ghost-like bookcase.

Kade reached out with his mind and felt the familiar presence of the dragon. Relief washed over him. He was not even aware that he was this worried for his friend until this very moment.

"And he will carry us as he has done for others?" Doren asked critically.

"He will," Kade responded confidently.

"Then have him ready. The Alluvium may have left for now,

but if it came to incurring the wrath of Morg, or keeping us captive, it won't be a difficult choice. Morg is brutal beyond words and knows no mercy," Doren said. Kade was sure there was just a touch of compassion in his voice for the earth creatures.

Just pawns caught in a game, he thought to himself.

Kade reached out with his mind and made contact. He felt the dragon come alive. There was intense relief along with happiness so strong that Kade could not help but to smile.

"He is ready," Kade said with a smile. His heart started to pound. He was eager to be back on the safety of his dragon with the feel of Darcienna behind him.

"Doren…," Kade started to say when the Master Chosen cut him off sharply.

"Master Chosen Doren, Master Doren or Master Chosen," Doren said tersely. Kade flinched at the scolding. He took a breath and started again.

"Master Chosen Doren," Kade said, using the full formal title. "The dragon is ready when I call. We must be quick. As soon as he comes, they will sense him and try to stop us."

"Very well. Let's continue," Doren said.

The group crept toward the front door and stopped. Doren moved slowly as he peered outside to survey the area. He started to take a step through the door when he froze, one foot hanging in the air. Ever so slowly, he moved back into the house. He wobbled slightly while moving from foot to foot, trying to keep his balance as he edged back step by step. Kade was certain the old man was holding his breath. It was almost comical to watch this old man, who had clearly enjoyed too much good eating. He could have lost half his weight and still been too heavy. His salt and peppered hair was cropped close to his head just so he would not have to put effort into taking care of it. His clothes were too large, making him appear even heavier than he was. He definitely had a slobish appearance about himself. Lazy was another word that came to mind.

Doren took a long, slow, quiet breath and let it out just as slowly. He silently turned as he sought Kade's eyes. He pointed at the wall just next to the door as he nodded. Kade's eyes came open as he recalled the way the giant had stood in that very spot earlier. Kade nodded back in understanding. Doren motioned for Kade to follow as they moved further back into the house. When Doren felt they were far enough away from the porch, he turned to Kade.

"Is there a way out the back?" Kade whispered. His lungs hurt from trying to control his breathing.

"No. We have to leave out the front. I had this mansion constructed on a cliff so that the house could not be approached from the rear. Anyone or anything had to approach from the front. I had to know when he was coming," Doren said as he breathed a sigh. "But, alas, it appears it was for naught."

"No," Kade said with confidence. "We have knowledge, and there are two of us now. We still have a good chance to defeat him," he added with confidence born from the determination to exact revenge. "No. This is far from over," he said as he probed at the hate that surrounded his heart. Doren studied Kade thoughtfully for a moment, and nodded once, a slight smile creeping across his face.

"Doren...Master Doren," Kade said quickly, correcting himself. "Are you able to make an illusion of me running from the house?" Doren looked at him and took on the air of patience born of years of teaching.

"Yes, I have mastered that calling," Doren said with forced patience.

Kade got the feeling that Doren was irritated and may even have felt slighted that Kade was actually asking the question. He mentally chastised himself. He should have known better. For a moment, he was surprised he was still alive after so many blunders. Of course the Master Chosen could perform the calling.

"Doren," Darcienna said sweetly, with just a slight glance at Kade. "Why not just do what you did to the one downstairs?" she asked.

"There are too many. I could get a few, but it would not take them long at all to overwhelm me," Doren said, again, with that forced patience.

Darcienna's smile faded ever so slightly. Kade grinned as she got to share in his misery. Darcienna turned and saw the look on his face and shot him a glare that could have frozen water instantly. When she turned back to Doren, the sweet smile was back on her face as if she had never been bothered.

"Kade is formidable with his Lightning Calling and I do have skills, also," Darcienna said confidently.

"There are thousands of them," Doren said, a slight condescending tone in his voice.

Kade saw the look in her eyes and cringed. Doren might be a master, but she was going to make him pay if he continued. She cared nothing for his skill, status, or anything else that the Master Chosen thought defined who he was. Kade quickly slid next to her and gave her a reassuring smile that said, "I understand your pain." With an audible huff, she gave up. Doren chose to pretend not to notice.

"If you were to make an illusion of me running from the house, they may chase after it, giving us a chance to get away. If we time this perfectly, I can get the dragon to us, and we can make a run for it," Kade said.

Doren grinned and sprang into motion. Within seconds, Kade was looking at an exact replica of himself. It was eerie. Darcienna looked from Kade to the replica and back to Kade. She nodded her approval, her previous frustration completely gone. She was impressed.

"They will not be fooled for long," Doren said as he inspected his work with pleasure. "Remember, they sense movement. This will not give them anything to sense. Let's just hope they are fooled long enough by what they see for us to get away," he said as he motioned them back to the front. Kade could see that Doren was focused on maintaining the illusion even though he talked casually enough.

Kade crept toward the entrance and barely breathed. He peered around the edge of the door and saw the massive shape of the giant Alluvium standing guard. There were a few Alluvium around the yard but not enough to concern him…yet.

Rayden, be ready to come when I call, Kade sent. There was a response, and his heart started to pound. His palms started to sweat.

"Now," Kade mouthed. Doren grinned and put his right hand out as if to catch a ball, and then, with a slight movement forward, the figure of Kade raced out the door. Kade looked at Doren and saw an intense look of concentration on his face. It reminded him of Zayle's last few moments of life when he had created the illusion of the dragon and its passengers.

The giant flinched in surprise as it looked down at the figure that had taken off at a dead run for the open field. Kade felt a vibration through the floorboards of the house. Shortly after, the field started to fill with Alluvium. Kade's image leapt easily over several of the beings and continued on in its race for freedom. The giant took a step forward.

"It's not following," Kade mouthed as he pointed at the wall where the one on the porch was. Doren was too focused on the illusion to respond.

Kade watched as the giant unfolded its arms and took another step forward. There were more strong vibrations that resonated through the house. Kade was certain that the giant was yelling now as it took another step forward. Glass in every part of the house vibrated. The creature clenched and unclenched its fists and there was yet another vibration so strong that Kade heard cups rattle in the den. This was too much for Rock-face to watch. The giant took off after the image. Kade watched in awe at the speed of the Alluvium. He had not expected this from such a large and cumbersome looking creature.

Now, Rayden! Kade sent as he readied himself to dispel the Transparency Calling. He could hear Rayden coming, and when he was sure the dragon was close, he let the calling go. The dragon popped into view and Kade felt his heart leap into his throat. There, racing after the image of the illusion, was Rayden. *NO,* Kade sent hard through the link. Confusion assailed him from the dragon. *We are back at the mansion.* Hurry, Kade sent. He glanced at Doren and knew he was going to hear about this later, but for now, the master had to focus. Doren had beads of sweat forming on his forehead.

Rayden veered hard, spraying rocks and dirt high into the air as his claws tore furiously at the ground and raced back toward the mansion. The giant hesitated as the dragon charged directly at it. Rock-face braced, expecting the dragon to attack and Kade was sure it was turning to stone as he watched. Rayden raced by the giant, spraying it with dirt as its claws dug at the ground for purchase. The giant spun, confused, and then turned back to watch the image of Kade race on. It tilted its head as if to listen for something and then held its hands out to its side. Kade got a sickening feeling in his stomach and knew they had mere moments before their ruse was up. He considered making them invisible, but trying to get everyone on the dragon would be a disaster. He had to wait until after they were mounted and on their way before perform the calling. He could not see any way around it. His heart raced. It was now or never. He watched as the giant looked back at the mansion. Even at this distance, Kade locked eyes with it. His heart pounded hard.

"Now!" Kade screamed as Rayden slid to a stop.

They raced out the front door. Kade reached for Darcienna and all but threw her up to land on the dragon. Without any concern about formalities, Kade grabbed the old man and swung him up to land heavily behind the wings. Kade vaulted onto the dragon's back, landing in front of Darcienna.

"Hold onto its wing joints," Kade screamed at Doren as he gave the dragon the mental command to go. Kade felt himself press back hard into Darcienna and did his best to pull himself forward by grabbing the dragon's ridges.

Rayden exploded with such power that Doren almost lost his grip. The dragon tore at the ground with all its might. Kade felt the muscles bunch and explode just as the giant was approaching them. It reached out to pluck them from the dragon. It was so close that Kade flinched back from that massive hand. The Alluvium missed and slid to a stop as its momentum carried it past. It turned and took off with amazing power and speed. Kade looked on in horror as the giant Alluvium continued to give chase. For something that appeared as though it would be sluggish, this thing was moving like the wind. In an instant, Kade realized that he was looking at the creature that had destroyed Darcienna's home. It was much smaller now, but there was no mistaking that this was the creature that had torn the house to pieces.

"They are creatures of nature. While connected to the ground, they have abilities that would stagger the mind," Doren yelled over the wind.

The dragon ran for its life. It dodged, twisted and leapt to avoid the smaller forms, any of which could cause the dragon to crash to the ground if they made direct contact. The dragon leapt and landed only to have to leap again to avoid the earth beings that were closing in. The field looked like it was coming to life as more and more of the beings sprang from the ground.

"Doren, can you do anything?" Kade yelled.

"If I let go for a second, I will no longer be with you," Doren yelled back, gripping the dragon's wing joint and holding on for his life.

Kade watched in horror as a rock flew through the air. He braced for the impact that never happened. Darcienna's shield sprang into life just long enough to intercept the rock and then winked back out. Kade felt her recoil from the impact, but she held her place.

Another disaster barely averted, Kade thought as he considered the Transparency Calling. He quickly dismissed the idea, as there was no way he could let go of the dragon's ridges long enough to perform the moves needed. The dragon needed to dodge and weave too much for him to even consider any callings that required his hands. It was all up to Darcienna and the dragon now.

"Kade," Darcienna yelled over the wind. "It's closing!"

Kade glanced over his shoulder and saw that it was, indeed,

closing the distance between them. As he watched, something brushed his leg in an attempt to grab him. He flinched and drew his leg up. He searched the land for an opening and found it. Ahead to their left was a field where there were no Alluvium.

That way, Kade sent to the dragon and Rayden turned hard, narrowly avoiding being grabbed. There was no way to leap them now as they were coming from every direction. The empty field was their only chance. Rayden put his head down and raced for it. The wind was so loud that Kade could barely hear that Doren was yelling something, but he could not make it out.

Kade looked down to see beings coming out of the ground as they passed and worried that Rayden might trip. If the dragon fell, it was all over. He glanced over his shoulder and saw the leader still coming. The Alluvium was growing with every step, and with that, his speed was increasing. Rock-face was looking more and more like the creature from the cabin as he grew. The ground shook with every pounding of his foot. Rayden raced on. The giant was twice its original size now and continued growing. The dragon was no longer pulling away but losing ground quickly.

It was obvious that they had mere moments before Rock-face had them. Kade tried to think, but his mind was whirling out of control. He started to look back when he felt Darcienna lurch. He expected her shield to pop into view but there was nothing. He glanced back just in time to see the little, black book collide with the giant, and then, a bright, blue flash exploded on the creature. Kade watched, stunned, unable to comprehend what had just happened. After a moment, he understood and turned as far as he dared to look at Darcienna.

"You threw the book!" Kade exclaimed, remembering the black book he had tucked behind his waist.

"I had to," Darcienna said defensively.

Kade nodded his approval, grateful for the small reprieve. For a fleeting moment, he was sure that Darcienna thoroughly enjoyed being rid of that book. He looked back, expecting to see the giant no more, but it was still coming. It had fallen back considerably as it swatted at the blue spark that danced around it in a blur. The giant faltered several times as it struggled to keep moving forward. Kade held his breath, praying that Rock-face would go down and stay down, but his prayers were not to be answered. Soon, the blue spark lessened and then winked out completely.

"It didn't kill it!" Darcienna shrieked over the wind.

Kade urged the dragon to increase its speed, but it was already running as fast as it could. Rayden just had no more to give. Kade knew the exertion had to be killing his friend. He looked back and saw that the giant was gaining on them quickly, once more. Doren yelled again. Kade could barely make out the words.

"Kade! NOOOOOO!" Doren yelled, but it was too late.

The dragon never saw the edge of the cliff as it ran full speed into empty air. The giant came to the edge and leapt after them. Kade's throat closed up, and his stomach felt as if it wanted to heave. They started to fall. Every muscle in his body clenched. His hands slipped from the dragon's ridges as he desperately tried to grip Rayden with his legs but it did no good. He started to float free. Darcienna screamed in terror. All in a flash he realized that they had been herded to this spot. The field was empty for a reason and they were the reason. The giant, most likely, expected them to be trapped and then caught, but that was not to be the case. Kade had run them right over the edge. That feeling of falling off a cliff was back, and this time, he truly knew what it felt like.

The Alluvium reached out as they fell, and just when it was about to close its hands on the dragon, there was a loud crack like the sound of an axe hitting a log and then a sudden jerk as the dragon's wings shot out to grab the air. Kade and Darcienna landed on Rayden's back with a jarring impact and almost bounced back off. The dragon grunted hard as its shoulder muscles strained under the force of the hit. Kade feared that its wings were going to collapse as it struggled to halt their fall and absorb the weight from the riders at the same time. Rock-face was not expecting the sudden change from the dragon and misjudged as its hand closed on empty air. It careened off Rayden's tail and tumbled through the air. The Alluvium let out a scream of rage as it fell away. It turned to dust, swirling away on the air currents. Rayden strained to force his half extended wings down, desperate to slow their decent. Kade could feel the dragon's muscles turn to iron as its wings came down and then fully extended. They stopped dropping and started to glide.

Rayden let some of the speed bleed off and then relaxed ever so slightly. He would pump his massive wings and then glide for a good distance before pumping again. The dragon labored for breath as he flew, still exhausted from the race for their lives. The run had taken too much out of it. Kade only hoped that the dragon could recover while in its gliding phase.

"I thought you said the dragon could not fly," Doren said breathlessly. The Master Chosen was so ashen that he looked deader now than he did back in his study.

"This is a first time for me," Kade said, still trying to unlock his muscles.

"And, it's Master Doren," the Chosen said, a small amount of color starting to return.

Kade rolled his eyes, recalling that he had, indeed, addressed Doren in the informal while running from the rock creatures. He shrugged and decided to deal with it later. For now, they were safe. That had to count for something.

Kade looked over his shoulder at the large man who was trying to situate himself. He desperately hoped that Zayle knew what he was doing, because from where he sat, Doren was no match for Morg. He could only hope there was more to the man than he had seen so far. His eyes shifted to Darcienna and she smiled for him. She was safe again and that was the most important thing to him. He recalled wishing he could whisk her away to someplace that was safe. Maybe now he could since the Master Chosen was safe. He would take the man where he needed to go and then be done with this. He had done his part. He had saved Doren. He was an apprentice after all so what more could they expect from him. He smiled to himself and reached deep into his boot, pulling out the precious amulet. He slipped it around his neck and breathed a sigh of relief. He turned forward and leaned back into the arms of the woman who was quickly stealing his heart and settled in for the ride.

THE DIVINE SERIES
CONTINUES
LOOK FOR

THE DIVINE

UNLEASHED

PLANNED RELEASE IN
JANUARY 2014